LOCO IN THE BADLANDS

LOCO IN THE BADLANDS

To Roger

Thank you for your support

[signatures]

Pedro Villegas
with William Scordato

Library of Congress Control Number: 2017913041
ISBN: Hardcover   978-1-5434-4595-4
             Softcover   978-1-5434-4596-1
             eBook   978-1-5434-4597-8

To order additional copies of this book, contact:
Xlibris
1-888-795-4274
www.Xlibris.com
Orders@Xlibris.com
762812

CONTENTS

My parents raised me to have respect for law-enforcement officers. It gave me an early perception of importance regarding them. Decades later, I met Pete Villegas. Soon after we agreed to work on a book detailing his exploits, my existing respect grew out the roof. My understanding evolved to a whole new level as to what our law-enforcement officers are up against on a daily basis. It was not only a pleasure to write about such bravery and courage, it was inspiring.

This book is based on the true case files of Mr. Villegas.

But, it was vital to make some changes as we went along. First, as there were still personnel working in the field, it was necessary to change names to protect them. It did not stop there. Names of informants and others involved were also changed. To further disguise identities, personality traits were mixed and matched. In other words, Mr. Villegas, over the course of his decades-long career, had to confront individuals who acted with traits of racism. He had to deal with individuals exhibiting incompetence endangering him and his fellow officers. There were corrupt government officials. Such traits, and others, were used to create composites of characters in the book.

Secondly, there were revisions made to benefit the reader. In order to make for smoothly flowing plots, there were dates and locations changed too. This allowed plots and sub-plots to successfully transition from chapter to chapter.

There could be incidents in the book that drew details from three different incidents experienced by Mr. Villegas. This will also be done in sequels to this novel.

So, once again, this story is based on his true case files. And Mr. Villegas along with his fellow officers are to be commended for what was accomplished in documented, record-setting busts in the arena of narcotics and illegal arms dealing.

I dedicate my involvement in this project to Pete Villegas and the brave men and women who continue to serve and protect our society.

William Scordato

PROLOGUE

6 June 1989, Philadelphia, PA

A young Colombian, in his black GTO, sped down the Schuykill Expressway. With the roof down, Manuel sang at the top of his voice to the heavy metal rock blaring on his car radio. His audience included everyone he passed as he made his way to Philadelphia. He felt on top of the world. It was only seven years ago when he had dropped out of school as a junior to be a full time drug runner. Now he had the resources to make deals in his own right. He had risen from a childhood of squalor to own property and a hot car that were his "babe magnets."

As he closed in on the city limits, Manuel needed to ensure his punctuality. *Time to check the roadways.*

He hit the button that switched the band from FM to AM and listened for the scheduled traffic report to ensure there were no surprises. The heavy metal rock disappeared, replaced by a deep, older male voice on the local all-news station.

"KYW news time, ten o-three."

Damn! Missed the ten o-two report. Now I have to wait nine more minutes. Better keep it on the station or I might miss the next one.

"Our top story this hour: State government leaders continue to press for new legislation proposing a Special Task Force in the war on drugs. The purpose of the Task Force would improve coordination between federal and state law-enforcement agencies in sharing information to apprehend dealers. Today, City Police Commissioner, Irving Nelson, added his stamp of endorsement."

The next voice spoke with the sound and emotion of a Martin Luther King.

"This legislation would greatly enhance our cause. We dream of a drug-free Philadelphia, but the current system ties our hands. We are currently battling the worst drug trafficking in our city's history. Without the Special Task Force bill we may as well be putting umbrellas up against waterfalls".

Manuel burst into laughter, causing some of the éclair to go down the wrong pipe. He choked as his tires strained to hold their grip on the highway. Manuel swerved to avoid one car pulling in front of him from the left and nearly forced another driver in the right lane off the road in the process. He hit the accelerator again. Both cars became smaller in his rearview mirror. Manuel finally got his breath, shook his head and resumed eating his éclair.

Waterfalls? Those poor dumb bastards! If they only knew the forces hard at work that will be turning the waterfalls into Niagara Falls for the new decade . . . and the ones after that!

But, until then, Manuel continued to do his part today.

The young dealer became distracted from the radio again when his car phone rang.

He finished one more bite and answered it. "This is Manuel."

The deep, gravelly male voice, associated with too much smoking, on the other end did not even bother to identify himself. "Are you on schedule?"

"I'm in route to The Badlands right now," said Manuel, "I'm closing that new buyer on 6th and Cambria, and I want to make sure I'm early. I've got to pick up some more weight before meetings with two regulars in the same area later."

"Where are you now?"

"I'm just passing the exit for the Philadelphia Zoo, so I'm already in the city. I've got plenty of time. You just try and keep your ass cool on that yacht of yours."

"Manuel," replied the man with a wheezing sound in his chuckle, "the temperature of my ass will be greatly enhanced after your call when you're done in The Badlands."

"Then I better bring my thermometer by so that I can stick it up your ass and make sure."

He pressed the "off" button on his phone.

On this late morning, the temperature rose as fast as the sun. Surprised when his air-conditioning unit failed him earlier today, Manuel put the top down on the GTO. But the wind in his face was still warm, and not nearly as nice as the air-conditioned comfort. Manuel used one of his short sleeves from a bright island button-up shirt to wipe some sweat from his corn-rowed head. The éclair was finished, so he ripped open a pack of TastyKake cupcakes and stuffed half of one of the crème-filled chocolate deserts into his mouth. Within twenty minutes, he would be in "The Badlands".

The Badlands featured the most hardened and dangerous of the drug dealers in the city. And these criminals showed no bias with whom they used in their activities.

Willing participants included a mix of children, senior citizens and all ages in between. All were used in a variety of ways to "work the real estate". Dealers owned "real estate" in the form of street corners where the drug sales took place. The more desirable corners could cost a dealer a healthy six-figure price tag per month in rent to the various drug outlets in the neighborhoods.

Manuel owned a number of such desirable corners.

The car phone rang again. He talked through half-a—mouthful of his sugar fix. Some of the crème was hanging out of the corner of his lips. "This is Manuel."

"I'm here."

Manuel recognized the man's voice. "Good, I'm just minutes away, so stay in that air-conditioned Benz of yours and keep your ass cool. It's hotter than hell out here today."

"My ass will be staying a little hot until you get here."

The man hung up.

"Shit," Manuel shook his head, and muttered to himself, "I have got to stop using that expression. Now my title is 'Cooler of the Royal Asses'." He put a finger to the corner of his lips and sucked off the crème.

The Badlands had gained its name and reputation in the early eighties – in various ethnic sections spread across North and Northwestern sectors of Philadelphia. By nineteen eighty-nine, high level drug-dealing was no longer limited to syndicates and cartels. And drug dealing was blind to race. Many had their fingers in the pie, including the Asians, Blacks, Organized Crime, those from the Dominican Republic and the white Irish Catholics – the Mac Boys.

Some had their specialties in which drug they dealt; some were a little more diversified. Puerto Ricans had made cocaine their commodity of choice.

Manuel had a realization and grabbed his car phone again. He hit a button that would redial the last incoming phone number.

"Yes?" came the reply.

"Hey! Did I hear your bitch laughing in the background when you called? Cause if I did, you get her ass out of there right now! We have rules – no bitches present during the deal!"

"I don't even see *you* present."

"Shit! I hear her laughing right now," said Manuel, "I'm telling you, if the bitch is there when I arrive I'm turning around and going to my next drop."

"You worry too much, Manuel."

"She's not your wife! She's your bitch! And bitches eventually get dumped. And when a bitch is resentful, they can use what they know to bargain with the cops when they get in their own trouble."

"I'm more concerned about cops being present than bitches."

"Don't you worry about the cops. That's *my* property you're waiting on. There'll be no cops. Just keep your ass . . . aw fuck! Just . . . just get her out of there!"

Shortly afterwards, Manuel arrived at 6th and Cambria, behind the black Mercedes of his buyer. He adjusted his aviator-style sun-glasses, tucked his three gold necklaces under his shirt and stepped out of his car.

Once out of the car, without even warm wind blowing in his face, the dramatic change in temperature made him almost as anxious to get into the fully air-conditioned, black Mercedes, as he was anxious to make the transaction.

A young Latino woman, wearing hot pants and a clingy, shoulderless top walked down the sidewalk on the opposite side of the shop-lined street. Manuel turned in the direction of her high heels clicking on the pavement at a rapid pace. *That better be his bitch leaving.* Manuel tapped on the driver's window of the Mercedes.

The window lowered, and the man behind the wheel motioned for him to enter through the back passenger door on the right.

The young Latino drew a deep calming breath. *All right, just make some small talk, take his money, and move on.*

He peered through the side window and was waved in by his thick-bearded, darkly sun-tanned customer, sitting in the backseat behind the driver.

Both the men in the car were dressed similarly with island shirts and short white pants. Both also had on their dark glasses. However, the man in the back had no gold necklaces. The high-rolling buyers never got into all the jewelry. Like Manuel, the buyer was trim, and less than average height. Manuel climbed in the back passenger side door, took a seat and closed his eyes. *Air—conditioning! Ahhhhhh!* He also enjoyed the new-car smell. But, Manuel knew the experience could not last.

The two men greeted each other and shook hands.

"So how about we pop the trunks and get this deal done?" asked Manuel.

The man behind the driver smiled. "I like you, Manuel. You're punctual and you don't waste any time with your deals. I'm on a strict time-table to deliver this. But, you said you would take my ass off the hot seat, and you did."

"Yep! That's me – 'Cooler-of-the-Royal-Asses'," replied the seller, as he admiringly looked around the interior of the Mercedes.

"Then maybe you and I can have a long-term relationship with each other," said the bearded man.

"Fine with me." Manuel responded as his eyes wandered downward. "You know, I have to ask you a question. What's that thin leather strap I always see hanging out of your pants pocket?"

His buyer's face became stern. "That's none of your fucking business. Any other questions?"

Manuel followed the lead. "What is this, an eighty—nine, XL?"

"Yes. And as you can see, it comes bitch-free."

"Yeah, I gotta get me one of *these*," said Manuel as he pulled out the open package with the second cupcake.

"With the prices you charge, how about if I just give you this one instead of the cash? *Then* you can eat in it. But, since it's still mine, you *don't* fucking eat in it."

Strike two, thought Manuel, as he quickly placed the cupcake back in his pocket. Manuel picked two crumbs off the seat and ate them. "The prices are more than fair. My overhead includes some cops working this shift on my payroll for this corner. And they ain't cheap. But that's why I can pretty much guarantee a safe place of business. Now I have to find some cops who I can buy off in the suburbs. I've just had a couple of groups of kids from The Main Line find me here in the city. And I'm not the *only* one these teen-agers are finding. That area will be snow-balling over the next year. So the time is now to begin marking my turf."

"Yeah, you better get up to The Main Line and start pissing on some corners."

"Funny. But mark my words. I'm going to set things up now, because soon I'll be networking with a new high roller getting his hands in the region and I may be able to get better volume prices. Then the next time we meet, I'll buy your car and eat in it all I want. Of course, you'll have to throw in your driver with the deal."

"Nah, he's my cousin," said the buyer.

"He's black!"

"Your time-efficiency is only exceeded by your powers of perception."

Manual knew he walked right into that one. "Yeah . . . funny. Speaking of time efficiency, I have two more appointments to keep with two white boys – a couple of dime bag deals. And I have to pick up some more dope before that. So, if we could kindly get on with the transaction . . ."

Manuel had better things to do than socialize, but, that was the way it was with the big buyers and sellers. Since the men had first been introduced three months ago by a lower level dealer, they had met frequently and developed a good, trusting, social relationship before scheduling this initial deal with themselves. Moreover, Manuel could smell the money now, so he relaxed. *I guess a couple of more minutes won't kill me.*

"Okay," said the buyer, "Take one more hit of the AC and step outside."

The trunks were popped open and they began making the swap.

"Here you go", said the buyer, as he grabbed a briefcase full of cash from his trunk. Check it out. Ain't no fucking white boys coming close to that."

"No," replied Manuel, opening up the briefcase and looking inside. He pulled out one of the bundles of hundred dollar bills and started fanning through it, "nothing close to this. By themselves, they can't do a lot, but you'd be surprised. Like I said, these boys are from the suburbs . . . Ardmore –some of the most expensive real estate in Pennsylvania. If they can't afford the good stuff right away, I get them started with a little weed, keep the relationship going and let things take their natural course. These kinds of kids have money from their rich parents, and they have lots of friends who want dope and crack. And those friends have rich parents. And what they don't get in allowance, they can steal from their own houses and sell it on the black market for more cash. Up until now, it's been an untapped market."

Manuel laid the briefcase in his trunk next to the duffel bag. With the money concealed from plain sight, he began to count the stacks of bills.

"Maybe I'll have to check into that rich, stupid white boy demographic myself," said the buyer. "So what do you do, go out there and give out some free samples at the schools?"

"Not yet. Like I said, these kids are coming to the city and finding us. So someone is out there. It's only a matter of time before the rest of us go out there and set up drug houses and sell corners. It's gonna be like the

California Gold Rush around here. Dealers will be rushing to stake their claims for the corners they want And then, there's some word on the street it'll expand again a lot in a little over a year."

"Maybe it *is* time for me to raise my bar."

Manuel raised his eyebrows, and cocked his head to the side. "Well, go to Northern Delaware and South Jersey, or you'll be stepping on a lot of toes in these parts."

"Of course," said the buyer, checking out the duffle bag of kilos. "So, who's this big ass high-roller coming here?"

Suddenly, the bearded buyer raised his eyebrows and did a double-take at the street to see a police squad car approaching from about one-and-a-half blocks away.

Manuel looked to see what was happening, and was equally surprised. "Shit!"

"You said not to worry about any cops?"

"The cops on this shift are mine! But one of them in the car is a *bitch*! I ain't *got* no bitches on my payroll!"

As he blurted out the announcement, he just as quickly, snapped the briefcase shut with one hand, snatched the duffle bag with his other and bolted down the street with the money and the drugs.

The bearded man yelled as he pulled a Smith and Wesson nine-millimeter hand-gun from behind his back and yelled as he ran in pursuit, "Hey, asshole! You don't get everything!"

Inside the police car, the Italian male officer hit on his young female partner. "So, what are you doing after the shift tonight?"

The woman put her tongue in her check. "Well, I don't usually fraternize with rookie officers. What did you have in mind?"

"Do you like Asian food? Maybe we could go down to China Town. I know a great little Thai place. If you like spicy . . ." The voice of the olive-skinned young man trailed off. He had been mildly oblivious to the surroundings.

But, now he had the sight of two Hispanic men running down the street. *Hispanics! Running!*

The female officer at the wheel hit the brakes, and she along with her partner opened their doors and jumped of the vehicle.

Her shrill voice hollered out. "Stop! Police!" Then she exclaimed to her partner, "Gun! The trailer has a gun!" as she drew her own weapon from its holster.

And that means I get to use this, thought the partner, grabbing a sawed-off shotgun from the back seat. He may have only had the status of a rookie, but he already had a reputation that preceded him from the training Academy.

This man was a marksman, and he looked forward to any green light to show off. He started to take aim.

The few passersby on the shop-lined area were already screaming, hitting the sidewalk and scurrying into shop entrances for cover. The men running heard the first warning.

"Stop! Or we'll shoot!" yelled the marksman.

The two men kept running and then the trailing man heard the unmistakable *last* warning prior to the discharging of a sawed-off shotgun – the loud double—clicking sound made just before the trigger was to be pulled. If there was anything worse than the entry wound from one of these weapons, it was the wide, exploding exit wound.

"They're gonna shoot us! Get down!" yelled the bearded Hispanic.

Manuel had heard the clicking too. He stopped and dropped to his knees. The briefcase and duffle bag plopped in front of him as he put his hands on his head. The bearded man did the same, laying his gun off to the side and putting his hands on his head.

As they closed in, the two officers were suddenly wide-eyed to see what looked like ten "citizens" including a street cleaner, two women with empty baby carriages, a hot-dog vendor and a homeless person springing out of the woodwork, all wielding hand-guns and flashing badges loosely chained around their necks.

"Prosecutor's Office! Don't shoot! Prosecutor's Office!" came the cries from the "homeless man".

Stunned, the two officers came to a halt as the agents converged on the two men kneeling on the sidewalk. The "hot dog vendor" straddled over the seller, and cuffed him.

"Okay! Okay! We got 'em now!" he yelled to the other officers.

The red-haired homeless person thrust his knee in the back of the buyer, who shot back a scowl at him.

"Easy, Dexter," said the vendor to his partner, "We've got 'em."

Both men had cuffs put on. One of the agents, a good—looking, tall Black man, dressed in a sweat suit, approached the officers. Despite all the bedlam that had taken place, he exuded a calm, confident manner.

"Okay, you two. We'll take it from here. We're on this case out of the Camden County Prosecutor's Office in Camden. My name is Thomas Bryant." He flashed his badge.

"DEA?" said the woman.

"On loan to the Camden County Prosecutor's Office.

The case started in Camden, and over the last two months it brought us here for the final bust. We've been after this pair for months. We were just ready to move in on them, when you flushed them out into the open. We'll need to follow you back to where your precinct is."

"So we don't get the collar on this?" asked the rookie.

"We'll make sure you both get an honorable mention," winked Bryant.

Mentally, the two officers rolled their eyes. As they turned to walk back to their squad car, the two officers paused to observe two more investigators cuffing the driver and putting him in another vehicle.

"Don't worry, Rook." whispered the woman to her partner. "I'll show you how, with some proper paper work, we can arrange to get more than an 'honorable mention'."

Bryant saw Manuel, with his chin up, glaring at him and the other agents. He knew Manuel would give anything to wipe the smiles off of all the arresting personnel.

But, Bryant could have no inkling of Manuel's earlier thoughts of waterfalls turning into Niagara Falls, and how this was a victory in name only. Nor would the agent on loan to the Camden County Prosecutor's Office foresee the nasty scene to be confronted within an hour of this arrest.

CHAPTER ONE

The men under arrest were driven six blocks to a plain brown building shaped like a big rectangle.

It was a very uninviting structure that seemed to tell passersby to "just keep moving along – nothing to see here". Mounted on the side of the wall facing the main street, ten-inch high, hard plastic block lettering identified the drab structure:

PHILADELPHIA POLICE DISTRICT 33

Around the perimeter of the building grew unkempt bushes planted in grass thirsting for water, having already been burned yellow by the summer sun. The building had only two floors—one floor just six steps above street level, and the other floor built mostly underground with a holding cell area.

With the back parking lot also below the street, the officers brought the three perpetrators in through a rear door. The precinct truly provided an early indoctrination for prison. At this level, the walls had grey cinder—blocks with no windows. The flooring had a matching drab grey-patterned vinyl tile.

The three culprits sat in the holding cell. The heavy-set, uniformed guard on the other side of the steel bars stared at a magazine with a bored, heard-it-all-before expression on his face as the three men pissed and moaned over their fates to three other men already in the cell.

There they waited until different officers came to separate them, and escort them to their individual interrogation rooms.

The driver was the first one to be removed from the cell by the man who had been posing as a hot-dog vender.

Next came Manuel, taken to his interrogation room by the agent who had been posing as the homeless man.

Agent Ray Diaz, the mustachioed man who was one of the "citizens" during the arrest, came to get his man – the one who had been left in the holding cell with three other detainees. He simply nodded to the guard. As the guard opened the door, he pointed to the buyer in the attempted cocaine transaction.

"All right, amigo. There's someone who's very interested in talking to you," said Diaz.

Quietly, the two men walked up some stairs and down an empty hallway tiled with a pebbled pattern.

The bearded Hispanic man looked at the little signs on the doors until he saw the one that read "Precinct Captain". Then he barked at Diaz. "If you try to follow me into this office, I swear I will fuck you up!"

The next instant, he quickly broke from Diaz's side . . .

"Hey!" yelled Diaz.

. . . and straight into the office, slamming the door and locking it behind him. The captain barely had time to get out a question.

"Who the hell are you?" blared the commander of the precinct.

The captain, in his late fifties, did not have the physique as when he used to drive a patrol car. He raised his paunchy body from the chair but that resulted in a big mistake. As he rose, his upper body leaned forward right into the lunging attacker, who grabbed behind the pin-on neck-tie and curled his fingers around the buttoned collar. He pulled the captain face down into a hot cup of coffee that lay next to an open box of Dunkin' Donuts. The captain could not even scream from the impact, because, just as fast, a forearm slammed down on the back of his neck. It felt like a two-by-four. All he could muster from his throat—a muffled choking sound – had no chance to be nearly loud enough for anyone to hear. His assailant leaned in to his victim's ear, speaking softly to answer the captain's question.

"Who the hell am *I*, you ask? I'm the most hated man in law enforcement! I *must* be, to have almost been shot by my own *man* out there!"

The captain could still only manage a choking sound.

"Do you remember the name 'Juni Neco' mentioned to you in a phone call from Camden County Prosecutor's Office earlier today?"

"Mmmmph!"

"Well, that's *me*, you dumb asshole!" Then Neco noticed the spread on the desk. "Is *this* why I almost got shot . . . because you're too busy enjoying your goddam *coffee and doughnuts* to order your men to stay clear of the area where I'm making a *bust*?"

Even through the contorted expression of pain, one could see the dawn of realization in the captain's bulging eyes. His morning misunderstanding had become very clear, but right now he had a far more pressing problem. This captain had a large frame, just a little over six feet tall and a bit on the heavy side. By comparison, Neco stood five foot eight and kept a well-maintained one hundred fifty pounds. It might as well have been *two* hundred fifty pounds for the way it felt on the captain's neck.

"I . . . can't . . . breathe," he sputtered.

Neco dialed the pressure back a small notch.

"I *know* you were told to keep the area clear of your men this morning. I *know* because I overheard the phone conversation this morning. And I *still* almost had my head blown off! The only reason I'm being *this* gentle is because we *still* caught the dealer." Neco took a deep breath. "Now *why* were cops patrolling the bust zone this morning?"

"I received a fax that the bust was moved up three hours."

"What?"

The captain lifted his right hand over his head and pointed toward the front corner of his desk. "The fax is right there."

Neco looked to the side and grabbed the paper with his free hand to read it. "It's not even from our fax number!"

"I don't have your fax number *memorized* . . . God let me up!"

Neco remembered what Manuel had yelled.

Don't you worry about the cops. That's my property you're on. They'll be no cops.

Neco barked his next question. "Where are the two officers originally scheduled for that shift?"

"They're dead."

That bit of stunning news took some of the fury out of Neco' voice. Without lessening the pressure from his arm, he spoke in a softer volume, "What happened to them?"

"This morning they were killed in the line of fire from a Jamaican shower posse. They weren't the targets.

They were just walking out of a coffee shop on a corner where some dealers were making an exchange. Witnesses said that neither of them even saw it coming. The cops, the two dealers and three other people were killed in the shower of bullets. That's why I never called to confirm the fax. I was a *little* distracted. My deputy is the one who called in the two other uniforms to work the rest of their shift."

Neco started to ease up with the pressure on the neck under his forearm, until the captain opened his mouth again. "I'm . . . reporting you to . . . the Commissioner."

Instantly, he reapplied the pressure with the captain's jaw hitting the top of the desk.

"Owww!"

Neco spoke uninterrupted. "Oh, but I haven't explained the *deal* to you yet. You report *me* and I have to report how you had at least two of your men on the take for a drug dealer, and, maybe how *you* knew about it. And maybe *that's* why the area wasn't secure."

"What?"

"Oh yeah. The dealer was *bragging* to me about it before the exchange. The two murdered cops were on his payroll. So, this can go one of two ways: 'A' we can report each other. And, my report will implicate you in my near death. With my office being higher on the food chain than yours, good luck. Then there's 'B'. We can forget this little incident and you use the information I've given you to look like a hero. So, what will it be . . . fucking with me, or not fucking with me?"

"You're nuts!"

Neco applied a little more pressure with his forearm.

The captain repetitively slapped his right hand down on the desk surface, like a World Wrestling Federation contestant tapping himself out. "*Not fucking. Not fucking!*"

Within the next fifteen minutes, Neco stepped outside the precinct and climbed into the passenger seat of Diaz's car. He had to get with the next person on his shit list.

Diaz turned the ignition key and pulled away from the curb still without the full news of the dirty cops reaching his ears. He had only heard some words through the captain's door without the full context.

Neco needed to schedule an emergency stress release session. He pulled out a cell phone and dialed a number in the Philadelphia suburbs.

The man on the other end answered the phone with recognition.

"Yes, Sensei?"

Neco heard the voice of his best friend – Ron Goldbach.

"Hello, Ron. I need a therapy session tonight . . . real bad."

"Preparation-before-a-big-job bad?"

"Police-screw-up-almost-getting-me-killed bad."

Goldbach let out a sigh. "All right, I better round up Mateo and everyone else for this one."

"Good, how about eight o'clock?"

"You got it, Sensei."

Neco hung up the phone.

"Yeah, 'therapy'", said Diaz. That's a good euphemism for it." said Diaz.

Neco got a gleam in his eyes. "It's the best therapy."

"So, you really learned about some dirty cops in this district?" asked Diaz.

"Yeah."

Diaz turned the corner. "You think that Philly Captain is in on it?"

Neco wrinkled his nose and shook his head. "No, I think he would have been even a lot *more* scared than he already was if he was in on it."

"I don't know," Diaz chuckled, "I couldn't make out all the words coming from the room, but his voice sounded pretty scared."

Neco did not acknowledge the last remark. He just stared ahead through the windshield, thinking about what he had been told. He replayed in his mind some of the last comments made by Manuel.

It'll be like the California Gold Rush around here.

Dealers will be rushing to stake their claims for the corners they want.

This new supplier had to be stopped before he could bring his goods to the region. And an example had to be made of whoever was planting seeds out in the suburbs for him. Before that, there had to be answers.

For now, that line of questioning had just been put in the hands of the local officials.

Neco would not be allowed to be in on the interrogation of Manuel. It would violate the whole point of him being included in the arrests during his busts — to keep his cover for future jobs. All the criminals brought into custody would see their "buyer" thrown into a cell with them. From their perception, Neco would go through the same process as them – tried, convicted and sent off to some prison.

And with Juni Neco as the lead agent on a bust, it would be the prosecutor's fault if the dealer did not get a life sentence. No law-enforcement official in the Philadelphia tri-state area was more meticulous when it came to proper documentation. He made sure all warrants were properly obtained, he provided plenty of tape from phone calls and face-to-face meetings with the criminal's first and last names repeatedly mentioned in the conversations.

The only leverage left to most defendants would be to sign a full confession and be located in a much nicer prison facility for the rest of their life in exchange for letting the State avoid a long and costly judicial process.

If they coughed up valuable information on their suppliers, they could plead down to something less than a life sentence.

That the dealers were helping the State by pleading was an acceptable truth, but, equally important was this kept Neco need to appear in court to testify at a minimum.

This was vital if the dealers were Colombian.

Colombian dealers would always have connections present in the court room during trials to identify any informants or undercover agents bearing witness against them.

Once visually identified, that informant or agent was as good as dead, along with any and all of his family members. And not just family members in the immediate household. Grandparents, brothers, sisters, cousins, and any pets would all alike suffer gruesome torturous deaths.

But, without the personal observation in court, it was impossible to pin down who Juni Neco was. The defendant himself could not provide enough information.

How would such a description read?

"Lean, dark-haired, good-looking Puerto Rican, a little below average height, with a beard that may or may not be there." Another descriptive reference about Neco included that he looked like a man in his early twenties. Juni Neco looked young beyond his years.

Hardly enough for any assassins to act on. Other than the beard, which could come and go, Neco had no physically distinct characteristics. His cover was always safe.

On the flip side, the same rules applied. Other agents doing the interrogation would not get much more than the signed confession solely implicating the defendant.

The dealers knew that testimony incriminating anyone other than themselves would be met with the same wrath beset upon any informers or undercover agents and their families.

Thus, the negation of value to the Witness Protection Program, if you were involved with Colombians.

Diaz drove Neco back to where his Mercedes had been taken, just a few blocks away, and gave Juni the key.

"I'll meet you back at the office," said Diaz.

"Yeah, I have to rush back and see our own good captain back in New Jersey."

"He's probably already in disbelief about you nearly getting shot by that cop."

"He wouldn't have mourned," replied Neco, shaking his head.

Diaz's face became serious, "That reminds me, Juni.

While you were waiting in the holding cell, I heard some of the other cops talking upstairs."

"About what?"

"Another agent from the Attorney General's office went missing this morning while working a case. They're presuming the worst."

Neco scowled at the news, "Damn it. You can bet it's the same son-of-a-bitch responsible for all the others. Let's find out if it ends up with a same signature style of a murder as the other three since earlier this year."

"There's nothing we can do," said Diaz. "So go get your mind off it and have a good one with your friends."

"I always do," said Neco, who then narrowed his eyes, "But first I want to stop somewhere for some bottled water and a sandwich. Then I have a score to settle back at the office."

CHAPTER TWO

Cherry Hill, New Jersey

Dr. Stanton Koblenzer rubbed at his right temple with an index finger, and forced himself to continue listening.

He felt mentally worn out.

If he had any doubt before . . . now he knew—*this woman is officially the craziest patient in the county.*

Koblenzer's psychiatric office had an office located on the seventh floor of the One Cherry Hill building in the huge parking lot of the Cherry Hill Mall.

Koblenzer grimaced, squinted his eyes and continued to utter soft, gentle acknowledgements at the beautiful woman lying on the couch off to the right. Silently, he reached out and pulled the cord to the blinds of the window to block the glare of the mid-morning sun. The patient did not notice. She just talked slowly, her face tilted towards the ceiling.

"And that's when I went to the kitchen and took the carving knife from the drawer to cut my wrists."

"Uh huh," muttered Koblenzer. He tried to resume with his notes but was further exasperated to find his Cross pen was running out of ink. Carefully, he took a small ring of keys from his pocket and unlocked a small side drawer on his desk. He fished around in the drawer and pushed aside a tiny spray bottle of breath freshener. He grabbed a new Cross pen.

In an effort to enhance that image of authority, he had his office decorated with conspicuous elegance: lush shag carpeting, leather furniture and oak paneling on walls decorated with two plaques of recognition. One read "Psychiatrist of the Year", awarded by the Cherry Hill Small Business Man's Association. Another "award" had been presented by the Jewish Community Center Women's Auxiliary Club.

In his thirty-odd years of practice, he had never experienced a patient quite like the one he had been seeing over these last several months. This woman could appear socially functional one minute, and then the next moment, display a side known only to a few family members. In the waiting room, she was normal. But, once she got into her private session, the dark side came out. And then it could disappear once she left. No other patient could actually produce the tiny beads of nervous sweat on his bald head like she could. He pulled a piece of tissue from a plastic dispenser and dabbed the beads before they dripped into his thick, dark-grey beard.

The patient had closed her eyes and trailed off in her speech. Koblenzer lowered his heavy black-framed glasses and spoke in his usual soft and deliberate "doctor voice".

"Sandy, tell me, why you were trying to slash your wrists with that kitchen knife last night."

"Because they were telling me to take the bad blood out," she said in a detached voice, as she rubbed her hands together.

Koblenzer scribbled down the answer. "Who was telling you to 'take the bad blood out'?"

"They said to take out all the bad blood, so that the good blood could get back in."

"Who told you that, Sandy?"

"The people."

Koblenzer frowned. *My God, it's like trying to yank a chew toy from my Doberman!* He gently repeated the question. "What people?"

Sandy opened her eyes, turned her head and just stared right through Koblenzer, unresponsive to the question.

"Sandy," Koblenzer repeated, "what people told you to take out all the bad blood, so that the good blood could get back in?"

"The shadows," she answered with no emotion.

"What shadows?"

"The shadows around the house. They talk to me."

Koblenzer continued in a condescending tone. "What else can you tell me about the shadows?"

"At night, they look like gargoyles. They said if I get the bad blood out, and get the good blood back in, that people would love me."

"Why didn't you take out the bad blood last night?"

The woman resumed looking at the ceiling. "The phone rang. My mother called me. I think the ringing of the phone scared the gargoyles away."

The doctor rolled his eyes. "Did the gargoyles come back?"

"No, while I was talking on the phone, my sister came by to visit me."

"Did you tell her about the shadows?"

His patient shook her head and began rubbing her hands again. She fought the urge to cry.

"Why didn't you tell your sister about the shadows?"

"I didn't think she would have believed me."

"How did you feel this morning?"

"I'm better this morning," she said, even as she made no effort to wipe a tear rolling down her cheek.

"No voices?"

Koblenzer watched his patient get non-responsive as she went into her blank stare again. *I'll bet I could put a brown paper shopping bag over her head and she wouldn't even notice.* He dabbed his forehead again.

"Sandy, did you hear any voices this morning?"

"No."

"Do you think these voices had anything to do with the accident?"

"What accident?"

Koblenzer mentally groaned. *Barely responsive and a memory like a colander.* "Do you remember the accident you had six months ago?" *You know, the one that made you a basket-case ever since?*

She did not answer.

"You were driving your car down a residential street."

Again, there was no acknowledgement.

"You were driving your car down a residential street in Philadelphia. A little eight-year old boy ran out from between some cars, chasing a ball. You hit the brakes, but the child was knocked to the ground. You thought that you had killed him, but he was only unconscious. Even though he didn't die, it was still very emotionally traumatic for you. Do you remember that?"

She nodded.

"That event was date-coincident with the onset of your borderline personality disorder. That's when you began suffering periods of depression. I'm asking if the voices in any way remind you of that accident."

Sandy shook her head back and forth in answer to his question.

Koblenzer laid down his writing pad and grabbed his prescription pad. "Sandy, prior to last night, your borderline personality disorder was limited to isolated minor anti-social tendencies and self-abnegation. But, now it has gotten worse. You have now manifested a potentially violent side. While this may have just been an isolated incident, I'm not taking any chances."

That statement got her attention more than any prior one. Sandy propped herself up on the couch by her elbows.

"You can't institutionalize me. The law says you can't institutionalize me without my husband's permission. And he has promised he would never do that."

Koblenzer looked at his watch in relief. "I'm aware of the law, Sandy. And I am not suggesting you be institutionalized. So allay your fears. I'm merely putting you on a stronger medication."

He quickly jotted on the pad. "This should keep you calmer longer. One pill costs one hundred fifty dollars, and you have to take one each day. But, your provider will cover it one hundred percent. The Camden County Prosecutor's Office has contracted a very good insurance program for you. Additionally, I am putting in my notes that you are to call me tonight and first thing tomorrow morning. If I don't hear anything, I will call you or your husband. I hope that's clear. Because our time is up."

Sandy slowly arose from the couch. She did not answer.

He finished the prescription, tore the paper off the pad, and handed it to his patient. "Go out and see Marsha.

Make an appointment for next week, and then walk right across the parking lot to the pharmacy in the mall for this prescription. Call my office if there is even the slightest inclination towards hurting yourself."

As the woman left, Koblenzer followed her out to the waiting area. He spotted his next scheduled patient on a seat, and exchanged furtive glances with her. Then he addressed his receptionist. "Give me a just a couple of minutes and then send in Mrs. Carpenter."

"Certainly, Doctor."

Koblenzer went back into his office and opened up the small side desk drawer again. He pulled out the tiny spray bottle of breath freshener and cleared his mind of Sandy.

She can be the ticking time bomb in someone else's life – not mine.

CHAPTER THREE

Over in West Philadelphia, a cheap digital clock read eleven-seventeen. Curtis Walker snapped out of a drug—induced unconsciousness as a strip of duct tape was viciously ripped from around his mouth and goatee.

Walker let out a slight cry.

Then he heard a deep voice with a Hispanic accent.

"Hmmph! If *that* makes you cry in pain, your black ass is in huge trouble."

The sting quickly subsided as Walker tried to orient himself in a room dimly lit by a single low-watt bulb swaying ever-so-slightly from a cord above him.

Reflexively, he took a deep breath and filled his lungs with a musty air. "Where am I?"

"All you need to know is that you are in a sound-proof room in West Philadelphia. As for the rest of your colleagues, who were originally staked out for your intended drug bust . . . well, they must be experiencing a substantial amount of panic at this moment. I can only imagine they have been completely re-deployed by now in a search for you, Agent Walker."

Walker's eyes widened. He could not move from a wooden chair in which he was seated – his arms tied to the arms of the chair him and his ankles bound to the chair legs.

"Yes, that's right, Curtis Walker – you have been m*ade*."

Walker's eyes focused on the tall, tanned, well-built man standing in front of him.

The broad face, covered with a thick beard, gave the dark brunette man almost a Cro-Magnon look that belied his ability to articulate himself. But, that is how it was with most of the higher-ups in the industry of drug dealing – they could be very well spoken. Walker did not recognize him. Even though each of the man's forearms had long distinctive scars – the kind associated with defensive wounds-they still offered no clue to his captor's identity.

"While you were setting things up for the bust on my employee, I've been behind the scenes, Agent Walker – diligently searching for any clues I could find as to your background until, finally, I found a match for a sketch I had secretly taken of you during a dinner meeting with my front man. You never should have had your picture taken with the mayor five years ago when you were still a cop walking a beat. You became a bit more of a celebrity than you give yourself credit for. But, then again, who knew at the time you would wind up working with the Office of the Pennsylvania State Attorney General?"

The windowless Spartan room had cinder block walls, and a concrete floor. Walker could not perceive any furnishings beyond the wooden chair in which he sat. From that, along with a wooden set of stairs going up off to his left, he concluded he sat in a basement. He tried to move, but could not.

"Who are you?" asked Walker.

The captor walked in a circle around his prey. Walker became aware of his heartbeat starting to race.

"My name is Alejandro."

"Who do you work for?"

"What name comes to mind when I say 'the most powerful drug lord in the world?'"

Walker took only a second to think. Then he closed his eyes in resignation.

Alejandro spoke from the direction of the stairs.

"That's why there's been a dramatic detour in the route to your intended drug bust this morning."

This morning! Curtis Walker tried to piece the images together. He was scheduled to meet a cocaine seller who he had been setting up for months. Today they were to make their first transaction. Walker was to go to a local precinct in Philadelphia, grab a briefcase full of cash and head out to his agreed-upon meeting place with the dealer.

His fellow law-enforcement officers would already be hidden in place for the bust.

The last thing Walker remembered was approaching his car in front of his house located in a Harrisburg suburb.

He had bent over to toss his jacket into the passenger seat. When he began to stand upright, a powerful arm wrapped around him from behind. A chloroform-laced piece of terry cloth was then jammed over the lower half of his face before everything went black.

Alejandro spoke again from directly behind the agent.

"Did you not realize you were dealing with Pablo Escobar?"

Walker could feel hot breath, smelling of tobacco, whispering into his right ear.

"Did you not realize you were dealing with . . .

Colombians?"

That last word sent a chill through Walker's whole body. Years ago, when he first became involved in law—enforcement, Walker had accepted the idea he might die in the line of duty. But that was *before* he learned of Colombian drug-dealers and how they disposed of their enemies.

Alejandro came full circle to the front. "I was hoping the failures of your past partners would have gotten the message across to your superiors by now."

My partners . . . Horrific images of three corpses flooded through Walker's mind.

The Hispanic man leaned forward to Walker's face.

"You're going to tell me everything you know about the state government's new Special Task Force. In not, well, I think we both know what happens then," said Alejandro, who smiled for the first time.

Walker's heart pounded. He did not have to withhold information out of bravery. He had nothing to tell.

"Everything to know is in the newspapers, man! The Special Task Force doesn't exist yet! Legislation hasn't even passed! It's still in the planning stages for Christ's sake!" shouted Walker, aware of a cold sweat on his forehead.

"We too have big things in the planning stages, Agent Walker. Granted they are at the opposite end of the spectrum from your camp. For that reason, it could only be beneficial to gather as much intelligence as I can on the enemy. Our plan will not be stopped regardless, but I will do *anything* I can to prepare for any of your government's plans. So I ask you again, what is The Special Task Force?"

"I don't know! I haven't read the bill?"

"Who has the bill?"

"I don't know . . . probably *everyone* in the state congress. They're the ones who have to vote on it."

"Who is heading it up?"

"No one has been named. But it would only make sense for it to be the State Attorney General."

"That's why I think you know more than you're telling me. You work for the Attorney General! He must have talked to you and the other agents about it."

"He sees no need to talk about it until it's official."

His interrogator pulled out a spring-assisted, Smith and Wesson M&P switch blade and snapped open its serrated blade.

Walker looked away. He thought of his wife and two sons. He wished he could say good-bye and tell them how much he loved them one more time. More than that, he wanted them immediately moved to safety. Then he felt the flat of the blade rubbing against his neck.

"I regret to say I don't believe you, Agent Walker.
We'll try this one more time. And then if you don't talk,
I will carve the black off of you."

"Alejandro!" interrupted a voice through a door creaked open several inches at the top of the stairs.

"There's somethin' you should see outside!"

Alejandro gave Walker a cold stare. Without breaking eye contact, he raised his voice and answered. "I'm coming!" Then he lowered his voice for the captured agent.

"I suggest you use this precious time to search the depths of your consciousness for any names or prospective locations for the Special Task Force."

Walker spoke, the resignation clear in his voice, "I'm telling you, I have nothing to reveal that you can't find in the newspaper."

"Then I leave you alone with your thoughts."

Alejandro, closed the knife, ascended the stairs and shut the heavy door to the basement. The other man, an African-American in his thirties wearing a white t-shirt, stood at the front window. He pulled his dreadlocks aside so he could see better and peeked through some blinds while he motioned for Alejandro to come over.

As Alejandro peered out to the street, he observed two uniformed men diagonally across the street talking to a resident on a front door stoop.

"The cops are canvassin' the neighborhood, man! I can't let them find me here!"

"That's right, Willie," said Alejandro. "That would be a real problem, because they know *you*. But, we don't have to answer the door, and this house isn't registered under 'Willie Greenwood'. However, the only reason I've worked with you was because you said you had a resource for a drug outlet that I badly need. Now, you've not only failed me, the cops are searching for us." In one motion,

Alejandro again pulled out his switchblade and snapped it open. He placed the tip over the location of Greenwood's right carotid artery. "Give me one good reason why I shouldn't rid myself of you along with Walker."

Greenwood spoke rapidly through quick breaths.

"There's another contact for you! I have another contact I can set you up with, to replace me as your middleman."

"What guarantees do I have you're not just setting me up with another agent?"

"That's impossible with this guy."

"And why is that, Willie?"

"I've been dealin' with him for years. And you'll have leverage on him," said Greenwood.

"What kind of leverage?" Snarled Alejandro.

"He provided a lead for a huge arrest in exchange for no jail time when he lived in California. If that cartel ever found out he was out here . . ."

Alejandro lowered the knife. "How soon can I meet this man?"

"As soon at the cops stop sniffin' around. The heat won't die down until they find their buddy."

"Oh, they'll *find* him, after I prolong his suffering to see what information I can get out of him. They'll just be surprised as to *where* they find him.

CHAPTER FOUR

Back in Camden, Captain John Blake peered through the blinds of his office window that overlooked the entrance of the parking lot.

The edifice, a significant upgrade in architecture over the small local Philadelphia precinct, stood equally uninviting in its own way.

While it did not tell you to just keep on walking, it did dare you not to be intimidated when approaching. The walls had been constructed with large blocks of off-white stone under a hipped roof. An iron fence with pointed tips across the top surrounded the parking lot. Words chiseled in a style associated with early Greek times identified the location.

CAMDEN COUNTY PROSECUTOR'S OFFICE

Blake recognized the Mercedes pulling into the parking lot. The Captain's emotions had been forty percent exhilaration and sixty percent apprehension until he learned about the successful bust, along with the details of the mishap with the two officers. Then the exhilaration-apprehension ratio became ten percent to ninety percent.

Maybe ninety-five percent.

What the hell did Neco expect me to do . . . triple and quadruple check the plan with the Philly captain?

Blake had heard the whispering among the staff.

Neco says when the day is right, he's going to beat the living shit out of Blake.

Juni says that on his last day in this office . . . Blake will be receiving an early 'retirement package'.

The captain, about the same age as his Philadelphia counter-part, stood a little shorter and had a similar paunch. His face had a slightly creased leathery texture associated with someone who enjoyed the sun in his younger days. That texture made the furrow in his brow more noticeable.

But, even in his prime, and with the reach advantage of someone four inches taller than Neco,

Blake would be no match for his junior in some improvised steel-cage match.

With Neco still out of sight, Blake gazed out the window as his front lower teeth nervously gnawed at the short hairs on the tightly cut mustache that matched his thinning closely cropped grey hair. Too occupied to notice the clicking action his jaw made while chewing, he contemplated how much easier life used to be before the hot-headed "Rican" came into his life.

Before then, Blake used to feel like he actually had a commanding presence. Behind his back, many in the office agreed his stone face could have been used for a portion of the outside walls.

Then it happened. His senior recruited this cocky—assed patrolman from the Philadelphia police and Blake suddenly became a lot more varied in expression – usually in shock and outrage. And his image never recovered.

His newest Hispanic field operator took on cases no one else would, while showing great instincts in the process. Within seven months, a new state record for a cocaine bust had been set in Pennsauken, New Jersey. It was a case that never would have come to fruition had Neco operated by the book.

Those Pennsauken drug dealers were one of those operations with a floating location. They could smoothly and efficiently transition their processing activity from one house to another throughout the town. Circumstances like those required two or more points for the arrests.

One location would be the corner where Neco was making his purchase. Additional locations would be where raids were simultaneously executed on any other houses with evidence involved. It took precise timing and execution.

Anything less could result in a person from one location alerting someone in the other. And that could bring about the enemy gunfire trying to be avoided with the element of surprise.

From Neco' intel, Captain Blake had been certain he detected a pattern for the time and sequence involving the switches of those Pennsauken locations.

Neco' instincts told him differently. He had asserted the agents and police needed to raid a different address than that surmised by his captain.

The captain could not even consult with Neco' partner for a second opinion. Neco preferred not to use partners. He would have a confidential informant come to some meetings to introduce him to a dealer. Sometimes he needed a body guard or a fine-looking woman to look credible. And every once in a while, he brought someone to act in the role of an underling. That was how Ray Diaz got involved in the Philadelphia case. Diaz's involvement was also a way agents with less experience could apprentice under someone who had a successful track record. But Neco liked to work alone, unencumbered by anyone who might get in his way. Blake had very little idea of Neco' methods once he left the office for a case.

After much debate over the choice of house for the Pennsauken raid, Blake agreed to where Neco wanted it, privately seeing it as an opportunity with a silent vow.

When he's shown to be wrong and blows the raid in the process, it'll be his ass!

Neco' choice of location and timing turned out to be perfect. The dealers had switched their mobile operation to another neighborhood house that very night, only to be surprised by the waiting artillery of the Prosecutor's Office and local police.

"Good job, Neco!" Blake had exclaimed at the time.

Dammit!

That night Blake lost any mystique with his crew – his respect had been taken down a few notches too. But, worse than both those things combined was that the whole incident seemed to bring out the condescending manner towards minorities Blake had once kept under better wraps.

He took a vow back then. *Neco will pay for this.*

But it would not be through a physical confrontation.

Instead he decided to make things miserable for Neco.

With luck it would be Neco leaving for early retirement . . . or at least a transfer out of frustration. It would be a beautiful day. And a day for which Blake would make sure to not be in the office.

For now Blake wondered if he should be in the office right now. He looked out the window and saw the answer driving through the entrance.

Down the hallway, on the same side as the captain's office, Ada Hernandez – Neco' "bitch" in the earlier morning drama, sat at her desk. Hernandez, a first-year investigator with the office worked in a larger room with working cubicles. First year investigators did not rate their own spaces yet. But from her cubicle, the young beautiful, sloe-eyed Latino with the light brown pixie haircut had a clear view of the parking lot entrance, from which she also spotted the much-anticipated arrival of Neco. Like Blake, she too had gotten a phone call.

She knew that Ray Diaz tried to curry favor with anyone he could— especially with someone the likes of her, by leaking rumors. Diaz always hoped that picking her as the first to have the juicy gossip would score some points in the romance department.

It never did.

Hernandez alerted the other two investigators, "Juni is getting out of his car. Sandra, sneak down the hallway and see if Blake is still in his room."

For the last seven years, Sandra Tomasson had been a patrolwoman in Burlington County before getting hired by the Prosecutor's Office. Recently, because she had paid enough dues, working some surveillance and had gotten through the necessary training, Blake promoted her to the position of field operator.

Much to Ray Diaz's disillusionment, both the young wavy-haired blond and Hernandez adored Juni Neco. And Neco loved it.

"I just came from down there" replied Tomasson, "He's still in his office.

Hernandez continued to look out the window. "He looks serious, but the eyebrow's not raised. That's when you know there will be trouble – when the eyebrow's raised."

A young man, posted in surveillance, by the name of Jerry Cohen, had been just transferred to Camden from Gloucester County. He did not know what to make of all this. "What 'trouble'? What's going to happen?" asked the baby-faced rookie with the weak chin and thick-framed glasses.

"Well," began Hernandez, "I've only been here a year, but to hear others tell it, Captain Blake has long been a thorn in Juni's ass. Oooh, wait! He's stalking around the parking lot. I bet he's looking for Opie's car."

"Who's Opie?" asked Cohen.

"Another one of our investigators, answered Hernadez, who was in on the case this morning. We got him from the Merchantville police for training. Rumor has it Merchantville sends any problem-child here to get them out of their hair for a while. It didn't take long after Opie's arrival to give credence to that. Right away, he started rubbing people the wrong way. It was clear he shares the captain's attitudes on minorities. Ray told me Opie was giving Juni a little of the rough stuff this morning when they 'arrested' him."

"His real name is 'Opie'?" asked Cohen. "That's pretty funny."

"No," answered Tomasson. "His real name is Dexter Rasche. Everyone just calls him 'Opie' because he looks like Ron Howard from the TV show *Happy Days*. He's got the red hair, a similar face and build as the actor. And *you* should talk. *You* look like a young Woody Allen!"

Hernandez laughed as Cohen tried to brush off the comment.

"Can't wait to meet him," said Cohen, sarcastically.

"Do you think Juni has found Opie's car?

"Oh, Juni's not going to find Opie's car," said Hernandez. "Opie was smart enough to get back here ahead of Juni, get the report in and vamoose already."

"Are you sure Blake is Neco' thorn?" asked Cohen.

"When the Captain was introducing me to everyone and we came up to Neco, Blake told me Neco was already his most accomplished officer."

"That's just how he acts socially," said Hernandez.

"It's different when his targets aren't around. He'll make a snide remark about the Blacks to the Hispanics. Then he'll criticize the Hispanics to the Blacks. He's not smart enough to realize we actually *talk* to each other.

Opie's the same way. Juni *is* our most accomplished officer. And despite successful jobs leading to one big conviction after another, Blake is always providing some kind of detriment to him."

Huh? Cohen looked puzzled.

"It's not that Blake *handcuffs* him," said Tomasson "but he *does* put a big fat rubber-band around Juni's waist.

Then he wraps the rubber-band around a stake in the ground."

Cohen looked only more puzzled, so Tomasson tried again. "Sometimes there aren't quite the funds available to Juni that are available to other investigators.

Likewise with getting higher tech surveillance equipment.

Hell, even Juni's cell phone is an older model – about four times the size of the newer, sleeker ones. But Juni always manages to snap that rubber-band!"

"Is Blake going to fit me for a rubber-band?" asked Cohen.

"It didn't help that Juni showed him up on the first case he was assigned," said Tomasson. "But Blake *does* have something against minorities. You'll get a rubber-band if you start making him look bad."

"Am I going to find . . . ?" began Cohen.

Hernandez finished his thought. "If you're probing to see if Jews are included in the abuse, the answer is 'yes'."

Cohen paused, looked away, and then turned to Hernandez. "So what's going on now?"

"Ray called me to say there had been some lack of coordination between county and the Philly P.D. which resulted in a mishap. It almost resulted in Juni getting shot by a patrolman during the bust. Now we're wondering if that was the last straw before he finally freaks out.

This might be the day Juni calls Blake out."

Neco entered the building and made a beeline for Blake's office. The three agents moved to the hallway door as the moment of truth came.

Blake stood behind his desk and high-backed chair. He spoke first in an effort to get a temperature reading on the agent coming through his door. "Juni! I got the good news! Great job!" Then he studied the reaction.

Neco entered the room as he whipped a piece of paper from his pocket. He shook it by one corner until it became unfolded. "What the fuck do you know about *this*?" he said with a snarl.

The palpable antagonism spread out of the room and down the hallway.

A confused Blake reached over his desk and grabbed the paper. He read the fax Neco had taken from the police station. "I didn't send this!"

Neco had suspected that would be the answer. "It isn't even from our fax machine. Someone decided to throw some *shit* up against the wall to see what would stick."

"Who would do that?" asked Blake. "Manuel?"

"Fuck no! He was just as surprised as me. This was done by someone who's got it in for me."

"Then again . . . who?"

Neco looked out the window and raised an index finger. "*That* bastard!"

Blake spun his head around and looked outside.

"Opie?"

He looked back and saw an empty room. The sound of Neco rapidly marching down the tiled hallway spurred Blake to yell after him. "Juni! Wait! We can't know who did it yet!"

Neco never broke stride as he hollered back. "I k*now* who gave me a good shot to the back with his knee when I was on the sidewalk this morning! Then he made sure to graze my head against the roof of the squad car as he was putting me in!"

"It's better for you! He was just probably trying to look convincing!"

"Yeah, I can be very convincing too!" said Neco, as he reached the glass door to the front steps. "He'll be convinced he's going to die!"

Blake yelled at the top of his lungs. "All hands! I need an 'all hands' *right now!*"

"*Opie?*" yelled Neco, now in the parking lot, "I'm going to *fuck* you up!"

Rasche looked across the parking lot to see an irate Neco storming at him.

"What the hell's the matter with *you?*" yelled Opie, as he quickly shuffled to the passenger side of his car.

"I *know* you sent that fax, Opie!" said Neco, closing in. "Did you think that was *clever?*"

"What the *hell* are you talking about? *What* fax?"

Neco darted to the passenger side as Rasche scurried to the back. Neco screamed as both men began serpentining through the other vehicles. "I was almost s*hot*, you bigoted son-of-a-bitch!"

In the background, Hernandez, Tomasson and Cohen stood riveted at their window. They watched as six officers led by Blake emptied out of the building and sprinted across the pavement. The prospect of Rasche's demise entertained them just as much as the prospect of Blake's had.

Cohen exclaimed, "I think I remember something like this on a PBS jungle documentary!"

"Stay away from me, you crazy bastard!" shouted Rasche, stumbling over his own feet, as he tried to run around another car.

The poor footwork cost him. Neco pounced on him like a lion on a fallen gazelle. With his prey on its back, Neco clamped a forearm on Rasche's neck.

"Gugh!" gasped Rasche.

"Do you remember that knee you jabbed into my back?

Well, *this* is what it feels like on your neck!"

As Rasche let out a high-pitched squeal, Neco suddenly felt each of his limbs being grabbed simultaneously. Four officers lifted him into the air as Rasche rolled over and writhed on his side, wheezing.

Blake ordered the men holding Neco. "Get him the hell into the conference room and keep him there until you hear from me!" Then the captain helped Rasche to his feet.

"You *had* to know he would be gunning for you. What the hell are you doing back here?"

Opie choked through his words. "I realized I left my cell phone in the office. I had to come back for it."

"Well, *that* was stupid. You should have left it here."

"The last time I did that, someone used it to make a bunch of prank international calls. I still don't know who it was, but I bet it was Neco! And then *I* was made responsible for the bill!"

Blake shook his head. "Opie, you leave right now, and just stay the hell out of the office for the rest of the week. Your damn phone will be brought to you. Do you *hear me*?"

Rasche, held his throat and nodded wanly.

"For the rest of the *week*!" repeated Blake. "And don't be coming back with any hair-brained ideas about how you're going to call him out to get revenge. That guy can kill you with one move! *Do you understand? No confronting him.*"

"Yeah," he said, finally breathing properly, as he lurched away. *There are other ways. There are other ways.*

Blake dialed his cell phone.

One of Neco' restrainers answered. "Yes, Captain?"

"All right. Opie's gone. Let Neco go."

"He told us you still need to see him, sir."

"Tell him to go home and I'll see him tomorrow."

"He says it really can't wait, sir."

Blake hung up and muttered, "Oh shit. Now what?" He jogged back to the office, but as he approached the conference room, he heard the sound of group laughter. He walked in the room to find Neco, sitting on a desk, describing how Rasche was screaming like a woman out in the parking lot.

"All right," said Blake over more laughter. "Neco will be appearing here the rest of the week. Everyone tip their waitress and go home."

All the officers cleared out and Blake stared at Neco. "Is it really necessary to keep making fun of Ray and Opie to everyone at the office?"

"I'm sorry, Captain," began Neco, hopping off the desk. "But that dumb ass gave the 'go phrase' just as one of the dealers was about to tell me the people behind the killing of those agents from Harrisburg. If I don't let off some steam joking about him, I'm gonna have to hurt him bad."

Blake's face took on a tired expression and he chose not to acknowledge the comment. He grabbed a chair and slumped into it. "What else do you have to say?"

"Our day's not over. We have to act quickly on something."

"What's going on?"

"While I was in holding over in Philly, I overheard one of the officers mention they had found a sheet of paper on Manuel during the pat-down. On the sheet were the places and times Manuel was going to be meeting some suburban kids he just started selling dope to. I bet I could grab Manuel's car, along with our crew who worked the job this morning . . ."

"Minus Opie," interjected Blake, feeling some energy again.

Neco grinned, "Like I said, I bet I could grab Manuel's car, along with our crew, minus Opie, go to the two corners, pass myself off as Manuel's rep and bring all those kids in."

Blake found himself feeling better by the minute.

"Turn this all into a triple-play today, eh?"

"Two teen-agers and all of their purchasing little rich friends we can get them to flip on – maybe beyond a triple-play."

"Okay, I'll set it up. Let me make some calls. When do we have to be ready by?"

"The first one is for five o'clock. The next one is just thirty minutes later. It'll pretty much be a replay of what we did earlier – some play clothes for everybody.

Only I won't need a driver. Manuel never had one," said Neco.

"How will you know these kids?"

Neco laughed with a snort. "Ardmore teen-age white bread in The Badlands? Are you kidding me? With the times, locations and names, I'll find them. Now I'm going to do my paperwork, go home and be back around four."

Blake got up. "I'll see you then."

"Oh, and Captain?"

"Yes?"

"Please make sure we coordinate this with a different precinct. I don't want any more surprises. I can't take many more before I *really* snap."

CHAPTER FIVE

The digital clock on Neco' desk flashed to two—ten. He finished his report and called it an afternoon.

Outside, he got into his Mercedes and pulled out of the parking lot. The route home entailed going through some back streets of Camden and then onto ramp for Route 676

South – perfect for Neco to indulge in one of his rituals to release stress. Speeding on expressways.

Neco hit the accelerator, quickly hitting ninety on the speedometer. This not only provided some regular exhilaration, but also served as a way to ensure the absence of being tailed.

The rear-view mirror revealed someone in his wake, gaining ground. Neco grinned as he observed the flashing lights. He immediately pulled over to the shoulder, opened his window and placed both hands on the steering wheel.

A young policeman stepped out of his squad car and his traffic violator. "Sir, may I please see your driver's license, insurance card and registration?"

"Certainly, officer," answered Neco, who reached in his pants pocket for this wallet.

"Sir, are you aware you were hitting eighty-five miles an hour?"

"Really?" said Neco, opening his wallet to flash his badge while going through the motions of taking out his license. "Man, I didn't realize I was going that fast."

"Oh," said the officer, recognizing the badge. "Who are you with?"

"Camden County Prosecutor's Office."

"Sounds more exciting than stopping speeders," said the officer, putting away his ticket pad.

"Yeah, I wouldn't call it monotonous."

"Are you on a case right now?"

"No, just going home. I'll be more careful."

"Okay, Mr. Neco. Have a good day."

Neco drove for two miles at sixty-five miles per hour. Then he floored the gas pedal again and raced to his hometown for an important meeting.

In about twenty minutes, the Mercedes pulled up on Chestnut Street in front of the Herma Simmons Elementary School in the borough of Clayton. A flow of kindergartners streamed out the front door as Neco quickly stepped out of the car. If there was one thing that brought a big smile to his son's face, it was the sight of his father waiting to pick him up.

"Daddy!" shouted Petey, as he ran up to the car.

"Hey!" said the father, who picked him up and hugged him. "How's my big guy? Did you have a good day in school today?"

"Uh huh."

"Little Petey" was the perfect nickname for the son.

When you looked at his face, you saw a little version of big Juni.

"What did you do today," asked the father.

"I made this for you. We were asked to tell about our daddies."

Petey handed his father a folded piece of light blue construction paper. Neco unfolded it. In crayon, he saw a crude drawing of a man with "My Daddy" written above it. Along the side he read a series of words with colon marks after them to describe the figure.

Name: Juni

Height: 50 feet

Weight: 60 pounds

Eye Color: Purple

Job: Zoo keeper

"Fifty feet tall and sixty pounds," laughed Neco.

"Mommy will like this."

"I didn't know what to put for 'job', so I put zoo keeper."

Neco had never had to confront this issue with his son. Today would not be the only time. "I see that.

Hey, big guy, are you in the mood to go to the Twin Kiss for some ice cream?"

The son nodded.

"Me too. What do you want, chocolate, vanilla or a twist of both?"

"A twist of both."

"Yeah, well, chocolate for me," said Neco as he folded up the paper and placed it in his pocket. "Let's get in the car *fast*, so we can be first in line."

Petey ran around to the passenger door and hopped inside.

Clayton, a small borough in South Jersey, was established in 1886. To some it seemed as if the Twin Kiss had been there ever since then. Mostly a residential community, the generations of town people never saw much in the way of commercial development.

The school stood just tenths of a mile from the Neco residence – a house with three stories, including the attic. The house had gray paint with red trim around the windows, except for the enclosed front porch, which had red paint with gray trim. The porch overlooked a lawn that extended level about fifteen feet in front before taking a steep forty-five degree angle drop towards the sidewalk.

Mowing that section was an absolute bitch. Neco never succeeded in delegating it to a lawn service.

I will pay you double your fee to come here and do my lawn.

I'm sorry, Mr. Neco. Between that steep drop and having to negotiate around the half dozen different trees you have out front, it would be murder on my peoples' wrists.

Neco hung up the phone.

I swear to God, my next house will be completely surrounded by gravel!

The two happy bearers of ice cream cones walked up five concrete steps, which had a metal railing on only the right side. Those steps took a person up that portion of the lawn having the forty-five degree angle. Then three more steps led to the porch where they stepped through the inside door and down a narrow hallway that separated the combination dining room and living room area on the left from the den on the right.

At the end of the hallway came the kitchen where they saw the surprised mother of the household. "Oh, honestly,

Juni, ice cream before dinner?"

Neco' wife shared his Puerto Rican descent. Five years ago, she and Neco had met while he was dating her older sister, Sheila, whom she lovingly called "Slut".

"Slut" referred back to her as "Ho". The two women had shared an apartment together.

Courtship with the slut lasted mere days. The briefest of introductions with Neco to their slightly unstable mother did not prepare him for the alcoholic that proved to be the older daughter. Neco thanked his lucky stars he had been subjected to her dark elbow-bending side in the early going.

Sheila was not ready when he picked her up for their first dinner date. Instead, she had already been wasted from swilling beer throughout the day. During dinner,

Neco persevered and tried to be a friend to the troubled woman – asking questions to see what might be driving her to the bottle so much. Instead, she chose to find fault with him that night.

"Why are you asking all these questions. What are you, like, a *cop* or something?"

"Actually, I am."

"Well, that's just great! That's just what I need – a cop for a date."

Had she not been drunk, Neco would have left her at the restaurant to fend for herself to get a ride home.

But he did give her a ride to her home and right after that he dumped her.

The younger sister had never played a day of basketball in her life. But any coach would have been impressed with how quickly she snatched that rebound.

Within a year they were married. Never having embraced "Ho" as a term of endearment, Neco instead went with the more traditional "Hon".

It was not too long after that the newlyweds were expecting Petey.

Giving birth to their one child had not had much effect on her shapely body, although she displayed a little more tummy than she wanted. Dark brunette hair running down her tank-topped slim torso made her look slightly taller visually.

Equally dark brown eyes looked up to her husband, who, again, had to divert his son's attention. "Petey, I forgot to ask for napkins. Go downstairs to the basement and grab a roll of paper towels for us."

Little Petey left and bought his father a few more moments to explain. He directed his wife into the dining room. "Hon, I had my first experience with him asking what I do for a living, so I quickly had to misdirect his attention. Ice cream was the first thing that came into my mind. I'm sorry." He licked some ice cream. "It won't become a habit."

"How long do you think it will be before we have to tell him?"

"If I have my way, it will be when he graduates college."

Little Petey returned, forcing another change in the conversation. His father took the paper towel gave his son one more request. "Petey why don't you go down the block and play with Johnny and Richie until dinner time?"

The son left the house, finishing what was left of his ice cream. His father waved good-bye and turned to his wife again. She spoke as she displayed the glare reserved for him until Petey left. "So are you staying home for dinner for a change, or is *that* your dinner?"

"Give me a break, Hon. I *have* to go back in. This ice cream probably *will* be my dinner. On top of that, I almost got shot this morning, and I'm still a little on edge."

His wife's response showed no sympathy. "Maybe you could just *lay* one of your fellow undercover agents. *That* oughta take the edge off!"

Neco narrowed his eyes in reaction as he shot back. "When are you going to understand I have *never* gone to bed with another woman? But when I'm on assignments,

I . . ."

". . . have to kiss them passionately and fondle their breasts! I know! It's all in the line of duty! My God!

How long will it be before you tell me you had to screw someone's brains out in order to stay alive?"

Neco bit on his lower lip for a moment. "I have to get back to the office."

"So when *will* you be home?"

"I'm not sure. After work I'm meeting with Ron and the gang."

"You were just with them *last* night. You spend more time with Ron than you do with *me!*"

"I know," said the husband, trying to calm things down as he put a hand on her upper arm. "But after what happened this morning, I need to do what I do. And tomorrow is my big job interview. There's more money on the line. If you want the bills paid on time, then let me spend the time I need to prepare . . ."

But before he could finish, she abruptly withdrew from his grasp and made her way back to the kitchen. "I'll have the bills stacked on the dining room table before you get back," she said, "Now I'm going to get dinner ready for your son."

Neco stood there for a few moments before he noticed the ice cream melting through the paper towel and onto his hand. Without saying a word, he marched into the kitchen and threw open the pantry door. He chucked his ice cream cone into the trash receptacle, slammed the door shut and stormed out of the house. The front door slammed as he left with an additional reason for his one-of-a-kind therapy session to be held later tonight.

The sound of an oven door slammed in the background.

In an effort to clear his head, Neco reviewed in his mind the events of the day again – especially the remark about what was being planned to take place with the drug dealing in a little over a year.

He only knew that for something to be taking place over that period of time, it must be bigger than the likes of which local drug-enforcement agencies had ever seen. He also knew it was highly unlikely the answers would come soon.

Neco just filed it away and planned to keep his antennae up.

Unfortunately his antennae could not pick up what was happening in South America at that instant.

CHAPTER SIX

Across the Atlantic Ocean, the temperature climbed to ninety-five degrees in Los Napoles, Colombia.

If the United States had their Roaring 20's, Colombia in South America had their Roaring 80's. Pablo Escobar personified the evil of Al Capone, Pretty Boy Floyd, Clyde Barrow and Baby-face Nelson all rolled into one.

Although with the mustache and a substantial double chin on his chubby forty-year old body, no one described him as "Baby-face."

By the time Escobar had arranged for the assassinations of police chiefs, local judges, Colombian Supreme Court justices and no less than three potential presidents of his country, he had personally changed the number one export of Colombia from coffee to cocaine. In the process, he became a national hero.

No, make that a god.

Escobar had created a whole new world. Prior to his rise to power, poverty was rampant. Homeless people tied scarves across their faces to ward off the stench as they scavenged through trash, looking for any items that could be cleaned up and sold for their only source of income.

Pablo Escobar rescued them from lives of squalor.

Neighborhoods were previously made up of countless ramshackle "homes" – structures made up of rotted termite—infested wooden boards. Those less fortunate had a cardboard box, or perhaps an "A-frame" of large sheets of plastic or tin attached together.

With the advent of Escobar's rise to power, all of this was cleared out and replaced with apartment complexes, nice restaurants and dancing clubs – discos. Their beloved hero had a passion for disco music.

The people working in his cocaine labs could afford to buy their own houses and cars.

Escobar constructed high-rise office buildings and sports complexes, complete with soccer fields.

And on the sixth day he created light – for the soccer fields, so his workers could play at night.

Gold-leafed frames with oil painting reproductions of Escobar hung in many a living room where people literally kneeled and prayed for him to have a long and healthy life.

In Escobar We Trust.

The analogy to a deity was not lost on Escobar. Just not only in a benevolent way. It was not long ago that he proudly asserted his power to the media.

Sometimes I am God. If I say a man dies, he dies that day.

With a time zone only one hour ahead of the Eastern Time Zone, Escobar did not have to be disturbed at unusual hours with calls to update him on drug dealings. News came on this afternoon as Escobar sunned beside an Olympic—sized, kidney-shaped pool – just one of six places he could swim, not counting any of his man-made lakes.

He dismissed a young Hispanic brunette, half his age, and answered the call he saw coming from America. "Yes?"

"It's me."

"Hello, Alejandro. What do you have to report?"

"There was a slight mishap."

Escobar noticed another young brunette walking towards him in the distance. He waved her off. "I do not like mishaps."

No shit, thought Alejandro, as he took a puff from a Parejo Cuban cigar. "Willie's buyer was an agent with the Pennsylvania State Attorney General's Office."

"When did you find this out?" asked Escobar.

"Last night."

"And you didn't call me?"

"You know me – I didn't want to present a problem without a solution," said Alejandro.

A wary Escobar asked, "And that solution is?"

"I am lining up a meeting with another prospect from Willie," said Alejandro. "And I have the agent."

"You *got* him?"

"Yes. I captured him right outside his house as he was leaving for the drug deal. Now I am working on making him spill anything he knows about the Special Task Force."

"Ah, yes. The Special Task Force," repeated Escobar.

The Colombian drug lord was not used to getting what he desired. Details on The Special Task Force continued to be elusive. Even his right-hand man, Alejandro, could not glean any incite from his previous prisoners beyond things reported in the news. Escobar wanted names and locations and anything else that would make this United States government project vulnerable to imposing his will on it.

"I would very much like to know what you have found out. Tell me." Said Escobar.

"Nothing yet."

"So this is no different than any of your other interrogations?"

Escobar could imagine Alejandro containing his annoyance by simply moving his head back and forth.

"All he has been submitted to is scare tactics. His real test is coming up within the next few minutes."

"Alejandro, you continue to press your luck. You should have just killed him at his house. It is not worth you getting caught, especially now that they know who Willie is. I need you finding a connection for Philadelphia, not rotting in jail."

Escobar translated the brief ensuing silence as Alejandro hinting that he did not like anyone telling him how to do his job. A second later, the response came.

"As I said, I am arranging to meet with someone. And as for pressing my luck, these narcotic groups haven't learned yet. Perhaps a *fourth dead agent* will be a lesson that will *stick*."

"While it was resourceful of you to capture an agent and attempt to do some intel on The Special Task Force, it remains a concern that, once again, we have failed to establish a new East Coast connection. Miami and New York continue to grow more and more risky for us to count on more than seventy percent of the time. That combined with our increased demand makes it a *priority* to find a new outlet." Then his voice became firmer, "And I want is *Philadelphia*."

Alejandro was not intimidated. "I'll get all the information I can from Willie Greenwood and have the meeting."

"Very well. Is this agent with you now?"

"Yes, downstairs, he is about to be submitted to more questioning."

Escobar arose from his chair. "I am going to take my electric car over to the steam room. Then I will get a much-needed massage. In the meantime, get things over quickly with this agent by the time I finish. Fit him for a tie."

"Yes, sir. He will receive one of my custom-made designs." He took another puff and expelled a stream of smoke.

Escobar had one more point. "Oh, and Alejandro . . . this agent? "I want to hear him scream all the way from here."

"Then I suggest you stay on the line and listen to what is about to happen next."

A blood curdling cry pierced the room.

Ron Goldbach grabbed at his groin in pain as he fell to the mat of a dojo in Levittown, Pennsylvania.

"I didn't target *there*!" Neco, attired in a black gi, screamed at Goldbach. "You stepped right into that!"

With Goldbach, dressed in a white gi like the rest of the students, curled up on his knees, it showcased the slightly long, dark brown, banged hair pressed to the top of his head with sweat. None of the others in the training room could see his goateed face.

"Get up and walk that off!" yelled Neco. "You should *never* allow yourself to be hit there!"

"Yes, Sensei."

Goldbach lifted himself up and nodded. He knew he had no other option but *to* walk it off. This had been included In the terms of the original agreement. He had met Neco at a Bally's Total Fitness in the Northern part of Philadelphia.

He remembered the night he was going to weight room when he happened to walk by a large studio normally used For aerobics classes. He spotted a Hispanic man working On his martial arts regimen.

After observing for several minutes, Goldbach walked In and extended his right hand down to introduce himself to Neco, who was laying on a mat stretching in gym shorts And a muscle shirt.

"Hi, my name is Ron."

The Hispanic man did not appreciate the interruption In his routine, but still managed to force a slight smile As he reached up and shook Goldbach's hand. "I'm Juni."

"I've seen you here before. You have an interesting regimen. I would bet you're pretty good."

"I do okay," said Neco, resuming his stretching.

"Maybe we could work out together."

"I don't think so."

Goldbach was not easily rebuffed. "We could learn from each other."

"There's nothing you are going to teach me."

"I'm pretty good. And I'm already in great shape," said Goldbach, using a hand to lift up a tight t-shirt and reveal a flat stomach.

"Believe me, you are not ready to work out with me," said Neco, not even looking at him.

Goldbach bristled, "You might think differently if you saw my collection of tournament trophies. They almost take up a whole wall."

Neco let out a snort. "I bet they're real shiny."

"You don't get that many awards without some speed.

And I'm fast! My friends call me 'White Lightning'. Check it out."

Goldbach demonstrated some combinations.

Neco began to stand up, containing his laugh to a soft chuckle. "You think that's fast? That's nothing."

"I bet I could give you a run for your money."

"It would be more like a run for your life."

Goldbach stood motionless, looking insulted.

"Go ahead," said Neco, getting up and placing his feet in position. "Try and hit me."

"The idea wasn't to fight right now. I'm just saying we should train together, set up some sparring . . ."

"What?" asked Neco, jutting out his jaw? "Are you afraid?"

"No. I just don't think two people should just start going at it . . ."

Neco stuck his jaw closer. "Are you afraid you'll? find out that you're not so fast after all?"

"You should know I can break six layers of bricks with one hand!"

"Wow! If I see you about to fight a pile of bricks,

My money will be on you. Because the last time I checked, bricks aren't too fast."

Goldbach was silent.

This time Neco gave Goldbach a quick poke to the chest. "C'mon, try and hit me."

That did it! Goldbach put up his hands and started bouncing up and down on his feet with quick lateral moves.

He saw Neco go into motion too, but he was not giving any ground. He was welcoming the attack.

First came some punches Neco did not even have to block.

"Oooh, I can see why those bricks never stood a chance," said Neco, dodging the blows.

Next came a kick. Again, not even a block. His fellow Bally's member was simply making him miss.

"Did you say 'White Lightning' or 'White Frightening'? cause you are scary slow."

Goldbach's eyes flashed with more intensity as he made sure he contained his smile. *And now he's set up for the "White Lightning" signature combination.*

Goldbach unleashed a flurry of punches and kicks.

Neco countered with some blocks to go with the dodges.

Which was fine with Goldbach because it was time for the climactic moment – *my debilitating roundhouse kick.*

It was a self-fulfilling prophesy.

Even as Goldbach was only one-eighth through his spin on one leg, he felt a punch to his diaphragm. His other leg was knocked out from under him by a Neco leg sweep. suddenly, Goldbach was flat on the mat, struggling for air.

He rolled over on his stomach; propped himself up on his elbows and pulled his knees up to his chest. As his breathing slowly got back in rhythm, Goldbach looked up and saw a hand reaching down to him. He grabbed it and staggered back to his feet as Neco admonished him.

"You need to get a lot better – and I mean a *lot* better, before you're working out with me, Mr. Lightning."

Goldbach could finally speak again. "Who the hell trained you?"

"I don't tell anyone that."

"I'll pay you for lessons," said Goldbach, rubbing his abdominal area.

"No," answered Neco, kneeling down to resume his stretching.

"C'mon! Am I *that* much slower?"

Neco paused and stood up again in front of Goldbach.

Before White Lightning could react, Neco punched and retracted his left fist from within a hair of Goldbach's right eye. Just as suddenly, Goldbach experienced the same eye being out of focus.

But he had not been hit!

Goldbach rubbed at his eye. "What the hell just happened? What did you do?'

Neco pointed to the bottom third of his own ring finger.

Goldbach dropped his jaw.

Stuck to the bottom third of the ring finger was his right contact lens!

"What are you, a god damn magician? How the hell did you *do* that?"

"My fist went towards and away from your eye so close and so fast, that, for an instant, it created a vacuum.

The vacuum sucked the lens right off your eye and stuck it to my knuckle. You *are* that much slower."

Goldbach watched Neco gently peel off the lens from his finger and hand it back to him.

"Now I'm going to finish my work-out, Mr. Lightning."

Goldbach left that evening. But on subsequent encounters at Bally's, he sustained his persistence in soliciting to be mentored.

Months went by, until one night Goldbach tossed out one of this token reaches.

"So, is this finally the day you let me into the inner sanctum?"

To his surprise, it was the day!

"Yeah. I'm taking you in."

After his double-take, Goldbach composed himself and asked what it was going to cost him. Not that it mattered; he would pay whatever he had to pay.

It was made clear to him money would not exchange hands. But the arrangement was not without conditions.

"You will not be doing any more drugs. You will not smoke. You will not drink. This training will have an intensity very few people can withstand. I am going to demand of you more than you can imagine. And then, I am going to demand more. So your conditioning must not be impeded by poisons in your body."

White Lightning nodded.

"We will train very regularly, but if I call you at any time to meet for a spontaneous training session, you will drop whatever you are doing and make yourself available to me – no questions asked.

He nodded again.

"You must be one hundred percent committed. This is just as much spiritual as it is physical. You must regard this with the same reverence as a religion. It will be a new way of life."

He gave one last nod.

"And one more thing."

There was a pause for three seconds before the last condition. "You will be unconditionally loyal to me. Do you have any questions?"

"Is the moment where we exchange blood?"

The irony was never lost on Goldbach that he actually had *begged* for this type of abuse. In retrospect know, he knew it had saved his life. Before his agreement with Sensei, Goldbach was in the fast lane for an early exit ramp from life. Drugs and alcohol made him feel immortal.

Even his own doctor warned him of how he was prematurely aging his thirty-year old body.

The doctor's advice had no effect. Nor did two incidents where he found himself waking up behind the wheel of his car, which was traveling fifty miles-per-hour. It was all to no avail until Goldbach committed to Neco'

"new way of life".

In present time, Goldbach freely shared his history with new recruits to the dojo. Two new such recruits watched in horror as Goldbach continued to walk off the pain.

Neco implemented his next-man-up philosophy "White Sam! Take his place up here!"

"White Sam" referred to Sam Schofield, a six-foot-two version of Goldbach – big-chested with arms to match. He looked like he could play tight end in the National Football League. Instead of a goatee, White Sam wore a thick bushy mustache. Still in his thirties, his short brown hair, also with bangs, sported no gray.

White Sam had gotten in on this elite "abuse" through Goldbach. The reason he was called "White Sam" was to distinguish him from "Black Sam" Whitmore, a six-foot five, fifty-two year old African American, also in attendance with the two new recruits not yet regarded as regulars. Mateo Meza rounded out the rest of the regulars.

Inspired by Neco, Meza, the youngest of the crew, in his twenties, joined the police and patrolled a beat which he would continue until he could realize his dream of working undercover. With a comparable height to Neco and Goldbach, Meza possessed a very fit frame, but he still lacked the ripped body of his idol.

White Sam took a punch to the jaw, toppling him over to the same spot previously occupied by his fallen comrade.

He winced in pain, a *huge* no-no. You were *never* to exhibit feeling pain.

"Oh, that *hurt?*" screamed Neco. "Well, then I better hit you *harder* next time!"

Out of the corner of his eye, Sensei saw the expressions of the new recruits. He had seen it before and could imagine what they were thinking.

These guys are freakin' nuts!

These crazy bastards are really trying to knock each other out!

The two men looked at each other, eyed the locker room door, looked at each other again, and rapidly walked out.

Those remaining acted as if nothing happened.

White Sam quickly bounced up and finished a few more minutes of sparring. Then White Lightning took his turn again. Sensei did not allow students to finish on such a bad note.

Neco made *Blocking Out Pain 101* mandatory study in this dojo.

Goldbach immediately took to the offensive. Sensei liked that – no back-off! White Lighting had become a very worthy student.

At the end of the session, Sensei directed everyone to meditate. Meditation took place both prior to training and after. Before working out, everyone would drop to their knees and bend over with chest on thighs. Some would stretch their arms out in front on the mat; others would bend their arms and prop themselves with fists at each knee.

The meditation cleansed their minds of anything not having to do with that night's lesson. Any thoughts of personal problems, stress from work, or domestic matters vacated their heads.

Anything less than total focus could result in experiencing some cosmetic damage. It was fortunate for Goldbach he worked as a sales representative for his cousin, who owned a company – Tri-State Container – that sold high quality corrugated packaging to corporations.

His cousin came to understand it would not be unusual for Goldbach to report to work with a black eye or a fat lip.

Or both. Amazingly, even his clients got used to it. And they all knew who inflicted it on him.

"Man, he really worked you over last night, huh?"

"Yep."

"You have to have us meet this guy someday – have him show us his stuff."

"He's not running a parlor act."

At the end of meditation, the students all stood up and bowed their heads towards their teacher, who returned the bow and went down the line to hug them individually before he officially ended the session.

"*Class dismissed!*"

"*Thank you, Sensei!*" they all yelled in unison.

At this point, everyone stooped down and laid their bodies on the mat. This included Sensei.

He had pushed everyone, along with himself, to almost complete muscle failure. And then he pushed them some more.

They all laid there for the next half hour – the silence intermittently interrupted by some short conversations alternated with various doleful moans and the sounds of dry heaves from White Sam.

Anyone who had entered the dojo with any anger, frustration or the slightest bit of irritation left depleted of any energy to devote to such feelings.

Therapy session complete.

Neco left to return home so he could go up the stairs to Petey's room and give him some attention and *his* nightly hug.

The applicant would be ready for his big interview tomorrow morning. He did not suspect the importance of the meeting would reach new heights before he awoke.

CHAPTER SEVEN

7 June 1989, Harrisburg, Pennsylvania

By six-thirty the next morning, Martin Shurmur drove down 3rd Street in his silver BMW to the Attorney General's office building. The middle-aged Shurmur, in his second year as the State Attorney General, still approached his job with the same energy he had as a newly graduated law student. He liked to be one of the first ones to the office, if not *the* first one.

However, no amount of enthusiasm motivated this morning's early arrival.

Last night had been sleepless. He had gone to bed after midnight, but lay awake having 'nightmares'. A missing agent did that to him.

Yesterday there was not only a bust that failed to materialize, but Agent Curtis Walker went missing before he even reported to the office for final coordination. Under the circumstances, it became a foregone conclusion that he was dead. If the whereabouts of an undercover agent became unknown during an assignment, his chances of being alive diminished with each passing hour.

Over twenty-four hours had passed.

Shurmur could not shake the sinking feeling in his stomach. Three other agents had lost their lives in separate narcotics assignments during the last six months.

The Attorney General figured he may as well get back to the office and be prepared for the worst.

As he closed within a block of Walnut Street where he would turn, Shurmur saw the street to the building taped off by the police and the whole area already littered with squad cars, crime scene unit vans and an ambulance. Red lights flashed throughout, and the street filled with the smell of exhaust from too many vehicles left with their motors running. A crowd of gawkers started to form outside the taped perimeters with three news vans.

Damn it! Why wasn't I called?

He pulled out his car phone and answered his own question.

The phone had not been charged during the night. His battery had died.

Shurmur double-parked the BMW by a squad car and stepped onto the street. Two officers recognized his vehicle and made way to let him inside the perimeter.

"Hello, sir," said one officer.

"Hello, Mr. Shurmur," said the other almost at the same time.

"What happened here?" demanded Shurmur.

"Someone tried to call you, sir. When there was no answer, the Assistant A/G was called. He's over near the steps. You better just go see for yourself."

Shurmur removed a handkerchief from his inside pocket, took off his wire-rimmed glasses, and gave them a quick cleaning. He looked beyond the barricade but did not see his assistant. Instead he saw object of all the attention.

The Attorney General walked over and got a better line of sight towards the steps leading up to his office building. He paused in his stride and grimaced.

On the steps he observed a body – a black man dressed in blood soaked clothes. Shurmur knew who it was and broke into a quicker pace. The other officers and crime scene investigators all took a few steps back to let him up the steps.

There lay the body of Agent Curtis Walker. Personnel from the Coroner's Office had seen their share of murders before, but never more grisly than these recent ones. A new member of the coroner's office tried to place Walker into a body bag, but vomited on the steps when he had to touch the agent.

A look below Walker's face revealed that someone had made a deep incision just below the jaw bone; the incision ran straight down to the area of the Adam's apple. Someone then reached through the incision and pulled out the entire tongue to hang there. Shurmur recognized it instantly. He had seen it done on three previous agents working undercover in Philadelphia.

The Colombian neck-tie – the signature touch of the anonymous killer or killers working behind the scenes of the dealers targeted by Attorney General's Office. The Colombian neck-tie warned anyone even *contemplating* to work undercover against the Colombian cartels to stay away.

One additional factor made it even more gruesome.

A Colombian neck-tie was administered while the victim was still alive.

The State's drug problem kept getting worse, and this latest casualty turned out to be another rock to push Shurmur against his hard place.

Shortly after his election in 1988, Shurmur invested a lot of time and effort to help a State Senator with a new bill. Together they pushed for the State Legislature to approve enough money into the budget to fund an unprecedented Special Task Force. They had submitted it earlier in the year and a vote loomed for it next month.

If approved, Shurmur would run it, including the addition of a new satellite office for him in Philadelphia.

The war on drugs came with three major barriers.

First, federal law prevented coordination between the FBI, the CIA, Customs, the DEA, local police and the Attorney General's Office. Second, the state had a severe lack of money allocated for battling drug dealers, which contributed to the third barrier – insufficient manpower.

The Special Task Force would address the lack of coordination with the creation of the satellite office.

The office would be headquarters for not only the Attorney General's Office, but all the other law-enforcement agencies as well. The bill also included substantially increased funding. A lack of manpower would no longer be a problem.

But the early indications showed the bill did not have enough votes locked up to pass. Other priorities came ahead of coming down harder on drugs. Agent Walker's death would make no stronger point than the deaths of those before him. The State Congress needed more pressure than this latest casualty.

Another member of the coroner's office took over for the one with the weak stomach. He zipped up Walker's body bag as the other investigators continued to look for clues.

Shurmur stood rigid at the top of the stairs.

His deputy walked up to him. Shurmur did not even say hello. The first thing he voiced was a question.

"Are the wife and two sons safe?"

"Yes," answered the deputy. "They were taken to a safe house before Walker's meeting. And, as you know,

Walker was an only child. His parents have passed away with any aunts and uncles he had. The deputy looked back at the body on the steps. "We've got to make a dramatic change in our methods."

"I may have a solution today," said Shurmur, still also staring at the body. "Meet me in my office in ten minutes."

The dismayed Attorney General made his way into the building where his agency occupied the last three of sixteen floors. Shurmur took the elevator to the top, entered his office and sat in his red leather, high-backed desk chair. There he reclined back and folded his hands across the receding dark brown hair on his head. *I've got to act fast.*

Six years ago, Martin Shurmur served the public as the District Attorney for Lackawanna County out of Scranton,

Pennsylvania. His reputation as a no-compromising DA quickly spread throughout the state as he zealously sought any death penalty to be had. Then two years ago, he parlayed some strong endorsements with political contributions that doubled those of his opponent. He sealed the election as State Attorney General and began confronting new heights of evil.

His eyes drifted to the morning newspaper that had been brought to his desk by the night security guard – part of the guard's daily routine.

A front page headline jumped out at him.

THREE DRUG ARRESTS IN PHILA.

Shurmur grabbed the paper and began reading.

He finally put the paper down, opened up a drawer in his red mahogany desk and pulled out a personnel folder he had reviewed many times over the last week.

The name on the file read "Juni Neco, Jr.".

Just then, the Deputy Attorney General, Anthony Sorvino, entered the room.

The two men went back together from Scanton, where Sorvino was Shurmur's Assistant District Attorney.

Sorvino had dark brown hair, parted to the side, olive skin and a slightly wide nose. At a trim six-feet in height, he only had an inch on his boss, who also took watched his weight. Both wore expensive custom-tailored Italian suits and silk ties with matching pocket squares.

And leather shoes imported from France.

"Hello, Martin," said Sorvino, "I'm sickened over the whole Walker scene. I know his wife. I'll break the news to her if you want."

Shurmur nodded. "Anthony, you're right. We can't keep functioning this way. Something dramatic has got to change with our agents' operating procedures."

Sorvino spotted the personnel folder. "When do *I* get to read that?"

"It's not classified material. Read it right now," said the boss, sliding the folder to the other side of the desk. "He's sent in an application to work for us. Maybe you can help me make a recruiting decision on this guy."

Shurmur then flipped the newspaper over to Sorvino. "But take a look at this first."

Sorvino sat down on a matching upholstered low-backed chair and grabbed the newspaper. "What am I reading?"

"The one on the three drug arrests."

"You think it was him again, don't you?" asked Sorvino, looking again at the personnel folder.

"I *know* it was him."

"They would never say it in the article."

Shurmur leaned forward with his hands and forearms on the desk. "Three arrests in one day? I'll bet you dinner with our wives it was him. I'll make a call to Camden."

Sorvino picked up the folder. "What's the issue with recruiting him – do you question some aspect of his qualifications?"

"Hardly. His qualifications are stellar. Look at that background. Read the reports."

Sorvino began reading out loud. "Very advanced martial arts skill."

"Yeah, he came that way right into the police academy.

He made a travesty of the police training for hand-to-hand combat."

"It *is* a joke. Have you ever seen the academy training while working your way up the ladder?"

"I've taken some tours," said Sorvino. "During one of them, I witnessed them being paired up for boxing matches.

It wasn't pretty. No coaching. They just put on their shorts and gloves and were told to go at it. Lots of flailing around, especially with the women."

Shurmur pretended to look surprised. "You could tell the difference?"

"According to stories I've been hearing, this Neco guy made *all* of them look like women. When Neco was first informed it was time for boxing, he refused to be put in the ring with anyone."

"Let me guess. He was afraid for the welfare of others?"

"Damn straight," said Shurmur. "He was finally ordered to participate. To hear this other officer tell it, Neco finally gave in, saying something to the effect of telling the coach to pair him up with someone he didn't like. He said once the bell rings, he doesn't hold back." Shurmur sighed. "The poor bastard fighting Neco was knocked cold with one punch."

"Where was he trained?" asked Sorvino.

"He's never revealed that. But people who are knowledgeable about martial arts say he exhibits the skill of a Tenth Degree Black Belt."

"How many of *them* are on the planet?"

"I don't know about the planet, but, here in the United States, probably not too many."

Sorvino looked down at the open folder again. "There are a lot of high commendations here. I can see why the Camden County Prosecutor's Office was anxious to snap him up. What's your consideration?"

"Almost every commendation is countered by a report of his disregard for authority and rules. That same police contact I have tells of a time when some female officer was soliciting donations for a project her kid was doing in public school. As an officer back then, Neco made it a habit to just carry enough cash for his daily needs – you know, lunch, whatever. He politely told the woman he would bring a donation the next day."

"And then what happened?"

"Well, apparently she was a bit of a bitch, and this rubbed her the wrong way. She marches out of there and tells her boyfriend, a big brute, that this Puerto Rican has diss'ed her, and she demands satisfaction. The brute, who is also a superior officer, goes back to confront this 'disrespectful' little punk. He and Neco start having words and a small crowd of other officers gather as the antagonism is escalating. Neco finally calls him out, right in front of everyone."

"Right there, on the spot?"

"No." said Shurmur. "The brute gets challenged to meet him on some little back street after duty. Neco also wonders out loud if the guy's wife knows he has a girlfriend."

"And?"

"Neco shows on time. The brute doesn't. Neco sticks around an extra two hours, making it a point to have any other squad cars passing by to see him waiting."

"So the other guy never shows up?" asked Sorvino.

Shurmur reclined back and started swiveling back and forth as he talked. "Word had it he was strongly advised by another woman on the force, who told him his showing up for the fight could be signing his death warrant – that Neco could kill him. While she outright admitted to this superior *she* didn't like him either, she also said she didn't hate him enough to see him dead."

Sorvino just stared back as his boss continued.

"Those few friends Neco *did* have warned him word was out he better not hold his breath during future incidents when he radioed for back-up, because it just might not be as fast as needed."

Sorvino put down the folder and nodded. "Have you ever met him?"

"No."

"Set up an interview. You read people well. See what you think after your experience with him."

"I'm way ahead of you. He's coming in at eleven this morning. Special Task Force or no, I can always strengthen our existing office."

"Yes. A Puerto Rican who speaks fluent Spanish would be invaluable to us for undercover work."

"Yup," agreed Shurmur. "As long as he doesn't get shot by his own troops!"

"As long as he doesn't get shot by his own troops," repeated Sorvino, as he rose from his chair.

Shurmur waved an index finger at Sorvino as he reminded him, "I'm betting you dinner with our wives it was him."

As Sorvino left, Shurmur picked up his ringing phone.

"This is Shurmur."

It was a man from the crime scene investigation unit.

"Sir, we may finally have a lead on the bastard doling out Colombian neck-ties."

CHAPTER EIGHT

Hours later, Juni Neco made his first appearance on the premises of the State Attorney General Office's building. He usually dressed in a scruffy manner – tee—shirts, faded jeans and sneakers. And so much the better if the jeans had a hole or two.

Today he looked resplendent in a navy blue pinstripe, three-piece suit, starched white shirt, red silk power tie and . . . a matching pocket square.

He also had a clean shaven face.

On this late morning, he crossed the marble flooring in the lobby for his interview with his prospective employer, Martin Shurmur.

As a police officer, he had pulled down about twenty—four thousand dollars a year before taxes. Plus the city provided a good health insurance package.

With his move to the Camden County Prosecutor's Office came only a modest increase in pay – about four thousand.

But the perks were substantial. Agents always drove around in only the finest of confiscated cars. They were reimbursed for all the gas used. All meals eaten while on an assignment were picked up by the taxpayers. And the agents kept all the fine clothes purchased by the county for undercover work.

Like the impeccably tailored suit he wore this morning.

With all these additional benefits, an agent really made sixty thousand a year.

Becoming an agent with the State Attorney General's Office, however, started with a salary of one hundred thousand *and* the agent received all the same additional benefits. It was the salary equivalency of one hundred and sixty thousand dollars a year.

So Neco figured he would be better served during the interview by looking like a million bucks.

"May I help you?" asked an overweight security guard, looking up from his newspaper, behind a desk in the lobby area.

"My name is Juni Neco. I have an appointment with Martin Shurmur for eleven."

"Please sign in," said the security guard as he picked up a phone.

Neco signed in while the guard announced him.

"Yes, there's a Mr. Neco here to meet Mr. Shurmur for an eleven o'clock appointment. Uh huh." He put down the phone. "Someone will be right down for you, sir. Please have a seat."

The applicant for the A/G office took a seat and turned off his pager to eliminate the last possibility of a disruption. His cell phone remained in his vehicle.

A few minutes later, a tall gentleman in a charcoal suit walked up to the security desk. "Mr. Neco?"

"Yes."

"Good morning. My name is Anthony Sorvino. I'm the Assistant A/G."

"Good morning. Please call me Juni," said Neco, shaking his hand.

"All right, Juni. If you'll follow me, I'll take you to Mr. Shurmur's office."

Neco motioned with his hand. "Lead the way."

They walked to the elevator.

"That's a nice suit," commented Sorvino.

"Prosecutor's Office purchase?"

"Thanks. Yeah, before nailing a dope dealer, I had to look good with my two crack-whores."

Sorvino almost spit as he laughed. *"Oh, Martin is going to love you!"*

The two men took the elevator up to the sixteenth floor. When they emerged, Neco was led down a hallway adorned with art that showed off Pennsylvania's rich history. Silver aluminum-framed and matted water colors from a local artist included the Liberty Bell, Independence Hall and Elfreth's Alley, featuring the oldest continuously-lived-in residential area in the United States – from the late 1600's to present time.

Within moments they arrived at the reception area for Shurmur's office.

The secretary, already knowing of Neco and his escort, did not get her boss on the intercom. She remained silent on her word processor and let them pass.

Sorvino opened the door and allowed Neco to enter first.

He made the introductions and left.

Shurmur motioned with his hand to a chair in front of the desk. "Have a seat, Juni."

"Thank you, sir."

Before he sat, Neco took in the view from the window behind his prospective boss. His office looked directly over the beautifully domed Capitol Building.

"Listen, Juni. I'm not going to take up a lot of your time. I've looked over your file extensively and wanted to meet you in person. I really have only several questions for you."

"Shoot," said a smiling Neco.

"What are you going to do for me if I hire you?"

Neco smile grew wider. "Mr. Shurmur, I have set records for arrests wherever I have been. If you hire me,

I will set a record for you. It's my understanding you will be running for governor in the primaries starting in less than two months. The damage I can do to the drug—dealers should be worth a lot to you in the eyes of the voters. You can be voted in for the Democratic nomination and ride the momentum right through to the general election."

"Yes, if highlight videos were composed of narcotics enforcement, you would be the lead performer on the screen.

My concern is your blatant disregard for the rules. You have a reputation for taking matters into your own hands with both assignments and internal affairs. How are you not a liability to me?"

"Sir, have you ever been out in the field?" asked Neco.

"You already know the answer to that question."

"As a matter of fact, sir, I do. You have not. May I speak off the record?"

Shurmur motioned with his hands for Neco to keep talking.

"As someone who *has* been out in the field, on all levels – from patrolman to working deep undercover – I can tell you there are two sets of rules. There are the rules of your office, and there are the rules of the street. And the rules of the street are so vastly different from what you are taught in your office, it takes great discipline to u*nlearn* those rules of the office."

"So you don't take the advice from those who have never been out in the field, eh?"

"Let me tell you a little story. Just several months ago, I was one of two speakers at a state Fraternal Order of Police convention. The agent speaking before me was bragging of his exploits, how he had worked deep undercover and survived being shot eight times. When it was my turn to speak, I voiced some disagreement with his manner of operating."

Shurmur asked, "Did he have anything to say about that?"

"Oh hell, yeah! He took offense over that and interrupted me from the door and shouted back into the room to protest how I was undermining him. And the audience became very quiet awaiting my response."

Shurmur leaned forward. "What did you do?"

"I asked the audience if they would rather listen to someone who had worked deep undercover and been shot *eight* times? Or would they rather listen to someone who had worked deep undercover and *never* been shot?"

"And?"

Neco chuckled, "A lot of them pointed to me and said 'you!' Boy, did that piss off the other agent! He just cursed under his breath and stormed out into the hallway."

Shurmur grabbed the personnel file for Neco and arose from his chair, "Juni, with all due respect for your past successes, I want to show you what you'll be up against if you come on board here. Walk with me."

The two men turned left around a corner and ten yards to the right was a glass door flanked by a glass wall sections revealing the conference room.

"Let's step in here," said Shurmur, opening the door.

"This is where we create and co-ordinate a lot of our tactical actions in the war on crime."

In the center was an eighteen foot, red oak table shaped like a slim football with its tips cut off. Six low-back leather chairs were positioned across the table from each other. At the head of the table was a high-back leather chair with arm rests and a manila folder laying in front of it.

Martin does like his thrones, thought Neco, wandering over to a full-length window that ran the width of the room. "Another great view of Harrisburg."

"Let me direct your attention to a less prettier view," said Shurmur, placing the personnel folder next to the other one on the table. He made his way to the wall behind his chair.

On the wall were twelve 20 X 20 inch sections of street maps for the greater Philadelphia area – each dry—mounted on foam board with wooden frames and no glass.

Neco studied the displays and noticed pins with two different colored heads punched into the maps. "What do the pins and colors represent?"

"Each section has two street maps," answered Shurmur, pointing to one. "The first one has red pins showing the locations of drug arrests for last year by the local police – mostly kids and some small-time dealers. We're not talking kilos here." He pointed to the next one." The second one has blue pins for the same area this year.

Tell me what you see."

"Two things are clear," said Neco, using his right index finger to make his point. "There are two to three times the arrests for this year over last year and there are more arrests in the suburbs this year."

Shurmur nodded. "And we're only in the middle part of this year. The wall on the other side of the room has street maps extending a little further from Philadelphia.

They're not nearly as bad yet, but, if you took a look, you would see the trend is going slowly in the wrong direction more and more throughout the state. And you know what really rubs salt in the wound?"

"What's that?"

"The big dealers have larger budgets than we have.

They can afford the best in automatic weapons. And their private warehouses have state-of-the-art security systems," said Shurmur, walking over to his conference chair.

Neco followed him over, stood in front of his prospective employer and looked him confidently in the eyes. "Well, you did indicate you wanted me to know exactly what I would be getting into with your office.

But I know I can be a big asset to you. You've shown me nothing I can't confront."

Shurmur took his seat, picked up the manila folder and opened it. "Then let me show you this." He grabbed an 8 ½

X 11 inch color photograph and handed it to his applicant, who followed his lead and sat in the chair next to him.

Neco held the photograph and grimaced. The picture showed a head shot of Agent Curtis Walker showing his Colombian neck-tie in graphic detail.

"I've already lost four agents to a cold-blooded killer," said Shurmur, leaning back in his chair and cupping his hands behind his head. "But, this office *cannot* back-off and we *won't* back-off. Are you still up for this?"

Still holding the photograph, Neco waved it at Shurmur. "This is someone trying to tell me that I can't do something. And when someone tries to tell me that I can't do something, that only makes me want it more. I have a mindset to follow some simple rules on the street that keep me alive."

"I see," said Shurmur, dropping his arms and placing them on the arm rests. "Tell me about these rules."

"Among my rules for the street are some very vital ones. One, you cannot be afraid to kill someone, and you cannot be afraid to die. Two, when you're working undercover, you have to recognize how insane these criminals are. Then they have to perceive you as just a little bit more insane than the craziest guy in the gang."

Shurmur did not say a word.

Neco continued. "Working out in the field is the supreme test of one's acting ability. In Hollywood, you can screw up and get as many takes as needed to get the scene correct. Out in the field, you don't even get a *second* take. One screw-up, and either the criminal gets away, or worse, he escapes and you lose your life.

The *only* reason I have remained alive to even *persist* in bringing down criminals; the only reason I am still around to make my *seniors* look good, is my strict adherence to rules 'one' and 'two'. Unfortunately, that can carry over into how I behave with colleagues and superiors. If you want me, you have to take me as I am."

The Attorney General let out a deep breath. "I like you, Juni."

"And why is that?"

"Because most everybody else around here wants to kiss my ass and tell me what they think are the correct responses."

Neco flashed a mischievous smile. "May I call you 'Martin'?"

Shurmur's face took on a suspicious look. "Sure."

The smile broke out into a wide grin as Neco talked through his laughter. "Martin, I will never, *ever* kiss your ass! But I *will* promise you this. If you do hire me, I *will* set a record for you."

"If I hire you, and you set a record for me, I will have you come out here for a personal acknowledgement."

"You're not listening. When I set that record, *you* will come out to see me."

Shurmur shook his head. "I'm actually following up on a lead we have for the murderer. I'll be Philadelphia this afternoon. God willing, we'll nail this guy before I have to hire you and put up with your antics."

There was a short rap on the door. The man, who then let himself in, was a little taller than Neco. He had a strong jaw, shortly trimmed salt and pepper hair, and and wore a charcoal grey suit. He had a few small age spots on his cheeks, but he still looked great for shaking hands and kissing babies. "Am I interrupting anything?"

"Not at all, Senator," replied Shurmur, as he and Neco stood from their chairs. "We were just wrapping up."

The senator reached out his right hand at Neco.

"Good morning, son. Donald Carvey, Pennsylvania State Senator."

"Good morning, Senator," said Shurmur's guest, shaking his hand. "Juni Neco, registered Clayton, New Jersey voter." During introductions,

Neco made especially good eye contact. He commented on the senator's. "You look like you've had a late night on the campaign trail, Senator."

Carvey pondered for a moment. "Hmm? Oh, you mean my eyes . . . yes! It *was* a late night. Are telling me my eye drops didn't get all the red out?"

"Doesn't look like it, sir," answered Neco.

Shurmur chimed in, "Juni here is an investigator with the Camden County Prosecutor's Office. "He's sent in an application to work with my office and we were just completing a hiring interview."

"Camden, eh?" chuckled the senator, "Well, I won't hold that against you, son. It's quite all right, since my next election campaign will be starting this September as a candidate for the Democratic Presidential Primaries.

I welcome votes from my Jersey constituents." Carvey noticed Neco' personnel folder on the desk and picked it up. "Do you mind?"

"Be my guest," said Neco.

"Hmmm . . . says here the person you're most proud of is your father. Is that right?"

"Yes, sir. My father was a hero to me. I was the youngest of five children, and before I was born, he had fought in World War II, and later, in Korea. My father earned Purple Hearts during both wars. The second medal came after he was shot, then missing in action for three or four months and presumed dead before finally making his way back to his troops. Later, as I grew older, I was able to fully comprehend how brave a man he was."

"If you're any indication, he did a fine job of raising his five children. I have two myself."

"Juni," said Shurmur, "your father and the Senator share something in common. The Senator has also been awarded a Purple Heart."

"Is that right, sir?" asked Neco.

"That's quite right, son," said Carvey. "The Attorney General is being very kind for bringing it up. I received my Purple Heart for action when I was serving in Vietnam."

"Then it's a double honor to meet you, Senator."

"Well, I can see you were on your way, so far be it from me to hold you up any longer trying to schmooze a vote out of you," said Carvey, chuckling again. "You get back to Clayton and tell those people that a vote for Don Carvey is a vote for a car in every garage, a chicken in every pot and a mailbox in front of every house."

"No problem, Senator," smiled Neco, who turned back to Shurmur and reached for his hand. "Martin, if you have no other questions, I'll be looking forward to hearing from you."

"Thanks for coming out, Juni," said Martin, shaking hands good-bye.

Neco left the room and closed the door behind him.

Carvey kept quiet until Neco was beyond the glass walls. Then he turned to Shurmur. "Keeping up with your EOE interview quotas, Martin?"

"I beg your pardon?"

"You're not seriously looking at hiring that crazy Puerto Rican, are you?"

Shurmur tilted his head and kept his jaw from dropping. "Do you have something against Puerto Ricans,

Senator?"

"Of course not! I've just got something against *that* Puerto Rican."

"What are you talking about?"

"Oh, come on, Martin!" said Carvey, throwing his head to the side. "I was meeting guests in the lobby, and while they were signing in, I saw the name 'Juni Neco' registered to see you. As I've been expanding my contacts over the last several months for this campaign, this guy's name has been popping up all over the place. And he doesn't even work in our *state*! This guy is an insolent son-of-a-bitch! And *you*!"

Shurmur leaned back and put his hands out, "Me what?"

"When I was coming up to the other side of the door, I actually heard you *validating* his flippancy! That only promises to beget you more flippancy!"

"It was harmless," said Shurmur, shrugging his shoulders.

"Are you aware there's a rumor that just last week, he absolutely *manhandled* a police captain in Philly?"

Shurmur's eyes slightly widened. Silently, he went back to the head of the table and sat back down.

Carvey continued. "An hour after that, he nearly strangled one of his own men back in Camden. I'm not supposed to know that. And now neither are you."

Shurmur felt there had to be a good reason. "Did you find out why?"

Carvey could not believe Shurmur would give the reason any significance. "Who *cares* why?" he asked rhetorically.

"You don't go around trying to put your own people in the hospital! For Christ's sake, the dealer they *caught* didn't get that kind of punishment!"

"He accomplishes amazing things. And now more than ever, we need some amazing things done here."

"Martin," said the senator, taking the seat just vacated by Neco, "we are both about to campaign for our party's primaries. I used my influence and gave you a strong endorsement for the Attorney General's job."

Shurmur bristled slightly. "I earned my stripes as a pretty good DA in Scranton."

"Hell, yes," said Carvey as he started shaking his index finger at Shurmur. "But, I included you in *every* speech, in *every* county, in *every* stinking town hall meeting I held while stumping for my re-election to the Senate. I pointed to you with pride as my endorsed candidate for Attorney General. I believe even *you* have to admit it made a difference in what turned out to be a tight race."

Shurmur looked impatient. "Is there a point on the horizon?"

"*Now* I'm pushing you for the gubernatorial primaries.

Do you really want some no-fear-of-consequences renegade on board who might call you out in front of everyone, or, even worse, hold you down by your throat on your own desk, like he did that captain in Philly? It's lose-lose! If you *don't* stand up to him, you're perceived as spineless with your own personnel. If you *do* stand up to him, you're still viewed as the idiot who brought him on board."

Shurmur countered, "I don't think it's a matter of him not being stood up to."

"What are you talking about?"

"Don, I once read about an ancient Asian army where an outstanding brave deed was recognized by an award of the title 'Kha Khan'. It wasn't an army rank. The Kha Khan remained the rank what he had, but he was entitled to be forgiven the death penalty ten times in case, in the future, he ever did anything wrong."

The senator shrugged. "What are you saying, this guy is a Kha Kahn?"

"Yes. Whether people are aware of it or not, Neco is instinctively, begrudgingly or gratefully being treated as a modern day Kha Kahn. He's forgiven the death penalty when he does something not in the rule book."

The senator chose not to acknowledge the last statement as he stood up and walked towards the door.

"While championing you, I will continue to push for support on my Special Task Force Bill. As it stands now, we don't have enough votes committed to this. The vote is coming up on the nineteenth of June. I am going to keep pushing it hard, and I'll get it! Then you won't need this Neco. So, please don't make me look like an idiot."

He closed the door behind him.

Down in the lobby, Neco turned on his pager. The instant beep told him someone had tried to reach him during the meeting. The "911" attached to the end of the phone number indicated it was a call regarding the evening's upcoming bust in New Jersey. Neco had to speed back to Camden.

CHAPTER NINE

West Philadelphia

Later, that mid-afternoon, a group of men in blue uniforms quietly took their positions at the front door of a row home just off the Baltimore Pike. The surrounding area had squad cars blocking off all traffic from that street. Other police officers, on foot, waved cars and pedestrians towards alternate directions for their destinations.

"Police! Open up the door! We have a warrant to search the premises." yelled the young officer, surrounded with a full complement of armed uniformed police with bullet-proof vests and helmets with visors. He pounded on the door of the row home again and shouted.

They heard no answer.

Martin Shurmur had flashed his ID to get through the road blocks and finally pulled up in his BMW about one block away from the targeted residence. He looked at his watch. It read several minutes after four o'clock. He had left shortly after the interview with Neco, but construction on the turnpike had delayed his arrival, so he had called ahead to make sure the search would not be delayed. He rolled down his window and motioned to a detective standing in the street. "Detective! What's the status here?"

"We got a solid picture ID from someone recognizing Willie Greenwood using that residence," replied a detective about Shurmur's age. "Either he's not there or he's not answering. But we have a warrant, so we're going in. If we can find Willie Greenwood, we're confident he can lead us to the killer."

As soon as the words were out of his mouth, the officers on the front stoop of the row home bashed in the door with a battering ram and rushed through the opening. They quickly checked out each room along with the basement and declared the area clear. The crime scene investigation unit made their way in and pulled out their tools to comb the premises.

The unit did not need any aids to make out the widespread splatterings and massive stains of dried blood on the concrete basement floor. They went to work.

Two blocks away, a Black man with dreadlocks wearing sun-glasses stood beyond the perimeter set up by the police.

Willie Greenwood reached up and slightly lowered his sun-glasses to get a clearer look. He allowed himself an ever-so-slight smile as a single thought went through his mind.

They'll never find anything useful.

Then he nudged his sun-glasses back up, turned and walked away.

CHAPTER TEN

Gloucester, New Jersey

Roughly four more hours passed as four unmarked police vans from the Camden County Prosecutor's Office drove down a dark street in Gloucester City. They carried agents from the office along with some of the town police.

Gloucester was not The Badlands. But they could be seen from there.

On the Delaware River, Gloucester had a little bit of Clayton in it – an old town with not much new development and the houses pretty much the same ones from fifty years ago. But Clayton did not have the redneck factor. And Clayton had a cleaner feel to it. In Gloucester the lawns were not as well kept and flower beds displayed a minimum of creativity.

Juni Neco' disregard for authority paled in comparison to that of the folks in Gloucester.

Outsiders did not get a good reception. Neither did minorities. Police officers driving through the neighborhoods stayed alert to the prospect of their squad cars being the target of rocks thrown from hidden sources.

So the combination of an *outside* law-enforcement official a*nd* a minority gave that person a triple whammy on their presence.

It was nine o'clock and the vans took parking places about a half-a-block from the targeted residence. The agents from the Camden office marched down a street all geared up for a raid. In the dark, the street was safer than the sidewalk where thick, developed tree roots fought to break through the concrete, causing lots of uneven footing. Four drivers stayed behind in the vans with their radios on.

Neco did not lead this operation. Blake assigned him as part of the crew to bust down the door. Neco carried a sawed-off shot-gun. Most of the other officers possessed their nine-millimeter handguns. Two in the group toted the battering ram.

In coordination with the local police, Blake orchestrated everyone's strategy. Those not storming the house would be positioning themselves for crowd control as well as to cut off potential escape routes.

Neco walked with his group and closed to within six houses of the targeted residence. Out of the corner of his eye, he noticed an old man sitting in a rocking chair out on his covered front porch. The old man looked like a hillbilly with unkempt hair and a long scraggly beard almost covering his sunken cheek bones. He placed his two thumbs behind the straps that held up his overalls.

As he rocked back and forth, he stared at Neco.

Neco shot back a look as if to say, "What the fuck are you looking at?"

The old man kept rocking. "Well! Well! Well!" he exclaimed, "What have we here? A niggah!"

Neco turned to him as his captain grabbed his arm.

The old man kept rocking. "Hey, niggah! What trash are you foraging through in *these* parts?"

Neco clicked his gun, without raising the barrel.

"Don't even play around, Juni!" admonished Blake, putting one hand on the barrel and keeping it down. "You are *not* going to fire on him."

"I won't shoot him," said Neco, pulling the gun away. "Just let me singe his beard."

Blake toned down his demeanor. "I know Gloucester doesn't have the best reputation for racial tolerance.

But, most of the people are good, honest, hard-working people. Don't let one of the smaller percentage get under your goat. Just keep it down and keep walking."

Another shout came from the porch.

"Hey, niggah! You let me know what you find foraging through the trash! Maybe I'll give you a shiny nickel for it!"

Blake pointed an index finger and flashed a scorching look at the man rocking. "I might not stop him next time.

If I were you I would just shut up!"

The old man just stared back and kept rocking.

Time for the raid.

The house had all of its lights on. Alternative rock music blared all the way out to the sidewalk.

Blake shook his head. *No wonder they never heard the old bastard down the street.*

Six officers, including Neco, crept up the front porch steps, two with the battering ram. Six others manned positions to the sides and rear of the house.

Captain Blake peered through a porch window. Inside with the Jamaicans, he saw the homeowner – a Caucasian, probably in his mid-forties. The Jamaicans faced away from the front window. The seller faced the window as he looked down to count the cash in his hands.

The lead officer saw Blake's signal. "Police Officers! Open the door! We have a warrant!"

It was only a formality – even as he yelled the words, the battering ram bashed into the door. Simultaneously, the officers in the rear kicked in the back door.

The three startled occupants never had a chance.

Within seconds, the agents and policemen swarmed in and wrestled them to the floor . . . right next to several small packets of heroin.

Neco and two other officers quickly turned them face down to cuff them.

"All right, my good man," began Neco to the seller, "I'm gonna pat you down here. Just tell me right now if there's anything that could stick me." He wanted to know about any drug needles, especially any used ones.

No reply.

"Answer me!" yelled Neco, jamming a knee on his prisoner's spinal cord.

"Uhh! No! No! There ain't nothing that can stick you, man! Now get your fucking knee off me!"

"Sure," said Neco. "Just let me get my balance here." Then he jammed the knee in harder.

"Owww!"

Neco took his knee off and found a small handgun around the waist area.

The officers yanked the prisoners to their feet and directed them back to the waiting police van.

As Neco marched his man down the street, he saw the old man still rocking in his chair. "Well! Well!

Well!" shouted Neco. "Look what the niggah found during his foraging! *White* trash!"

All the other agents and police officers burst into laughter.

The old man got up, scowled, flipped everyone the middle finger and went inside his home.

Back at the crime scene, the lead officer called out to Blake from the basement. "Captain! Captain Blake!

We've got a surprise down here!"

CHAPTER ELEVEN

8 June, Camden, New Jersey

The next morning, an unshaven Neco, dressed in tattered blue jeans and a tee-shirt arrived at the Prosecutor's Office a little after ten o'clock. Those involved in the previous night's arrest could come in late.

So after the usual dropping off of his son at preschool,

Neco had gone to Bally's for an extended workout before reporting to work.

He sat at his desk when the realization suddenly set in that he had left his cell phone at home. Mentally kicking himself, he picked up his desk phone, called his wife and asked her to bring it to the office. Today she must have been having a good day, because she agreed with no resistance, almost cheerful. Security would alert him when she arrived and he would go to the front entrance to meet her and retrieve his phone.

About an hour had passed when he left his desk to go to the men's room.

By the time Neco returned to his office, someone had already pinned up on one of the walls a large poster of a hillbilly staring straight into the camera.

Handwritten on the poster was the following inscription:

Well! Well! Well! What have we here?

Neco' lips curled up and he let out a long laugh.
This cued a chorus of laughter throughout the hallway.

One source of the laughter walked into his office.

Sandra Tomasson took a position in front of Neco' desk. At roughly, five-foot five, one hundred sixteen pounds, the striking, tressy blonde, rivaled Ada Hernandez for the title of Miss Prosecutor's Office 1989.

Today she wore her skinny blue-jeans, and a collared blue pull-over shirt. This brought out the sharp blue eyes she had compliments of a pair of colored contact lenses.

She smiled at Neco. "I just had to see your face before I grabbed some lunch and left for my doctor's appointment."

"Did you do this?"

"When I learned what happened in Gloucester City, I pulled out that poster I had gotten at a flea market as a gag gift for my grandfather. This was a *much* better purpose." Then Tomasson put a little twinkle in her eye and put out a tease. "Hey, come give me some company at Amy's Deli. They're still serving *breakfast*."

She knew Neco enjoyed having breakfast for lunch.

And Amy's served the best breakfast in Camden.

That got Neco' interest. "Good idea. I really haven't started here yet." He paused. "And if we go now, it'll be before the lunch rush. Good idea, Miss Sandra. Damn, you're pretty smart for a woman."

Then he laughingly half-defended himself from a punch to the upper arm.

A minute later, the two agents approached the man sitting at the security desk by the front entrance.

"If Blake is looking for me," said Neco, "tell him I went to Amy's and will be back in less than an hour."

Amy's Deli, just a few blocks away, could be reached within minutes by foot. By the time the two agents were less than a block away, the aroma of French fries and grilled sausage began stimulating their appetites.

But, Neco prediction was a little off. Already a line formed at the counter where people stood to place their order. And seats were already about three-quarters taken.

As the background noise of conversation in the air mixed with the sounds of metal utensils and plates clattering into bussing trays, Tomasson quickly proposed a strategy. "You secure a table for us near the window and I'll put in our orders. I know exactly what you want – scrambled egg whites, turkey sausage, home fries, wheat toast and green tea."

"I guess I'm getting too predictable," said Neco now starting to point with his index finger. "I'm gonna get that table in the corner over there."

Neco walked over and sat in the chair facing the door. For seven minutes he stared out the window at the passersby, doing some girl-watching, until Tomasson was back standing at the table with a ticket showing the number that would be called out when their food was ready.

"So what did *you* end up ordering?"

"I ordered my own rendition of breakfast: An egg salad sandwich with bacon and pepper-jack cheese on rye."

Neco looked approvingly. "Oh, that sounds pretty good. Maybe *I'll* have to try that next time."

"You'll enjoy it." Then she sidled up behind him.

"And while we're waiting, I think you'll enjoy this." And she began massaging his neck and shoulders. "My goodness, you have to learn how to relax. You're all knotted up back here. Have you been under more stress than usual lately?"

Neco reached back with his hands and gently removed hers. "Sandra, you have a husband," he said softly.

"From whom I am separated. He said he doesn't like my 'dark side'. Believe me we are *not* getting back together."

"You're aware that *I'm* married."

"I also know you have a wandering eye."

It was true. Neco did have a wandering eye – there was nothing secret about it. He openly appreciated the female body. Always did. He loved the way a woman's hips swayed back and forth when she walked. And if she had a little bounce in her chest, so much the better. By the time he was in college, he was in the best shape of his life and never at a loss for having companionship. Women hit on him all the time. And back then, he was happy to oblige them.

Years later with marriage came his vows and the end of his promiscuous days. Neco remained loyal to his wife.

"I told my wife that was part of the package when she married me."

"Honoring a marriage is unusual in a profession where the divorce rate is fifty percent higher than the rest of the country. What about all the stuff I hear about making out with other women when you're under cover?"

Neco half twisted around in his chair. He extended his arms out with his palms up and shrugged his shoulders. "Things changed when I came over here from the Philly P.D. I was just telling the Pennsylvania A/G yesterday that working undercover demands the ultimate in acting ability. Making out with other women is no different than in Hollywood. The spouses of actors know that sometimes their partners will be called upon to do romantic scenes. It's the same when you're hanging out with dealers – a vital part of the image is having your way with women. It comes with the territory."

Tomasson grabbed him by the shoulders and made him face front again. "And you're bound to your duty." She began massaging his shoulders again.

Neco grinned, stood up from his chair, turned around and took a step back from her. "I am bound to my duty. However . . . I never shit where I work."

Tomasson's face winced.

"That phrase is my mood killer," said Neco.

"I see how that could be effective," said Tomasson, her lips pursed. "How about if I started working for the A/G?"

"I would still be married."

"Then maybe someday, I'll just have to shoot a scene with you," said Tomasson, as she reached out and stroked Neco on the cheek.

The next instant, they both looked toward the window with widened eyes. There stood Neco' wife with his cell phone in one hand – equally wide-eyed. Only *her* eyes had *fire* in them. Without saying a word, she spun around and ran down the street back towards her car.

"Mrs. Neco!" shouted Tomasson. "What's she doing here?"

"Aw shit! No! She brought up my cell phone! Security must have told her I came here," yelled Neco, as he darted around the table and jostled between other customers going to their tables.

Tomasson muttered to herself, "Now *that's* a mood killer."

Neco burst through the door and out onto the sidewalk. He saw his wife already climbing into her car.

Neco ran up to the vehicle but the window was up and the door locked.

"Hon! Listen to me! It's not what it looked like!"

"Don't worry!" she shouted through the window. "You were clearly acting in the line of duty!"

And with that, she peeled back several yards in reverse, shifted into drive and floored the gas pedal again. Another driver, coming down the street, slammed on his brakes to avoid hitting her *and* Neco.

Neco stood frozen with his hands pressed against the sides of his head.

Behind him, he heard another unwelcome voice in the distance.

Captain John Blake marched across the street.

"Neco!"

The frustrated agent dropped his hands and turned around to see Blake closing in.

"Neco, you know the policy on bringing domestic problems into the office. Whatever that was, I need you to put it aside until later." Blake did not wait for agreement. "I have something to show in the conference room."

"Regarding what?" asked a still distracted Neco.

"Regarding the raid on that house last night."

"What happened?"

"After you left with the three perps, our men found more evidence."

"A whopping extra shitload of heroin? I saw the packets when we came in."

"No." said Blake, the furrow in his brow becoming more pronounced. "Much worse. You're coming back with me to the conference room."

Breakfast would have to wait.

Back at the office, Ray Diaz looked up from his desk in response to a fellow investigator entering his work area. With the man, walked a tall Hispanic civilian. He had a pear-shaped body and thick, matted-down hair, as if he were overdue for a shower.

The man, somewhere in his early thirties, wore handcuffs. His tanned skin made his oil-stained hands look even darker in areas.

"You sit here," said the investigator, directing his prisoner to a chair. Then he turned to his colleague.

"Ray, I need you to watch this guy while I find the captain. Where's Blake?"

"He followed Neco outside. He should be back any minute," replied Diaz, "What's happening?"

"His name is Roberto Quintero. He's a dealer we caught two days ago. I just need you to watch him while I go talk to the captain. Can you *do* that, Ray?"

"Yeah, sure. He won't be going anywhere."

The other investigator walked off and left the two men alone.

Diaz looked at his 'guest' and spoke in a low whisper.

"So they finally caught your fat ass, eh, Gordo?"

"Just shut up, Ray!"

Diaz began laughing under his breath.

Gordo glared at him, "What's so fuckin' funny?"

"Back when we were growing up in the neighborhood, and I was entering the Academy, you always laughed about how I would die as a cop before you ever got caught as a dealer.

Pretty funny now, huh? They didn't nab you at the garage, did they?"

His reluctant guest looked down at the floor. "No.

69

You know I never do deals at my garage, man. I'm not gonna risk involving my mechanics with my outside business. The cops got me in a back alley over in Northeast Philly with a buyer, who got shot and killed while trying to escape."

Why aren't you with the Philly police?"

"I'm cutting a deal."

"So you're just tired of living?"

"Not that kind of deal. I'm not diming out any of my suppliers."

"What else do you have to offer?"

Gordo did not answer until someone walking by the door moved along out of sight. "My competitors."

"Isn't that just as dangerous?" asked Diaz.

"No. With my buyer being shot, none of my peers will even know I got caught. They won't even know there was any incident involving me. As far as they're concerned, some careless little shit got himself killed. What's really going down is that I'm going to help your agency bring down other dealers."

"And *that* doesn't scare you?"

"Shit, no!" said Gordo. "You guys got it down. I deal in cocaine, but, as you know, I'm pretty small-time.

One of your boys will pretend to be a buyer who wants more than I have access to. So, I introduce him to someone who can produce the goods. Me and the other dealers agree that I get a nominal finder's fee for the first deal. At that point, I just drop out of the picture. Your boy makes a couple of more purchases, and then he ups the ante again.

The dealer won't be able to handle it, and he'll hook up the agent with a bigger fish for the first deal for a finder's fee—just like I did. Then *he* drops out of the picture. The agent's credibility as a buyer grows with each new deal . . ."

"Until he finally meets the biggest fish in the pond," finished Diaz.

"By that time, I'm three or four levels removed from the game. The bigger fish don't even know I was ever involved. That's when the investigator finally pulls off the final step – both him and the dealer getting busted together by your agency. In the eyes of the higher-ups, that's just two criminals getting caught."

"And you get your nominal finder's fee from the first dealer."

Gordo became smug. "That's just the icing on the cake, Ray. I'll make additional cash with the government helping me in my efforts."

Diaz sat back and pursed his lips. "Ah, that explains the canary feather poking out of your mouth."

"Well, that too," said Gordo. "But I was referring to how it keeps the competition from growing in my area!"

"What do you mean, 'keeps the competition from growing'? This kind of puts you out of the game now,

'doesn't it?" Then came the realization. "Holy shit!"

"Keep your fucking voice down!" Gordo said in harsh whisper.

Diaz looked out the door, leaned forward, and whispered back. "You still intend to *deal*?"

"Hey! I have to, my man. Think about it. If I'm seen turning away business from my customers while hooking up people with buyers . . . now *that's* dangerous."

"Do *we* know you'll still be selling stuff?"

"Nobody knows nothing, man. Just like you haven't 'known nothing' over these many years. I say nothing.

Nobody knows nothing."

"They didn't grow up with you like I did."

"It'll be fine. I can help them get much bigger players than me. I just have to be smart about it. All I need is the right man to work with."

"Ooh, ooh! Me! Me!" said Diaz, his eyes widening.

"You're shitting me, man," laughed Gordo.

"What? I would be *perfect!* We've known each other forever. Who would know how to work with you better than me?"

"Ray, you need to stick to working on the wire taps and stuff."

"I've been out in the field!"

"Not undercover. You just stake out the area where a bust is going down. No one would believe you're a dealer."

Diaz bristled. "I just led a bust the other day!'

Gordo stared back in disbelief.

"I did! I busted two Colombians! Plus, I'm Puerto Rican. I speak . . ." Diaz shut his mouth as another person walked past the door. "I speak fluent Spanish!"

"And you look, dress and *act* like a preppie," scoffed Gordo. "Look at you – designer slacks, a collared pull—over shirt and a sweater tied around your neck by the sleeves."

"So?"

The two old friends buttoned their lips as two of Ray's fellow investigators walked by and looked in on them.

"Yo, Ray! Are you working today?" asked one man.

"You got a hot date this afternoon?" asked the other.

The two men did not wait for a reply and continued walking down the hall.

Diaz looked down at his outfit as Gordo continued.

"And I've seen you in the chillier weather, man. Then it's *designer* sweat suits."

"I can dress differently."

"You could, but you would still look out of place.

People look at you and want to ask where the polo game is."

"That's bullshit!"

"Ray, do you remember that man last month in D.C., who was riding that train and just pulled out a gun and randomly started firing at people?"

"Yeah?"

"If he saw you standing in that train dressed like this . . ."

"Yeah?"

"You would have been the first person he shot!"

Ray persisted. "I'll prove it to you. Let me be the first one to work a case with you. If it doesn't fly . . ."

". . . you might die," said Gordo. "And I might too. No, my dear, naïve dumb ass. I will not work with you. The person I work with will be someone who can pull off being the baddest of bad asses. Someone who looks like they would be right at home in a back alley to cut a deal.

It'll be someone who looks like they would kill you just for looking at him the wrong way."

Just then, Captain Blake walked by the door, returning to his office from the conference room. Several steps behind him stepped the investigator who dropped off Gordo.

Neco, holding a folder, brought up the rear. He still had a scowl on his face from the earlier moment with his wife.

"Him!" shouted Gordo, pointing at Neco with both the index fingers of his cuffed hands.

Neco stopped in the doorway. Blake and the other investigator came back to join him. Ray Diaz's long-time friend asked to meet his prospective partner.

After the introductions, Neco sized up his new informant. "Mr. Gordo, you finalize all your agreements with these two good people here, and then report to my office. If you pass your interview with me, we'll get right to work." He held up the folder. "I have something a little different to show you."

CHAPTER TWELVE

As soon as Gordo had passed his interview and made his agreements with Neco, he wished he had not.

Gordo stared, his mouth slightly agape, at the photographs Neco had spread out on his desk.

"I didn't sign up for this!" said the Prosecutor's Office newest informant.

"Oh, but you just did," replied Neco, "Your involvement with us is not selective on your part. You don't pick and choose your cases here."

"The spirit of the agreement was *drug* dealers, not a*rms* dealers! *Look* at this shit!" Gordo pointed to the photographs. "Those are Uzi's and Mac-10's . . . Mac-fucking-

10's! I'm no gun expert, but I recognize *those*, they're assault weapons! Uzi's are used by Jamaican Shower Posses!

Have you ever heard of a Jamaican Shower Posse?

"Yeah," answered Neco, matter-of-factly. "If some Jamaican gang wants to take over a corner that someone won't sell them, they do a drive-by shooting with a shower of bullets when the reluctant seller is back at his corner.

Then they take over the corner. That's another reason the two Jamaicans we caught were connected with the seller – they were also purchasing arms to take over some real estate."

Gordo put a finger on one of the pictures. "What's in the boxes?"

"Ammo – hollow points."

"What's different about hollow points?"

"More stopping power. On impact with soft tissue, they expand out instead of passing through the body. And since those are forty-five millimeter, anyone charging you will be knocked on their ass," said Neco. "But there's a bigger concern."

"What?"

Neco pointed to a photograph of some rifles.

"*Those* are Russian Kalashnikovs. See the scopes? They're high-powered sniper rifles – the last damn things cops want in the hands of the enemy."

"The last damn things I want in the hands of the people I'm informing *against*! Listen, the arms dealers are whack jobs! You don't even have to screw them. They'll shoot you just for the fun of it!"

"Have you ever heard of a man by the name of Arnie Schmidt?"

Gordo shook his head back and forth.

"That's the name we got from the seller we caught."

"Great!" said Gordo, "Then go arrest him."

Neco gave him a cold, steely look.

Gordo got the message and took a deep breath. "I've never worked with arms dealers. What do you expect *me* to do?"

"All we got is the name. The only prints on the guns were those of the ones in the house we raided. We *do* know his address. He lives in a room above his mother's house in Pennsauken, New Jersey. The only problem is that we're told he doesn't keep the weapons there. His supplies are somewhere else. And there's another problem."

"I'm afraid to ask."

Neco placed his finger on another photograph.

"Those are M-16's."

"What makes them worse than anything else there?"

"You could go out and buy an AR-15 rifle . . ." began Neco.

Gordo stopped him there. "Could you just stop with the ABC-20's and the XYZ-30's, and just tell me what makes those so bad?"

Neco flashed back half a smile. "Here's the bottom line. They're both automatic weapons. The AR-15 is semi-automatic. But the firing mechanism is set to fire only one round at a time. One pull of the trigger equals one bullet. The M-16 will empty the entire clip with one pull of the trigger."

"Still doesn't sound like a huge difference to me."

"Oh, there's a huge difference."

"What?" asked Gordo.

"M-16's are military issue." Gordo stayed silent as Neco continued, "It would appear our friend, Mr.

Schmidt, has a contact in the armed forces."

"Gosh, if I beg, can I help you *now*?" said Gordo, his voice dripping with sarcasm.

Neco began wondering if this new relationship was going to be worth it. In his mind, this new informant seemed to spook way to easily. And yet, he *still* felt more comfortable with the idea of working with him than working with Diaz. And this man could generate valuable leads. He decided to maintain patience. "Just relax.

This will work the same way as with the drug dealers. You scrounge around and put out the word you have someone in the market for some guns. Hook me up and get out while I go on and make a small purchase. Then I'll come back without you and ask for some heavier artillery he can't provide. I'll work my way up the ladder until I meet this guy. By that time, you are *way* out of the picture."

"*If* you even meet him. There's no guarantee they will lead to Schmidt."

"No, there's not. But I figure when we ask for Kalashnikovs, that'll start greatly improve our odds. In the meantime, we'll also obtain a warrant to tap his phone, try to put a tail on him, and see what produces a result first," said Neco.

"Fine. I just hook you up once and get the hell out."

Neco crossed his arms. "Do you know someone to get the ball rolling?"

"Yeah, I know someone who likes his guns."

Gordo's assignment had begun. So, Neco finally escaped from the office. As he sped down the highway, he tried to reach his wife on both her car phone and the home line. A recording came on each time asking to leave a message.

Neco called a third number.

"Hey, Sensei!" greeted Ron Goldbach. "What's up?"

Neco told of how his wife surprised him while receiving an unsolicited backrub from Sandra Tomasson.

"So she storms out of the Prosecutor's Office and now she isn't picking up either phone," Neco summed up. "*Now* what the hell am I supposed to do?"

"Let sleeping bitches lie."

Neco thought to himself. *Serves me right for seeking advice from a person who hates her.*

The marriage was already on the decline by the time Goldbach had come into Neco' life. Neco knew Goldbach could sympathize with someone who had bad luck, but he had no tolerance for anyone using underhanded ways to control others. That was all he observed with her. It would have been fine with White Lightning if his sensei had gotten a divorce long ago.

"You are no goddam help." said Neco.

"C'mon, Sensei," replied Goldbach. "You know what'll happen. In a day or two, she'll thaw out, and it'll be just another incident in her rear-view mirror that will disappear in the distance."

"I don't know, Ron. We had just had an earlier confrontation over the whole issue with my female partners, and then *that* happens. I think 'objects are closer than they appear' in the mirror this time."

Neco turned onto Chestnut Street. Up ahead he could see Petey standing out in front of the Herma Simmons Elementary School.

"Ron, I gotta get off the phone. Petey's about to get in the car."

"All you can do is come from the truth. You tell her what really happened."

"That's all I ever do."

"Let me know if you defuse the bomb."

Chapter Thirteen

Scranton, Pennsylvania

Over two-and-a-half hours away, out in Lackawanna County, the Northeastern side of Pennsylvania, Senator Donald Carvey, orated like a televangelist. He stood behind a podium inside the Town Hall and addressed the packed attendees at a noon town hall meeting.

The senator had come a long way since his youth in New Hope, Pennsylvania.

His parents still lived on the same estate, a moderate drive from a marina where they docked their yacht. His father, a retired military general, and his mother, still a passionate activist for the environment, had decided early in little Donnie's youth that he would be groomed for the highest office in the land. The young boy not only bought into it early, he reveled in it. For their only son, it was nothing but private school followed by enrollment for political science in Yale University and a subsequent hitch in the United States Marines out in Vietnam.

War heroes make good presidential candidates, they told him.

Donald Carvey served, earning a Purple Heart in the process for a minor flesh wound.

By the time he returned from overseas, his father had further greased the runway and lined up a governmental entry-level job in Bucks County, north of Philadelphia.

A couple of favors called in brought back a nomination for local town councilman in Doylestown and later more campaign contributions for a higher office. The son continued to climb up the political ladder to his current position as a state senator for the Commonwealth of Pennsylvania.

Carvey continued to rev up the crowd.

He held up an article cut out from a local newspaper. "First it was Merion County! Then Lancaster County! Now teen-agers are being arrested for peddling drugs in Lackawanna County!"

A murmur shot through the crowd. He put down the article and held up an eight-by-ten color photograph. It had the face of a smiling Caucasian teenage boy. "This is Gerald Waterson. He's been going to a private school in Merion County . . . straight-A student, fourth in his class.

Slowly his grades started to dip. The parents could not understand it. The boy had a history of high grades. It made no sense. Until . . ." Carvey put down the photograph with his right hand, and grabbed another from the podium with his left. " . . . *this* was found in his bedroom!"

He held a picture of drug paraphernalia: spoons, matches, straws and cocaine—the items needed for free—basing. Carvey switched to another picture. This one was a Caucasian teenage girl. "This is Tiffany Grayson – valedictorian for her high school in West Chester County.

She had been given a full scholarship for Swarthmore. Not anymore. Tiffany has been selling heroin to her fellow graduates this summer."

The senator put the picture down. "This is no longer someone *else's* problem! This is no longer just the government's problem! This is *everyone's* problem! And right now, our narcotics officials are not operating at full capacity! Our agencies are not in coordination with each other! They lack funds! The drug dealers have bigger budgets to *sell* drugs than we have to *fight* them!

The drug dealers can purchase higher technology for surveillance and better weapons than *we* can!"

This provided the loudest murmur of disapproval from the crowd.

Carvey knew he needed to set up his biggest applause line. "I'm *not* here tonight to ask you to enlist in law enforcement. I am *not* asking you to become vigilantes. am not even asking you for money. But I *am* asking you to help me pass my bill for a Special Task Force that will provide *more* funds, *more* manpower, and *more* coordination between our agencies! Call your local representatives!

Call them and tell them to vote on the nineteenth of June for this bill! Tell them that *you* want Pennsylvania *safe* for your children!"

A series of "Yeahs" began to build. The timing would never be better.

"As your senator, I will help make Pennsylvania a model state in the war on drugs. And if you vote for me in the Democratic Primary and then the general election, as your President, I will take this model and export it to the rest of the states in this great nation! But I need *you* to start making a difference in America right here in Pennsylvania! Start making a difference right here in Shurmur Country! What do you *say*, Lackawanna?"

Carvey pumped his fist in the air and basked in the resounding applause and cheers.

He would send another video to his mother and father.

Next he would dial up the pressure on the public to a new level. First he would have to do what was necessary to separate himself from his security. He would pretend it was time to go home. No one could know of his next destination.

Chapter Fourteen

14 June 1989,
Fort Washington, Pennsylvania

First, George Martinez privately cussed himself out for even answering the office phone. Then he cussed out the caller. "Dammit, Willie! Why are you calling me at my work number? *Have you lost your mind?*" Martinez caught himself speaking too loudly and dialed it back. He used his other hand to steady himself on his knee to lift his tall, corpulent body from his office desk chair. "What the hell are you doing? I've made it clear you are *never* to call me at this number!"

Computer Resource Dynamics, a business software company, had set up shop in an upscale office complex just off the Pennsylvania Turnpike, northwest of Philadelphia.

George Martinez, hired on the ground floor of the company to head the programming department, earned his way to the title of Vice-President for Research and Development – a more impressive title if one did not know the company only had eight staff members.

"Sorry, Bro. This is an emergency and I dialed without thinkin' of the time," said Willie Greenwood.

"My boss is coming to see me and he could walk through my door any minute. I'll call you back on my car phone."

"You've got five minutes."

"*What?*" exclaimed Martinez, who caught himself again,

"You don't dictate to me when . . ."

"This ain't comin' from me, bro . . ."

"There's no one else *besides* you and me! Who . . . ? I have to go. I'll call you back."

"Five minutes, for your own good."

Martinez hung up the phone and snapped his briefcase shut. Quitting time arrived, but his boss wanted to see him before he left.

Despite their small staff of fourteen, Computer Resource Dynamics continued to grow incrementally and Martinez had been a big part of that. Even better, he could do more and more work out of his home– a farmhouse on some extensive property in Exton, about an hour further west.

His boss entered the room and addressed him. "That was a fine presentation this afternoon, George. I told you shaving your beard would make you look younger. You still may want to reconsider my advice to shave that tanned head of yours, or at least coloring the flecks of grey in the micro-mini afro."

"I'm not even forty yet, sir. But thanks," said Martinez, removing his hands from the briefcase. "It's having a body like Barry White that adds a few years."

"From all indications, the sales department will have this deal closed on Thursday."

"I feel good about it, sir."

"Then you're about to have an even better feeling, George."

"Why?" asked Martinez, giving his watch a furtive glance.

"I'm giving you off tomorrow and Friday. Take a four-day week-end. Leave early tomorrow, beat that shore traffic and get down to Wildwood or someplace. Have some fun with your family."

"A four-day week-end! And I told my wife I had to come in and work on the project this week-end. Man, if we can leave on Thursday, I'm going to Saratoga Springs in upstate New York!"

"Saratoga Springs. Great mineral spas, a national award-winning Main Street with great antique stores, and wonderful bed and breakfasts."

"And horse-racing," added Martinez.

The sound of a ring interrupted the conversation.

Both men checked their phones.

Martinez recognized the number – Willie Greenwood's – and let out a suppressed sigh followed by a lie. "It's the wife. I better take this. Don't let me hold you up."

"Have fun, George."

You too, sir. And thank you!"

His boss exited. "Lock up!"

"Will do, sir!" said Martinez, stepping over to close the door. He hit the "talk" button on his phone and answered. "Christ, Willie! What the hell is going on?"

"Hey! My brother from another mother!"

"Just get to the point, Willie! What couldn't wait fifteen more minutes until I got to my car?"

"You need to meet with me at the Carlyle Hotel in Philadelphia in an hour."

"An hour?" Martinez grimaced. "Do you understand what the expressway will be like now?"

"That's why I couldn't wait another fifteen minutes.

There's a surprise waitin' for you. A nice one."

Martinez braced himself to hang up. "I've already had the only surprise I need – a four-day week-end."

"Perfect!" said Willie. "You'll need it. You're goin' on a trip."

"That's right . . . to upstate New York. Bye Willie."

"George, don't hang up, man! There'll be consequences . . . serious consequences."

Martinez steeled himself. "Is that a threat?"

"Not from me, bro. This comes from someone who knows about you."

Martinez gritted his teeth. "Knows *what* about me?"

"About you giving up state's evidence out West . . . where you're hiding, and he knows who still wants to know where you are. Everything, man."

Martinez felt a shiver through his whole body. All his years with a perfect cover, all of his hard work to remain undetected was now crashing in one bone-chilling moment. His eyes flashed with anger as he darted towards the door, opened it, and peered both ways down the hallway.

He spoke in a loud whisper. *"Who the hell have you been talking to, Willie?"*

"Chill, my man. I've been just as blindsided by this as you. You don't think the water is just as hot for me? Walk to your car while we're talkin'."

Martinez went back to retrieve his briefcase and rapidly strode to the door and down the hallway, as Greenwood kept talking, "The good news is that this doesn't have to be a bad thing. This is a golden opportunity for you. Now I suggest you get your ass down to the Carlyle by six-thirty. Otherwise, by six-thirty—one, a man by the name of Alejandro is going to start tellin' people where you are, and what you've been doin'"

Martinez knew if that information was ever disclosed, he would be doomed. The only question would be how he would die. A car bombing? A hail of bullets from a Jamaican Shower Posse? A shiv from behind in a prison shower? He spit out the only answer he could, "I'm on my way."

Who the hell is Alejandro? And what does he want with me?

Chapter Fifteen

On Interstate Highway 95, just north of Philadelphia,
Goldbach answered his car phone and heard Neco. He could tell just
from the "hello" his best friend felt down.

"What's happening, Sensei? You don't sound too good," said Goldbach.

Neco, also driving, spoke from South Jersey without the usual energy
in his voice.

"As I was leaving the office, I got a call from Shurmur.
He's not hiring me for the A/G's office right now."

"Damn! Did he say why?" Goldbach felt his sensei's voice rising more
from dejection to suppressed anger.

"He gave me some bullshit about how he had to address some other
priorities that suddenly came on his plate.
Said he has some shit he has to handle before he takes on more
personnel."

"Like what?" asked Goldbach.

"He wouldn't say. But it doesn't make any sense. I thought we really hit
it off during the interview. He knows my record. His office has already lost
four agents this year to drug dealers. There's *something* he's not telling me."

"So that's it? That's where he left it?"

Neco settled down. "Nah. He didn't close the door, but he has no idea
when he'll be addressing more hiring. This is *not* the news my wife will
be expecting to hear. She's still sulking over the incident with Tomasson.
It couldn't have hurt to have her think I would be transferring away from
'that woman'."

Goldbach knew how to make his sensei laugh. "Would you feel better
beating the living shit out of me?"

"Very tempting," said a chuckling Neco. "But I'm working late tonight. Something big has fallen in our laps and we're doing a raid. Maybe *tomorrow* night I'll beat the shit out of you."

"Give me a call later, if you need to."

"Thanks. And stay away from Camden tonight."

"I *always* stay away from Camden. Don't let Diaz screw you up on this one."

"Diaz is in no position to screw me up this time and I've personally coordinated with the local police. All I can say is, there better be no more surprises."

CHAPTER SIXTEEN

Dexter Rasche stood in the back parking lot of the Prosecutor's Office and looked at the light fog creeping over the city of Camden as he and the rest of his unit donned their bullet-proof vests.

Beautiful night for a raid, he thought to himself.

Should be memorable.

For this assignment, no one wore "play clothes" as the unit called the various disguises used for some stings. No hotdog vendors, no homeless get-ups. Tonight the plan only called for the vests, helmets with visors and dark blue jackets with the words "PROSECUTOR'S OFFICE" written in large, white, block-print letters.

Baby carriages and walkers stayed in the huge garage with the other props. Captain Blake's crew packed electronic megaphones, 12 millimeter sawed-off shotguns, and sniper rifles. Lastly, one barrel-chested officer also added a one-hundred-fifty pound cylindrical hunk of cast iron with metal handles as part of the mold —a battering ram, or as it was known to the police, "the ram". The investigators holstered their standard issue 9 millimeter automatic handguns.

The targeted residence waited in Camden, just minutes away.

Captain Blake addressed his personnel. "Okay! Let me have everyone's attention! Everyone face this way."

Sixteen men and two women, Hernandez and Tomasson, moved away from the four vans being used and gathered around.

Blake turned and pointed to a high-rise office in the distance. Everyone watched as he continued. "We'll be heading towards the row homes about eight blocks behind that abandoned office building. Juni and Gordo will be arriving shortly before nine o'clock. We will close in right behind them and await the signal to the surveillance van. Juni estimates no more than six men, including the dealer, armed with handguns. But, they will have quick access to boxes of high-powered artillery. There is no rear entrance and no access through the windows. So when that signal comes, our entry through the only door must be swift and blinding."

The captain finished his briefing and everyone began climbing into their vehicles. Ray Diaz went in the surveillance van. Blake's lead van left with the others following behind.

The last van pulled out from the garage with one notable item left on the concrete garage floor.

The ram.

CHAPTER SEVENTEEN

Out on the Western side of Pennsylvania, Senator Carvey also worked late. In the town of Greensburg, a little over an hour northeast of Pittsburgh, he addressed a large constituency of local law enforcement officials from Westmoreland County in the Hempfield Area High School auditorium.

Carvey spoke from behind a podium holding a microphone, "You are all working in small towns. The current law limits your activity to the jurisdiction of your municipalities, making it impossible for you to do undercover work. How are you supposed to do undercover work in a small town where everyone knows you?"

"We can't!" shouted one man's voice from the group.

"You're damned right, you can't!" acknowledged Carvey, pointing at the man. "That's what makes this Task Force Bill so effective for the suburbs. This will allow officers from one jurisdiction to be assigned to another, where he or she is *not* a recognizable face! Those undercover will have a car assigned to them with all gas expenses paid for. In addition, you get full reimbursement for your meals and other expenses."

A hand raised in the back of the room.

"We have a question," said Carvey, pointing to a woman.

"Is this bill providing money for more officers to replace those who had to leave their community to work undercover?"

"No. It's even better. I can tell you the budget will address that issue in two words – overtime!"

The room filled with appreciative loud laughter and nodding heads.

"Call your local reps, officers," said Carvey. "Tell them to vote for this bill!"

Once again he had stoked a crowd to a rousing ovation.

He privately laughed, wondering how these people would respond if they knew the truth – how he covertly brought about the inflamed emotions that were so easy to manipulate for his bidding. Within days the vote for his bill would be held and he would get what he wanted.

If there could be such a thing as "emotional substance abuse", for Carvey, *this* was it.

CHAPTER EIGHTEEN

Camden, New Jersey

About an hour later, Neco rotated the steering wheel of his black van and made a left on 9th Street. Gordo sat in the passenger seat, fidgeting with his seat belt.

The silence needed to be broken.

"You realize no one expected it to go down this way?" said Neco.

"I know. I know," frowned Gordo, who continued to fidget and stare straight ahead at the dilapidated homes they passed.

By ten minutes of nine, the sun had long set on Camden. Back in the early nineteen fifties, Camden used to be a respectable little city. Located on the other side of the Benjamin Franklin Bridge from Philadelphia, along the Delaware River, it was a cleaner and more affordable area than its Pennsylvania neighbor. Some major corporations had set up camp there, including Campbell's Soup and RCA.

As the fifties turned into the sixties, the sun set again as things dramatically went downhill. The only evidence of new construction had, ironically, been a prison. Crime went on the rise and that included heavy drug trafficking.

On this night in Camden, Gordo found himself being forced to confront the exact circumstances he had resisted all these years – Jamaicans with guns.

"Gordo, how were you supposed to know your first lead was loaded-up-the-ass with weapons in their own right? We *had* to shit-can our plan to move up the ladder when the leader said he could provide whatever we needed. It was like getting our bluff called in a poker game. We never thought the other guy could bet that high," said Neco.

"The search for Schmidt is on hold while we bring these guys in."

Gordo popped a stick of gum in his mouth and gnashed at it between words. "Yeah, if I don't show up for my finder's fee, they'll know for sure I set them up. *No* one lets someone else collect their *cash* for them."

"It's going to be okay," said Neco as he put an assuring hand on Gordo's shoulder. He wished someone would put an assuring hand on him. *I really need this guy to keep it together.* "Look, Gordo, I've done this before.

I've never lost a partner and I won't let anything happen to you. Just stay in character and everything will be fine. I've got your back, okay?"

"I'm fine," said Gordo, feeling far less than fine.

Neco glanced at the buildings long deserted by Campbell's Soup and RCA off in the background. Then he pulled the van over to the curb and parked in front of their destination.

They climbed out of the car and looked at the row homes in front of them. With the exception of the abandoned ones, each home had iron bars on all the windows.

Both Neco and Gordo wore expensive, yet casual clothes. Neco had on a button-up, short-sleeve Hawaiian shirt, untucked at the waist. The top three buttons remained undone to reveal his rock-hard pectoral muscles. A wire stayed hidden around his stomach. Between the waistband of his pants and the small of his back,

Neco carried his 9 millimeter Smith and Wesson.

Gordo wore a silk Hawaiian shirt and long black pants.

He turned back to the side passenger door and slid it open to grab a briefcase full of cash.

"Now remember," began Neco, "we go in, make sure they have the guns, give them the cash, and I give the surveillance team the trigger phrase . . ."

"Which is, 'It looks like everything is in order here,'" completed Gordo.

"By then my people will be right outside the door.

The *instant* they hear the go phrase, they bust through the door and the bad guys never even have a chance to grab their guns. It's over and we all get taken away."

Gordo nodded weakly and gave a disconsolate sigh really wondering if this was better for him than jail.

They walked up to the stoop and Neco assumed the proper posture for his part – shoulders back and chin up in the air. He knocked on the solid metal front door and heard footsteps approaching from the inside.

The two sting operatives waited for someone to check them out through the peephole.

The sound of a heavy metal bolt clicked, the door opened and a young African American man silently admitted them into a sparsely filled living room area. Offensive wisps of pot and tobacco from the dining area greeted the visitors. An arch coming out of the ceiling and going down the walls separated the two spots. The middle of the room had ten heavy cardboard boxes, about thirty-six long, twenty-four inches wide and eight inches deep. Smaller boxes contained ammo.

Five other men sat at the dining table. The men's ages ranged between the mid-thirties and early-forties.

On the table lay some playing cards, stacks of poker chips and opened beer cans.

Between all these items also lay six handguns.

Four of the men, also African American, smoked joints.

The last one, a Jamaican, spoke to Neco through a cigarette in his mouth. "Mr. Neco, I'm so glad you and Gordo could join us."

"We wouldn't have missed it for the world, Julio," said the man called Neco.

"Neco" was one of a handful of aliases used by Neco during his undercover jobs. "Juni" he kept as his first name, so he would not be thrown off from being addressed with another name – or worse, *responding* to "Juni" being called out in a crowd when it was not how he had introduced himself. For this job he was "Juni Neco."

The host extended his hand with an open pack of Marlboro cigarettes. "May I offer you a smoke?" Then he noticed his guest's grimace. "Oh, that's right. You're too fuckin' healthy for that."

"I don't even like *standing* in all the smoke," said Neco, who walked towards the boxes and started opening them.

One of Julio's men motioned towards Neco' pants pocket. "What's this leather strap coming out of your pocket?"

The man called Neco snapped, "Keep your fucking hands off of me! What the hell's wrong with you!"

The man stepped back with his hands held out in the air. "Hey, chill! I was just ax'in, man!"

"Well, *no* one touches the strap! I'm here to get my *guns*, not answer your questions. So let's just get back to our deal."

The room turned quiet and Gordo quickly decided to break the tension.

"Well, *my* health is fuckin' poor," said Gordo, who put down the briefcase and reached for the pack as his partner checked out the contents of the boxes. "Let me have one of those cancer sticks."

Gordo spit his gum out into a wastebasket, pulled out a cigarette and reached for a matchbook on the table.

Julio swiped the matchbook back towards him and motioned at one of the other men, who held up a butane lighter for Gordo.

Outside the row home, the men from the Prosecutor's office emptied out of their vans and Blake used hand signals to direct them to their positions. Some crouched behind the hoods of the vans. Rasche led nine others to the front door. Inside the surveillance van, Hernandez and Tomasson looked out the window and listened intently with Diaz for the trigger phrase.

Hernandez opened the van door.

"Where are you going?" asked Tomasson.

"I noticed something," said Hernandez, who stepped out without shutting the door. She ran up to Rasche and whispered. "Opie! Where's the ram?"

"How the hell am *I* supposed to know?" said Rasche, whispering back. He turned to the other men. "Who was supposed to pack the ram?"

"Burt," answered an officer.

Everyone looked back to look for Burt. What they saw was a Black man, who looked like an enormous child frantically involved in an Easter egg hunt as he ran from the back of one van to another.

Rasche marched over to Burt, "Where *the fuck* is the ram?"

"I know for sure I packed it!" said Burt.

Blake saw all the extra animated motion and came over to find out the cause. "What's happening here?

"Burt was supposed to pack the ram, and now he can't find it," replied Rasche.

"I could have sworn I packed it, sir," said Burt. "I can't understand why it's not here!"

"And you looked in all the vans?" asked Blake.

"Yes."

"Well, we're expecting the go phrase any minute! And if we have to blow through that metal door without the ram, it's going to be with your *head!*' said Rasche.

"Everyone get to the door," ordered Blake.

"Now that you've inspected my merchandise," asked Julio, "have you got something for me, Juni?"

Neco grabbed the briefcase and placed it on a sofa with badly worn upholstery. Julio and the others watched as the opened briefcase revealed bundles of hundreds stuffed to the top.

"That's payment in full," said Neco.

Julio, stuck his handgun in his pants, walked over and flashed a wide, toothy smile. "My men will help you get those boxes out to your van."

With that, all the dealers holstered their handguns and approached the boxes.

"Thank you, sir," acknowledged Neco, who paused while Julio's men lifted up the boxes filled with weapons.

He thought to himself. *Five of them have their hands full with boxes and the other one has his hands full of cash.*

Neco determined the timing to be perfect. "All right.

It looks like everything is in order here."

Diaz heard the trigger phrase and told Tomasson to flash the van's headlights. Blake saw the signal and yelled at Rasche's team "That's it! Go! Go!"

"*Police!*" shouted Rasche, "*Open the door! We have a warrant!*"

Burt never waited for another "Open the door!" He threw his six-foot-three, two-hundred-fifty pound frame at the metal barrier.

It did not give a millimeter.

The searing pain in his shoulder did not stop him from instantly lunging at the door again. Another officer joined him.

They threw their bodies at the door.

Again, it did not budge, as they both felt like crash test dummies.

Inside, Neco found himself stunned to hear no evidence of the ram being used. Just as quickly, boxes dropped to the ground as the arms dealers drew their handguns and trained them on Neco and Gordo. It felt as if the walls of the room were rapidly moving in on him.

Gordo's face went ashen.

Neco thought, *This might be it . . .*

"*Police! Open the door now! Right now!*" screamed Rasche.

Burt and his partner continued to block out the pain and kept hurling themselves at the door.

"This was a set-up!" yelled Julio, "And we fuckin' know that it wasn't any of us that set it up! So it had to be you two! Kiss your asses good-bye!"

Six hammers clicked into position. Neco had less than a second to act. Options did not include a shoot-out.

He and Gordo would be riddled with bullets before he could even make a move to pull his weapon. That left one last desperate chance.

Neco got wild-eyed. "I can't go back to prison!" he yelled.

The men aiming their guns froze for a moment as Neco whirled his body around and screamed at the shell—shocked, gape-mouthed Gordo.

"It wasn't *me!* That means it was *you, you son-of-a—bitch! I'll fucking kill you before they take me!*"

Julio and his men stood paralyzed with confusion, their bulging eyes darting back and forth between the relentlessly pounded door and the crazed Puerto Rican.

They watched Neco assail Gordo, grabbing him by the throat.

"I'll fucking kill you with my fucking bare hands!"

Neco had Gordo around the neck so tight the big Hispanic could not speak, as he rapidly shoved him towards the door. He slammed Gordo against it and took one hand from his informant's throat to release the metal bolt holding the door shut.

With the bolt up, the door flew open, slamming into Gordo's back and Neco' forehead. It sent them both reeling to the floor.

While falling backwards, Neco drew his Smith and Wesson and fired off a couple of rounds into the living room as the officers poured through the door and opened fire. Two of the dealers took shots to their chests and fell to the floor.

The remaining dealers returned fire as they scattered for cover behind furniture.

A wounded Julio flipped the dining room table on its side for protection.

A pair of officers screamed from bullets to their upper bodies. The force of the bullets repelled them back, as Rasche and more officers behind them replaced their fire with more semi-automatics and sawed-off shot guns.

Neco, still on his back, saw Julio starting to bring his gun around the side of the table to fire at him.

But Neco already had his gun trained on the Jamaican.

Gordo, also still on the floor, saw Julio aiming at Neco. Without knowing his partner already had Julio in his crosshairs, Gordo reflexively pushed himself off the floor on top of Neco. "Juni! Watch out!"

He pinned Neco' forearm to the floor and shrieked in pain as he felt a bullet enter his shoulder.

Neco summoned up the strength to slightly lift Gordo with his forearm and fire back at the gang leader, hitting him in the wrist.

Julio's gun flew from his hand and he yelped with his second wound.

Less than five seconds later, the only sound left came from the semi-automatics.

Four arms dealers lay dead. Another lay unconscious from wounds.

The bullet-proof vests succeeded in protecting the two officers leading the charge. Their chests hurt like hell, but they remained alive to tell about it.

Julio raised an arm from behind the overturned dining table and begged for his life. "Don't shoot! I don't have a gun! Don't shoot!"

Gordo rolled off of Neco' arm and clutched his shoulder. "Nobody shoot me anymore either!" Then he whispered to Neco, "The deal's off! Send me to jail, because I am *done* with this shit."

Burt yelled outside, "We're all good! All the officers are good!"

Hernandez and Tomasson both let out deep breaths.

Neco, still a bit dazed from the impact of the metal door, did not respond. He became aware of a trickle of blood running from the middle of his forehead. Before he could reach up with a sleeve to wipe at it, he saw the barrel of a sawed-off shot gun put within three inches of his face, followed by the double-clicking sound no one wanted to be on the wrong end of.

On the other side of the weapon, Rasche smiled and whispered down to him. "We still have to put on a show for the audience outside. You never know who's out there looking." Then he ordered his team. "All right! Let's get these scumbags in the vans and bring 'em in for questioning." He barked at Neco. "Roll over on your stomach! Now!"

A livid Neco turned face down. It took everything for him not to retaliate as he felt the cuffs put on him.

Outside, Blake waved the ambulance personnel into the row home.

Before they made their way in, Gordo observed that the matchbook, earlier palmed by Julio, had been thrown off the dining table when it was overturned. Now it lay right in front of him. The informant palmed it and placed it in his pocket.

Hernandez and Tomasson ran the crowd control on those souls who had waited until the gunfire died down before daring to come back for a look. Most watched through the iron bars from their windows as officers placed Julio in an ambulance.

Next came Neco with Rasche right behind him.

"Opie," whispered Neco through heavy breaths, "I am going to fuck you up!"

"We have to treat you just like the other guy," said Rasche quietly, "It's more convincing for your cover. The better the credibility, the better to keep your ass alive.

Besides, I didn't lay a finger on you."

The loud blare of the first ambulance siren filled the air. All eyes focused on the vehicle starting down the street.

Neco saw the everyone's attention on the ambulance, "Then I won't lay a *finger* on you."

With that, he kicked his foot back like a horse right into Rasche's crotch. Rasche expelled a loud grunt and began to double over. Before he could finish a subsequent moan, Neco whirled around and swung his leg upward to kick his captor across the face.

Rasche's universe went dark. His body twisted and collapsed in a heap on the street.

"Shit!" bellowed Blake, who figured out what happened.

"Grab him!"

Two investigators grabbed Neco' arms. He gave no further resistance. "I want three men with that son-of-a-bitch in the other van!"

An EMT tended to Rasche as the investigators hauled Neco to the waiting van.

Blake, stride away, spoke in an angry whisper, "Are you fucking loco?"

Neco kept walking, looking straight ahead as he snarled back, "Opie advised that I needed more credibility as scum.

Then he was placed in seat of the back row.

Blake grabbed the seat on the front passenger side and in a slow burn spoke to Burt, who was already behind the wheel. "Give us some privacy."

Burt dutifully slid out of his seat and left the van.

The captain vented through the cage behind the headrests, as Neco sat with his elbows on his knees, staring at the floor. "I will *never* understand why you prefer to work without a partner. I will *never* understand why you often prefer your knife to your gun. And the way you go about putting yourself in the dire circumstances you do? Well, you maybe *are* loco! Maybe you just have a *death wish!* But you have *got* to cease and desist on trying to put a fellow cop in the hospital! Am I making myself clear?"

Neco finally looked up. "Where *the hell* was the ram?"

Blake turned his head away, but before he could respond, he found himself distracted by the sight of his men removing box after box of weapons from the row home, including more from a huge cache found upstairs – enough to supply a platoon of soldiers.

No one noticed Gordo escorted with an officer and another EMT, who had given him his first aid and now led him to one of the ambulances. Nor did anyone notice him studying some words handwritten on the inside cover of the matchbook.

Neco continued stewing inside his van. A big decision resulted.

Chapter Nineteen

15 June, Harrisburg, Pennsylvania

Martin Shurmur walked across the street from Strawberry Square to the Capitol Building. Using his ID and name recognition with the lobby security and his charm with Carvey's secretary, he continued unannounced to his destination. Carrying a newspaper under his arm and one large covered Styrofoam cup of coffee in each hand, he made his way to Senator Donald Carvey's office and surprised his fellow politician, seated behind a cherry wood desk full of paperwork.

"Good morning, Senator. Just thought I would deliver your coffee and daily paper for you."

He laid a copy of The Patriot-News on Carvey's desk.

The front page had a headline circled.

RECORDS ARMS BUST IN CAMDEN

The senator snorted as he placed a form in his out—basket. "I know you're just as proud as hell over your boy there. But are you also aware he put one of his own men in traction?"

"How do you *find out* this stuff?"

"I have some people," said Carvey, who opened his middle desk drawer to grab two packets of sugar and one of powdered cream with a plastic stirrer. He tore open the sugars and emptied them into the cup. The he rapidly flicked the cream packet back and forth to get all the contents to one side.

"Anyway," countered Shurmur, checking to see how hot his coffee was with a test sip. "I'll bet the guy deserved it."

"My sources tell me this last incident has earned him a nickname – 'Loco'. I think they should have gone with 'Psycho' myself." Carvey added the powdered cream and began stirring the contents together.

"Don, between recent retirements and actual casualties we've suffered, I'm being forced to use men with minimal undercover experience. They certainly don't come with the qualifications of Neco. It's like he told me, wherever he goes, he breaks records."

"Apparently he also breaks necks."

Shurmur did not crack a grin. "We could use some records broken around here, Senator."

"When I get this bill passed, you'll set your *own* records. Give me two more days. If I don't get those votes, you can hire the psycho that same day."

Shurmur spoke suspiciously, "Is that a real deal, or just a political promise?"

Carvey grabbed his cup of coffee. "That's a real deal."

The Attorney General walked out as Carvey glared at him behind his back. He blew on his coffee and sipped at it.

A deal I'll never have to make! Because I'm getting those votes!

Putting down his coffee, *he* looked at the newspaper with a frown, angrily snatched it up with both hands and crumbled it into the trash can underneath his desk.

CHAPTER TWENTY

19 June Camden, New Jersey

After the high stress of the illegal arms arrest last night, Captain John Blake simply wanted a peaceful morning.

The first three hours had been just that – minimal phone calls, no screaming demands, no sting operations scheduled and, most important of all, no internal strife with his own people. He needed to *not* be the captain for an hour without anyone *seeing* him not being the captain.

All he wanted now was to take a little time for an early lunch and enjoy one of his guilty pleasures in the privacy of his office – a deluxe Italian hoagie from Amy's Deli. Amy's featured a version of the sandwich using genoa salami, prosciutto, soppressata and extra sharp provolone. The captain paid additional money to have them add hot capicola. And any of the staff at Amy's knew to automatically drizzle twice the usual amount of extra virgin olive oil over the oregano-sprinkled lettuce, tomato, onions and hot banana peppers.

Whenever he went in to order it, all he had to say was, "I'll have 'The Blake'."

"The Blake" cost almost fifty percent more than the regular Italian hoagie but budget and blood arteries be damned!

As he opened his mouth in anticipation of his first bite of Cop Heaven, a mildly surprised Blake looked up from the sports section of his newspaper and did a double-take through his office window. Out in the parking lot, he saw a wound-up Juni Neco getting out of his car. Blake could not understand why his problem child drove in to the office on his day off.

He put his sandwich and wiped his mouth with a paper towel. *This can't be good.*

The mystery did not last long. Neco strode right by his own office and came directly to him.

"Loco!" said Blake. "I'm amazed to see you here today. You should be taking some well-deserved time off."

"Well, there's going to be *plenty* of time for that,

Captain," said an adversarial Neco.

Blake squinted his eyes, "What does that mean?"

"It means that I'm taking two weeks of vacation due to me right now." said Neco. "And during that time, I'll be exploring other options for employment.

I was wrong! Thought Blake. *This* can *be good! This can be* better *than good!*

The captain of the Prosecutor's Office suppressed the emotion swelling within him. He wanted to jump for joy, but then he recalled the earlier whispering campaign among his staff.

Neco says when the day is right, he's going to beat the living shit out of Blake.

Juni says that on his last day in this office . . . Blake will receive an early 'retirement package'.

The lid stayed on. *Don't say anything stupid, John.*

"Whoa, Juni! Is this because of the missing ram yesterday?"

Neco ranted, "It's because of the missing *ram*!

It's because of the mysterious *fax*! It's because of *Ray Diaz* assigned to a bust, which he almost blows, after *I* set everything up! It's because I have someone in this office who has it in for minorities and takes it out me during the busts. It's because there's too much fucking crazy-per—square-*foot* around here! And I've *had it!* I went through this shit back with the Philly P.D. and one way or the other, I'm not going through it again!"

"I regret what you've been up against. And I ripped Opie's face off after what you told me. I made him *swear* he would never take advantage of you again during an arrest. Not that it would make any difference if you don't come back. I mean, we would obviously miss you around here. But I'll respect any decision you make," said Blake.

"Do you have any prospects? Where would you go?"

"Some place where I won't have to keep looking behind my back," said Neco, reining it in. "But right now,

I'm going to my office to make sure all my paperwork from yesterday is caught up before I leave."

Then Neco turned and left the room. He walked back towards his own office.

The captain called out to him. "Juni, let me know if there's anything I can do – a letter of recommendation – anything." He walked out the door, then hurried back to his desk and stuffed "The Blake" in a white paper bag.

With paper bag and sports page in hand, he briskly strode out of the building.

Chapter Twenty-One

Fort Washington, Pennsylvania

George Martinez sat behind his desk with his head resting in his palms. He sat up as he recognized the sound coming from the heavy footsteps of his boss coming toward the door to his office.

"Good morning, George," said the boss as he entered the room.

Martinez raised his head from his palms. "Good morning, sir."

His boss studied the expression being displayed. "How was Saratoga Springs?" he asked warily.

"We never made it there."

The boss looked puzzled.

"Yeah, something came up," added Martinez. "We couldn't go."

"What happened? Is everything okay?"

Martinez stood from his chair. "Actually, no. I'm afraid that I have to turn in my resignation, effective immediately."

The boss's voice became a little shrill. "What? You must be joking! What's going on here?"

"There's been a personal emergency."

"Well, good lord, just tell me what's going on. We can arrange for a leave of absence. You're an important asset here. I don't think I deserve to be *blind-sided* by this."

"I regret to say it's not that easy, sir. I'm here to get my things. I'm very sorry. The four-day week-end did *not* go as planned."

The past week-end had been a whirlwind of activity for George—the memory of that whirlwind still vividly etched in his mind, starting with the shock of who Alejandro wanted him to meet.

Welcome to Hacienda Los Napoles, George!" said Pablo Escobar from the shallow end of one of his Olympic size swimming pools.

In the pool with him stood three of South America's recent beauty queens. One, a brunette. The other two, dyed blonds. All in skimpy bikini tops and thongs.

As impressive as the plane had been, these surroundings had him even more wide-eyed, as did his surprise host. It was all Martinez could do to spit out an acknowledgement. "Thank you, Senor Escobar."

"I trust you had a good flight."

"I'm not big on flying, but a fully stocked bar helped. I must say, your plane makes the ones used by commercial airlines look like flying trash cans."

Escobar kept a matter-of-fact expression. "As intended."

Indeed, thought Martinez. He had flown first class on 747's before, but this experience had been in a class by itself.

While a standard 747 would seat one hundred twenty people, the hull of Escobar's model had been gutted and redesigned to meet his exact specifications. The new spacious cabin area included a dining area and a kitchen worked only by world-class-level chefs. Behind that came the lounge with its high-backed, extra-wide leather seats.

Martinez remembered fastening himself in with seat-belt buckles made of 24 karat gold. The lounge also included a bar, and a six-by-four foot TV with a VCR to watch movies.

Finally, there was a bedroom with a queen-size bed with Escobar's private bathroom featuring a gold-plated sink.

Ten museum-quality oil paintings hung throughout the whole cabin.

The flight proved almost as intimidating as the experience with the estate.

"Um . . . you'll have to excuse me for a moment. The women and I were just about to hold a little contest." Escobar turned to women. "Ladies . . ."

Martinez did not recognize the contest. But he saw Alejandro walking up to the pool, and Alejandro apparently *did* recognize it, as he watched very matter-of-factly at the event unfolding before him.

The three women climbed out of the pool and removed their swim suits. From the pool, they walked over to a grassy section where someone had chalked a white line.

The Lord of Hacienda Los Napoles gave a signal to the driver of a Porsche, who climbed out of his car and planted two long wooden stakes into the ground just off to the side. The stakes, about twenty feet apart, had a wide yellow ribbon stretched out between them at the top.

"We are about to have a race," said Escobar to Martinez. Then he directed the contestants. "Assume starting positions!"

The naked women bent over into four-point stances like track runners.

Escobar explained to his guest, "The first one to break the tape gets the Porsche." Then he turned back towards the women and yelled, "On your mark . . . get set . . . *go!*"

The three contestants burst off the starting line and ran nothing like accomplished track runners. Escobar never tired of it.

The brunette broke the tape first, just nipping out the two blondes.

After the race, the Martinez and Alejandro were told to go to the changing room, put on some swim suits, and join the drug lord in the pool.

Martinez had suspected that Alejandro was in great physical condition – after all, that would be an important asset when "assassin" was part of the job description. The sight of Alejandro in a swim suit reinforced this.

Martinez, never thrilled to wear a bathing suit, admired Escobar's right-hand man in Philadelphia, who had a well—defined six-foot frame built for hand-to-hand combat. Two long scars, one on each forearm, added to the evidence.

Martinez heard Escobar address him as he and Alejandro began wading in the pool towards the drug lord.

"George, I'll get right to the point. You are here with me to discuss your future."

Martinez already knew that. He returned an expectant look.

Escobar motioned with his arms in an outstretched manner. "Look around, George. Do you know what it takes to have a lifestyle like this?"

"I could only venture . . ."

"Fleets of planes carrying one thousand kilos per flight," interrupted Escobar, answering his own question.

"Small, remote-controlled submarines carrying one thousand kilos from here to the waters just off of Puerto Rico, from where divers remove the shipments and transport them in speedboats to Miami."

"That's more cocaine than I can envision," said Martinez.

"Up until now, customs and narcotics agents in Miami could only intercept a small fraction. Lately it has become a bigger fraction. The same is happening in New York. Alejandro has worked behind the scenes with four different Philadelphia liaisons, all of them resulting in the execution of an undercover narcotics agent, and the subsequent transfer of our liaisons to work in another country."

"Pardon me, sir," said Martinez, "but all I know is Alejandro said if I didn't board the plane with him, my current drug dealings would become known to the authorities, and my name would be leaked to any and all dealers I was hiding from. So rather than become a man without a country, I now find myself here. Is Colombia my new country?"

"Not at all," reassured Escobar. "Yes, you are in Colombia now, but I need you back in the United States.

That is why we are meeting this week-end. You fit the profile for what I need as a front man in Philadelphia.

You are smart, experienced in dealing drugs, you have connections, and I have something to hold over you – your wonderful secret life. I want you on my payroll full—time . . ."

"Oh! Um . . . well, I guess that certainly beats the hell out of the alternative. I know that with a proper transition period . . ."

". . . immediately," finished Escobar.

"Senor Escobar," began Martinez, "I need a little time to formulate a plan. I have to figure out what I am going to tell my family. They don't know what I do when I'm not working at my company. Right now they are at home thinking I had to leave for a business trip to Rio de Janeiro."

"Again, that is why you are here. We will work out a plan to tell your family, and we have the resources to paint a good picture for them." Escobar signaled for a bartender to have three drinks brought into the pool.

"Getting a connection in Philadelphia is turning out to be a more arduous process than originally thought. It is going to take far more attention than you can devote while reporting to your office. So, effective immediately, you are now working for me full-time."

Martinez failed to keep an entirely good poker face.

"Do not look so sad, my friend," assured Escobar.

"This means more days like this. Instead of rushing into agreements with prospective liaisons, you will form a relationship. You will spend a lot of time with them over a long period. You will wine and dine with them; learn everything you can about them. And during that time,

Alejandro here will also be checking things out behind the scenes. He will scour for who else knows the prospective liaison, check out caller ID names and locations. We will make sure we get our man."

A waiter waded into the pool, carrying a small round tray with three snifters from the bartender. He handed them to Escobar and his guests.

"This is one hundred-year old brandy," said Escobar.

"Sounds more appealing all the time," said the new recruit.

Martinez held the snifter, swirled the brandy around and put his nose up to it. He breathed the bouquet and took a sip, moving it around to the different taste buds on his tongue, fully savoring the flavor before finally swallowing it.

"Imagine being able to do that anytime you like. You will be living a life of luxury. But to start, as a show of good faith on your part," said Escobar, holding up his index finger, "there will be one simple condition."

In a reflex action, Martinez downed the rest of his drink in one gulp and braced himself for what he was about to hear.

Chapter Twenty-Two

Camden, New Jersey

Ada Hernandez knocked on the open door making Neco look up from the word processor on his desk. "Is it true?

You're leaving the Prosecutor's Office?"

Neco swiveled from the screen. "As of now, nothing is official. But I'm working on it."

"I understand you've had some rough spells, but you knew what you were getting into when you got into law enforcement. You've always confronted the challenges and the dangers. Are you sure this is what you want?"

"I know I don't want a job where I'm battling the enemy and the people on my own *team*."

"What are you going to do for your livelihood? How will you pay your bills?"

"I haven't quit yet. I'm going down to Puerto Rico to sort that all out in my mind. I have enough money to cover my bills while I'm down there. And one way or the other,

I'll have work when I get back. Hopefully not here."

"Puerto Rico?" asked Tomasson, entering the office.

"When are you going to Puerto Rico?"

"I'll book a flight tonight. Then we head on down tomorrow. My older sister lives in Cabo Rojo. The family will stay with her for a while. Preschool is done for the year, and Petey loves it down there."

"What did your wife have to say about this?"

"The reaction wasn't exactly enthusiastic, but she took it favorably."

"Go ahead," said Tomasson, "say it. She's *relieved* that you won't be having any more assignments with us, right? In fact, she probably can't *wait* for you to be out of our sight."

Neco shook his head, "I think it's more because we seem to get along better down there. It's gorgeous! The water is a beautiful blue-green, and yet you can still see through it to the bottom. It's a calming environment. And I have my own sanctuary along the shore."

"One of the beaches?" asked Tomasson.

"Even better. About thirty yards off the shore is a little sandbar. You start wading out there and quickly the water is about chest high. But then you go out a little further and you begin emerging again. Finally you go out a little further and you're almost above the water again.

Your feet are only about six or eight inches under the water and you can feel a layer of vegetation you're walking on."

"Yuck!" said Hernandez, curling up her nose. "And that's your 'sanctuary'?"

"Resting on this sandbar is a large piece of driftwood – about twelve feet long, five feet wide. I go out there and lie on that driftwood and it makes me feel like I'm laying out on the ocean completely surrounded by the water.

God created a serene spot for me to use for meditation. So I use it every morning I'm down there. And to get the maximum sense of tranquility, I make sure I'm there to enjoy the sunrise . . . God! Maybe I'll leave tonight!"

"Sanctuary aside, you'll be back," said Hernandez.

"You may have come to hate this place, but you could never leave your band of brothers from the dojo."

"They helped me address my stress last night and I anointed Ron to take over the training sessions. They're throwing me a little party after work. They hope I can find employment in this area. But they're facing the fact I may stay down in Puerto Rico. I'm also gonna check around for private investigator work."

"You'll be back here," said Tomasson.

"I can't even imagine what could take place to make that happen."

CHAPTER TWENTY-THREE

With his wife still under the belief he worked for Computer Resource Dynamics, George Martinez drove his cobalt blue Lexus from Ft. Washington to his next destination – a storage facility in North Philadelphia.

Escobar's terms still rang in his ears.

"I need you to operate quickly. As incentive, your weekly 'allowance' will be withheld until you have begun cultivating your first lead for our Philadelphia connection. Once that happens, you will receive regular checks from a fictitious company each week as part of your cover."

As Escobar spoke, his newest recruit mentally planned to make a quick personal deal with one of his small-time contacts for some quick cash.

Martinez rolled into the parking lot of the storage facility where he had a unit rented under a false name. He drove up to his space and stepped out to the roll-up, garage-style door with the heavy combination lock. After he dialed the numbers, Martinez pulled open the lock and rolled up the door.

Inside, over a dozen cardboard boxes of various sizes rested on risers spread throughout the concrete floor.

Most of them contained junk from his house – an old TV/VCR set, some lamps, and other things he told the wife he was throwing out. Those boxes served as decoys in the event of anybody invading his privacy. One particular group of boxes buried a small, heavily taped container.

Martinez took a pocket-knife to it. In this box he kept his private stash – cocaine he had skimmed here and there from various jobs – far less than enough to retire on. Just enough to get through some rainy days.

This should provide enough to keep that demanding bitch at home off my back for a while.

With the container in his possession, he locked up, got into his car and pulled out his address book. The time had come for an unscheduled visit with someone who could quickly move the weight for him. Martinez thumbed through the pages and stopped at "Q".

There he is – Roberto Quintero.

For Martinez, it was a short drive to go a little further south where Roberto Quintero owned a mechanic shop on a small side street off of Castor avenue. The shop, moderate in size, possessed three working bay areas. It not only provided some steady income for him; it, more importantly, provided the illusion of him being a fine, upstanding business man in the community.

The man nicknamed "Gordo" heard a vehicle pulling into his parking lot and looked up from the hood of a car. To his surprise, he saw George Martinez parking his luxury sedan. The mechanic shop owner left the car with one of his people working on it, sprayed some solvent on his palms, grabbed a rag and began wiping his hands.

Gordo emerged from the garage and called out, "George! To what do I owe the honor of this visit?"

"Good afternoon, Gordo. I'm holding a personal fire sale, and you were the first person I thought of to capitalize on it. Where can we talk?"

"Let's go to the diner around the corner. Let me turn things over to the guys," said Gordo. "I'll treat you to an early dinner."

Martinez grabbed at the sleeve of his host's greasy overalls. "*You* take *your* car. I'll follow you." He noticed Gordo when he tugged at the sleeve. "Something wrong with your shoulder?"

"Garage accident. It's fine. Let's go talk business."

CHAPTER TWENTY-FOUR

Levittown, Pennsylvania

At those times the dojo gang just wanted to hang out, no bars or nightclubs would do. No one drank alcohol and no one could stand the smoke at such establishments.

Tony's Family Restaurants operated a small regional chain in the tri-state area. Their policy of being open twenty-four hours a day made it particularly appealing for Neco and his students. Except for Black Sam, who had an early bedtime. But that did not matter for an early dinner party.

Still before five o'clock, the restaurant had no other patrons beyond the five of their regulars – Juni Neco,

Ron Goldbach, White Sam Schofield, Black Sam Whitmore and Mateo Meza. Having been banned for loud and obnoxious behavior from other eating establishments, Tony's still accepted them and remained as a place where they had not worn out their welcome.

Goldbach spotted Kira, the only waitress on duty, also doubling as the hostess. She instantly recognized the rowdy bunch when they came through the door. Kira knew what the crew lacked in decorum, they more than made up for in tips.

She greeted them with hugs, starting with Goldbach.

"Good afternoon, boys! A little earlier than usual, aren't you, Ron?"

Meza interjected, "I wanted to get here early enough for breakfast!"

"Once again," said Goldbach, "I want to apologize for our friend. He only *sounds* like he came from a bar. He's really just couth-challenged."

"Couth-challenged?" bellowed Meza. "That's not even a real expression!"

"I believe you can find it in the 'Goldbach-to-English dictionary' at the library," said Neco.

Goldbach watched Kira roll with it all. "It's okay, boys. We serve breakfast all the time."

"Well as long as you don't discriminate against the couth-challenged," said White Sam.

"Shut up, Sam!" said Meza. "You're like . . . stupid—challenged!"

"That would mean he's *smart*, you dumb dipshit!" laughed Goldbach.

"Let the lady escort us to our usual booth," said Neco.

"This way, gentlemen," said Kira, grabbing some menus.

Everyone sat down in a red, upholstered, half-circle booth. Neco took a position facing the entrance. The waitress handed out the menus and went to get five glasses of ice water with a dish of lemon wedges.

"What is the *matter* with you, Mateo?" asked Goldbach.

Meza stood up and broke out into a loud sing-songy voice, as he extended his arms above his head. "I just want to be *looooud!*"

"You shouldn't be acting all brazen and shit," said White Sam. "I still owe you for the sucker-punch during Shark Attack last night."

"What's 'Shark Attack'?" asked Kira, bringing back the water and lemon wedges. She pulled out her order pad.

"Sensei surrounds one student with the other four," explained Goldbach, as Meza sat down again. "Then he whispers a number in each of their ears. When Sensei randomly shouts out one of the numbers, the person with that number kicks or punches the guy standing in the middle. And he rapidly shouts out the numbers, forcing the student who's surrounded to raise his reaction time to an attack from any direction."

"Oh, my!" sighed Kira. "You people are nuts."

"He never puts us through something he's never done himself," said Goldbach.

"What's the purpose of it?" asked Kira.

"It trains proper breathing," answered Neco.

"Your body is more vulnerable to a blow when inhaling.

Your muscles are tighter when exhaling."

"And Mateo sucker-punched White Sam during Shark Attack?" asked Kira.

"Damn right, he did!" said White Sam.

Black Sam snickered and nodded.

The answer to Kira's innocent question no longer involved her. She put her order pad back in her pocket.

"Signal me when everyone knows what they want."

No one heard her.

"They're *all* sucker-punches during Shark Attack!" countered Diaz. "That's *another* point of Shark Attack – to be ready for *anything* in a fight!"

Goldbach came to White Sam's defense. "You still have to wait for *your* number to be called, Mateo! Sensei called *my* number, and I was still mid-kick when you kicked Sam in the head!"

"My number *was* called!" said Meza.

Goldbach turned to Neco, "Sensei, did you call Mateo' number?"

"Nope," said Neco. "You were out of turn, Mateo."

Meza looked away from White Lightning.

"You owe White Sam one," said Goldbach.

"I owe him one what?"

"You owe Sam one free shot at you."

"That's right," said White Sam.

"Fine!" said Meza. "Next sparring session you get the first shot."

"Nooo," said Neco. "He gets one *free* shot anytime he wants. That means you can't strike back. And it also means you can't say shit about it. You'll just take it like a man, and then everything will be even. Otherwise you answer to me. And don't think I won't fly back from Puerto Rico to kick your ass."

Goldbach and the two Sam's broke into wide grins.

"Fine! Anytime, Schofield! You hit like a pussy anyway," said Meza, getting up again. Then he broke out into that sing-songy voice again. "I'mmmmmm going to the baaaath-roooom!"

As Mateo left the table, Goldbach heard Neco' pager go off. "Do you have to take that?"

"Yeah," said Neco, looking at the number. "And there's a 911 at the end. I'm going outside to the car phone."

"I'll keep everyone in line," said Goldbach.

Their sensei made his way to the door.

Before he could exit, a burly, bearded, barrel-chested biker came through the door with his equally black leather—clad girlfriend.

The woman softly whined, "I still say you shouldn't have parked in the handicapped spot."

"The place is empty. There's plenty of spaces left for the handicapped."

Intent on getting to his car, Neco accidentally brushed against the woman. "Pardon me, I'm very sorry,

Miss."

"You need to watch where the fuck you're going, boy," said the boyfriend.

Neco paused and turned to the biker. "You heard me apologize to the lady, didn't you?"

The woman elbowed the boyfriend. "He said he was sorry, T-Bone. Let's sit down."

Neco smirked.

"Just what's so amusing? Do you find my name funny?"

"I'm going to my car now, Mr. Bone."

"That's a good idea. You better run off now and drive the hell away from here."

Neco raised his eyebrow and clenched his jaw.

"You know what? I'm going outside to answer a page. If you're still here when I return, I am going to bring you outside so I can kick your big . . . fat . . . *overweight* ass and drag you up and down the parking lot by that frizzy patch of steel wool you call a beard!" Turning, he exited the restaurant.

Goldbach saw Diaz observing this as he returned from the bathroom. He motioned for Meza to be silent. The gang watched T-Bone glare back at their sensei.

"Just let him go, babe," said the woman.

"Shut your yap! We're gonna get some food, and then we're gonna go back to my pad where you can do what you do best. That little fuck is just lucky I'm hungry."

T-Bone and his cowed girlfriend by-passed Kira and took a booth across from Neco' students.

Goldbach winked at the others, "Follow my lead," and called over to the biker. "Hey, you're going to go kick the shit out of him after you're done, right?"

"Just mind your own business, boy" answered T-Bone.

To his surprise, the nosy patron stood from his booth and stepped over.

The biker shifted his feet to get up, but Goldbach spoke again. "You don't understand. We're on *your* side.

That chump is in here all the time trying to intimidate people. We were hoping you would go out and teach him a lesson."

"Nobody here cares what you're hoping for."

"Hey," continued Goldbach. "You heard him. He's coming back in to call you out. You're gonna have to confront him anyway. I just wanted to share a secret of how to make a spic your bitch."

That got the biker's attention. He stared at Diaz.

"It's okay," said Goldbach. "It's no secret to *them!*

They *know* it.

Meza took his cue and hung his head in resignation.

The leather-clad pigeon slid off his seat and stood next to Goldbach. "What 'secret' are you talking about?"

"C'mon, Ron," said Black Sam, with a straight face.

"He's already got a size advantage. Don't get into this."

"No, Sam. The four of us have seen it enough. He's has this coming to him, and this guy is just the person to give it to him."

"What's 'it'?" asked T-Bone.

"You know, Ron, you're right," said Black Sam. "He d*oes* have it coming."

"We see him in here all the time dissing people in front of their women. I'm going to tell you how to totally intimidate a spic. What you do with the information is your business."

"What do I do?"

Goldbach leaned towards T-Bone. "First you have to stare them down . . . just for a few seconds."

"Stare them down," repeated a suspicious T-Bone.

"Yeah, you stare them down. At first, they might give you some false bravado – you know – like 'What the fuck, man?', but you just keep staring. For some reason this mentally paralyzes them." Goldbach turned to his booth.

"Am I right, Mateo?"

"I think it has something to do with the way our Hispanic mothers raise us," answered Meza.

"Then, after the staredown, *that's* when you do it," said White Sam.

"That's when I do what?"

"You bitch-slap him right across the face," answered Goldbach.

"Not a punch?"

"No," said Goldbach, "It *can't* be a punch. It has to be with an *open* hand. Just give him five fingers across the eyes. That's *far* worse with these people than any punch."

"Then what happens?"

"It just freezes them. It represents like total degradation or something. I don't know why; it's just something about people from the other side of the border."

"What a buncha bullshit," hissed T-Bone.

"It's true," said Goldbach, "We'll prove it. White Sam, show him what happens."

Schofield got up from his seat, facing away from a slightly apprehensive Meza.

In the next instant, White Sam spun around and gave Diaz a blistering slap across the face. Between the force and the surprise of the blow, Diaz's eyes felt like they had popped out of their sockets.

The words were still fresh is Meza's mind.

He gets one free shot. That means you can't strike back. And it also means you can't say shit about it.

Anytime Schofield!

Meza shut his eyes and bent over the table, burying his face in his arms.

It sold T-Bone. He turned and marched towards the door. "Wait there," he called back to the woman.

"Five across the eyes, man!" shouted Goldbach, making the slapping motion. He turned back to the booth. "We are n*ot* going to have a good afterlife, are we gentlemen?"

"We just scammed someone into trying to *slap* Sensei – the *worst* thing anyone could try to do," said Black Sam.

"We all know the story behind that. *No* one tries to slap Sensei!"

"Sensei says we can still have a good afterlife as long as we die like warriors," said White Sam.

"You're all going to die like fucking *dogs*, you bastards!" said Meza. "I am going to fuck you *all* up!"

"*After* we make sure this guy doesn't die," said Goldbach, getting up. "C'mon, twenty bucks says the Bone's hand never gets a third of the way up!"

"You lay two-to-one odds and I'll take a piece of that," said Meza.

The two Sam's agreed.

The girlfriend sat silently, looking not unpleased.

Out in the lot, Neco hung up the phone and got reminded of the other reason he was out in the parking lot.

To his great surprise, he saw his adversary coming out for the showdown.

Sensei's students stared through the glass of the front door.

"Here we go . . . he's staring Juni down," said Goldbach.

"Now Juni's saying something," said Meza. "But the dude's still staring . . . getting ready to make his move . . ."

"Oooooh!" said the two Sam's simultaneously.

"At least he's justified to use that handicapped space n*ow*," said Goldbach, holding out his palm.

The other three reached into their pockets and pulled out their cash.

Neco saw them and came back to the door. "I'm sorry, guys. Something's come up. I have to go."

"Right now?" asked Goldbach.

"Right now. It's an emergency. Make sure no one runs over Mr. Bone."

CHAPTER TWENTY-FIVE

With his other mechanics holding the fort, Gordo and Martinez sat in a corner booth of Lou Ann's Diner.

"Twenty percent off. That's a good price, George . . ."

"It's priced to move," agreed Martinez.

They paused in their conversation as a waitress approached.

"Good afternoon, gentlemen. My name is Lou Ann. And no, I'm not the owner. I get asked that all the time, but I'm . . ."

Martinez turned and gave her a cold stare as he cut her off. "We'll call you over when we're ready."

With her social circuitry broken, the waitress became a little taken back, trying to figure out what to say next.

Gordo, a regular there, quickly smoothed things over.

"Lou Ann, we have some serious business, and we may take a little longer than usual. Now I don't want to get so engrossed that I forget about you, so let me give this to you in advance." He pulled a ten dollar bill out of his pocket and palmed it over to her. "I'll just give you a little wave when we're ready, okay?"

"Yeah, sure. You just call me when you're ready."

With Lou Ann gone, Gordo picked up where he left off.

"Yes, it priced to move . . . and ordinarily I could move that quickly, but I'm a little low on cash right this instant.

Just bring back the stuff in another three days. I have some money coming to me. Then I can take that off your hands."

"Three days! We're only talking one hundred k.

That's nothing compared to what you usually get."

"I know. I know. And like I say, it's a great price.

I want to do it, but my cash flow is tied up until I collect on some money owed me."

"I told you that my employer ordered me to quit my day job. My cash flow is 'tied up' too. I need a favor here."

"Once I get this other deal closed, you can bring it back to me, and I know I can move it the next day. I can't act any faster than that."

Martinez looked down and rapped his fingers on the table for a few seconds. Then he started his counter—proposal. "I start with my new employer tomorrow. That means I will be on a tight leash – I may even be under some surveillance. He doesn't know I'm doing this, and *believe* me, it would be counter-productive if he found out. And on top of all that, you know me. I'm *more* than uncomfortable carrying weight. I *hate* it! I have a real phobia about it. That's why I have other people do that for me. So I'm going to front you the coke today. You meet with one of your customers tomorrow, make the deal and I'll come by to get my percentage."

"And you're comfortable with that?"

"I'm *un*comfortable carrying it around anymore than I have to. And I need this expedited as fast as possible.

Just take it and make your deal. Tomorrow."

CHAPTER TWENTY-SIX

Cherry Hill, New Jersey

Dr. Stanton Koblenzer, in the middle of another session with his most exasperating patient, kept on a good face and took a seat in the chair behind his desk. "I want to commend you, Sandy. In light of the near tragedy last night, I think you've made the right decision to let your husband know what's been happening lately." Then he turned to the husband seated on the couch next to his patient.

"And I want to thank you for coming in."

The husband nodded.

"Sandy, I want you to tell your husband what happened last night."

The woman stayed silent, not even looking at anyone in the room.

"Sandy, we agreed it was time to tell your husband about last night's incident. He's here for you now. It's okay."

"What's okay?" she asked.

Koblenzer bit his lip. Then he spoke. "To tell him what happened last night at home."

She responded slowly and deliberately. "Last night . . . I found your handgun in the top bedroom drawer . . . and put it to my head . . . and . . . I nearly shot myself."

Juni Neco sat frozen in his seat – the only visible motion, the widening of his eyes.

"It happened twice . . . I wanted to handle a really bad migraine."

Neco had known about the 'shadows', the imaginary 'gargoyles', even the incident with the knife to let out the 'bad blood'. He had even been

---

121

present for some of them. And except for the incident with the knife, they had all happened quite regularly since the day his wife ran into the young boy with her car back in Philadelphia.

From that time on, she had been nearly catatonic with one psychiatrist after another. Dr. Koblenzer was the seventh one to see her, and for some reason, the first one able to coax her into communicating.

Unfortunately, this willingness to communicate with a doctor was the only "gain" in her case progress. The medications were failing to help. In fact, the side effects were being compounded by her drinking problem.

Ever since the day involving the car and the young Philadelphia boy, Neco was no longer a husband.

He had become a caretaker.

Koblenzer continued to present him with the latest news. "Somehow she figured out where you hid your gun.

The only reason she could not successfully pull the trigger was her inability to switch the safety off.'"

Neco endured it all in silence until the end of the session. He watched the doctor stand and see his wife to the door. Then the husband stood and addressed his wife. "Hon, would you stay in the waiting room for a minute. I have to ask the doctor a question."

"Okay," she said.

Neco closed the door behind her and turned to Koblenzer. He spoke in a soft voice. "I have one question to ask you: Is she a threat to my son?"

"Well, up to date, any tendencies towards violence have been limited to self-destructive behavior . . ."

Neco cut him off. "Right now, do you see her as any kind of threat to my son?"

"I don't believe she would manifest her psychosis by hurting anyone other than herself."

Neco pointed both index fingers at Koblenzer and continued to speak softly. "If you are wrong, I will *kill* you. And I mean 'kill'."

Koblenzer bristled and took a step back. "You can't hold me responsible for her behavior!"

The index fingers remained up. "That seems only fair.

If *he* dies, *you* die. If *she* kills Petey, *I* will kill *you*."

"You're the one who has chosen to remain married to her. Why haven't you divorced her?"

"Because I'm in a line of work where I could get seriously hurt, perhaps severely disabled. Should that ever happen, I would like to think she wouldn't desert me – that she would stay loyal and see that I was taken care of, just like I have stayed loyal and made sure that she was taken care of."

Koblenzer just stared back.

With that, Neco opened the door. He stepped through halfway and stopped to turn around and face the doctor. He looked into Koblenzer's eyes, and, once again, pointed both index fingers at him before he left the office.

CHAPTER TWENTY-SEVEN

In the middle of the night, little Juni woke up from his sleep with a scream from the sudden pain in his pinkie finger. The four-year-old immediately reached over and hit the switch to the lamp on the night stand. The room lit up to reveal his brown wooden floor had turned completely black. But the change in color turned out to be an illusion created by the countless cockroaches covering it.

They looked like crude oil oozing away as they scurried for cover in reaction to the sudden brightness.

Little Juni trembled and found his attention back on the reason for his awakening – his right pinkie finger.

He saw blood running down the side.

Little Juni had always wondered why his mother insisted he wash his hands with soap and hot water every night before bed. On this evening, he decided to secretly see what would happen if he did not follow his mother's instructions.

One of a pack of filthy vermin had just demonstrated the consequences.

The pain had been caused by the bite of a rat smelling the aroma of food on his hands.

He cried out for mommy and daddy.

Juni Neco screamed as the upper half of his body snapped straight up in the air. The scream initially startled Sandy, lying next to him, then she immediately realized what happened.

"Another nightmare?" she asked.

"Yeah," replied Neco, as he swung his legs to the side of the bed. "One of when I was a little boy. I'm going downstairs to get some water. You go back to sleep,

Hon."

"Fine". She rolled over and closed her eyes.

Neco walked down the stairs to the kitchen and poured himself a tall glass of purified water. He drank it down and made his way to the den where he stretched out on the couch as childhood memories flooded through his head.

Young Juni Neco had been brought from Puerto Rico to the Harlem section of New York when he was four years of age – the youngest of four children with a brother and three sisters.

His father, although a twice-decorated war hero, never had the formal education needed to secure a job with the pay commensurate to support a family of six outside of a ghetto. So Juni Neco, Sr. worked hard in a city factory, often staying after his shift to see if he could substitute for anyone calling in sick for the second one.

The apartment they rented was below street level. The windows were so close to the walls opposite them, it was almost impossible to tell the weather unless you stepped outside. And when someone *did* step outside of the apartment, they were exposed to the absolute stench of the cumulative garbage from the other tenants.

One of the advantages of his youth was that little Juni had no earlier memories of better times to which to compare things. With no better times to recall, it was easier to acclimate to the financial circumstances.

Not afforded the usual toys given to other children by their parents, little Juni could improvise.

"Where did you get that toy?" his mother would ask.

"I found it outside in the trash. The people next door threw it out."

But poverty was not the only detriment to survival.

The streets were littered with prostitutes, homeless people sleeping on the sidewalk and teen-age gang members and young bullies.

Juni Neco, Sr. realized that his family would be raised in a world of violence. He provided an opportunity for everyone to learn some self-defense. As a former drill instructor, the father had become well-versed in martial arts.

But it was the seven-year-old Juni and his older brother by eight years, Raymond, who were most receptive to extensive lessons. The father had them practice on each other.

The teachings quickly became of use in school as little Juni was now in a level of school where bullies were becoming more prominent in the area.

Neco, Sr. had sternly told the boys that they had to be responsible with their new skills. If he ever learned that they had started a fight, he would personally beat their asses. But, if bullies were to come at the two sons, they were authorized to knock the shit out of them.

Predictably, it was not long before little Juni had his first encounter. A Black child in the next grade up from Juni told him to give him his lunch. When Juni refused, the older boy tried to initiate a fight with a sudden shove. But, just as suddenly, he found his arms being thrown to each side and his face being on the receiving end of a right-cross that staggered him six feet to the left where he fell to the tar surface of the fenced-in school playground. The boy rose to his feet and ran at Juni with his fist raised to strike. In one motion, Juni dodged the boy and tripped him to the ground again. Jumping on his opponent, Juni started wailing away with punches to his back, neck and head until the boy yelled that he gave up.

By the next day, the boy brought Juni a piece of candy during recess and the two students became friends.

Juni thirsted for more training from his father and continued to improve his skills.

The threat of violence at school did not end when leaving the playground.

Inside the school proved to be no sanctuary from bodily harm either. Back in that neighborhood, there was nothing to prevent a teacher or administrator from striking a student.

His father's words continued to wring in his ears.

"If I hear of you starting *any* trouble at school, you will answer to *me!*"

It stuck. Juni never created a problem for his teachers. He did, however, watch disrespectful students get slapped in the face or hit on the hands with yardsticks.

Juni never actually *saw* what happened to the real trouble makers. They were removed from the class and taken to what came to be referred by the students as "The Ass-

Whuppin' Room." This room was reserved for administrators to mete out corporal punishment.

Within the next four weeks, there was another bully confrontation, another victory and another new friend.

The two incidents provided Juni with more and more confidence in his ability to fight. But this had a downside.

Juni could get over zealous.

Summer vacation came and Raymond took Juni to a local movie theater.

As the crowd was emptying out of the theater, gunshots could be heard. Two local gangs were in a turf war.

Raymond grabbed his little brother by the hand and began running as Juni stumbled behind him through the screaming bodies fleeing in all directions.

Raymond found an open lane and continued yanking Juni behind him. But before he could get another thirty yards, they were stopped by five Caucasian members of one of the warring gangs, who quickly pushed them against a wall.

The five thugs, dressed in black pants and black leather jackets, surrounded the two brothers in a half—circle. They closed to within six feet as one them angrily identified Raymond as a member of their rival gang.

As Raymond tried to convince them they had made a mistake, he found Juni yelling and adding egg-beater to troubled waters.

"You leave my brother alone, or I will kick your ass!"

"Shut up, Juni!"

"You hurt my brother and *I* will hurt *you*!"

The gang members each reached into their back pockets.

Two pulled out knives and the others each pulled out a Colt revolver.

Raymond put his hand over Juni's mouth. "What is *wrong* with you? I said 'Shut up!'"

A moment later, a sixth gang member walked up and tried to size up the situation. "Hey, what the hell is going on over here?"

One of the teen-agers with a knife replied. "We've just caught another one of the Dragons! Then he looked at Juni. "And one of their little iguanas."

The sixth member held up a hand. "Cool it! I know this guy. He's not a Dragon. He's a friend of mine at school."

The other five lowered their weapons.

"Raymond!" asked the friend. "What the hell are you doing here?"

Raymond, trembling, took his hand from Juni's mouth and dropped it down to his brother's chest to clutch him.

"Just trying to go home from a movie with my brother, man.
We're not looking for trouble. All we want to do is go home."

Sirens from blocks away filled the air.

The friend put a hand on one of the other member's shoulder and another hand on another's back and slowly parted the waters to make a path as he spoke. "All right, you guys, let 'em go. We're cutting out before the cops get here." Then he looked at his friend. "Ray, run! Get out of here!"

Raymond nodded and began to run, again, yanking Juni by the hand.

He admonished his little brother all the way home, and made sure that Juni knew there would be no more movies for a month.

Juni improved at containing his fights to any of the local neighborhood bullies that picked on him.

Year by year, bully by bully, Juni took them on, won his battles and gradually increased his circle of friends.

However, more converted bullies never reduced the stress of a constantly challenging environment. The ever—present potential threats from teen-age gangs and older criminals kept young Juni wound pretty tight. It continued to be a miracle that he did not experience nightmares *every* evening.

Juni, Sr. eventually relieved the stress when he finally saved up enough money to move his family to Camden,

New Jersey in 1966. By then, Juni was ready for high school.

From Harlem to Camden, Juni's father knew he had to keep Juni's eyes on the prize. He constantly preached the value of school. In fact, he had routinely used Harlem to make his point.

"If you don't want to continue living like this for the rest of your life, you make sure you do well in school and go to college."

The message hit home.

A highly motivated Juni did work hard. After attending Woodrow Wilson High School, he was accepted on a scholarship to Rutger's University in New Brunswick, New Jersey. He chose to major in law.

While his study ethic was inspired by his father, the choice in major was inspired by life's vicissitudes. For Neco, that meant being routinely subjected to what, in future years, would come to be labeled as "racial profiling".

"What's the problem, officer? I know I wasn't speeding."

"No, sir. You weren't speeding," the officers would say, as they shined a flash light in his face. "This is just a routine spot check."

"The police are very 'thorough' in New Jersey. You know, I've only had my license for several months and already I've been 'spot-checked' four times."

"Driver's license, registration and insurance, please."

He chose law as a major for the purpose of infiltrating the other side.

Neco studied and played with equal intensity. His roommate once overhead two faculty members talking in the hallway.

"Juni has as many women as he has textbooks."

"Yeah. And he hits them both hard."

But even at that age, the partying did not include drugs or alcohol. As a part of having been indoctrinated to martial arts learned by his father, Neco indulged in no substance abuse. Those two factors had him in better shape than any of his peers. Still, he was always looking to raise his martial arts skills to new highs.

Midway through his upper education, during the month of November, he was presented with such an opportunity.

Word had spread to him of a dojo in the lower income section of New Brunswick. Some drop-outs from the dojo came railing to him what a chamber of torture it was. In fact, it was simply known by anyone who could not cut it, as "The Hell Hole."

"Forget it, dude! Even *you* wouldn't last a week there!"

Motivating young Neco included telling him there was something he could never hope to accomplish.

At his next opportunity, he packed his gym bag and found his way to The Hell Hole.

It was an unassuming community center in a lower commercial end of New Brunswick. There he was greeted by a lean, dark-skinned Black man, who stood several inches taller than Neco. He wore a black gi and loose—fitting pants.

"I'm Sensei Richard Gorell, director of the community center. I'm a Fifth Degree Black Belt. Our class is about to begin and I invite you to join us. If you like it, we can then discuss your enrollment."

"Thank you, sir. I've heard a lot about your class.

I'm eager to begin."

"It will be more important to see how anxious you are when you finish, Mr. Neco. Most do not persist. The students you will see before you are relatively new to my dojo. And the exercises we do tonight will only get tougher."

Undaunted, the young law student quickly changed outfits and joined the others in the basement. His gi was white.

Sensei Gorell introduced his new recruit to the group of eleven other men. Then he got right down to business.

"Mr. Neco, first we warm up."

Gorell pointed towards the wall to Neco' left where eleven pairs of shoes and socks lay grouped together.

Neco took the cue and placed his footwear along the wall.

The "warm-up" was a sequence of one hundred jumping jacks, one hundred sit-ups and one hundred push-ups.

Gorell walked among his students as they went through their push-ups. Abruptly he stopped and wrinkled his nose.

"Something stinks!" He paused and took a deep breath. "I smell lotion! Who has lotion?"

All the students ceased their exercise.

One with an uneasy look on his face spoke up. "I put some moisturizer on my feet . . ."

"Feet are *not* to be pampered! There will be no lotions! The balls of your feet are to be made hard and calloused! You are not being trained to kick your opponent with feet like a *baby's bottom!*"

The student in violation nodded rapidly. Everyone else remained silent.

"Run and wash that off before you come back here!" shouted Gorell.

"Yes, Sensei."

"Everyone else back to your warm-up!"

Neco watched as the cowed student sprang up to his feet and quickly slinked to the locker room.

By the time he returned, the students were well into their stretching.

Gorell put the students through an extensive period of combinations and, finally, paired them up for sparring.

Throughout the workout, Gorell had kept a particularly intent eye on Neco, who was making a favorable first impression with his focus, stamina and precision of movement.

The session ended after two hours. Neco showered up and changed back into his street clothes. He went upstairs and approached Sensei Gorell. "So how much does it cost to enlist in your dojo? I'm a college student, so if it's a lot, I may have to work out a payment plan, if that's okay."

"Don't worry about money," said Gorell.

"You're not going to charge me?"

"We'll make a deal. I will not charge, and you will not quit."

Neco laughed and the two shook hands.

From there, the workouts became only more intense.

Gorell added a one-mile run outside on the streets of New Brunswick. It steadily increased to five miles.

Also in bare feet.

Dressed only in gis.

In the dead of winter.

The jumping jacks, sit-ups and push-ups were raised to five hundred each.

During the course of this there were some drop-outs and some new recruits.

Gradually there was a stable core of participants.

And Neco was the star pupil.

One day, Sensei Gorell pulled him aside after a workout. "Soon you will 'graduate' from here and be introduced to your next mentor."

Neco squinted his eyes and paused to wipe some sweat from his forehead. "Who's my next mentor?"

"You will find out next week when I introduce you. He has worked with only a handful of people on the planet.

None of which have lasted with him."

Neco went back upstairs and got back in bed. He could not hear the dark thoughts emanating from the other side of the bed.

Juni may have bad blood. I might have to let out the bad blood so that the good blood can get in.

CHAPTER TWENTY-EIGHT

20 June, Harrisburg, Pennsylvania

Senator Donald Carvey strode out of the elevator on the sixteenth floor of the State Attorney General Office Building. With a spring in his step, he carried two cups of coffee in a cardboard tray in one hand and a bouquet of roses in the other.

After he cajoled Martin Shurmur's receptionist to keep quiet, he marched in unannounced to the Attorney General's office. "I just came by to bring some coffee to our next governor." Carvey held out the tray. "Take the one on the left."

A half-startled Shurmur rose from behind his desk and grabbed the cup. "And the flowers?"

"I always bring flowers to a funeral."

"Funeral?"

"To mourn the death of your dream to hire Neco."

"What are you talking about?"

"You haven't heard?" the senator asked rhetorically.

"Neco walked out of the Prosecutor's Office yesterday.

He's done with law-enforcement." Then his smile became wider. "I couldn't resist the flowers. I got them from the vendor down at the corner."

Shurmur paid no attention to the flowers remark.

"Neco is done with law-enforcement? What the hell happened?"

"He's had enough of his comrades . . . he marched into Blake's office and announced he's looking for a different job. If you hurry to the airport you can wish him 'bon voyage' on his flight to Puerto Rico."

Shurmur took off his wire-rimmed glasses and wiped them. "I should have hired him right on the spot. Who can tell me where he is in Puerto Rico?"

The smile on Carvey's face instantly turned into a frown. "You must be joking! You don't hire a man who quits because of his own men!"

"There's got to be more to it than that. Neco is *not* a quitter. Your sources may be just telling you what they want to believe themselves."

"He was yesterday. Cheer up, Martin. By tomorrow I'll bring you two more presents – a gold-plated, guaranteed-not-to-tarnish big budget with the Special Task Force, and the perfect man for you to hire."

Carvey tossed the flowers on Shurmur's desk. "Just be a good man and lay those at the grave of Neco's career."

CHAPTER TWENTY-NINE

Gordo stood on a corner in Bristol, Pennsylvania, as he waited for his buyer. He shuffled over to a deli with an awning to get out of the sun and looked at his watch.

It read 9:35.

All going well, this will just take minutes. Then my buyer, George and me are all happy. Another feather in my hat.

Within a few more minutes, his appointment arrived – a young Hispanic who looked no more than twenty years of age. He had a least three days of unshaven peach fuzz on his face. Gordo saw the young man clutching the handle of a briefcase in his hand.

"Gordo! Sorry, I got a little behind."

"It's okay. We're both here now."

"And that a good thing. I needed this to meet some pressing demands this week. Then it was like the clouds parted and a beam of light came through to shine on me when I got your call yesterday. You just don't know, man."

"Maybe I *do* know," said Gordo, as he walked over to his car where he popped open his trunk, revealing a brown shopping bagged holding two kilos.

Gordo removed the bag and handed it to his buyer, who went to his car and used his other hand to grab a brown paper bag full of cash.

An off-duty cop emerged from the pharmacy half-way down the street and returned to his unmarked vehicle.

The two men at the corner momentarily froze, catching the cop's attention with a scene all-too-familiar to him.

The officer opened the door on the passenger side and put down his own shopping bag on the seat. From the glove compartment, he removed his nine-millimeter hand-gun and from under the seat he grabbed his radio set.

The baby-faced buyer spotted the reflection of sunlight from the gun.

He did not hesitate. "We've got a cop!" Still holding the bag, he turned, grabbed his own bag with the money and ran.

"Hey! Drop my bag!" yelled Gordo.

"Stop! Police!" shouted the officer, now wielding his gun and breaking into a sprint.

Gordo tried to chase his buyer. It quickly became clear to Gordo he could not keep up with the young man.

He heard the buyer call back to him. "I know where I can reach you! Get to a safe place, so I can get the money to you!"

"I said 'Stop'," yelled the cop. "Police!"

"Shit!" exclaimed Gordo. He ran across the street through traffic as the cop closed in on the corner.

The officer made a snap decision. He could only go after one man, so he chose the one with his hands full –

The son-of-a-bitch with the evidence!

Gordo turned and stole a look behind him. He heard the cop, still in full sprint, yell into his radio for back-up. With the officer committed to the opposite direction, Gordo reversed direction and raced back to his own car. He jumped in, turned on the ignition and peeled out of his parking spot, almost hitting another car in the next lane. Within seconds, he heard police sirens blaring in the background.

In his rear view mirror, he saw the source of one of those sirens drive through the red light of the intersection he crossed.

Gordo knew he was in the clear. That relief lasted only a moment and he began pounding his steering wheel and cursing. *What am I going to tell George?*

CHAPTER THIRTY

That same morning, George Martinez drove down a little side street in Northeast Philadelphia. His thoughts wandered back to Colombia and Escobar's voice. "You'll tell your family how you have been plucked by a headhunter to work in the United States as an independent contractor for a company in South America. Your new job will entail some late nights and long distance travel from time to time. But your wife will be delighted to learn that your new company will be paying you many times over what you earned at Computer Resource Dynamics."

While he predicted an adverse reaction from the wife, he knew Escobar was correct. What the family would lose in face-time would more than be made up for with shopping sprees!

Martinez parked his Lexus on the little side street several blocks off of Bustleton Avenue. Several car lengths from him, he saw his destination – a little hole—in-the-wall tavern.

The sign above the door read, "Benny's Place."

Benny had assisted Martinez with moving some weight in the past. So, yesterday, Martinez gave Benny a call to see who he might know.

His comrade had a much-desired response for him.

"I've already started meeting someone who has the contacts you need at the Philadelphia Airport."

Inside, he spotted the bartender he had not seen before – a balding Irishman with a paunch hanging over a dirty pair of pants that needed pressing. The sweat—stained dark blue tee shirt contrasted against the short red hair that remained on his head. Four days' worth of grey stubble on his face combined with chipped, yellow—stained teeth made him look like a man in his early sixties.

He fit right in with the décor – a rundown, smoke—filled bar room.

Martinez stepped inside and winced at the cigarette smoke complimented by the wafting aroma of greasy deep—fried food from the kitchen. He grabbed a stool and observed six men at a table drinking beer and chomping on chicken wings, curly fries and onion rings. *The breakfast of champions,* he thought.

Escobar's new associate got the bartender's attention and motioned for him to come over. The man took his time.

"Hey, I'm here to see Benny," said Martinez.

The bartender sized up Martinez' suit. "Who's askin'?"

"Just a friend. I'm meeting him here. Is he in the back?"

The bartender broke into a lascivious grin. "Oh, he's in the back all right! He's in the back gittin' some."

"Getting some what?" It took a second. "Oh, for God's sake! Just go back and tell him George is here!"

"Can't."

"Why?"

"Benny told me he ain't to be interrupted for about another hour . . . or it would be my ass!"

Martinez inhaled some more of the bar room smells, wrinkled his nose and sighed. "Tell your boss I'm waiting outside!" He stepped back outside and climbed into his car where he nodded off to the sound of classical music.

An hour passed when Martinez heard a rapping sound on the windshield. He lowered the electronic tinted window to reveal the grinning, sun-burned face of Benny O'Toole.

O'Toole stood with another man, who also looked of Irish descent.

"Good afternoon, George," said O'Toole, reaching through the window to shake hands. "My bartender told me you were hanging around outside. You should have stayed in the bar."

"I didn't feel particularly welcome," answered Martinez, looking at the stranger. "Is this the friend I'm supposed to meet?"

"George, let me introduce you to Timothy O'Brien."

O'Toole, O'Brien . . . this is what you get when you deal with the Mac boys, thought Martinez, as he switched from O'Toole's hand to O'Brien's. "Where were *you* during Benny's last appointment?"

"I kept myself busy at the pool table," said O'Brien.

"Glad you could be patient. Should we join you in the car?"

"Tempting, but let's go inside," said George.

They all walked back in the bar and took a table by the kitchen door. The bartender came over and took their order. During this time, some of the patrons finished their drinks, plopped some money on the bar and departed.

Three teens, a Hispanic man and yet another Irishman came through the door and took stools by the bar.

"So, Timothy," began Martinez, "how did you meet Benny?"

O'Toole answered for O'Brien. "I had a regular buyer, who eventually asked for more weight than I could deliver.

So, this guy tells me that he knows someone connections in the Philly airport – Timothy here. Well, as soon as I found out that, I couldn't meet him fast enough. I told him about your phone call and how you needed a connection for Philly and here we are."

"And what do you bring to the table at the Philly airport, Timothy?" asked Martinez.

O'Brien put his elbows on the table, clasped his hands below his face and leaned forward. "I have some people who can look the other way on arriving charter planes. Benny tells me you actually need more than just some sporadic deliveries. According to him . . ."

The Irishman quit talking as the bartender came back to the table with their drinks.

As this happened, another man entered the bar. Still in the doorway, a look of recognition came across his face and he started to raise his arm to wave at the friend he recognized as Timothy MacKenzie. With Martinez and O'Toole still preoccupied receiving their drinks, they did not notice a suddenly concerned "O'Brien" raise one index finger from his clasped hands to his lips to make a "be quiet" sign. The Hispanic man at the bar *did* notice.

The Irishman got the signal and asked one of the teen-agers if they knew where the nearest convenience store was located. They shrugged their shoulders, he thanked them for nothing, told them they should be in school and left.

When the bartender left, O'Brien resumed. According to Benny, you need to have a regular schedule accommodated."

"It would be weekly. Can you handle that kind of volume?" asked Martinez.

"Given a predictable schedule and the right money, you bet."

"What kind of costs are we looking at?"

"Are you prepared to tell me the frequency and volume right now?"

"No, this is just some reconnaissance to see what you can handle. But, you'll be looking at high triple figures of kilos on the volume."

"Get back to me with the frequency and volume, and I can throw more exact numbers at you.'

"All right, I'll call my people, get some specifics for you, and we'll set up our next meeting."

They wrapped up and stood from their chairs.

Now I can take some of the pressure off Gordo, thought Martinez.

The Hispanic down at the other end of the bar scratched at a scar on his forearm. *All right, Mr.*

Shurmur. If you're behind this, the stakes have just gotten higher.

CHAPTER THIRTY-ONE

North Philadelphia, late evening

Roberto Quintero sat in Lou Ann's diner like a man awaiting his sentence before a judge. He watched out the window anxiously as the silver Lexus pulled into the parking lot.

Rita the waitress had learned her lesson with Martinez – speak when spoken to. This time she kept her distance as the hostess directed George Martinez to Quintero's booth.

Then she observed the animated conversation.

Martinez pressed two fists against his mouth and contained himself to a loud whisper. "So there's no money *and* no drugs?"

"I told you we had a little surprise in the form of an off-duty cop," said Gordo. "The guy just ran off with both the bag and the money. Turns out he got whacked in a shoot-out."

"Which will be *pleasant* compared to what might happen to you!" Snapped Martinez. "Shit, Gordo! Even a cashier in a drive-through window knows to get the money in hand before forking over the bag of burgers."

Gordo looked down at the table.

"So what are you going to do, Gordo? This is my full—time job now. I don't have a regular paycheck to fall back on and a prospective deal just went very bad today. You were supposed to buy me the time to have some money to back up my story for the new job I have. This is *not* helping me with my transition. So, I repeat, what are you going to do?"

"I don't know. I've been thinking of nothing but *this* since this morning. But I told you yesterday, my cash flow is down right now. I might need a week or two," said Gordo, looking down at the table again.

Martinez scowled. "I'm going to tell you who my new employer is, so you can understand why you don't have 'a week or two'. I have just started working for Pablo Escobar . . ."

Gordo's head snapped upright, "Please tell me you're not serious?"

Martinez put his hand up, palm down, to indicate his seller better keep his voice down. " . . . you heard me. Pablo Escobar. *No one* lets down Escobar. And if *I* go down with no connection for him, I swear that before I die, *you* and all of your family will suffer gruesome deaths. Call in any markers you have, look in any rat holes where you keep your secret stashes. You tell me right now, what you're going to do."

Gordo took a lengthy pause. "What if I had something more valuable to give you than the hundred grand?"

"And just what would *that* be?"

"Information on a man you should be aware of. He could determine whether you succeed or fail with your assignment."

CHAPTER THIRTY-TWO

21 June, Cabo Rojo, Puerto Rico

The island had a very calming effect on Sandy Neco. The fresh air, the tropical rainforests with their majestic waterfalls, the coast line overlooking the vast horizon – they all combined to have a naturally tranquilizing effect on her. The usually introverted wife and mother became far more responsive down here.

Petey loved it too.

Even though the sun rose on the east side of the island, a person could still enjoy the ambiance of early morning on the west side. Plus, the west side had the more beautiful water of the Caribbean Sea, versus the Atlantic Ocean on the other side.

The sun began to rise as Neco walked in his swimming trunks. He recalled the family walking along the beach last night after their flight.

"Look at the water, Daddy!" cried Petey, sitting on his father's shoulders.

"I see, big man! It looks beautiful, doesn't it?"

"I like it in Puerto Rico," said the son.

"Mommy does too," Sandy said softly, as she stroked her husband's arm.

And it does you more good than any of the quacks you've seen, thought Neco.

"Can we live down here, Daddy?"

"Maybe, big man. Maybe."

And that scenario made the husband more at ease about leaving Sandy and Petey with his sister.

As he continued walking, he finally could see this sanctuary coming into view up ahead – the driftwood. It sang to him like the Sirens from the Odyssey, beckoning him to come and enjoy the sunrise.

Neco began wading through the water and the image in the distance came more into focus. The image included an unwelcome addition.

Someone already occupied his space!

He drew closer until he had a clearer view—a woman!

Out on *his* island! On *his* driftwood!

A pair of sunglasses hid her eyes. A blue string bikini hid little else.

Neco' eyes squinted just before they widened in recognition.

The tressy blond-haired woman had the figure of a dancer – a figure he was used to seeing in tight blue jeans.

"Miss Sandra! Is that *you*?"

"It's me, Mister Juni!" said Sandra Tomasson, removing her sunglasses.

"What the hell are you doing down here?"

"When you described Puerto Rico the other day, you made it sound so inviting, I just had to come down and see for myself. Back at the office, you said you were coming to Cabo Rojo, and this is the *only* driftwood along the beach forming a little island of sanctuary for your morning ritual." said Tomasson, stroking one of the branches. She began to chuckle, "Ada will be furious when she finds out I switched off days with her to be *here*."

"Perhaps I didn't make it clear that this is *my* island."

"I don't remember you flashing a deed in our faces," said Tomasson. "And even in Cabo Rojo, possession is nine—tenths of the law. But I am nothing if not a benevolent dictator. Come on," she said as she slid over. "There's enough room for two."

Neco joined her.

As he lay down, Tomasson sat up and unzipped a plastic carrying bag hanging off a protruding branch. She pulled out a bottle of suntan lotion and began applying it to her long shapely legs as she spoke. "It's my understanding the rays of the sun can be more than a little deceptive down here during the early morning. You think the sun isn't up to full strength and then . . . wham! You've got a bad case of sunburn."

She continued applying the lotion on her arms and stomach.

"That's true for you foreigners," said Neco, as he took a position on his back. "We natives have skin more acclimated for the sun."

"Here," she handed him the bottle. "Help me get some on my back."

Neco closed his eyes for a moment. *God give me strength!* Then he sat up and took the bottle as Tomasson turned over on her stomach with her chin resting on her folded hands. With her feet held up on her toes, it accentuated one of the many things Neco admired about the female body – the small of the back. He started applying the lotion there first and worked his way up, despite the feeling as if his wrists were strapped to some powerful elastic material connected to her thighs.

He had to fight the urge to reach down and massage her toned, defined legs. It almost made him wish he was working a case. *I'd be all over them . . .*

"I can see why you like it down here," she said, "It's everything you described it to be."

"Tomorrow I'm looking for prospective locations to start a gym."

It dawned on him that he had spent more time than necessary on her back. He stopped and lay down beside her.

Tomasson rose up, grabbed the lotion and spread some on her hand. "With all due respect to your finely acclimated skin, you should get into this habit too." She began spreading lotion on his back – with both hands. Her motion was not that of applying suntan lotion. It was the action of a sensual massage.

Neco closed his eyes and conjured up threatening images in an effort to counter the reaction occurring under his swim suit. *Okay, I'm being held at gun-point by six arms dealers in Camden . . .*

She began reaching underneath his swim suit and Neco willed his hand to reach back and grab her hand to withdraw it from the area. "Sandra, we've been over this. There's no future here."

The massage continued on his back.

"Look me in the eye and tell me there's a future with your wife."

He stayed face down as Tomasson kept talking. "You told me that you didn't . . . well, you know . . . where you work.

So, what if you're not with the Prosecutor's Office soon?

Then there's no more an issue of you having a relationship with a co-worker – which is a lot more eloquent than the way you phrased it."

"True. I may no longer be with the Prosecutor's Office soon. But I *am* still with my wife. And *you* are still married. And we're *not* working on a case right now.

I told you I can live with the fooling around when undercover. It's a necessary job perk, like in Hollywood.

Only we have to be the best actors in the world, or we die. But, we're not on stage right now. We're not even rehearsing."

"So what *are* we doing," she asked.

"You and your husband never had any kids, right?"

"Lucky for me and him. What's your point?"

"Sandy and I had Petey. Having a kid changes a person. You get exterior from your body and pop into your child's. From there you perceive how that child is looking at you through his eyes. And you want it to be a good perception."

"Was that *your* father's philosophy?"

"I don't know. But I had a great perception of him.

He passed away while I was in college – had a real bad effect on me. We had the services down here . . . that's when I discovered this spot. I spent a lot of time out on this piece of driftwood. I *understand* I wasn't perfect then, and I'm not perfect now. I *understand* I'm a caretaker, not a husband. That's what comes with the wedding vows – in sickness and in health. But, I *do* have a tremendous relationship with my son. Since that first time on my little retreat here, I decided I would work hard to create that same relationship with any children I had."

"Someday you'll stop being a caretaker too."

Neco stood up. "I know you must have shelled out some good money to get down here. So I'm going to look upon this spot like a timeshare. You take your turn as long as you want. I hope you can get as much benefit from the spot as I have." He began wading through the water.

"I'll see you around, Miss Sandra."

Both Neco and Tomasson heard a buzzing noise.

"Where's that sound coming from?" asked the bikini—clad blond.

Neco pulled a small plastic zip-locked bag from his trunks. "That's my pager. Who the hell is trying to reach me at this time of day?" He studied the number. It had a 911 attached at the end.

"Do you recognize the number?" asked Tomasson.

"Yeah," said Neco, as he waded back into the water towards the shore. "I have to get to a phone.

A subdued Tomasson remained on the driftwood and watched her partner reach the beach. Neither she or Neco saw another female figure hiding behind some bushes off the shore.

The woman stayed in a crouched position. A solitary thought went through her mind. *Juni has bad blood!*

Chapter Thirty-Three

Harrisburg, Pennsylvania

At the same time that morning, Martin Shurmur pushed his way through the crowd in front of Strawberry Square as if he was furious at everyone in his path.

The coroner standing on the stairs of the building that housed the Attorney General's Office spotted Shurmur and drew a deep breath. The Asian forensics specialist knew that look in Shurmur's eyes. It would not matter what words came out of the his mouth, Shurmur would not be appeased. But he had to try.

The Attorney General broke into the opening in front of the stairs and yanked the "crime scene" tape over his head, where the coroner tried to intercept him.

"Martin! Martin!"

The words fell on deaf ears, so the coroner decided to let him have some space for a few minutes. He motioned for the surrounding personnel to do the same.

Shurmur closed in on the spot where he saw two bodies in blood-soaked clothes lying on the steps. "Oh, no . . . no . . ." he whispered.

He knelt beside the corpses. One was the body of Timothy O'Brien. The other was O'Brien's wife, who had had her throat slit. Her husband had received the full Colombian neck-tie.

"Lorraine . . ." he grabbed the woman's hand and spoke softly as his eyes welled up. "I'm sorry. I'm so sorry . . . You were never meant to be put in danger."

As he spoke, he heard a phone ring. Shurmur had no desire to take a call. He pulled out his phone to hit the "off" button when was shocked at the name on the caller—identification – "Timothy O'Brien".

The expression in his eyes changed from mournful to hatred. The Attorney General clicked the "Call" button.

He answered with a low hiss in his voice, "Who is this?"

A voice with an Hispanic accent replied, "Good morning, Marty. I see you have received your latest lesson. You have not been heeding previous lessons, so I have upped the stakes. I trust I have your attention now."

Shurmur's eyes reflexively scanned the crowd, but saw no one with Hispanic features using a cell phone. "The only thing you have is my *undying* oath to see you brought to justice, you sick bastard!"

"Such language . . . and just when I've done you a great favor."

"Favor? What favor?" asked Shurmur.

"This time I have spared you the burden of having to call the wife."

Shurmur became aware of his breathing beginning to get labored as he spoke, "Then perhaps I can return the favor.

What's your favorite music?"

There was a slight pause on the other end. "Of what concern would that be?"

"I just want to play the right song for you when I'm *dancing on your grave!*"

"Amusing . . . We'll have to see if you're still as witty if the next agent has any children. Because that agent will watch them die, just as this last one watched his wife die.

Enjoy the rest of your day, Marty."

The next sound was the click of the killer hanging up.

Shurmur let out a guttural cry and heaved his cell phone out into the street.

The surrounding personnel remained frozen as Shurmur stormed through the door to the lobby.

The coroner shouted to the surrounding officers.

"*Well, somebody find his damn phone!*"

Over a dozen policemen scurried into the street.

CHAPTER THIRTY-FOUR

Cabo Rojo, Puerto Rico

Neco finally got back to his sister's house.

Everything remained as quiet as when he left earlier. All the bedroom doors were shut, so he assumed the family to still be asleep. He stayed downstairs and grabbed the phone receiver as he dialed the number on the pager.

A familiar voice answered. "Hey Loco, I'm sorry to have to page you so early."

"You were supposed to lose my number, Gordo."

"Are you home?"

"No. I'm in Puerto Rico. How's your shoulder?" asked Neco.

"It's still bandaged up. But, I'm making do."

"What's going on? Why did you page me?"

"I've got a big one for you," said Gordo.

"You've got a big what?"

"A narcotics case."

"Not interested. Call Opie. I'm going back to the beach."

"No! Don't hang up! Please! There's more."

"Gordo, I don't want to be impolite, but I'm on vacation. I am *not* the person to call right now. I'm serious – call Opie . . ."

"Opie's *not* an option. The word around the office is that Opie is going to be hired by the Pennsylvania State Attorney General's Office." Gordo could not see the what—the-hell look on Neco face, so he just continued. "I'm in serious trouble. Please listen to me."

Neco clinched his jaw. "What are we talking about here?"

"The Colombian Cartel."

"*The* Colombian Cartel? *Escobar?*"

"Escobar," repeated Gordo.

"How the hell did you get involved with Pablo Escobar?

What kind of trouble are you in?"

"Escobar is desperate for another connecting point for his crack here in the East. One of my regulars got hired by him to find someone. I've referred him to you."

"What! You can't just go . . ."

"If I don't deliver you, it'll cause problems. I'm really in a jam and only you can help me. No one has put a hurt on Escobar. And this could be *huge.*"

Pablo Escobar had an aura—the unattainable Holy Grail of narcotics enforcement. And if something was unattainable, Neco wanted it.

"You can give me Escobar?" asked Neco.

"Will you get Escobar? Probably not. Can you hurt him? Absolutely," said Gordo. "I need a hand-to-hand here. And you're the best. I really need you, Juni."

"You've just given me some chips, Gordo. I have to think how I want to play them."

"I need you to call me back today for two reasons.

First, and most importantly, if you leave me hanging, you sign my death warrant."

"And secondly?" asked Neco.

"I have a big piece from another puzzle you'd be very interested in."

CHAPTER THIRTY-FIVE

Harrisburg, Pennsylvania

Late that afternoon, as the hail turned to rain,
Senator Carvey sat back in his high-backed red leather office chair,
ignored the ringing of his phone and continued to light a cigar. He took
a long satisfying puff, blew a few rings of smoke and finally picked up the
receiver. "Yes? . . . Sure put him through . . . Hello, Martin.

Please accept my condolences for the loss of agent Timothy O'Brien
and his wife. They were good people."

"Thank you, Senator. I was calling to congratulate you on the passing
of the Special Task Force Bill."

"It's a congratulations for all of us. Now you'll have the money to ramp
up your staff and begin coordinating with the other agencies to get the
son-of-a-bitch who's killing your men."

"And you're really endorsing I recruit Dexter Rasche?

"Rasche has been involved in many a bust for the Prosecutor's Office."

"Not as the one undercover."

"With your recent losses, he'll be the most experienced person you
have. He'll be a fine resource for you. And he'll be respectful to you, not
a loose cannon."

"Fine. I'm scheduled to see him tomorrow."

"You won't regret it, Martin," said Carvey, as he stood up, "Now if you don't mind, I have to get back to the phone and endorse my favorite gubernatorial candidate."

Carvey hung up the phone, went over to the coat rack and put on his raincoat.

CHAPTER THIRTY-SIX

23 June North Philadelphia

Neco sat in an air-conditioned rental car reunited with Roberto Quintero on a side street several blocks from the mechanic shop.

"So what did your wife have to say about all this?" asked Gordo.

"She's okay, but she would rather I don't return to the Prosecutor's Office."

"Because of Tomasson?"

"Probably. It seems that the incident with the massage in the deli has gone dormant for now. So I just need to keep it that way. I told her I didn't want to go back to Camden either. And that's the truth anyway."

"I don't know about you, Loco," said Gordo, "but, I can't just be working with you as some independent, rogue agent. I'm going to need the help of *some* type of law—enforcement agency. This is not a case where I put you on a ladder of drug dealers and move out of the picture while you climb it. This is the top of the ladder. Any bust will bring about the wrath of the worst drug lord on the planet. I'm gonna need the Witness Protection Program for me and my family before this is over.

"Of course. But let's just get your ass off of death row first, and I'll get some bargaining power to approach a certain agency with. Do you have any problem with that?" asked Neco rhetorically. "Now who am I being scheduled to meet?

"His name is George Martinez. As I mentioned, he's under tremendous pressure from Escobar to find a Philadelphia contact to bring in shit loads of crack. He wants to see you tomorrow at The Chart House restaurant for dinner."

"Good. I've always wanted to try their prime rib.

What else can you tell me about him?"

"He's not native to the area. I met him about a year ago. George hasn't worked with me regularly – we've only done some small-time stuff. So, it's my thought he's *never* dealt with having to move *this* kind of weight. You should be able to blow some real smoke up his ass," said Gordo.

"I'm still on vacation with The Prosecutor's office, so I still have all my fancy clothes, but it *was* necessary to give back my fancy car while away. I can't meet this guy with a rental."

"I'm way ahead of you, man. Just have your story together. You're 'Juni Neco' again."

"Juni Neco will get his foot in the door. Set it up when we're done here. Now what else were you talking about when you called me?"

"Ah, the piece of the puzzle you'd be interested in.

I have it right here." Gordo reached into his pants pocket and pulled out a matchbook. "No one saw me palm this during the raid in Camden."

"What is it?"

"Something the Jamaican didn't want us to see. While you were taking inventory on the guns, I tried to grab this to light my cigarette, he quickly snatched it back and gave me a lighter. Look what's written on the inside cover."

Neco watched Gordo open the matchbook. On the inside cover was a single name:

Arnie Schmidt

CHAPTER THIRTY-SEVEN

Center City section of Philadelphia

Alejandro pulled back the drapes from one of the windows in his penthouse suite and finally let some sunlight into his room. He had a call scheduled for overseas.

"Hello, Alejandro!" answered the boisterous voice of Pablo Escobar. "What's new?"

"George is scheduled to meet someone tomorrow," said Alejandro.

"Anyone we know?"

"No, but it's been set up through someone George already knew."

"George already knew Benny O'Toole too. And we both know how that turned out," snorted Escobar.

"Which brings me to my point. In light of our recent string of undercover agents, I want to implement a change in our operating basis."

"What are you proposing?"

"I've been in the vicinity with Martinez or Greenwood when they tried to cultivate a relationship. I've no doubt inflamed the local and state law-enforcement groups by dispatching dead agents out in Harrisburg. It wouldn't surprise me if the agencies somehow place more visual surveillance on them. This time, I'll switch things up and stay completely out of the picture—work totally behind the scenes – start investigating this Mr. Neco to see if I can sniff out any information about his background."

"As always, Alejandro, do what you have to."

"I already have a couple of things in place for The Chart House tomorrow."

CHAPTER THIRTY-EIGHT

Carlyle, Pennsylvania

Senator Donald Carvey's wife greeted him with a flute of champagne as he walked through the door of his estate.

Carvey had divorced his first wife over ten years ago and quickly rebounded with his current trophy redhead.

"Congratulations, Donald," said the much younger woman, kissing him on the cheek.

"Thank you, darling," said Carvey as he took a sip from the flute. "We've leaped over another hurdle on the track to the White House. Now, I hate to drink and run, but I'm scheduled to make a private call. I'll go upstairs and make it on the balcony."

"All right. I'll go confirm the reservations for our dinner party tonight.'

Carvey made his way upstairs and stepped out on the balcony overlooking the expansive, well-landscaped front yard. There he dialed a cordless phone he brought out with him.

"Hello?" answered the voice of Rasche.

"Good evening, son."

"Oh, hi, Senator! I heard the news on the car radio. Congratulations, sir."

"Thanks, lad. It's a big win for everyone." *But especially me.*

"It sure is."

"Listen, the reason I've called you is to give you some last minute tips in preparation for your interview with Martin Shurmur. Get some pen and paper."

"Hold on. I'm driving. Let me pull over."

"Okay, son."

Rasche had been supplying the senator with information from the Prosecutor's Office. Now it was important to have him as an inside man in the Attorney General's Office. The tips for Rasche would seal the interview. Carvey knew the questions to be asked and the buzz words and phrases that would impress Shurmur. Various traits that scored points with the Attorney General included someone who had done his homework. With the interview focused on hiring for The Special Task Force, there could be no one better than Carvey to orient Rasche on the fundamentals. If Rasche could demonstrate a solid grasp of what the bill was trying to accomplish and ask intelligent questions, it would greatly enhance Schurmur taking on the prospective recruit.

Rasche found a supermarket with a parking spot isolated on the perimeter of the lot. He pulled into it and positioned his pen and paper for his lesson.

"Okay, Senator. I'm ready," said Rasche.

"Then pay attention, son. I really want you in that satellite office."

Chapter Thirty-Nine

24 June, Philadelphia, Pennsylvania

The Chart House, a premier restaurant in Philadelphia, had off-white cement siding with long, twelve-inch wide, bright copper-colored metal sheets coming down from different angles on the roof. The restaurant featured wrap-around bay windows that provided a panoramic view of the city and the Delaware River. To the left of the building, patrons could see another company that ran an entertainment cruise business. The company had a large double-decker yacht and an even larger cruise ship that regularly hosted parties traveling along the river.

By four-thirty, Neco and Gordo pulled into the circular driveway where a parking valet came to take Neco' black Mercedes Benz.

Pulling out a twenty-dollar bill, Neco held it out to the valet, "I'm giving you this up front. If the car comes back with no nicks, there will be another one for you before we drive off with it.

The car, "on loan" from an unwitting customer at Quintero's mechanic shop, contributed more than amply to the aura of success Neco required for his undercover work.

Neco welcomed a cool breeze blowing off the river.

It made the transition from the air-conditioning of the car to that of the restaurant almost seamless.

The two men walked up the stairs to the front door where George Martinez already awaited.

All three of them wore sunglasses.

"George! Good evening," said Gordo.

"Good evening, Gordo," replied Martinez.

"George Martinez, I would like you to meet Juni Neco. Juni Neco . . . George Martinez."

"Nice to meet you, Mr. Neco."

"You can call me 'Loco'," said Neco, as he shook hands.

"I like you already."

As introductions and small talk concluded, a van with dark-tinted windows drove into the parking lot. The van by-passed the valet circle and pulled right into the parking lot to find a spot. From the inside, Alejandro, accompanied by a Caucasian man, woman and teen-ager, studied Juni Neco.

With his sunglasses still on, Neco did not provide a good look at his face. But even from that distance,

Alejandro perceived Gordo's friend to be quite a physical specimen.

They waited until the three men entered the foyer and allowed several minutes for someone to seat them.

Alejandro dropped off the "family", who walked inside the restaurant without him.

They observed a bored-looking host taking Neco,

Quintero and Martinez towards some tables with the river side view. a square table cloth with white linen near one of the windows with a riverside view.

Neco took off his sunglasses and sat facing the front door as the host passed out three menus.

The host smiled, muttered a perfunctory, "Enjoy your dinner, gentlemen," and left to greet the man, woman and teen-ager waiting at the host station.

"So, today," began Neco, "we just have some fun, and get to know each other a little. How about if we start off with some drinks?"

"Sounds good. And everything's on me," said Martinez, opening a menu. "What do you like, Loco? Beer? Wine?"

"Nah, I'm just getting some bottled water. I'm not a drinker. I like to stay in shape."

"I can see that. One of these days, you'll have to show me your regimen," said Martinez, who used his hands to indicate how he was wedged in the booth.

"That can be arranged. I can get you a guest pass to my gym."

"Hey!" said Gordo, "*I* drink!"

Martinez chuckled and signaled an young, attractive brunette waitress, who came over right away.

"Good evening, gentlemen. Welcome to the Chart House.

My name is Tiffany, and I'll be your server today. May I start you out with some drinks?"

Martinez pointed to Neco, "A bottle of sparkling water for this man, and two mojitos. Gordo, I want you to try one of them. They make them great here."

Gordo hid his reluctance and nodded with a smile.

The waitress spotted the protest anyway.

"You won't be disappointed," assured Tiffany.

"And we'll need some appetizers," continued Martinez.

Bring out some oysters Rockefeller, the calamari with citrus chili sauce and the fried asparagus with bleu cheese butter."

That got the attention of Neco, looking at and taking in the aroma from the vapor-trail of a rib eye steak platter being carried by him. "Ah, George, I don't want to sound ungrateful, but I don't like any of that stuff."

"My friend," snickered Martinez. "Those are for *me*.

Perhaps I will take you up on that guest gym pass later today."

The host took the "family" to a booth they requested along the opposite wall from the other three men.

Suspended above the booth hung a huge fish sculpted from sheet-metal painted with brown and turquoise shades. The teen-ager positioned himself in the center of the booth where no one could stand or walk behind him. The man and woman flanked him on both sides.

A waitress approached them. "Good afternoon, and welcome to The Chart House. My name is Lauren and I'll be serving . . ."

The man in the role of father interrupted her.

"Lauren, we know what we want for starters. Bring us three appetizers – the 'East Meets West Tuna', the lobster and shrimp egg rolls and the crab-stuffed mushrooms. Also a bottle of Charles Krug and a Pepsi for him. Just leave those menus. We love this place and we're going to take our time with picking the entrees."

Lauren gave a confused smile and handed out the menus.

"Okay. Let me tell you the unlisted specials. Today we have . . ."

"Thank you, Lauren. No specials." said the man,

"Please leave the menus and place our order for the appetizers and drinks. Let me give you this in advance."

Then he handed her a fifty dollar bill. "There'll be more when we're done."

"Yes, sir!" she beamed, "I'll get those in right now.

Take *all* the time you need with the menus."

As soon as she turned her back, the teen-ager opened his menu and rested it upright against the table ledge.

Then he pulled out a folded white, eight-and-a-half by eleven inch sheet of white paper from his pocket. The woman handed him a drawing pencil from her purse. The young boy casually looked across the room. He had an unobstructed view of Neco. Between the glances he looked down at the menu and began sketching the face of George's guest on the paper inside the menu. The man and woman pretended to engage him in conversation while he drew.

To his surprise, Gordo found himself actually enjoying the mojito ordered for him. It went just fine with his jumbo lump crab cake as he sat pretty much in listen-mode.

He already knew Martinez, so he let his long-time acquaintance and his contact from the Prosecutor's Office get familiar with each other.

Neco, savored a jumbo shrimp cocktail. He recognized the chef's use of tiger shrimp for the appetizer. It had more snap to the bite. And the cocktail sauce had just the right amount of tang from the horseradish.

The new agent from the Attorney General's Office had his standard procedure underway. He would not rush into things with a dealer – found it to be counter-productive.

Neco knew one of the important details – never appear the least bit eager. Today would be about women, cars, sports – everything except drug trafficking.

At this point, he especially wanted to know what Martinez did for entertainment. Neco noticed that his eyes lit up when they discussed the Philadelphia Phillies, sailing and gambling casinos.

The better to schmooze him with later.

The dinner meeting took over an hour-and-a-half.

Martinez paid the whole check over Neco's friendly protest.

The man two booths away, polished off the last of the Charles Krug and signaled for their waitress.

Lauren approached, "Can I get you anything else?"

"No, Lauren. We've gotten *everything* we came for.

Please bring our check."

Different valets brought the two vehicles for Martinez and his new friend.

Neco quickly gave his loaner the once-over.

Satisfied, he kept his promise and slipped the valet another twenty.

"Next time it's on me, George," said Neco as he got into his car with Gordo.

Martinez nodded. "Let's make it soon, Loco.'

As the two cars left the parking lot, the man, the woman and the teen-ager came out and Alejandro picked them up. He brought the tinted van back on Columbus Boulevard, drove past the restaurant and made a left on Walnut Street.

From there, Alejandro found a small side street in the Olde City section and parked.

Escobar's right-hand man stepped out of the car carrying a baseball bat. He studied some nearby windows and doorways, and noted that some trees cut off sightlines from them. The street remained vacated except for him.

Satisfied with his privacy, Alejandro smashed in the left front headlight of the van. Immediately, he signaled the man seated in the passenger seat, who pulled out a car phone and dialed.

"This is the operator."

"Operator, I need the number for the nearest police station. I'm at the corner of 2nd Street and Walnut. Thank you, I'll hold."

A uniformed policeman answered the call in less than five minutes. He climbed out of his squad car and approached the lone "victim". "Are you Mr. Walker?"

"Yes, officer."

"You reported a hit and run?"

"Yes, sir."

"Was anyone hurt?"

"No. It happened about twenty minutes ago. Some man parked in front of my car just backed up and smashed my headlight as he was pulling out. He obviously didn't see me walking back to my car and drove off hoping no one saw him. I started yelling, but he kept on driving, so I memorized his license plates."

"Did anyone else see this?"

"Unfortunately, no. I was the only one on the street and no one came out from their home."

"All right, Mr. Walker. Let me have your license, registration and insurance card. I'll write up a report.

Here's my card. Call that phone number next week and you can get a copy of what we come up with. Then you can forward the information to your insurance company if you wish, but, to be truthful, this kind of thing will probably have to be handled under your deductible,' said the officer. "What was the license number?"

The man handed him a paper. "Here. It was a Jersey plate."

Less than a mile away, Neco parked on a side street in South City. Gordo got out of the passenger side and walked around to the driver's side.

"You're on your own now, my friend," said Gordo.

"I'll take it from here," replied Neco, as he climbed out of the car with a screwdriver.

"You need to give me as much notice as possible before you make your big move."

"I understand," said Neco. He walked stepped around to the front of the car and squatted down. "But nothing is happening overnight. You should take the time to plan out your part of the exit strategy, so you're ready when the time comes."

"I will."

"And Gordo?" began Neco, as he removed the front license plate.

"Yeah?"

"Keep your nose clean. No more deals with him or anyone. Cause that's how you got into this predicament."

Neco walked to the back of the car and started the same action on the rear license plate.

"Thanks for reminding me. Just let me know how big a deal this turns out to be, so I can negotiate my price.

I'm going to need lots of money."

"I will when the time is right." He handed the screwdriver to his partner and kept the license plates.

"It's a good thing my office never thought to ask for these bogus plates back. Your customer's plates are under the driver's seat."

"I'll handle them right now."

Neco went to his rental car and gave some parting words. "Take care, Gordo. I'm telling you again, keep your nose clean."

"What are you going to do with Arnie Schmidt?

"Let me execute my strategy for getting hired first."

CHAPTER FORTY

26 June Harrisburg, Pennsylvania

Martin Shurmur looked out the window from his office at the capitol dome while wrapping up a phone call.

"Training for the Special Task Force starts on July 6th,

Dexter. It's held out in Indian Gap, Pennsylvania. It'll take about two weeks. Then you'll be placed in our Philadelphia satellite office."

"I'll make you proud, sir," said Rasche.

"See you out there."

"See you there."

As soon as Shurmur put down the receiver, the intercom line rang. He punched the button. "Yes?"

"Security says there's a Juni Neco down in the lobby to see you. He says he doesn't have an appointment."

Shurmur froze for a moment. The announcement totally caught him off guard. "Did he say what he's here for?"

"No, sir. He won't tell security. He just says to tell you he has some . . . 'records' . . . you might be interested in.

Shall security tell him to call and make an appointment?"

The Attorney General knew he would be able to concentrate on very little else until he found out what this was all about. "No. Send him up. I'll see him."

Security escorted Neco to Shurmur's reception area and the secretary motioned for him to go in to the office.

Shurmur met him at the door.

"Juni! This is a surprise. I heard you had split for parts unknown."

"I did. But circumstances dictated I return. Now I have to see where I land."

Schurmur did not know what to do with that remark. He gestured towards a chair.

"Please have a seat. May I offer you a drink? I have some cold bottled water."

"Cold bottled water is always welcome, sir. Thank you."

Schurmur went over to his mini-fridge and pulled out two one-liter bottles of Evian. He put one near his desk pad and handed the other to his guest, who stood to reach it.

As Neco twisted the cap open and took a big swig,

Schurmur left his untouched and got the ball rolling.

"Tell me what's going on. And what are these 'records' you wanted to discuss?"

The two men sat and Neco opened up as Shurmur slowly rocked back and forth in his chair. "I'll get right to the point. I've never understood why you didn't hire me after my interview."

Shurmur stopped rocking. "I'm apologize. I should have been clearer . . ."

Neco held up his hand to stop him. "The reason really doesn't matter. What matters is that I heard the Special Task Force is underway and I want to work in the Philadelphia satellite office."

"Juni, again, I apologize, but hiring was pretty much grooved in as an anticipation of the bill passing. Once the bill passed, we pretty much called the prospects and confirmed them as on board. This poker game is filled."

"What if you had a new player that had two very valuable chips to throw in the pot?"

"What are you talking about?" asked Shurmur.

"Hypothetically, what if the new player could help you get to Pablo Escobar?"

Shurmur stopped swiveling. "Escobar is in Colombia.

He won't be wandering the streets of Pennsylvania anytime soon."

"No, but if he was planning a massive delivery of crack to be channeled through those streets, a well done undercover operation could hurt him."

"What do you know?"

"It wouldn't be right to make the new player throw his chip in the pot if you weren't going to ask him to play."

"Juni, this is not a game. If you have information that could thwart a big delivery of cocaine, you're obligated to . . ."

"I may *not* have the information. We're talking hypothetically here. What's not hypothetical is that I set a record arrest for illegal arms since I last spoke with you. I'm sure you read about that by now. So you know that I don't just blow smoke up people's asses when I talk about records. I back up what I say."

"It's a pretty hot chip. You wouldn't want it to get cold."

"And there are *two* hypothetical chips?"

"That's right. And both could set two records in the name of the A/G's office *or* The Special Prosecutor's Office. Are you interested?"

Shurmur sighed. Images of the two prior newspaper headlines regarding Neco' cases flashed through his mind. He weighed those images against ones of the Senator's protests. The he reached across the desk.

"Welcome to The Special Task Force."

"Thank you, sir. Now let me tell you about that second chip I have to work on tomorrow."

"Tomorrow?"

The Attorney General finished coordinating with Neco, gave him his paperwork for hiring and some orientation which included the details of the Indian Gab training center. He then sent Neco on his way when his private line rang.

"This is Shurmur."

"Martin."

The Attorney General recognized the voice. "Hello, Senator. What can I do for you today?"

"Just calling to congratulate you on your new hire today."

"Which one?" asked a coy Shurmur, as he noticed the predictable, subsequent pause.

"I was referring to Dexter Rasche," said the senator.

"Who am I missing?"

"I've just brought on Juni Neco."

The answer created a longer pause.

"I thought we had an agreement," Carvey said sternly, "And how the hell did you find him?"

"You know, Loco. He found me. And I just buried another agent. We are *losing* this war on drugs, Senator."

"You have The Special Task Force! That's why you have Dexter Rasche!"

"I *do* have The Special Task Force. But if my choice for a lead undercover agent is between Juni Neco and someone from Mayberry, I choose Neco."

"This guy put a fellow officer in a neck brace, in essence tells his captain to shove it and then he waltzes into your office and comes out of it smelling like a rose with a promotion in stature!"

Shurmur thought to himself, *Kha Khan!*

"I have to go," said Carvey.

The senator hung up the phone in his office. *Okay, Mr. Attorney General, if that's the way you want to play . . . I've been prepared for this contingency.*

CHAPTER FORTY-ONE

Levittown, Pennsylvania

With the exception of Black Sam, all the other students, dressed in their white gis, awaited for their sensei in the gym.

Black Sam had been excused from the running that took place first. Neco did not excuse him because of his age – fifty-two – or lack of fitness. Black Sam Whitmore, already a Second Degree Black Belt when he met Neco, made men half his age jealous with his six-foot-four trim and toned frame. He had the reflexes of a cat and his sensei spared him no quarter. But Black Sam's routine already included a lengthy run during the day, so he reported later.

Neco came up the stairs, dressed in his black gi.

Those students present included Ron Goldbach, White Sam Schofield and Mateo Meza.

After they greeted their sensei, White Sam began to tell Neco of a tournament they participated in while he was away.

Every once in a while, the students would register for some local kick-boxing tournaments to see how they stacked up against outsiders under live-fire. Then they would proudly tell their sensei how they kicked the opposition's asses.

White Sam started to chuckle.

"What's so funny?" asked Neco.

"Mateo lost his fight," said White Sam.

"What?" said a suddenly stern-looking Neco.

167

"He lost by decision," added Goldbach, also smiling "because he was knocked on his ass more than one time."

Neco turned to Meza. "Then you weren't breathing right! Why do we invest so much attention on proper breathing?"

"No. No. My breathing was fine, Sensei," said Meza.

"Your breathing was *not* fine!" said Neco, his voice more intense.

"I just got caught off guard a couple of times."

Only Neco' dark sun tan kept his face from turning beet red. Spittle shot out of his mouth as he shouted.

"Don't you *dare* question me! I'm your *sensei*!"

Goldbach and White Sam wiped the smiles from their faces and replaced them with somber looks – not out of any sympathy for Meza. They did not want to bring any of the ongoing wrath in their direction.

"The only thing wrong with you was your *breathing!*" screamed Neco, with a look burning a hole in Meza's skull.

"I'm sorry, Sensei . . ."

"Get in the straddle position!"

"Sensei, it's okay. I get it."

"Get in the straddle position! Now!"

Meza assumed the position.

"Now shut your eyes!"

Shaking off great consternation, Meza closed his eyes.

"Now breathe properly!" yelled Neco. Then he let loose with a vicious kick to Meza's abdomen.

Meza's five-foot-nine one hundred seventy-pound body jolted back about five feet. But he kept his balance.

"Breathe properly!"

Another kick.

Another five feet backwards.

Two more times Neco screamed the command and followed it with a kick until Meza finally went thudding into the dry wall. But he still remained on his feet.

The wall did not come out of it as well. Meza's torso created a big crack.

White Sam knew this incident would add to the list of times he had to put his professional construction skills into use to replace a sheet of dry wall in the gym.

"Any more questions, Mateo?" yelled Neco.

Meza replied softly, "No, Sensei.'

"All right! Everybody out to run!'

The evening session eventually concluded. Only Neco and White Lightning remained in the locker getting dressed.

"Yeah, I knew you'd be back," said Goldbach.

"What can I say?" said Neco. "The universe conspired against me."

"Well then 'Bravo' to the universe. Everyone's glad you're here . . . even Mateo."

"I've done worse to students," smirked Neco.

"Yeah, like suddenly leaving me in charge in the first place," said Goldbach.

"I've been thinking about how I was going to make it up to you."

Then Neco tugged at the leather strap coming out of his pocket.

"Don't tease me, Sensei."

"I think it's time."

"You mean . . . ?"

"That's right. Tomorrow night . . . you finally learn 'The Cut of a Thousand Deaths'."

Chapter Forty-Two

27 June, Exton, Pennsylvania

Over in the outskirts of Exton, George Martinez and his family lived in a beautifully renovated and spacious old three-story stone farmhouse. Like most old farmhouses, it was custom-built with its own unique design.

What made it distinct was that when someone looked from the side, it could be seen the home had been built on ground so *uneven* there was a floor constructed half *underground* with a rear one-story stone wing extended perpendicular from the floor that was *above* the ground.

From an aerial view, the structure looked like a T.

The half of the story in the main structure that was underground was considered the *first* floor, and the above—ground portion was considered the *basement*.

Martinez had, as one of his guilty pleasures, a passion for barbequing. So much so, he had the top of the above-ground section that was the basement converted into a deck with wooden railings. The back had stairs leading up from the back yard to the deck.

This morning, Martinez heard the heels of his wife's shoes clicking louder and louder as she walked through the kitchen towards the deck. He finally felt prepared to handle her on his latest career move.

The wife poked her head out the door onto the deck, "I thought I heard someone out here. What are you still doing home with a can of propane gas in your hands?"

"I'm off today and I'm going to slow roast some ribs for lunch," said the husband.

"You're off?"

"Actually, I'm more than off. I'm transitioning to a new job, Yolanda."

"A new job? When did this happen? What happened with Computer Resource Dynamics?"

"I've had a headhunter approach me for a company in Colombia. And I've accepted," said Martinez.

"When were you going to tell *me* about this? How could you decide to work in Colombia without consulting me?

What's supposed to happen with the kids and their schooling? My mother will have a heart attack when she finds out we're supposed to move . . ."

"Whoa! Time out, sweetie," said Martinez as he hooked up the new container of propane to the gas grill. "No one said we're moving to Colombia. That's the beauty of this.

We stay right here and I work out of the area. Yeah, there may be some overseas travel called for, but for the most part, I'm working out of the area."

"Fine," said Yolanda, "But you *still* should have consulted me."

"Sweetie, I *told* them I had to consult you. That's why I indicated I couldn't start right away. But when I told them that, they doubled the money and put a clock on it. So, you see, *you* inadvertently helped drive the offer up. And for that, you get rewarded with a nice clothes shopping spree this week! We're going to have to attend some nice dinner parties, and they want you to be ready."

Martinez saw the look in his wife's eyes change to a very favorable one. He knew the moment was right to put a big bow on this thing. "Oh, and they want your mother in on the shopping spree too."

"I'm going to be going to dinner parties?" asked Yolanda.

"Some," said Martinez. *Just not the ones I go to with other women.*

"So this is all official?"

"Yes," said Martinez. *Pending the results of Alejandro's canvassing The Badlands with that drawing.*

CHAPTER FORTY-THREE

Pottsville, Pennsylvania

After an inspired morning work-out, Neco drove from the Bally's in Deptford, New Jersey to Pottsville,

Pennsylvania. He found East 2nd Street and followed it until he arrived at the Schuylkill County Jail.

Neco flashed a letter from The Office of the State Attorney General Pennsylvania to security and the guard admitted him into the cell block. Another officer brought him to a cell at the end of the row. The cells before it had no prisoners, which afforded Neco the privacy he desired. He looked through the bars and stared at a Jamaican man lying on a cot.

The man stared back. His look quickly changed from one of apathy to one of unpleasant surprise. "Neco!"

"Let me in,' Neco told the officer.

"I've got nothing to say to him," said the prisoner as he sat up from the cot.

"You might want to keep the bars between you and him," replied the officer. "He's a cold-blooded bastard."

"I'll be fine. Let me in."

"Okay. The Attorney General told us it's your show."

The officer unlocked the door and slid it open.

Neco stepped inside.

He motioned for the officer to leave and glared at the lone occupant in the cell.

"Hello, Julio," said Neco.

"Neco," said the arms dealer, "I don't know what the hell you're doing here, but I ain't got nothing to say to you."

"What did I ever *do* to you?"

"You got me *shot* you son-of-a-bitch!"

"And you shot at me. You see, I thought we had a nice bonding moment there. And in the spirit of that, I come bearing gifts – your favorites." Neco reached into his jacket pocket, removed a fresh, unopened pack of Marlboro cigarettes and tossed them to a mildly surprised Julio, who snatched them out of the air with one hand.

The convict opened up the pack, closed his eyes and placed his nose over the top. He took a deep breath and savored the aroma of the tobacco.

The he opened his eyes and the serene expression turned back into one of suspicion. "What do you want?" He pulled out a cigarette and smelled the tobacco.

"I understand you have a friend I would be interested in meeting."

Julio squinted his eyes and shook his head. "My friends are dead. You know that. You were there."

"The friend who gave you military-issue guns isn't dead."

"I've been over this with the detectives and the D.A. already. You're wasting your time. You have nothing linking me to anyone."

Neco pulled a matchbook from his pocket and opened it. He lit up a match and held the flame and open matchbook up to Julio's face. "*This* says I do." The inside of the matchbook cover, palmed by Gordo in Camden, displayed the name "Arnie Schmidt" in Julio's handwriting.

The aloof eyes that were just half-closed, widened in fear.

For a few moments, Julio silently looked at the evidence that displayed his handwriting on it. He finally composed himself to respond and accepted the light. "My sentence wouldn't be lessened if I flipped on him."

"You could serve your time at a much better facility."

"There's no prison where I would be safe if I gave that guy up to you," said Julio, as he took a deep drag and blew out some smoke rings. He closed his eyes again.

"I've almost forgotten how much I've missed this brand."

Neco suppressed his disdain for the smell filling the room. "You'd be safe if Schmidt didn't know it was you."

"Who else would tell you? As I said, all my friends are dead."

"You know he has other buyers. For all he knows, one of them could flip him."

"Schmidt is smart. He lives in a room at his mother's house . . ."

"We know where Schmidt lives,' said Villages, who kept himself from wincing at the smoke. "We need to know where he keeps his arsenal."

"That's what I'm getting to. He never tells the buyers where his stash is. He just meets you at a location where you look at pictures to choose from. Then he gets it dropped off and you never know where it came from."

"What's the location where he shows the pictures?'

"He floats it around. But the last one was in Camden.

And *you'd* have to get his military source out of him. He would never tell us." Julio blew more smoke rings.

"Have you been in contact with anyone who knows Schmidt since you were caught?" asked Neco.

"No, man. I couldn't even tell you if he even *knows* I've been caught. We concluded our deal and there was no need to speak again until it was time for the next order – which had no scheduled time."

"I would bet he doesn't know for sure. We withheld all your names from the media. Hell, who knows if he even reads the paper or watches television."

"What if he does? What if he knows about your raid?"

"That wouldn't be a problem if he found out you weren't there," said Neco.

"I don't know, man . . . what's in it for me?"

"Do you know where they want to put you after you're convicted?"

"No."

"East Graterford."

"The *'Rectum'*? They're gonna stick me in The *Rectum*?

Oh, fuck! I *know* guys in The Rectum! I knew a guy who d*ied* in The Rectum! The people that run that place are worse than the inmates! They're thugs! If Schmidt doesn't have someone kill me, I'll die from the filth and disease!"

"Schmidt will never know you were in on it," assured Neco.

That prompted Julio to take a deep draw on his cigarette. "How does this work?"

"Just like it worked with you. Only you play the role of Gordo. You tell Schmidt you found a big buyer for which you want a piece of the action. As soon as we get what we get all the evidence we need, the good guys charge in and arrest all three of us. You're not the enemy and you serve your sentence in much nicer accommodations."

"All right. Anything but The Rectum. Two more things."

"What?"

"One, who's going to make sure the cops remember to bring the ram?"

"Don't get me started," snorted Neco. "What's the second thing?"

"I have to tell you what's required to even *meet* Arnie Schmidt."

CHAPTER FORTY-FOUR

Levittown, Pennsylvania

A man could count on one hand how many people on the planet knew about "The Cut of a Thousand Deaths".

And he would still have three fingers left on that hand.

Ron Goldbach waited anxiously to become a middle finger. He decided to kill some nervous energy in the dojo until his sensei arrived.

Neco pulled up to the gym and made his way back to the entrance of the room they rented for private use. He saw White Lightning engaged in one of his own cathartic rituals. Respectfully, Neco kept quiet and did not even make his presence known. *Just let him concentrate.*

His best friend and confidante wore a sleeveless brown tank-top tucked under some tight black pants. A thick, dark sweatband covered his bangs. Around his neck hung three gold necklaces.

Neco often commented, *"If you put on one more necklace, you could work a corner in The Badlands."*

Goldbach showed a built physique – definitely distinguished from his mentor's. Neco' lean and chiseled body looked like it was about six percent body fat. White Lightning's torso was fleshier. But anyone who doubted how much of it was muscle only had to observe the scene in the dojo.

Goldbach stood before two cinder blocks, standing upright about two feet apart. Across the cinder blocks laid eights slabs of brick, each about two inches thick.

Thin sheets of fiberglass separated the outer edges of each layer. A terry cloth draped across the top of the stack.

Ron's getting in his zone now, thought Neco.

Goldbach paced back and forth from the stack. Then he held his bent arms out about mid-chest and swiveled his torso several times. His breathing became more and more deliberate.

He began some practice swings. First came the motion of the hand coming down and tapping the towel. The same hand swung "through" the bricks from three inches away.

He paced some more, he swiveled some more with very audible breathing.

After some final practice swings, Goldbach let out a loud yell.

His hand crashed down with the force of a sledge hammer on the toweled area, breaking every layer of bricks and pushing the cinder blocks over on their sides. A brief cloud of powder from the bricks rose in the air.

White Lightning, you bet.

Goldbach turned to see from where the sudden applause came. His mustachioed mouth broke into a smile.

"Eight bricks now . . . very impressive," said Neco.

"That's the first time I ever tried that many," beamed Goldbach, still breathing hard as he walked over to his mentor.

"I've brought a new toy for you tonight."

"The Cut of a Thousand Deaths," said Goldbach, with the appropriate reverence in his voice. "I've waited a long time for this.'

"It will have been worth the wait. Now you just stay right where you are," said Neco, as he took a position in the center of the room. "Watch and learn."

While Neco assumed a safe distance, Goldbach noted from which back pocket the thin leather strap hung.

Neco turned back and faced his student.

In a smooth, rapid motion, Neco reached back with his right hand, speared his middle finger through the leather loop and formed a fist to yank out what was attached to the other end of the strap – a knife.

Neco did not use any old knife for this feat.

This action needed a 007 switchblade. The "007" name had no relation to Neco' lifelong favorite movie character – James Bond. The company arbitrarily assigned the number to that particular model.

The combination that made the weapon inspirational for this unique style of combat included three features. Most importantly were the three holes bored through the stainless steel handle. This allowed the leather loop to be threaded through the middle hole for perfect balance.

The second feature was two slim strips of wood down the middle of the handle, providing just enough friction for the grip to be right. Lastly, when opened, the blade had a locking mechanism to hold it in position.

Neco' motion never stopped as he put on a display that would take slow motion replay to fully appreciate. As he swung the blade over his head, Neco snapped his wrist to open the blade and lock it in position before whipping it in front of him. From there the combat style compared to that of a person wielding a nunchuck in fast—forward speed. In this case, one end of the nunchuck had a razor sharp blade.

The master unveiled a blinding fast sequence which alternated whirling the knife in slashing figure eights, snapping the handle back to his hand for direct stabs, all mixed in with kicking motions. The leather strap, combined with the opened blade, gave the user an extra two-foot advantage in reach for hand-to-hand combat.

Awesome! Thought Goldbach.

Within one minute, Neco had unleashed an attack the magnitude of which could have debilitated or killed at least six attackers.

Neco snapped the handle to his fist one last time and ceased the exercise.

"Holy shit! That was amazing!"

Now come out here," said Neco, "And I'm telling you right now, you're going to have to take this slow and easy. We don't want any mishaps with that handsome face of yours."

They practiced until the dojo closed.

"So you haven't told me where you learned how to do that," said Goldbach.

"That's a long story that only two other people know.

I'll tell you soon, but not tonight. Petey's waiting for me."

CHAPTER FORTY-FIVE

28 June, Camden, New Jersey

Two unmarked police cars escorted Neco, who drove Julio to a pay phone booth outside of a vacant, boarded-up delicatessen. A nearby van contained personnel ready to tap the call.

Julio understood the necessity for the call to be from this neighborhood as he punched in a phone number.

On the receiving phone, the caller ID screen read "Camden".

The Jamaican heard a familiar voice mannerism in the answer – a short, distinct, expelling of a breath.

"Kih! Yeah?"

He held the phone receiver so that "Neco", who stood next to him, could listen in on the call.

"Arnie, this is Julio."

No response came back.

"Arnie, are you there?"

"Kih! Weren't you caught in a Camden raid this month?"

"No, man. That was my men. I was *supposed* to be there, but the cops stormed in before I arrived. I came just in time to hear the fireworks starting from three blocks away. Then I high-tailed my ass out of there."

More silence ensued. "I've had to lay low for a while, Arnie. Listen, man, I need more guns. The cops got everything you sold me last time and more. They even got what I had waiting to be sold. I have to make another purchase. When can we meet?"

"I don't know what the hell you're talking about.

Kih! Don't call me again. The phone number won't be good."

Julio heard the click and then the dial tone. "Shit!"

Neco leaned back from the receiver, "He didn't buy it."

"I told you he was smart."

"Which is unfortunate for you," said Neco. "We have to take you back to the jail now." He grabbed Julio around the upper arm and turned him facing away as he pulled out a pair of handcuffs.

"But, you'll put in a good word for me with the D.A., right, Neco?"

"No," Neco snorted and put the cuffs on him, "Why would I do that? You produced squat for me."

"I did everything you wanted! I said exactly what I was told to say! I even gave you his phone number to tap before this. You got to give me something!" pleaded Julio.

Neco yanked him from the booth and over to one of the unmarked cars. "There's been no calls to monitor until now, and you just spooked him into changing his number.

For that, you get a roll of ass wipe for The Rectum."

"Ass wipe?"

"Two-ply."

One of the officers stepped out of his vehicle and opened the back door.

Neco placed his other hand on Julio's head to guide it under the roof of the car.

"Neco, wait!" The Jamaican straightened himself up.

"I have another idea! I have another idea!"

Neco withdrew his hand from Julio's head. "I'm listening."

"I know some other people who might be able to help."

"Who?" asked Neco.

"Remember I told you I knew some people serving time in East Graterford?'

"Yeah . . ."

"One of them is serving time for a drug bust."

"What good does that do *me*?"

He's *also* bought from Schmidt before. Only Schmidt wouldn't know he was in the slammer. This guy was arrested out in the Pittsburgh area for drugs. It didn't involve guns and it wouldn't have been covered in this area. You get what I'm saying?"

"That this guy could be persuaded to call Schmidt with the right deal?"

"Yeah! Schmidt will *take* that call. This guy can set you up to meet Schmidt. Pretty smart, huh?"

Neco shook his head. "Yeah, Julio. Very smart.

We'll have to add the word 'savant' to your title."

Julio looked pleased.

CHAPTER FORTY-SIX

Cherry Hill, New Jersey

That same Thursday morning, Sandy dropped off little Petey with her mother. School was out for the year and she needed help watching her son so she could keep her second appointment with Dr. Koblenzer since returning from Puerto Rico. Now she made her way to the One Cherry Hill building and took the elevator to the top floor.

"Sandy," began Koblenzer, "initially I was encouraged with your first session since you came home. You looked more relaxed, you started getting out of the house and were actually more conversant. But on the down side, I've not been encouraged with your choice of company."

"My husband is going to be gone for days at a time," said Sandy, who sat on the couch instead of having her usual position. "His training out at Indian Gap starts soon. How am I supposed to be conversant without people to talk to?"

"Certainly not your sister. She's an alcoholic."

"It's my understanding that the whole purpose of our sessions has been to have me socialize more, to . . . how did you put it? Oh yeah, to get me out of my 'shell'."

"The purpose *has* been to get you out of your shell, but *not* with friends who suffer from being alcoholics."

"Can I share a secret with you?" asked Sandy.

Koblenzer looked back with suspicion. Sandy did not wait for him to answer. "While we were down in Puerto Rico,
I saw Juni with that slut, Tomasson."

"What? I can't believe Juni would ever initiate any . . ."

"I don't care who initiated what. That's the *second* time I've caught the two of them getting touchy-feely when they weren't even on a case. Would you rather I take to the bottle or the gun?"

"I don't approve of either!" said Koblenzer in a huff.

"Relax, I have no access to a gun. Juni has a new hiding place. Besides I think the alcohol has been helping me more than your pretty-colored little pills."

Koblenzer regained some composure. "Your use of alcohol has given you a false sense of courage, Sandy.

Yes, you're talking more, but it's not helping your sense of responsibility. And the label on your prescription clearly warns of the potential dangers for people taking it with the consumption of alcohol."

"Then I should tell you another little secret."

"That you're drunk right now?"

"No. Not right now. That's not the secret." Then she stood from the couch, went to the door leading to the reception area and slightly opened it, as if checking to see if anyone was listening on the other side. Satisfied with their privacy, she shut the door, went back to the couch and continued. "The secret is I don't have to worry about the effects of the alcohol being mixed with the pills, because I haven't been taking the pills since returning from Puerto Rico."

Koblenzer again lost his usual monotone demeanor.

"Sandy! If you do not adhere to your program of care, I cannot be responsible for what happens to you. I may have to discharge you from care!"

"Maybe. Or maybe I'm discharging *myself* from care . . . period!"

"I strongly suggest you remain under care and adhere to your program! You are hardly in a state of mind to determine your own program."

"I don't know. I seem to be having more fun now than I've had in long time."

"But the 'fun' is *immoral* fun. You're not thinking clearly. The alcohol is lowering your ability to confront reality; thus you can't even perceive problems. Your 'fun' is in the form of doing irresponsible things!"

"The pills were doing the same thing, only without the fun part," she looked the clock on his desk. "I believe our hour is up. I'm leaving now."

Koblenzer stood from behind his desk. "Sandy! Are you going to adhere to my program or not?"

CHAPTER FORTY-SEVEN

West Philadelphia

The man baring scars on his arms heard his cell phone ring and saw the number from Colombia. "Yes."

"Alejandro! What are you up to today?" asked his employer.

"My eighth day of working the bars and pool halls in The Badlands. No one's recognized Neco's picture yet."

"Or no one has *dared* to recognize it."

"I'm flashing one hundred dollar bills. I'm confident I would have some takers if someone knew him."

"I told you that dead-end with the license plate could mean he was a criminal, "said Escobar.

"And I told you it could also mean he was a cop," said Alejandro.

"What's next for George?"

"He's having a dinner with Neco on Saturday. George is excited because they're bringing women – neither of which is George's wife."

"That's our boy."

"After that, Neco's shelled out money for premium seats at a baseball game on Tuesday," said Alejandro.

"Make sure he starts to mix in business with the fun now."

"If I don't find anything before then."

"Listen, my friend, I have to go now. I have some women competing in another contest," said Escobar.

"I'm almost afraid to ask . . ."

"Naked tree-climbing."

"Good-bye, sir."

They ended the phone call and Alejandro entered a place called "Dewey's Bar and Grill". He went up to the bar where six other people sat on red upholstered stools.

"Hey, good afternoon, darling," said a woman bartender, mixing a drink. She wore a low-cut, pull-over white top, with a black mini-skirt. "What can I do for you?"

"You can get me a brandy," said Alejandro, who flashed his picture of Juni Neco, "and any information on *him*." He held the picture at an angle where everyone near the bar could see it.

"What are you, a cop?" asked the bartender.

"No," replied Alejandro flashing a one hundred dollar bill in his other hand. "I'm someone passing out *these* to anyone who can tell me information on this guy."

She put the mixed drink down and stared at the picture. "I have seen him! He's been in here. I remember him because he never touches alcohol . . . drinks only bottled water."

"Looks like you just made a quick hundred dollars, Cindy!" said one of the men.

Alejandro shot a disapproving look at the fellow, and turned to Cindy. "I'm going to need a little more than his drinking habits. What else can you tell me? Who was he with? What was he doing?"

The bartender resumed pouring the drink as she pursed her lips. "He was here about three or four times a couple of months ago . . . always with the same guy . . . and the same woman.

The guy was some young Hispanic. I remember him too. No matter what time of day it was, the younger one always ordered cake or ice cream to eat. And your guy's woman was a hottie! She was also Hispanic . . . all over your boy there."

"Could you hear what the men were talking about?"

"No. But when things got serious his woman was dismissed and sent outside. *That* tells me they were probably discussing drugs. When the dealers start talking about their business, *that's* when the women are sent away, you know? That way if the woman ever gets dumped or upset, they can't get even by going to the cops, you know what I mean?"

"I know what you mean," said Alejandro.

"Hell hath no fury like a woman scorned, you know?" she laughed.

"Yeah, I know, I know."

"So do I get the money?'

Alejandro smiled, reached out and tucked the bill under her bra. "There's more where that came from, if you remember anything else. Never mind the brandy." He got up to leave and then heard a voice call from behind him.

"Sir. Wait a minute!"

Alejandro turned and looked at a Caucasian man, who seemed to be in his mid-thirties with a shaved head.

"If I give you a *lead* to someone with information on your boy, do I get some of those c-notes?"

"Sure. Who do you know?"

"Can I talk to you in private?"

Alejandro shrugged his shoulders and motioned to follow him.

Once outside, the man resumed talking. "I *know* that guy."

"You *know* him?"

"Well, I don't know him by name. But, I'll never forget the face of the man who kicked my ass years ago."

"Why did he kick your ass," asked Alejandro.

"I got fresh with one of his girlfriends in a New Brunswick bar – one of the college student hang-outs. She told me to lay off, then *he* told me to lay off. I never thought that skinny little fuck would be able to lay me out like he did – thought he was gonna kill me! I had some nightmares of that face for a while after that," said the man.

"I need to know if you can connect me to someone or someplace in New Brunswick. Did you report this incident to anyone – the police, the college?"

"No, after he knocked me on my ass, I saw this *look* in his eyes. There was this expression – 'Don't you even t*hink* about fucking with me!' This wasn't someone playing hero to a damsel in distress. This guy had the eyes of an assassin. Since he let me live, I decided it would be better for my welfare if I never mentioned it again."

"What was the name of the bar?"

"Shouldn't I get some money?"

Alejandro handed over three hundred dollar bills.

The man looked in both directions, took the money with a smile and put it in his pocket.

"What was the name of the bar?" repeated Alejandro.

"Shit, I don't remember."

Alejandro glared at him.

"But I remember it was only five blocks south from the campus library. I went to that bar a lot. At least until the incident with him. You know, for another hundred bucks, I might remember something else."

Escobar's right hand man kept his expressionless eyes trained on the man as his fingers pulled another bill out of his pocket.

The man looked both ways, took the money with a smile and put it in his pocket. "I was a student. I think he was too. We were wearing the same New Brunswick college tee-shirts."

"What year did this happen?"

"Is that worth some more money?"

"I give you a hundred dollars and you tell me about tee-shirts? Just tell me what year this happened."

"I was a junior, so it must have been 1971."

Alejandro held out the photograph again. "And you're *sure* this was the man?"

"If it's not him, he's got a twin. And that bartender? He was the owner. I'll bet he's still there."

The assassin walked away.

Neco seems to make lasting impressions. Tomorrow I'll see if he made any lasting impressions in New Brunswick.

Across the Delaware River in Clayton, Neco parked in front of his house. Working with Julio and the Pottsville authorities kept him from picking up Petey.

But Julio came through with the name needed for getting into Arnie Schmidt's inner circle.

Neco found the home to be dead quiet. He marched upstairs where he saw his wife fast asleep – her open mouth had some drool dripping onto her pillowcase.

"Sandy!"

Awakening seemed painful to her, but she mustered a response.

Sandy rolled over and closed her eyes again. "What? What's going on?"

Her husband stepped into the room. "Where's Petey? Why are you sleeping in the middle of the day?"

"Petey's at my mother's," said Sandy, her eyes still closed.

"Look at me. Why is he at your mother's?"

She rolled over and opened her eyes. "My mother picked him up from here earlier."

"I smell alcohol!"

"Petey was already at mother's. I didn't drink until after I left Koblenzer. I went out with my sister and some friends. Can you understand why Petey's still at mother's?"

"Because you're *drunk*?"

"Because I'm being responsible!" she said with a taunting smile. "I knew I shouldn't drive him home."

Neco began pacing, working to contain himself.

Sandy sat up in the bed. "I was out with my sister and some friends! God! I don't understand! Everyone wants me to come out of my shell, and when I finally do, you guys are angry at me."

"What 'guys'?" asked Neco.

"You and Dr. Koblenzer."

"Koblenzer is angry with you?"

"I don't know . . . maybe more like disappointed – let down."

"That makes two of us! We wanted you to come out of your shell, not run away from your problems." He paced some more. "How long has he known you're mixing alcohol with your prescription?"

"I'm not on my prescription anymore."

"He took you off your prescription?"

"Nooooo. I deprescribed myself." She chuckled admiringly over her talents as a wordsmith.

"I going over to your mother's to have her watch Petey when I'm not home. Then I'm calling Koblenzer." As he went down the stairs, he yelled back up to the room, "And your *sister* is the *last* person you should be socializing with!"

Neco got into his car and pulled away. As upset as he was, he had to stay focused and plan out his little bomb to drop on George Martinez tomorrow.

CHAPTER FORTY-EIGHT

1 July, Philadelphia

Neco sat in the backseat of a fully-loaded white Cadillac approaching the Benjamin Franklin Bridge en route to Philadelphia for his dinner meeting with Martinez. He and Martinez agreed to discuss business tonight. But Escobar's latest front man had no idea of the playing card Neco would put on the table this evening.

In the meantime, the agent sat in silent appreciation.

He could believe the driver he had, but he *still* could not believe who had been assigned to be his woman this evening.

His mind briefly wandered back to his conversation in Harrisburg with Martin Shurmur on Friday.

"Martin, for this next meeting with George, it's time to show off. I told you I'm going to need a bodyguard to drive me around and a woman to be my bitch."

"I don't have any female agents here. But, in anticipation of your needs, I've made arrangements to borrow someone from another agency who's willing to play the part of slut to your womanizer."

"I don't mean to be disrespectful, but it's important that I'm in on the selection process. This woman has to look right for the part. She's got to be hot," said Neco.

"You'll find her to be what you want," assured Shurmur.

"I mean really hot! These dealers have high standards. I can't be set up for a 'blind date' and get a nasty surprise."

"Then perhaps you should meet her now."

Neco squinted his eyes. "She's here?"

Shurmur leaned over to his intercom and buzzed his receptionist. "Please send in our slut."

The door opened to reveal the smiling face of Ada Hernandez, who did a little dance with her entrance.

"Miss Ada!" said Neco.

Ada embraced her former partner in a hug. "Hello, Juni! It's so great to see you back. I can't wait to work with you again." Neco, still a little flustered, smiled at Shurmur.

"How did this happen?"

"You're doing this assignment out of Philadelphia, so I called your old office across the river and asked Captain Blake who you were comfortable with for such cases. He told me that he had someone available who you'd be very happy with. And Blake says "Hello" by the way."

"Yeah," snorted Neco.

It was not his only surprise.

Shurmur buzzed reception again. "Please send in the muscle."

The opened again and Thomas Bryant made his entrance.

"I'm not dancing for you, Loco!"

"Mr. Thomas! This is great! Now I got me a bitch *and a* dumb *son*-of-a-bitch!" said Neco, shaking hands and hugging Bryant.

"I trust you find, Mr. Thomas acceptable," said the Attorney General.

"Are you kidding?" said Neco, "It's the dumb, out—of-shape bastards that I can't stand. They can't protect m*e*. I have to protect *them!* With Thomas, I know I won't have to worry about that at crunch time."

"And he's got street smarts," added Ada. "He's not someone who's worked solely behind a desk. Oh . . . no offense, sir."

"None taken, Ada. Juni here made that point when I first interviewed him."

Neco' mind snapped back to the car when he felt the Cadillac slowing down for the toll booth. As Bryant threw some quarters into the exact change basket, Hernandez broke the silence.

"So tell me about where we're going tonight—The Moshulu," she said.

"The Moshulu is this big-ass ship that's been converted into a restaurant. In fact, if you look out the left window, you can see it from here."

"Where am I looking?"

Neco pointed, "Do you see those strings of blue light bulbs down there along the river?"

"Yes."

"That's The Moshulu," said Neco. "The lights are outlining the bare masts."

"My God! It must be huge!"

Permanently docked perpendicular to the Delaware River in an area of Philadelphia known as Penn's Landing, The Moshulu spanned four-hundred and nine feet from stem to stern – a little more than a third longer than a football field. The middle of the ship at its widest covered about fifty-feet. No other four-masted ship still afloat in the world could match that.

When patrons walked up to board the ship, it greeted them like a Philadelphia tour guide – immediately sweeping them into history.

The Moshulu, originally launched out of Germany in 1904 under the name of "Kurt". It had a long career working the ports of the United States, Europe, Africa, Australia and South America. In 1968, it was purchased in Naantale, Finland, converted into a restaurant and towed to Philadelphia in 1974. The next year, it opened as a five—star restaurant with an Asian decor. As terrific as the earlier dinner with Martinez had been, The Moshulu, less than twenty-five yards from the Chart House, would give Neco the one-upmanship he wanted when picking up the tab tonight.

Bryant pulled up to the parking attendant's booth, paid for the parking and grabbed the ticket. The attendant hit the switch to raise the horizontal bar and let them in.

"Here we are, Miss Ada. I see George outside the door there with his skank and his muscle. Are you ready for this?"

"It's like we never stopped."

Patrons entered the ship on a heavy canvas-covered walkway that took them over the water and brought them into one of the ship's side entrances. Martinez and his party waited at the front end.

"Right on time, Loco," said Martinez. "That's how I like to conduct my business."

Neco began the introductions. "George Martinez, this is Ada Ramirez. Ada this is George." Then he turned to Martinez' date, "And whose this lovely young lady?"

"Juni Neco, this is Holly Rivera. Holly this is Juni."

"You can call me, Loco," smiled Neco.

"So, I hear," replied Rivera.

"These two are a lot prettier than Gordo, huh?" said Martinez.

With high heels, Rivera stood almost as tall as Martinez in height. Like Hernandez, she wore a form—fitting gown, tastefully low-cut at the neck and with a slit going up the bottom of a hem line that began above the knee. Unlike Hernandez' red gown, Rivera's blue gown had sequins.

Neco grabbed Hernandez by the butt and led the way to the hostess. The two bodyguards followed at a distance.

The two businessmen requested a table in the dining area that did not feature the bar. They asked for a booth in the corner. The booth had a glass partition rising from the upholstery. It would provide ample sound-proofing for when the business portion of the dinner took place.

Bryant and his counter-part adjourned to the bar area and took two low-backed, wooden stools from where they could monitor the entrance to restaurant from the windows.

A wine steward approached Neco' table and asked what the party would like to drink.

Martinez and the two women agreed on a bottle of white wine for the table.

Neco noted that the selection was priced at one hundred ten dollars.

Remembering that he agreed at The Chart House to pick up the next tab, he quietly breathed a sigh of relief.

Thank God I'm back on the job with an expense account!

Instead of his traditional half-dozen oysters Rockefeller, Martinez had them with a light tropical-style sauce. His six oysters were accompanied by ahi tuna tartar and Asian-spiced crispy calamari.

Neco upgraded from his jumbo shrimp cocktail at the Chart House to a colossal shrimp cocktail tonight.

The women each had the Moshulu chopped salad – an artistic presentation of iceberg, frisee, Belgian endive, smoked bacon, sweet potatoes, bleu cheese, craisins, pumpkin seeds, red onion and bleu cheese dressing.

Other patrons alternated stares and the averting of their eyes from Neco' table, as the two couples alternated kisses and caresses throughout their appetizers and entrees – exotic dishes of filet mignon and lobster.

Again, the conversation was all chit-chat about recent movies, where they liked to vacation – everything but smuggling cocaine while the women were present.

Neco took a desert menu being passed out by the waitress.

Hernandez rubbed her date's leg under the table as he spoke.

"Let's order some dessert, and then . . ." He flinched upwards for a second as Hernandez' hand found its way above his thigh. Neco closed his eyes for a second and smiled. "And then, we'll conduct some business."

After dessert, the men dismissed the women to take a couple of seats at the bar.

Martinez opened things up. "Tonight I want to get into the details on your set-up. What are you bringing to the table here?"

"I've worked to create very simple, but very valuable circumstances for dealers."

Martinez leaned in. "Which is good. I like simple."

"I have two guys with Customs at the Tioga Marina off Interstate 95."

"I know that one," said Martinez. "That's the one off the exit for Allegheny Avenue."

"Right. What happens is, someone like yourself gives me all the shipping information – the complete schedule from departure to arrival. I want to know exactly what's coming, exactly how much, and how it's going to be packaged."

"We manufacture fake Bibles and put packets of dope in them. Then they come in boxes packed inside big wooden crates."

Neco nodded approvingly, "Bibles . . . I like that . . . nice touch. So as I was saying, you give me all the details, including a copy of the bill of lading. Then when the shipment arrives, my guys insure that they are the ones who will 'inspect' your cargo and handle all the paperwork for receiving it. With that done, two more of my people pick up the merchandise out on the loading dock and come out of the marina . . . usually at Gate B . . ." Neco paused to let a server bring more beverages. "You'll recognize Gate B because there's a set of old railroad tracks coming in from the street there. The van is then driven to where the goods can be switched easily and quickly to your vehicle.

The street in front of the marina is very wide. If it's okay with you, we'll make the switch there."

"If that's your standard mo. that's fine with me," agreed Martinez.

"That's my standard mo." said Neco.

"You'll get five percent of the haul."

Neco rebutted. "I'll get *ten* percent of the haul."

Martinez raised his eyebrows. "We give five."

"Then we shouldn't waste any more time. The ten percent is non-negotiable."

"We're talking about a lot of weight, Loco. Five percent will be *very* substantial."

Neco shook his head. "No . . . no. This is high-risk, high-reward. I have to pay top dollar to these customs guys. They don't do shit like this for some piss-ant amount. They give me the service I need. And that's what *you* need. For that I get ten percent of what I touch."

Martinez, crossed his arms and rested them on this stomach area. He looked at Neco and then down at the table and then back at Neco. "I have to get back to my boss and run this by him."

"I understand. There's a lot involved with something of this magnitude. Remind your boss that's why he wants to work with someone that comes with a one hundred percent guarantee. Do you *lose* more than ten percent trying to move things through New York and Miami?"

Martinez let out a sigh. "I'll be sure to ask." But he already knew the answer.

"Without someone on the take in customs, you have to hope the inspectors are careless enough to think the Bibles you use are real. Smart ones will check them."

"Every box has two layers of real Bibles on top."

"That's fine. But thorough inspectors will check the items on the bottom or randomly bring in the dogs. When the inspectors are on *your* side, neither of those things happen. Oh, they'll make it *look* good. They'll poke around, take out some Bibles, but your weight *always* gets through. Combine that with the fact security on the docks isn't as tight here in Philly like those other cities,"

Neco leaned forward, "Your boss will more than make up the ten percent with one hundred percent of your shipments getting through."

"Like I said, I'll run it by him."

"Take your time. *He's* the one coming to *me*. I don't need this, but if he wants to play ball, I will do a first—class job for him like I do for everyone else."

They signaled their respective bodyguards to go out and have the vehicles brought to the entrance. The women came back to the table as Neco paid the bill.

"Good night, Loco. I'll have an answer when we meet at the ballgame."

"See you then."

Bryant started to drive Neco and Hernandez back to their cars in Olde City. He looked back in the rear-view mirror at Neco. "How'd it go?"

"The way I like it to go. I told him I want double the standard rate. He tried to negotiate me down and I didn't budge So, he's going to get back with Escobar and meet with me again. And just when he thinks things are under control, I'll drop the *next* bomb on him."

When he got back in his own car, Neco turned his pager on again. The number had "911" tacked on at the end.

He pulled out his car phone to return the call.

"This is Dr. Koblenzer."

"This is Neco. What's going on? What's the emergency?"

"Since her last session, I have been trying to confirm Sandy for her appointment on Monday. I haven't been able to reach her. Do you know where she is?"

"She said she was staying at her sister's tonight."

"Where's your son?"

"I keep him at his grandmother's whenever I'm not going to be around."

"I felt I had convinced her not to discharge herself from care. But I still have my concerns. Before her last appointment, she told me that she did have her last prescription filled. Now she's indicated that since her recent binging with alcohol, she hasn't started her prescription yet. Mr. Neco, should she take those pills concurrently with alcoholic beverages, she could experience mood swings like we've never seen before."

"What should I do? What *can* I do?" demanded Neco.

"On an immediate basis, someone has to get a hold of her pills so that she has no access to them until we get her stably off the alcohol. Ultimately . . . you may have to look at having her committed."

"Committed? Like to a mental institution?"

"She's never followed through on her suicidal attempts with the knife and the gun, but there's no telling what she's capable of if she pops one of those pills before or after one of her visits to the neighborhood tavern."

"So it's come down to this? I have to put her away, and tell Petey that his mother is nuts?"

"Let's see if you can get those pills first."

Neco ended the call and slammed the phone to the passenger seat. *Jesus Christ! What am I supposed to do?*

What the hell is he saying?

CHAPTER FORTY-NINE

Clayton, New Jersey

Neco sped home and rushed to the front door.

Sandy had not answered her cell phone and there were no cars at the sister's house when he drove by. The mother—in-law *had* answered her phone and assured him Petey was fast asleep in bed. She was not made aware of the doctor's information.

Once inside, he ran up the stairs, two-at-a-time, and went straight to the medicine cabinet in the master bedroom's bathroom. Sandy often kept her prescriptions in there.

He swung open the mirror and saw it – the bottle from the pharmacy. Neco allowed himself a quick sigh of relief before realizing he had to do one more thing – count the pills.

The count came up two pills short.

Satisfied Petey was safe, Neco decided the time had come for sleep.

Neco rolled over in bed awakened by the sound of his home phone ringing. He glanced at the alarm clock which read two-thirty-seven.

"Who is this?"

"Mr. Neco?"

"Yeah. Who is this?"

"Mr. Neco, this is Officer Patton with the Gloucester County Police. We have a situation at your mother-in-law's home involving your wife and son,"

Neco felt his heart jump. "What? What situation?"

196

Neco quickly threw on some clothes, ran down the stairs and out to his car. Some lights came on in the neighborhood as he peeled out of his parking spot and sped down the street.

Within ten minutes, he arrived at his mother-in-law's house, which already had a half-dozen squad cars flashing on the scene.

He unlocked his glove compartment, removed his badge and nine-millimeter handgun. With the gun tucked behind his back, Neco jumped out of his car and waved his badge at the closest officers. "I'm Neco! Where are they? Where are my wife and son?"

"They're upstairs, Mr. Neco. But you can't go up there alone!"

Neco darted past them towards the front door.

"Hey! Somebody grab him!" screamed the officer.

Two other officers positioned themselves at the front door.

"Stay right where you . . ." began one of them.

A left cross interrupted his attempted command. As the officer blacked out in his fall to the front porch deck, the second officer grabbed Neco from behind with a bear-hug.

Neco stomped his foot down on the officer's arch, which loosened up the bear-hug enough to jam his right elbow into the man's sternum. This freed up the same arm to deliver a back-fist to the face. The second officer fell in a heap on the first one's body while Neco bolted through the door and up the stairs.

Halfway up, he could make out the sound of Petey crying.

A third police officer, stationed in the hallway, stared into the bedroom and never heard Neco coming up the stairs. Within seconds the officer would hear nothing else for a while as he received a chop with the side of a hand to the back of his neck.

Neco stepped to the doorway of the master bedroom and stood in stunned amazement to see Sandy brandishing a pistol at Petey. Off to the side lay the bruised and bloody body of her mother – unconscious, but still alive.

"Daddy!" screamed a crying Petey. "I don't want to die!"

"Sandy! What the hell are you doing?"

"She wanted to take Petey from me!" said Sandy, her words slightly slurred. "I told her *nobody* is taking Petey from me! And that means *you're* not taking Petey from me either! Petey has bad blood! The bad blood has to come out! Then he can love me again!"

Neco drew his gun from behind his back and, with both hands, trained the barrel on his wife. "Sandy, put down the gun, or, I swear to God, I will put a bullet in you!"

Sandy took on an expression of pretending to think.

"Hmmm, how would the great Loco handle this if he was in *my* shoes?"

Neco' finger tightened on the trigger. "Put it down *now!*"

"Oh, I know! The great Loco would say, 'How are you going to kill me, if I kill you first?' right?" And with that she turned the gun on Neco and strode toward him.

Neco did not hesitate. He squeezed the trigger with the intent to begin unloading the clip.

But nothing happened except for a clicking sound.

As she grew closer, she started to laugh maniacally and stopped just short of her husband, who could only produce the sound of empty clicks from his weapon.

Before he could react, she swung her gun into his face and sent him to the carpet.

With a final laugh, Sandy spun around and screamed,

"Petey has bad blood and it has to come out!"

She took dead aim at Petey and fired.

Neco screamed as his upper body went involuntarily upright from his mattress. He breathed rapidly with a cold sweat across his forehead.

It came back to him – Petey stayed at his grandmother's house and Sandy spent the night with Sheila.

He went downstairs for a cold glass of water,

Well, fuck any sleep before my meeting with Arnold Schmidt tomorrow!

Chapter Fifty

1 July, Harrisburg, Pennsylvania

Senator Donald Carvey shut the door to his bedroom and dialed up a number on his private line.

"Good morning, Senator," answered the voice of Dexter Rasche.

"Dexter, my boy! Where are you?"

"Home, enjoying a four-day week-end."

"I was calling to see what you could tell me about the latest activities of that crazy Puerto Rican."

"Senator, I approached Shurmur on Friday. I told him that I was surprised that I was hired first and yet Neco was already on two cases."

"What did he say to that?" asked Carvey.

"Something awfully strange."

"What?"

"He said 'Neco kind of assigned himself to the cases'."

Rasche could not see Carvey biting on his lower lip.

"Son, did you ask Mr. Shurmur what the two cases were?"

"I tried, but he said that Neco demanded that I am to know nothing about his cases. All he was willing to tell me was that they involved something out in Western Pennsylvania. It *sucks!*"

"Who the hell is *running* that operation over there, Shurmur or that crazy son-of-a-bitch? The Special Task Force is my ticket to the Presidency. And I'm not going to have loose cannons around to screw things up."

"I'm sorry, sir. I know you were as upset as me over his hiring."

Carvey took a deep breath and regained his composure.

"Dexter, let me tell you how much this worries me. When I learned about his hiring, I called up my butler and told him to order me a three hundred dollar bottle of Remy Martin Cognac. And I told him when he gets that bottle, I want him to put it in the center of my display table in the dining room. And when I finally make it so that Neco is no longer a distraction, you and I are going to open that bottle and have ourselves a fitting celebration.

That's how much he worries me."

"Sounds great, Senator. I only wish Shurmur wouldn't treat me like a second-class citizen."

"Don't you worry about Shurmur. Just keep your ear to the ground and keep me posted on any news with Neco' cases. Somebody somewhere must know something about them.

I'll see you out at Indian Gap this week."

CHAPTER FIFTY-ONE

Camden, New Jersey

Julio's contact had come through with the goods. As the Jamaican predicted, Arnie Schmidt had no idea that the man setting him up called him from a phone booth in the next town from the prison where he was serving his time.

Schmidt scheduled the meeting with Juni Neco near an old elementary school that had been closed for ten years.

Untended weeds surrounding two sides the building had grown to the size of tiny trees. The other two sides of the school were flanked by the concrete of a playground area.

And even *that* had weeds muscling their way through cracks in the surface.

Like a lot of the buildings in Camden, all the lower level windows had iron bars.

Neco parked across the street at a park the size of a small block. He scanned the deserted park which had a sidewalk around the perimeter and two more sidewalks cutting through the middle like an "X". Old maple trees took up enough space to prevent kids from playing wiffle-ball and other team games.

Sunburned patches of grass cried for water to no avail.

Where the hell is this guy?

Then he spotted the lone person in the park.

The center portion of the "X" had four benches heavily bolted to the concrete. A man sat on one of the benches.

He wore a dark pair of wire-rimmed shades and looked to be in his late thirties, early forties.

Neco grabbed a briefcase, got out of the car and walked towards the center of the park.

The clean-shaven man sported a crew cut and wore camouflage attire. His sleeveless shirt revealed well—toned arms heavily covered with tattoos – Chinese dragons, big-breasted females and more than several names of women he was supposed to love forever.

Julio described him well, thought Neco.

As Neco approached the bench, the man remained seated, not even looking in his visitor's direction.

When he got within six feet, the man dressed like a war veteran finally spoke, still not looking at Neco.

"Eleven hundred hours. Kih! Right on time. Have a seat, Mr. Neco."

Neco remembered Julio telling him about the "Kih!". Schmidt had some type of chronic inflammation in his throat which caused him to have a recurring throat—clearing sound. Julio warned him it was like Chinese water torture to have to listen to it.

"Mr. Schmidt?" responded Neco, as he sat on the other side of the bench, still holding the handle to his briefcase.

Suddenly the man held up an index finger to his lips.

"Ssssh!" And he quickly swiveled his head from one side to the other.

Neco looked around and saw nothing more than trees rustling in the wind.

"Yeah, I'm Schmidt. Arnie Schmidt. I understand you're in the market for some weapons."

"You understand correctly, Mr. Schmidt. I have lots of business to attend to . . . pending the quality of your wares."

Schmidt stared at the briefcase. "First we see if requirement number one has been met."

Neco placed the briefcase on the bench and opened it enough for Schmidt to see the contents. "Your five hundred thousand dollar retainer."

"Stand up, Mr. Neco."

"Why would I do that?"

"I have to pat you down."

"I'll tell you right now, I'm carrying a weapon."

"I don't care if you're carrying a weapon. Kih! I'm going to check you for a wire. No pat-down, no deal."

"You're going to pat me down out here . . . in the open?"

"There's no one else in the park and no one in their homes will care."

Neco released the briefcase and stood up. "You won't like what happens if you touch my gun."

"Acknowledged," said Schmidt as he stood up in front of his customer. He began the pat-down. "You're in good shape, Mr. Neco. Kih! Did you ever serve?"

Neco raised his arms. "I suppose, if I count myself as my own country."

"Me, I served in Nam. Kih! Marine Corp. Three years until I was finally honorably discharged with a respiratory disease from Agent Orange."

"I've heard of that stuff," said Neco. "Nasty shit."

"The shrinks also said I was unemployable. Kih! Claimed I had developed a paranoid disorder from too many traumatic incidents with Charlie."

"Ummm . . . Charlie . . . oh, right! The Vietnamese. The bad guys."

"Mr. Neco, I learned a military pension and government disability check don't feed the bulldog. But America is the land of opportunity. Kih! With the proper attitude, some rugged persistence and the right illicit contacts, even a disabled veteran can live out his dream."

"As can an illegal immigrant looking to expand his own illicit contacts. Can you help me with that, sir?"

Schmidt rose to his feet. "Walk with me, Mr. Neco."

Neco grabbed his briefcase and followed Schmidt across the street and over to the school playground.

As they walked, it hit Neco. "You're the owner of this property?"

"For the last year."

"And *this* is where you store all your weapons?"

"No, Mr. Neco. Kih! This is just a showplace for buyers. The school is where I keep a modest display with a catalogue of everything I sell. I float the merchandise between other locations I own."

"A lot of space for an 'office'," commented Neco.

"It's a great way to ensure there are no neighboring offices. Kih!"

"This is Camden. Aren't you the least bit worried about vandals breaking into the building and stealing what you *do* have here?"

The two reached the back entrance to the school.

"Check out this door," said Schmidt. "Kih!"

Neco recognized the type of door – the same type that dislodged the shoulder of his colleague, Burt, when he substituted his body for the ram left behind at the station.

His host continued. "All the doors are like this – each with an electronic security system from which I can shut down a series of motion detectors inside. Unless you know the right combination of numbers to punch on this pad, the motion detectors stay on."

"But wouldn't it be better to have a place with your own muscle securing it?" asked Neco. "Here, if someone forces their way in, your alarm goes off, and they run away. Then the police arrive and discover what you have here."

"Oh, there's no alarm. I've customized the system.

If those motion detectors are tripped . . . BOOM!" said Schmidt as he suddenly clapped his hands. "The whole place goes up!" He punched in the numbers and opened the door.

Stepping inside, the ex-marine suddenly stopped. His finger went up to his mouth again. "Sssssh!" His head swiveled back and forth.

Neco squinted his eyes. "What the *fuck* is wrong with you?"

With no answer, Schmidt ran up a flight of stairs.

Neco bit his tongue and followed with the briefcase.

The war veteran did not stop until he reached the third floor, where he went down a hall and into a classroom overlooking the park. Neco watched him go over to a closet and remove a sniper rifle that already had a silencer attached to the barrel. Schmidt quietly raised one of the frosted glass windows about eight inches and peered through it.

"Just tell me what the fuck is going on," demanded Neco.

Schmidt brought the butt of the rifle up to his shoulder and trained the barrel through the opening. He placed his eye on the scope. "All of a sudden, there are a lot of people in the park. Kih!"

"So what?"

"When there are a lot of people around, I get a little nervous. Kih!"

"Well then setting up next to a park was just the perfect decision, wasn't it?"

Schmidt looked through the scope. "Do you see that small, skinny Black boy down there on the corner?"

Neco put down the briefcase and peeked through the window. "Yeah, what about him?"

"You know," said Schmidt, "I could shoot that kid from here right through the temple. *Pop!* And no one would even know where the shot came from."

Neco' eyes widened as he riveted on Schmidt's index finger, still around the trigger guard. He slowly reached behind his back and gripped his handgun. If that finger was placed on the *inside* of the trigger guard, he would have to either blow his cover or take Schmidt out.

"Oh shit!" said Schmidt, as he lowered the rifle.

"Wait! Kih! He's one of mine!"

"Huh?" said Neco, his hand returning to his side.

"That one is one of your what?"

"A runner. He runs some drugs for me."

"He looks like he's ten."

Schmidt did a double-take through the window and ran towards the door and shouted back to his customer. "I have to go let someone in."

"Schmidt! I'm here to purchase some fucking guns! Are you going to talk about my order or what?"

By that time, the gun dealer yelled from the hallway near the flight of stairs.

"There's another buyer I have to let in."

Neco quietly trailed a short distance behind.

Schmidt ran down the stairs and punched the numbers needed to admit the young kid and his other client, holding his own briefcase into the building. "Hey, Baseem!

Greetings, Mr. Tortelli."

Tortelli looked to be somewhere in his early forties.

He stood around six-feet, two in height. A little too much girth challenged the buttons on his pin-striped jacket. An excessive amount of gel slicked back a full head of dark brown hair.

The unctuous Italian put down his briefcase, let out an annoying sigh and raised his arms as Schmidt patted him down.

"Is this really necessary?" asked Tortelli. "This is the second time we've met, I've already given you the retainer and now . . ."

"You've brought your final payment," finished Schmidt, who already opened the suitcase to check the money. "Sorry,

Rico. Kih! But my protocol is my protocol." Then he turned back towards the stairs and yelled, "Mr. Neco! Come down to the basement!"

Neco quickly removed his shoes and silently ran back up the stairs, pretending not to hear Schmidt. This new arrival potentially could potentially set the stage for an arrest without Neco having to blow his cover. He would keep alert for any information that could be used to make Tortelli the fall guy.

"Mr. Neco!" repeated Schmidt. "Come down to the basement!"

Neco yelled back from the third floor. "I'm fucking coming!"

The basement had seedy furnishings. An old, scratched up teacher's classroom desk had a ratty swivel chair with rips on multiple spots placed behind it. For his guests, a couple of slightly rusted metal folding chairs would have to suffice. Two three-ring bound notebooks laid on a well—used desk pad.

Schmidt's clients walked over to the desk where he handed them each a notebook.

Neco looked over at the young Black kid sitting at a cafeteria table on the other side of the basement. "Mr.

Schmidt, what the hell is your boy doing here?"

"He's here for class," said the arms dealer, as he walked towards the boy. "Come over here."

Curiosity overcame the irritation felt by his two customers. They stepped over to the table where the boy sat.

Schmidt opened up a leather case on the table to reveal a dismantled Russian Kalashnikov sniper rifle. He slid the open case to his runner.

Neco recognized the weapon that matched up with those found in the Gloucester City and Camden raids.

Schmidt pulled a stopwatch from his pocket. "Ready,

Baseem?"

The boy nodded.

"Go!"

Neco and Tortelli watched in astonishment as Baseem rapidly assembled the weapon and held it ready to aim and fire.

Schmidt looked triumphant. "Twenty-one seconds!

That's the best you've ever done, boy! Kih!"

The Special Task Force agent pulled himself together.

"As impressive as that was, class is over. I want him out of the room."

"As you wish, Mr. Neco. Baseem, report here tomorrow.

Same time."

The boy dutifully left.

"Okay, is everyone happy now?" asked Schmidt.

Tortelli joined in on the communication. "No. I don't even want *him* around when I'm conducting business."

Neco turned to the Italian, "Then you better schedule another appointment for yourself."

"Listen, pal," said Tortelli, "I work for 'The Dictator'. Now if that name from South Philly means nothing to you, it will real soon if you mess with me."

Schmidt broke out into a gleeful high-pitched laugh.

"And just what do you find so damned funny, Mr. Schmidt?" asked Tortelli.

"I always find all the nicknames amusing. Kih! 'The Dictator'!" he laughed again. "Maybe you two should have nicknames." He looked at Neco. "You could be 'El Presidente'." Then he turned to Tortelli. "And you could be 'The Little Fascist'."

The frowns on his guests' faces stayed on their faces as Schmidt remained the only one finding any humor.

"Hell," Schmidt continued as he walked back to the table with the catalogues. "I'm going to start calling myself 'The Czar'! Yeah, 'The Weapons Czar'!"

The two men ignored him.

Tortelli stepped right in front of Neco to ensure Neco knew he was being looked down on. "You don't know who you're messing with, Neco!" said Tortelli. "You mess with me and you mess with the family."

Neco planted his feet for action. "And just who would tell the family I messed with you if you were dead?"

Tortelli made a sudden reach inside his jacket. "Why you stupid little spic . . ."

Neco answered with a back fist to the Italian's jaw. Mr. Tortelli staggered backwards. Before he took his third step, he felt a foot plunging into his sternum which lifted him up and into the air, ass over heels. His body landed in a heap on the tiled basement floor.

The ex-marine enjoyed the display. "Whoa! They never taught that in the Corps! Kih! Now be careful, Neco! We don't want to have an international incident!" And he let loose with the high-pitched, gleeful laugh again.

Neco stood over the semi-conscious Tortelli, and removed a revolver from the man's shoulder holster. "Spics have 'families' too. So if I were you, I wouldn't mess with *me*. I already *have* a nickname – 'Loco'. Plus I'm already armed . . ." Then Neco jammed the barrel of the revolver in Tortelli's mouth, " . . . to the *teeth!*"

That snapped Tortelli out of his daze. Neco removed the gun from his mouth and yanked him up off the floor to his feet. He kept his hand clinched on Tortelli's lapel and pushed him against a wall as he continued. "In the spirit of our new understanding, I'm going to read my catalogue while you take the first turn with the 'Czar' here. Then you'll leave and we'll work to never have our paths cross again. You'll understand why I'm going to hold onto your gun until you leave. And when you *do* leave, the bullets stay with me. Capiche?"

When Tortelli begrudgingly nodded, he released him with a shove in the direction of Schmidt. The mobster straightened his jacket, dusted off his sleeves and walked unsteadily over to the arms dealer.

"Okay!" exclaimed a wide-eyed Schmidt with a loud clap, "If that concludes our little one-act drama, we can finish conducting our business."

While Neco emptied the revolver, Tortelli gave Schmidt his list of selections and quantities from the catalogue.

"Need any training on these?" offered Schmidt.

"Remember, it's included in the price."

"No, I have people familiar with what I'm getting."

"Kih! When do you want your merchandise?"

"Monday," answered Tortelli "My boss has some competition to eliminate. He wants to address the matter this month."

"Did you want some drugs with your order?"

Tortelli's expression took on a look of mild surprise.

"I didn't know you had drugs in your inventory."

"I have an old war buddy, now in the government – he asked me if I could do a little drug running for him. I don't handle the drugs personally. Kih! I've got a local boy who I give your money to, minus my finder's fee. Then he gets your stuff to you. Initially, I got my hands on some dope, but since then he's raised his demand. He's graduated up to coke now."

"So you can get crack and LSD?" asked Tortelli.

"I'm your one-stop shop."

"What kind of weight can you accommodate on the dope?"

"Right now, I can easily get you up to ten kilos.

Above that it gets a little difficult to accommodate change that. In a little over a year I'll have contacts who can move all the weight I want."

The words triggered a file in Neco' mind.

Manuel. Sixth and Cambria. "And then there's word on the street it'll expand in a little more than a year."

Neco continued to see the inception of the new drug wave unfold before his eyes.

And who's this "buddy" in the government he's supplying drugs to?

"How soon will that be?" asked Tortelli.

"Too early for me to say. Kih! But I'll keep you posted as the date nears. What number do you want to be called at?"

Tortelli reached into his pocket and handed him a card. "This one."

"Good," said Schmidt, "Kih! We'll meet at eleven hundred hours."

"Where?"

"I'll make sure one of my locations is secure and then I'll call you and give you directions."

Tortelli, already in motion for the door, said, "Can I leave without blowing up the building?"

Another amused expression came over Schmidt. "I have to let you out. Kih!"

The two men left the room, leaving Neco alone with his thoughts as he pretended to go through the catalogue.

"Your turn, Mr. Neco! Oh! I'm sorry, I mean" said Schmidt, as he made air quotation marks and shook his head,

"Loco!"

Neco went through the catalogue with Schmidt and made his "order".

Then Schmidt informed his buyer the amount due, handed him his phone number and escorted him to the door.

"Arnie," said Neco, as he opened the door. "Don't go popping people from your bell tower up there. I'm going to need you for more guns. I don't need you in jail."

Schmidt got a steely look in his eyes. "Oh, I'll never be in a jail."

Neco quizzically squinted his eyes.

"And that's because, I will *never* be taken alive.

I'll either be dead or disappear. All my exchange locations are like this one – wired to blow up, if needed. And when I say 'disappear', I mean *disappear*. I can stay under the radar for years. I'm a survivalist." Suddenly his head swiveled and the index finger went up to his mouth.

"Ssshh!"

Crazy ass . . . Neco left it at that. He had some useful information and grabbed his phone.

From his office at Strawberry Square, Martin Shurmur awaited Juni Neco' call from Camden. When he worked on a Saturday, it meant he had to answer his own phone.

The light flashed on his private line and he picked it up in anticipation. "This is Shurmur."

"Martin. Hello."

"Loco! I've been waiting. What kind of news do you have for me?"

"I know when Schmidt's next deal is. Our boy has hooked up with a South Philly thug – Rico Tortelli.

Tortelli needs a big shipment of guns for some kind of massacre his boss wants. Let's meet and we'll go over a plan, including what kind of manpower is needed."

"That's why I'm here," assured the Attorney General.

"I have all the people I need, either here or on call."

"Good," said Neco. "The Prosecutor's Office will have some more information on Schmidt too."

"I know Captain Blake. I'll give him a call."

Neco laughed. "Give Captain Blake my love."

Shurmur had forgotten about the emotion around Neco' departure from Camden. "I'll blow him some kisses for you. Then I'll see if we have any files on Tortelli." said the Attorney General, swiveling in his high-backed leather chair. "So Arnie Schmidt is a bit of a nut, huh?"

Neco chuckled. "Nut? He's a full-blown whack job! When we collar him we're going to have to put him in a psyche ward with a straight jacket and throw away the key."

"All right. When do you want to talk strategy?"

"Let me get out of here and I'll call you later in the afternoon. We have to make every effort to take him alive.

He's got some vital information, including from where he's getting military-issue weapons."

"I'll be here."

Shurmur hung up the phone and pressed the intercom button.

His secretary answered, "Yes, Mr. Shurmur?"

"Mary, call the Camden County Prosecutor's Office and get Captain Blake on the phone for me."

"Yes, sir."

Within minutes, Shurmur pressed the line for his call on the speaker phone.

"Captain Blake! Martin Shurmur here. We haven't spoken since our offices combined on that case in Chester.

Good to speak with you again."

"The feeling's mutual, Mr. Shurmur. What can I do for you, sir?"

Blake's words sounded nice, but with all the emotional delivery of a drill sergeant speaking to a superior officer, Shurmur did not sense that the feeling was mutual.

Just as well, I'm not all that thrilled to be making contact with him either. Hmmm. Maybe the feeling is mutual. "Looks like we're going to be collaborating again,

Captain."

Blake paused. "You have a new case moving over to our sector?"

"No," said Shurmur, "One of my agents has just made a breakthrough with one of your cases. And now we need to coordinate."

A longer pause followed. "Why is one of your agents working on one of my cases?"

Shurmur enjoyed the tease. He swiveled in his chair and decided to extend it just a little longer. "It was just one of those spontaneous things where my agent came upon some important information, and, fortunately, it turns out he already has some background with this case."

The third pause was the longest. "Who is the agent you're talking about?"

God, I wish I could be there in front of him for this!

Thought Shurmur. It was time to end the cruelty. "You know him. It's Juni Neco."

The Attorney General heard the sound of what he could only imagine to be a fist slam on the top of a desk.

Blake's voice became less deliberate. "Neco, you say. I knew he was with the A/G's office. Imagine that he's the one working on this case."

"Yes. He's my newest hire. It seems I'm ending up with your people for my new satellite office in Philly. I hope you don't mind."

"No, sir. Not at all," the captain lied. "Please fill me in."

Shurmur filled Blake in on the information, omitting the part of Neco acting on his own before being hired.

As far as Blake was concerned, Neco had another informant that provided him with a new lead on Schmidt.

He finished the briefing, ended the call pushed the button to disconnect with a bit flair. Shurmur needed to feel like things were looking up. His office needed to start accumulating some wins. Just as he stood from his chair, Shurmur saw the light for the private line blinking again with another call. He picked up the receiver.

"Okay, Loco, what did you forget?"

"Mr. Shurmur, my name is Michael Owens."

Shurmur sat up straight in his chair. "Who are you?

How did you get this private number?"

"As I said, my name is Michael Owens, I'm with the Pennsylvania State Bureau of Elections. I just tried to reach you at your home and your wife said you were at the office today. She gave me this number."

Shurmur pretended to not know what the call was for,

"What is this about, Mr. Owens?"

"There's no easy way to say this, Mr. Shurmur, so I'll get right to the point. I'm calling you today because I'll be coming to your office on

Monday morning to meet with you. I wanted to provide the courtesy of informing you first before anyone in the press finds out about this."

"And what is 'this'?"

"We've received an anonymous tip concerning your finances during your term as District Attorney in Lackawanna County. Since then some subsequent research has come up with some discrepancies that merit a formal investigation into the funding for your campaign for State Attorney General."

CHAPTER FIFTY-TWO

Pennsauken, New Jersey

The Camden County Prosecutor's Office had gotten Arnie Schmidt's address when they collared the three dealers back in Gloucester.

This section of Pennsauken was more upscale than that neighborhood. But it did not take much to accomplish that improvement. The lower middle-income residential area had houses mostly from the mid-sixties, with well-developed magnolia trees lining the streets.

Schmidt did, indeed, live in a room above his mother's house – a two-story colonial with tan brick and tan aluminum siding. The roof had faded black shingles and the front entrance featured a covered porch.

The good son provided his mother with money to contract a lawn service to keep the grounds in good order.

The grass was a healthy blend of Kentucky bluegrass and various fescues. A Japanese Red Maple tree accented the left side of the front yard and a towering elm tree highlighted the other two thirds, surrounded by an island of various flowering plants.

The branches from the elm tree obscured the view to Schmidt's bedroom, but binoculars provided some limited surveillance – enough to tell if Schmidt was passing by or looking out either of the two windows.

On the left side of the dwelling, Schmidt had constructed a set of stairs as a private entrance to his bedroom. The stairs were narrow by design – wide enough to accommodate only one ascending body. In the event that any group of cops tried to charge up the stairs, they could be picked off one at a time.

Since the arrest in Gloucester, the Camden County Prosecutor's office had kept a constant stake-out and wire—tap on the house. But it had been to no avail. Now time was running out before his deal with the member from South Philadelphia.

A half-a-dozen streets away, Juni Neco drove a tan Chevy Camaro into the neighborhood. The digital clock in the car read 4:03, still well before sunrise. Ray Diaz sat on the passenger side and slurped at his piping-hot coffee.

It was one of the two cups along with two bottled waters they had gotten from a Wawa convenience store.

Neco grabbed at one of the bottles from the cardboard box in Ray's lap. "Something has to give soon.

The deal with Tortelli is scheduled for today."

Good old Juni, mused Ray, *He leaves the Prosecutor's Office in a rage, somehow lands on his feet with the A/G's Office and he's still finding a way to help us.*

Neco parked the car three blocks away from the stake-out location and the two agents began their walk.

Neco carried a valise with food for the shift and Diaz carried the four beverages. Still under cover of darkness, the two agents walked up to the house and went around to enter through the back door. Making their way upstairs, they were greeted by the two agents being relieved.

Neco set down the valise and grabbed his water back from Diaz. Then he faced the other two male officers.

"Your expressions tell me it was another uneventful night."

Jerry Cohen, one of the officers on the overnight shift, answered him. "Well, the wire-tap remains a colossal waste of time. You know, only his mother continues to use the house phone. But there *was* a break in his usual routine."

Diaz had already reached into the valise and began eating a cold ham-and-fried egg sandwich on a bagel. He spoke through food in this mouth, "What changed?"

Cohen continued, "It was the same old, same old, until after his usual late dinner. Then instead of staying up until 2:00 am to sleep past 9:00, he never turned out the lights. He left the house and drove off around 3:30. He hasn't been back since."

Diaz began thinking out loud, "I've always wondered what the hell he does until 2:00 am – watch the late night talk shows?"

Cohen stretched as he arose from his desk chair, "I've always figured he was paging through *Mercenary Digest* and reading books on how to make bombs."

While the three men laughed, Neco' mind calculated the odds that the early departure had anything to do with Tortelli.

The Prosecutor's Office learned early that both Schmidt and Tortelli were too methodical to put a tail on.

Both men drove routes with unnecessary and repetitive turns that would make anyone following them stick out like a sore thumb in the rear-view mirror.

As the two agents left, Neco sat in one of the vacated office chairs and stared out through the blinds at the street-light lit neighborhood. There was no probable cause to justify any action with searching the house. And the agencies really wanted to try and avoid blowing up a building in Camden to search for weapons that evidence that may have already been shifted to another location. But time continued to run down.

The sound of a vehicle coming down the street brought him out of his thoughts.

Neco recognized the van as Schmidt's.

"Ray!" he whispered. "He's back!"

Diaz stuffed the rest of his sandwich in his mouth and took a seat at the other window.

They heard the sound of a slight scrape from the rear bumper hitting the top of the cement incline bridging the street to the driveway.

A perturbed Schmidt emerged from the driver's seat.

He angrily snapped his head forward several times, his lips accompanying each snap with a soft one-syllable utterance, as he paced back towards the rear of the van to assess the damage.

He squatted down and rubbed his hand back and forth along the bottom of the bumper. As he finished the inspection, Schmidt rose up and looked at the surrounding area to see if anyone had noticed the noise.

Neco and Diaz quickly shifted to the sides of their windows. But Diaz began choking on his sandwich.

I should just finish the job started by the sandwich, thought Neco, who instead threw a roll of paper towels at him and frantically waved for his partner to exit the room.

Diaz ripped several towels off and used them to muffle his mouth as he moved awkwardly towards the hallway.

Neco, his heart beating rapidly, moved one eye back towards the blinds.

Schmidt opened the back of the van and removed one of many large metal containers. His manner of exertion manifested how heavy it was.

Neco grabbed the binoculars. He could see the words on the containers. They each had a name and address.

"Son of a bitch! 'Fort Dix', whispered Neco.

"Somehow, that's where he's getting his merchandise. I bet that's Tortelli's order. Jerry, get the video cam on those boxes right now, before he shuts the door."

Cohen did so and zoomed in as close as he could on the boxes. The street lights provided just enough light to get a clear image.

"I got 'em," said Cohen.

The stake-out crew watched Schmidt move several of the containers to the passenger seat.

"Looks like he's trying to redistribute some weight," said Hernandez.

"Okay," said Neco. "We need to quickly get some more units out here and take measures to secure the area."

CHAPTER FIFTY-THREE

Harrisburg, Pennsylvania

By eight-seventeen, later that morning, Martin Shurmur was rifling through his desk calendar. He stopped on the page for July 16th and circled the date. His intercom buzzed. "Yes, Mary?"

"There's a Mr. Michael Owens here from the Board of State Elections. He says he has an appointment, but I see nothing for eight-fifteen in your book."

"That's okay, Mary. I made the appointment over the week-end. I'm sorry I forgot to tell you. Please send him in." The Attorney General greeted Owens at the door and directed him to a seat in front of his desk. Owens wore a tailored tweed suit and wire glasses. Shurmur's nose twitched at the scent composed of too much cologne on Owens' neck and a hairspray holding medium length blonde hair way too rigid. He did find *one* favorable thing.

He looks even younger than he sounded over the phone.

I bet he's only been at this several years.

Shurmur got Mary's attention. "Please hold all calls until I'm done with Mr. Owens here."

The two men walked to Shurmur's desk and Owens took one of the seats in front.

The Board of State Elections representative placed his briefcase on his lap, popped it open and pulled out a paper from a file. "Mr. Shurmur, let me get right to it, this paper shows a list of taverns that my staff and I have been visiting in Lackawanna County. Next to the names of the taverns are

---

217

the current owners or former owners who ran them during the time of your tenure as the District Attorney for the county. Their lawyers have them not admitting anything, but, upon completion of our initial interviews with them, there's a mosaic beginning to form that illustrates a tacit agreement of some sort that allowed them to operate video poker games in their establishment back in the earlier part of the decade."

Shurmur looked attentive as Owens continued.

"I don't have to explain to you how it's illegal to have unauthorized bookies for gambling activity. But, when public are shelling out money to participate in these games . . ."

"It's tantamount to having an 'electronic' bookie," finished Shurmur.

"Correct. But, for this many establishments to be operating in such a fashion undetected, there have to be people looking the other way – like the local cops on the beat."

"I don't understand." The Attorney General leaned back in his chair and cupped his hands behind his head.

"You seem to be suggesting that some cops were on the take.

But, your office has nothing to do with investigating crimes like that."

"Ordinarily we would never investigate this behavior unless . . ."

"Ahh! You suspect that I was getting some type of kick back in exchange for the cops looking the other way while the taverns used the video poker games."

Owens squinted his eyes. "Interesting you would conclude that for someone who was just confused."

"I'm an attorney, Mr. Owens," said Shurmur leaning forward. "It doesn't take me long to put together the pieces. Am I under arrest?"

"No, Mr. Shurmur. But, you'll understand why we're having audits done on these taverns for that time period.

If there were kick-backs used for funding your campaign for State Attorney General, then that *does* become my domain.

So, my office is going to need to have you submit your books to us for that period." Owens pulled out a second piece of paper from his briefcase. "This is a subpoena for those records."

"My personal attorney keeps all such records for me."

"Then I think it would be a good idea to call him up and set up a meeting for the three of us."

"Of course, Mr. Owens. I have nothing to hide and I intend to fully cooperate with your people on this investigation. Let me call them right now."

Shurmur punched in the number and hit the speaker phone.

Over at Warner and Associates, the receptionist heard the phone ring and noticed a private line to the office light up. "Attorney General" flashed on the caller ID.

She let it ring until the answering machine picked up the call.

"You have reached the office of Warner and Associates.

The office is closed for the day, but your message is important to us. Please wait for the tone and leave your message. Someone will get back to you as soon as possible . . ." A soft beep followed.

Owens raised his eyebrows in surprise as Shurmur hung up the phone. "Their office is closed? It's Monday morning!"

Shurmur shrugged. "They're probably taking a four-day week-end for the 4th of July holiday. But it *is* only eight—thirty. I'll try again . . ."

A female voice over the intercom interrupted him.

"Mr. Shurmur, you have a phone call."

"I said to hold all calls, Mary."

"Yes, sir. But this is from Captain Blake with the Camden County Prosecutor's Office. He says it's urgent.

It has something to do with Agent Neco."

Ah, this sounds doubly beneficial for me, thought Shurmur. "Okay Mary, tell him to give me a minute." He looked back at his visitor. "I'm sorry, Mr. Owens. I do have to take this call. I'm coordinating with Captain Blake on a huge illegal arms dealer case. And I'm pretty sure Warner and Associates are closed through Tuesday anyway."

Owens closed his briefcase and rapped his fingers on it. "Let's arrange to meet there on Wednesday morning when they open."

Shurmur began to rise from his chair. "Absolutely!"

He noticed his desk Calendar still turned to July 16th.

"Oh wait," he flipped his calendar back to July 5th. "On that day, I'm scheduled to be in Indian Gap to prepare for the Special Task Force orientation. It's pretty vital.

I'll be back on July 10th. But you really don't need me to be at Warner's to get those records. Now you'll have to excuse me, I have to make sure everything is in order for a huge arrest today."

"Fine." Owens pulled pocket calendar from his inside jacket pocket and began scribbling. "I'll see Mr. Warner on Wednesday and you on next Monday. Good day, Mr.

Shurmur." He got up and walked out the door.

The Attorney General picked up the call from Blake and jotted down quick notes as they spoke.

Shurmur nodded to himself as he ended the call. *So far, so good. I'd feel better if I knew who the 'anonymous call' came from. But right now I have to call Neco.*

The intercom buzzed again. "Yes, Mary?"

"Senator Carrie is on line one for you."

Shurmur took the phone off speaker and picked up the receiver. "Good morning, Senator."

"Martin! You sound resigned, my friend."

"Funny you should mention that."

"What?"

"Nothing."

CHAPTER FIFTY-FOUR

It was after nine, and most of the surrounding Pennsauken residents with jobs had left for work. Arnie Schmidt's mother had already left to do grocery shopping.

Now officers had sealed off the street to any new traffic.

The only vehicles driving past the house were their own unmarked cars, providing the illusion of the usual street traffic for the neighborhood.

Ada Hernandez had joined and took over Neco' place in the upstairs bedroom with Ray Diaz. She studied Schmidt's bedroom window. Hernandez was to alert Diaz on when Schmidt was not in view so Diaz could radio the communication to the officers on the ground and they could gradually take their positions for the arrest.

With the radio up to his face, Diaz peeked through the blinds of the window on the second floor of the vacant house from where he would give the green light in stages.

Ray Diaz loved giving orders. It gave him a sense of importance. He felt like a puppet master. "Unit Number One: Go!" He watched three agents run from behind the house he was in and position themselves behind parked cars on his side of the street. "Unit Number Two: Go!"

Additional agents then ran and crouched behind more parked cars on the opposite side of the street. They took their position under the stairs to the private entrance. And finally his most eagerly anticipated command – he got to give an order to Juni Neco. Even though he was operating under the exact sequence ordered by Neco, it still felt empowering to Diaz. "Unit Number Three: Go!"

Hernandez lowered the binoculars and became riveted on Juni Neco, as he moved quickly, taking a position around the corner from the stairs to Schmidt's room.

Neco took a stand next to some perfectly manicured bushes along the front wall. This morning he wore dark blue shorts with a navy-blue, short sleeve shirt with the initials "CCPO" on the back.

Hernandez and Diaz, along with the other shifts, had been recording Schmidt's routine for weeks. Another of his predictable activities, included his breakfast schedule.

Hernandez whispered, "Okay, Arnie, time to go hit the diner for your steak and eggs . . ."

With everyone in position, Diaz turned to Hernandez.

"Juni told me that Schmidt has some mystery contact in government and because of that Schmidt can't know that Juni was in on this arrest. How the hell is he going to do that as the point man?"

Hernandez flashed a knowing smile. "Juni said he knows this guy and he knows exactly how it has to work without being identified by Schmidt."

Neco did have a plan. He had heard Arnie Schmidt vow he would never be taken alive. Thus a surrender, peaceful or otherwise, was out of the question. So the new hire for the Pennsylvania Attorney General's Office aimed to do his boss proud *and* keep his cover.

All that remained was for Hernandez to alert the crew when Schmidt was leaving the house. Neco listened intently into his earpiece.

Two blocks away, a uniformed police officer stood on the street and waved a tan Lincoln Continental to pull to the side of the street.

A frail, elderly woman rolled down her window. "What seems to be the problem, officer?"

"License, registration and insurance, please, miss."

"I know it's a twenty-five mile per hour zone, but, surely, I was doing no more than thirty," said the woman, complying with the officer.

The officer read the driver's license. "Miss Gertrude Schmidt?"

"Yes?"

"Miss Schmidt, I'm going to have to ask you to come with me. Please park your car over there."

"C'mon, Arnie," said Hernandez, looking through the binoculars. "Can't you just smell that sizzling steak . . ."

Then she straightened up in her seat and lightly punched Diaz in the shoulder three times. "Okay. Tell everybody, I just saw Schmidt move in the direction of his door!"

"Attention, all units," said Diaz into his radio,

"Attention all units. Our man is now moving towards the door."

"Here he comes!" said Hernandez.

"All units. Schmidt is now coming down the stairs!"

As soon as Schmidt's feet touched the grass, the agent under the stairs jumped out with his gun trained on the arms dealer. "Arnie Schmidt! This is the police!

Put your hands . . ."

Schmidt did not let him finish the command. With an expression filled with anger and hate, Schmidt whirled in the direction of the voice and reached for a hand-gun tucked under his shirt behind his back.

His hand never reached the weapon. As soon as his left foot lifted off the ground to complete his turn,

Neco sprang from the corner. With lightning speed and the precision of a surgeon, Neco dropped to the ground and swept his right leg at the foot Schmidt still had in the air.

Just as Schmidt felt his whole body being lifted flat into the air, the next instant he felt a powerful right arm lock around his neck as he came down.

His military training had made him aware that a man had ten seconds before he would go unconscious in such a grip. Schmidt had already lost precious seconds just realizing what was happening as he hit the ground with another body underneath him. He wasted another several seconds trying to break the vise-like grip.

He tried to let out a scream, but it was just a loud gurgle. And just before things went completely black, he heard a low whisper from his unknown assailant.

"Ssssh! You're about to be taken alive!"

"Kih!"

CHAPTER FIFTY-FIVE

New Brunswick, New Jersey

By eleven that same morning, a tall dark-skinned Colombian walked into Ott's Tavern, three blocks south of the New Brunswick College. He wore a brown pin—stripe suit with a gold and green patterned power tie, his right hand wrapped around the handle of a black leather briefcase.

He stood next to the bar where he was greeted by a bartender, who looked half his age. The bartender wore a green Ott's Tavern tee-shirt and dried off a wine glass as he spoke. "Hey, good afternoon, sir. What can I get you?"

"Is the owner in?"

"He's in the back office. Who should I say is here?"

The reply came in the form of a business card.

Carlos Jimenez, Esq.

Attorney at Law

The young man placed the glass in the rack above his head, took the card and disappeared to the back.

Minutes later, another man, twice the age of the first one, wearing an identical tee-shirt, walked around to the side of the bar where the Colombian stood. "I'm the owner.

Should I be calling my attorney, Mr. Jimenez?"

"Certainly not, Mr. Ott. I represent the estate of someone recently departed, and I'm here to see if you could help me find someone who stands to inherit a lot of money."

"I don't know if I can help you. Why would *I* know this person?" asked Ott, as he scratched at his beard.

The "attorney" rested his briefcase on the bar, popped loose the latches and opened it. From a file folder, he picked out a manila envelope, pulled out a picture from it and handed it to the owner. "Do you recognize this man? I understand he used to frequent your establishment in the early . . ."

Ott's eyes widened in fear. "No. I'm afraid I can't help you, Mr. Jimenez. I'm sorry." He slid the picture back to its owner.

"Are you sure, Mr. Ott? Upon execution of this will,

I make a substantial percentage. I am prepared to give you cash for information that helps me locate him."

"I said I can't help you, Mr. Jimenez," repeated Ott.

"No one has to know we talked," said the visitor, "As I stated, you would receive a handsome reward for what you know."

"I'm sorry. I have to go back to work now." And he went back to his office.

The man who identified himself as Mr. Jimenez lost his image of congeniality. *Mr. Ott, you could have made this a lot easier on yourself.*

Back down south at the Camden County Courthouse, the bailiff raised his voice to address the people in the courtroom. "All rise! The Honorable Judge Stephanie Grey presiding!"

Judge Grey entered and took her seat behind the bench.

This morning, for the first time in a long time, Arnie Schmidt did not wear his camouflage attire. Today he wore an off-the-rack suit from a department store purchased by his defense attorney.

"Be seated," said the judge, who turned to the bailiff. "What's the first case?"

"Case number 1014. The People vs. Arnold Schmidt, Possession and Dealing of Illegal Weapons."

The District Attorney walked to a center position in front of the judge as the defense attorney joined him.

"Your Honor, David Sokolic for the prosecution. We request, Mr. Schmidt be held with no bail."

"Harold Patterson for the defense, your Honor. We waive reading and enter a plea of 'not guilty'. We object to being held with no bail. Mr. Schmidt has no prior record and represents no flight risk."

"No flight risk?" retorted Sokolic. "He's an arms dealer! He has merchandise that's military issue! And on top of all that, he's a drug dealer!"

"Is the prosecution now playing the role of jury?" said Patterson sarcastically. "Again, your Honor, no previous record. He's served his country and was honorably discharged."

"Oh well, that just *substantially* upgrades his character," said Sokolic.

"All right!" said Judge Grey. "I've heard enough.

Bail is set at one million dollars."

Schmidt, still in his seat, did not bat an eye, but Patterson raised his eyebrows.

"Your Honor! A million dollars? That sounds a little harsh."

Judge Gray's face took on a sudden hangdog expression.

"My heart pumps peanut butter for your client. Trial date is set for August 14th. Mr. Schmidt, you are not to leave the county." She slammed down her gavel. "Next case!"

CHAPTER FIFTY-SIX

South Philadelphia

The assignment of Ada Hernandez to another case necessitated that someone else be paired up with Neco for the day's meeting with George Martinez. A conflicted Sandra Tomasson drew the straw as the only other credible beauty between the agencies.

The drive to Veterans Stadium, home of the Philadelphia Phillies had minimal conversation, punctuated by comments related to the case.

The two field operatives arrived at the stadium and met Martinez along with his date at the agreed-upon gate.

Martinez had four seats along the first base side, right behind the home team's dug-out. The weather was perfect for a day game – bright and sunny, not too humid.

Throughout the early-to-middle stages of the game, conversation remained strictly social. During the seventh inning stretch, the two women were told to remove themselves until they were waved back.

With the seats around them temporarily vacated,

Martinez took the opportunity to talk a little shop.

"Loco, you'll get your ten percent."

Neco nodded approvingly. Then he dropped his second bomb. "Your boss won't be sorry. Now when can I get something up front?"

"What?" Martinez realized his reaction was louder than intended. He looked around to see if people had returned to their seats.

Still empty.

"When can I get a little something up front?" repeated Neco.

"What are you *talking* about? You get a percentage of the value. *Ten* percent! This is the Escobar cartel! He doesn't give anyone *anything* up front."

"For me to begin setting this up, I want a show of good faith."

A stunned Martinez forced himself to reply. "Like what?"

"I don't know . . . something good – maybe a kilo or something," said Neco.

"Who *does* that? Who gives something *up front*?"

"The clients *I* deal with. I have people to take care of on the inside to insure things go off without a hitch.

That takes some time and money on my part. And I'm not shelling out either because when I have no guarantees that anything is going to happen."

"If Escobar says it's going to happen, it's going to happen."

"Oh, please! George, you know that even Escobar has failed deliveries. A shipment from Colombia is going to take days to arrive from the time it leaves. And they're going to have to make at least one stop between there and here. The longer the runway, the more opportunity there is for tacks on the runway. I couldn't care less what Escobar decrees. If he was so high and mighty, he wouldn't need me. But he does. Tell him that I want something good up front."

Neco noticed fans starting to return to the surrounding seats as action resumed on the field. He waved the women back. Martinez continued to stare into space as he contemplated what he was going to tell Alejandro.

The Phillies player at the plate swung and missed a curveball. In the process, he accidentally flung the bat from his hands in the direction of the home team dug-out.

Right at the oblivious Martinez.

A collective gasp rose from the crowd, which snapped Martinez back into the present with only enough time to throw up his arms and shut his eyes. The bat helicopter—bladed within two feet of his head.

He waited in the darkness for the impact that never came. A rousing cheer from the fans replaced their previous gasp.

With his arms still around his head, Martinez opened his eyes.

Right in front of his face, he saw the bat – in Neco' hand.

Neco stood to acknowledge the crowd, as he made sure to keep on his sunglasses.

Tomasson and Martinez' date jostled back to their seats to see what all the noise was about.

Puzzled, Tomasson looked around the stadium until she finally noticed spectators pointing at the animated scoreboard.

She saw the screen replay Neco snatching the bat in midair with one hand. Then the camera went live to Tomasson and the hero of the day. To stay in character, she clung admiringly to Neco, only to be surprised, as he clutched her around the waist and planted a long, deep kiss in her mouth.

The scene prompted another roar from the crowd.

At Jack's Tavern in Clayton, Sandy Neco sat at the bar with her sister, Sheila.

Sheila nudged her younger sibling. "Sandy! Look at the television!"

Sandy raised her head from a glass of scotch and focused on the screen.

"Isn't that Juni?" asked Sheila. "He's wearing sunglasses, but I recognize those pecs under the Hawaiian shirt."

Sandy studied the image being replayed on the animated scoreboard.

"Isn't that the same slut you said was on the island with him? Didn't Juni say he wouldn't be seeing her at his new job?"

The wife frowned and sighed, "That's my husband, all right." She impatiently clinked the ice cubes in her glass to signal the bartender to refresh her drink. *Juni has bad blood!*

In the privacy of Neco' car on their way back from the game to the Prosecutor's Office, Tomasson spoke up. "It took everything for me not to react with surprise to that kiss back there."

"If you're going to be surprised by kisses, you're playing the wrong game," said Neco. "Because this game requires showing passion."

"I wasn't surprised by the *kiss*. I was surprised by the *nature* of the kiss."

"Too much passion for you?"

"Passion is fine, but that 'passion' seemed a little on the vengeful side. Are you okay?"

Neco bristled. "Vengeful? What the hell are you talking about?"

"Whenever I've been kissed like that by a man, that was a revenge kiss. Who are you trying to get even with?

Your wife?"

"We were on a case in public! We've been over this!

We're on stage! If you're too fucked up to confuse role—playing for 'revenge', then you're not qualified to be on assignment with me. Next time you're asked to work with me, you make sure you have something else to do."

"I'm trying to have an honest communication with you!" said Tomasson.

"When I plan out how a day undercover is going to play out, I stay up for hours at night examining every contingency. I try to keep my level of prediction so high that I can anticipate how to stay three steps ahead of these scumbags! I have enough to look at! The last thing I need is more sabotage from my own partners!"

"Sabotage?" said Tomasson with wide eyes. "Don't you compare this to your mishaps with the Prosecutor's Office!"

"If you drop out of character for one instant, that's sabotage!"

"I was fine! The crowd ate it up!"

"You know, you can just forget about coming with me to meet him in Atlantic City next week-end!"

Chapter Fifty-Seven

New Brunswick, New Jersey

Ott chased the last of his customers out of the bar by midnight. Twenty minutes later, he turned out the lights and stepped out into a steady rain.

Figuring out the receipts can wait until tomorrow, he thought.

The owner of the bar clutched a zipped vinyl pouch with the day's receipts and cash. He looked around the empty street and prepared to lock the door.

A peal of thunder surprised him.

Before his hand could insert the key, a figure darted from behind an automobile and grabbed him, muffling his mouth and shoving him back inside the bar.

"Don't hurt me!" pleaded Ott, "Just take the money!"

"I don't want your money!" said the assailant, who flipped open a switchblade and pressed it against his victim's neck.

Out of the corner of his eye, Ott recognized the man as Carlos Jimenez. The power suit and tie had been replaced with a tight black pull-over, collared shirt and black khakis. "You!" Ott exclaimed through the hand covering his mouth.

"Mr. Ott, I have the feeling that you were not being completely forthright with me during our conversation this afternoon. Now we're going to discuss that picture again.

But instead of money, I am offering you your life. So let me ask you again, who is this man?" He withdrew his hand from Ott's mouth.

"Okay! Okay! His name is Juni!"

"Last name?"

"I don't remember."

The knife dug in a bit.

"What's his last name?"

"I don't remember! I swear it! It was seventeen years ago! We weren't friends. He was just someone who came into my bar every once in a while."

"Juni Neco?" asked Alejandro.

"It could have been. Maybe. Definitely some Hispanic type of name. I really just knew him as Juni."

"Why did seeing his picture unnerve you so much?"

"Because he and his gang were crazy!" replied Ott.

"What gang?"

"There were around ten of them. They ran the streets barefoot in the dead of winter, wearing only a martial arts robe and pants. They had a director – some light-skinned Black guy from a community center on the other side of town. That director . . . he was a Fifth Degree Black Belt . . . he held martial arts training sessions. The place was known as 'The Hell Hole'. And from everything I was told, it couldn't have had a better name."

"You can't tell me that men running barefoot in the street terrorized you," said the man called Jimenez.

"It wasn't that. But, I didn't want anything to do with him."

"Why?"

"After about two years in The Hell Hole, the director hooked him up with some other Black guy . . . a little shorter than Juni. This guy was also light-skinned. What was his name? Dammit! What was his name? Nothing against the color of his skin, but he just looked like evil personified. Oh yeah! Tony! His name was Tony! Tony something!" said Ott, his voice trembling.

"What do you know about this Tony?"

"He was very mysterious," said Ott. "If anyone asked him about what he did, he wouldn't answer. And from his reaction, you didn't dare press him. Only the people in the gang knew about Tony, and even *they* didn't know much.

But they *did* know that Tony had received his training from some master in Asia. And eventually, I *did* find information about him in the newspaper."

The storm outside let loose a series of loud crackling sounds. The wine glasses in the rack overhead clinked as they gently touched each other.

Not too many people knew all the details of what happened back in 1973.

"Juni," said Sensei Gorell, as the two men walked across the floor of The Hell Hole training room. "There is someone I want you to meet." This is Tony Echevarria.

Sensei Tony has been personally trained by Master Instructor Gogen Yamaguichi, a Tenth Degree Black Belt.

Sensei Tony himself is an Eighth Degree."

"It is an honor to meet you, Sensei Tony," said Neco, shaking hands.

"Sensei Gorell has told me a lot about you. It is his belief you have gotten all you can out of his training. I am here to find out how much interest you have in moving on to the next level."

Neco contained a sense of absolute exhilaration rushing through his being. "I would like that very much, sir."

"I'm going to let you two talk alone now,' said Gorell.

"Let's take a walk, Juni," said Tony.

The two men walked along the residential streets of New Brunswick in a cool breeze with dark clouds swirling overhead.

Tony Echevarria had five years in age on Neco, and like his potential protégé, possessed a lean and muscular body. He stood slightly shorter, but his afro hairstyle made him look a little taller.

Echevarria gave Neco his history with Yamaguichi out in the Orient. Neco listened intently. As with Gorell, there would be no money accepted for this training – only the acceptance of Echevarria's terms.

"Sensei Gorell assures me you subscribe to a life of no alcohol, no smoking and no drugs. It is absolutely necessary that you never deviate from that. Your conditioning must never be impeded by poison in your body."

"My father brought me up on that from an early age. I do not put garbage in my body."

"I will give you my gift from Yamaguichi. But you must be totally committed. If you thought training at The Hell Hole was demanding, the discipline entailed with me will be more than you can imagine," said Echevarria.

Neco nodded.

"Your dorm life will be over. You will have to move in with me. We will be training very regularly, and your availability must be high. If I call you at any time for a spontaneous training session, you must drop whatever you are doing and make yourself available to me, no questions asked."

He nodded again.

"You must be one hundred percent committed. This is just as much spiritual as it is physical. You must regard this with the same reverence as a religion. It will be a new way of life."

Another nod.

"And one more thing." Echevarria paused for several seconds. "You will be unconditionally loyal to me. Do you have any questions?"

"When do we begin?"

Thunder roared in the distance from Ott's Tavern.

Beads of sweat covered Ott's forehead. He breathed heavily between his sentences. "Those two were hooked up for several years. And if this bar was packed on nights when those two walked in, the public parted for them like the damned Red Sea parted for Moses. Juni was okay – real friendly . . . but this other guy . . . no one wanted any part of him."

"So if Neco was 'okay', you still haven't explained to me why you went white and couldn't bring yourself to answer my questions when I showed you the picture."

"Years after Juni left, there was a headline in a New York City paper with a picture of this Tony guy's face. He had been found dead in an apartment. The paper reported his body had been riddled with bullets . . . and it also reported who he was."

"Now it's your turn to tell me," said Alejandro, as he pressed his knife a little more into Ott's neck.

"A professional assassin!"

Alejandro froze, but only for a moment as Ott continued.

"The FBI said he was a gun for hire. Only I bet he never used a gun. He looked like someone who would kill you with his bare hands . . . or maybe a knife. When I learned your boy was associated with a professional killer, I never wanted to see his face in my bar again. Fortunately for me, Juni had long disappeared by the time I read that headline."

"Where can I find The Hell Hole?"

"The Hell Hole is gone. It's just a regular community center now. The people who used to be associated with that group have long disbanded for parts unknown," said Ott, as sweat dripped into his eyes. "Now you've gotten what you want. There's nothing else I know. I don't know where your man is, and it's my prayer that I never see him again – or any other professional hit man!"

"Hmmph! What were the odds you would meet another one in your suddenly abbreviated life?"

Once again, he firmly cupped his hand over Ott's mouth.

Minutes later, Alejandro dropped the dead body to the floor. He stepped over a puddle of blood as he scanned the tavern and located a lit red sign for the restrooms.

In the men's room, the assassin washed his hands and arms of the blood from Ott's throat. The tavern owner had not received a Colombian neck-tie. After all the man had not been a squealer to be made an example of for other potential squealers. No, Ott had been just too pig-headed to answer questions during the first meeting. If he had just freely given the information like the people at the Philadelphia bar, everything would have been okay and Ott would still be alive. But now it had become necessary to eliminate the witness.

Alejandro studied the blood stains on his shirt and pants.

And this is why I don't wear suits for these occasions.

Alejandro left the men's room and walked behind Ott's bar.

Now here's a bonus . . .

He grabbed a bottle of Johnny Walker Double Black and poured some into a shot glass. Between sips he noticed a pack of cigars near the beer taps.

I know I'm going to regret this . . .

Pulling one out and using a lighter next to them, he lit it up and took a drag.

He winced and tossed it to the floor where he put it out with his shoe.

How do people smoke that garbage?

He stared at the corpse in front of him on the floor until the ringing of his phone took his attention.

Escobar had finally returned his call from his master bedroom, where he had finished "rewarding" one of his contest winners.

Escobar dismissed the young girl and spoke into the phone. "You called, my friend?"

"Yes, I'm done in New Brunswick. I've gotten another piece of the Neco puzzle and news from George."

"So your trip to New Jersey was fruitful?"

"As I've said, Neco leaves a trail of lasting impressions," said Alejandro.

"What can you tell me?"

"He learned a very high level of martial arts in this town."

"And that helps your beloved drug lord how?"

"He was trained by a professional hit man out of New York City."

"It makes me wonder, Alejandro, if this man is even more evil than you. Are you satisfied yet?"

"No," answered Alejandro. "There's always a 'but' with this guy."

"Such as?"

"His plates aren't registered. He could be a criminal, but he could also be a cop. He's trained by a cold-blooded professional hit man, but George tells me Neco risked injury to himself to prevent George from being injured by a flung baseball bat. And the bartender in New Brunswick says Neco is a friendly guy."

Escobar chuckled. "I'm a friendly guy too! But somebody better not rub *me* the wrong way either." He got no response, so he kept talking. "You are the best,

Alejandro. But Neco is what we've been looking for. What news do you have from George?"

"George says that Neco wants something up front as part of the agreement."

Seriousness replaced the light-hearted tone in Escobar's voice. "What do you *mean* he wants 'something up front'? He wants something up front on *top* of the ten percent? Does he know who he's *dealing* with?"

"Neco wants a kilo in advance to pay his customs people something right now. If there's nothing up front, there's no deal."

Escobar paused. "You were right, Alejandro."

"About what?"

"A 'but' keeps coming up with this guy."

"What are you talking about?"

"Tell George to make Neco wait a little while. Then we'll give him his kilo. *But*, if our shipment results do not live up to expectations, there will be no place Neco can hide to escape my wrath. And there better not be any more surprises."

Chapter Fifty-Eight

5 July, Harrisburg, Pennsylvania

The firm of Warner and Associates occupied the top floor of a mauve-colored granite high-rise building on North Front Street. From their western windows, a person could look out over the Susquehanna River and look at City Island, a sixty-two acre piece of land featuring Riverside Stadium – home of the Harrisburg Senators, a minor league baseball team for the Philadelphia Phillies.

The man investigating Martin Shurmur walked through the door to the law office of Warner and Associates as they opened up for business.

He flashed his identification badge at the woman behind the reception desk. "I'm Agent Michael Owens with the State Bureau of Elections. I need to see Christopher Warner. I don't have an appointment."

"One moment, Mr. Owens," said the receptionist. "I'll go back to his office and tell him you're here. Please have a seat."

"I'd rather stand, thank you."

Several minutes later, the receptionist returned and addressed her visitor. "Please follow me."

She led Owens through a couple of hallways until they arrived in the spacious office of the senior partner –

Christopher Warren, who rose from his plush leather chair to greet them. "Good morning, Mr. Owens."

"Good morning, Mr. Warner."

"Please call me Chris," said Warner as they shook hands. "Thank you, Louise. I'll take it from here."

The receptionist left the room and the two gentlemen got down to business.

"How can I be of service to you today, Mr. Owens?"

"I'll get right to the point, Chris," said the agent, as he pulled a two-way folded paper from his suit jacket pocket. "This is a subpoena for the records of Martin Shurmur from the time period listed. Mr. Shurmur informs me that they are under your auspices."

Warner studied the subpoena. "Everything seems to be in order. What's the nature of the investigation?"

"I'll brief you while the files are being brought out," said Owens.

"Fair enough, Mr. Owens," said Warner. "We will fully cooperate on this matter until its resolution. I can have my assistant bring them out for you. Make yourself comfortable. May I have someone bring you some coffee?"

"No thanks, just the files will be fine."

"Okay. Oh, what kind of car did you drive here?"

Owens looked a little puzzled. "Umm . . . a Honda Civic. Why?"

"Ohhh, a compact, huh? Well, I suppose you'll have enough room."

"Enough room for what?" asked Owens.

"The files. They're quite voluminous."

"Mr. Warner, I just need the files from the very select time period listed on the warrant. That can't be too much."

"But, the files aren't sorted by subject matter.

They're filed chronologically with other accounting," smiled Warner. "Agent Owens, if you prefer, I would be happy to assign someone to go through the boxes and pick them out for you."

"Boxes?" repeated Owens, "No. That's okay. Just have the boxes brought out for me."

"Whatever you wish, sir."

CHAPTER FIFTY-NINE

6 July Indian Gap, Pennsylvania

Neco listened to Goldbach on his car phone as he drove along the outside of an expansive complex enclosed by a barbed-wire fence. The grounds belonged to the State Police Barracks located west of Harrisburg.

"Good morning, Sensei. Where are you right now?"

"Out in Skunk Lick, Pennsylvania!" said Neco.

"Man! Talk about being out in the *sticks*. This place is really tucked away from civilization. It's just winding roads and trees out here."

"Did you see the newspaper this morning?" asked Goldbach.

Neco looked down at a copy of the Harrisburg Patriot News on his passenger seat. "Yeah." He took in the headline.

Election Bureau Probes State Attorney General

"What's going on with your boss man?"

"I only know what they said on the evening news last night. I really hoped he could be someone I trusted. Now I don't know *what* the hell is going on. Now I have to watch what I say to *him*," said Neco, as he turned left onto a long driveway. "I have to get with security. I'll call you later about how you're going to run the training session tonight."

Once the bill passed for The Special Task Force, the State Police Barracks became designated as the new unit's orientation location. It looked just like a military base.

It featured a variety of unimaginative one-story buildings for training and dorms with cots. A building in the center area contained a large cafeteria that served all the meals.

Neco flashed his ID to a man at the guard booth, who admitted him to the complex. He did a double-take at a car in the parking lot in front of the building holding the orientation lectures.

It belonged to his old pal from Camden – Opie.

Neco walked into the reception area. A woman behind a linen-covered banquet table greeted him and gave him an adhesive name tag. Across the room Dexter Rasche engaged in 'conversation' with a Black recruit.

Rasche repeatedly nodded without opening his mouth.

The recruit finally excused himself prompting a silent grin from Rasche. The good mood quickly disappeared when he spotted his nemesis approaching.

"Look, Neco," said Rasche, "We're here to get training. Don't start with me."

"Don't worry about *me*, Opie. I've actually decided to help you," began Neco. "I'm going to make the rounds and inform the minorities to edit their conversations around you. All going well, I'll have all their agreements n*ot* to discuss their religions and cultures around you."

Rasche scoffed. "What? People can say whatever they want around me. I've never asked anyone to edit their conversation."

Neco held up his hand to make a "stop" sign.

"Maybe not with words, but make no mistake, you do it all the time. I can tell from across the room what's going on with you."

"Oh, you can," snorted Rasche.

"All I have to see is all your closed-mouth nodding at a minority and I know that they must be trying to discuss religion or culture with you. You'll just nod until they get tired of talking to themselves. But I'll alert them to not waste their breath. You should be very pleased. No . . . I take that back. I *expect* you to be pleased. You *should* be ashamed of yourself, Opie." Then he leaned over to Rasche who flinched back a bit. "But, hey, no worries. Like you say, you're 'not a perfect human being'." With that,

Neco walked off to the meeting room.

The staff set the room up seminar style. Long tables had cushioned seats facing the front of the room where an overhead projector sat in front of the aisle between the tables.

Neco chose a chair in the front next to a man who looked to be somewhere in his fifties. Like Captain Blake, he had some creases in his face and like Senator Carrie, he had short salt and pepper hair.

The fellow trainee opened the conversation with Neco. "Hey, I couldn't help but hear your talk with that Opie guy. He sounds like a real butt load."

"That's okay. I've not only gotten used to it, it motivates me."

"Then you're in for a lot of motivation. I've seen some others around here who are going to get along with him just fine. Now me? Not a prejudiced bone in my body.

Spics, chinks, darkies . . . I consider them all equal.

Everybody should own one or two."

"Imagine my relief," snickered Neco.

The man extended his hand. "My name is Stan. Stan Logan. Looks like we're going to be seeing a lot of each other."

"I'm Juni Neco. You can also call me 'Loco'.

And I always appreciate someone who can help me mock Opie."

"Somehow I believe there'll be no shortage of opportunities," said Logan. "So what does Martin want you doing for the Task Force?"

"He wants me to keep doing what I'm doing – deep undercover work to make him look good," said Neco.

"And it sounds like he's going to need a *lot* of that."

"Yeah, how about that probe, huh? That'll drag on a bit before we find out anything."

"What does he want you doing?" asked Neco.

"I'm going to head up the SWAT team."

"Oh, well, I wasn't going to be that nice to you. But I better change my thinking."

"You want to hit a bar tonight after training?"

"No, thanks. I already have to be in Atlantic City tonight."

"Hot date?"

"Someone I intend to introduce to you and your SWAT team in the near future."

CHAPTER SIXTY

Atlantic City, New Jersey

The Special Task Force did not hold training on the week-ends, so Neco did not have to miss any orientation to keep his appointment with George Martinez.

Once again, Martinez sent his wife and mother shopping for the day. That freed him up to be with his woman du jour.

Neco brought Ada Hernandez with him for this meeting at Caesar's Palace, located at the foot of the Atlantic City Expressway. Once they drove past the overpass with the big, blue "Welcome to Atlantic City" sign,

Neco rolled down the window and took a couple of deep breaths of the salt air.

"You seem to be enjoying that," commented Hernandez.

"It's much better than what I have to breathe in North Philly," replied her partner.

Neco drove past Atlantic Avenue and made a left into the parking garage for the casino. They left the car on the fourth floor of the garage and walked through the entrance and into bustling crowd of the casino.

As the undercover couple made their way past one of the bars, a Hispanic woman seated on a stool tapped the shoulder of her sister next to her.

"Are my eyes deceiving me, or is that your husband with his arm around another woman?"

Sandy Neco turned from her drink and raised her eyebrows in surprise.

"Do you recognize that one?" asked Sheila.

"That's another one of the women he said he wouldn't be working with again," said Sandy in a soft, resigned voice.

"I am so sorry, sister," said Sheila. "But a Puerto Rican doesn't change his tan. C'mon. Let me buy you another drink and figure out a plan for him."

Neco and Hernandez kept going until they reached the front door cubicle on the boardwalk. They stepped through the huge columns where they found Martinez gnawing on a big hunk of strawberry salt water taffy.

"George!" yelled Neco.

"Loco!"

"You remember Ada."

"I sure do. Hello. Ada."

"Hello, George,' said Hernandez.

"Where's your date?" asked Neco.

Martinez pointed to a striking Black woman walking in the distance down the boardwalk.

"Whoa! George!" said Neco. "Score!"

"Yeah, she's a knock out," added Martinez.

"She's an Amazon."

"Her work-out is probably something like yours, Loco.

Along with weights, she throws in some kick-boxing for her cardiovascular routine. She almost makes me ashamed to take my clothes off," said Martinez. "I said 'almost'.

But, hey, I would certainly take my clothes off for Ada too."

Ada resisted the temptation to throw Martinez through the plate glass window. Instead she smiled and clung to Neco, grabbing at his buttocks.

"George, if you want to get in shape," said Neco,

"I should have you come to my gym as a guest. I can show you a good beginner's routine."

"You're on, Loco. I'd like that."

A short distance away, a tall, dark Colombian man, wearing a short sleeve, button-up shirt that revealed scars on his forearms stood near a fried dough concession stand.

He sipped at a liter-size bottle of spring water.

"Loco, while we're waiting for my date, I need a moment of privacy with you," said Martinez.

"Sure," said Neco, who turned to Hernandez. He reached into his pocket and pulled out some cash. "Babe, take this and go buy some bottled water from that stand over there."

Hernandez smiled. "You got it, sweetie."

Martinez waited until Hernandez was out of earshot.

"You'll be happy to hear that you'll be getting your kilo up front."

Neco smiled and nodded his head. "You're all right, George! That's good news. When can I expect that?"

"Soon. Probably sometime next week. I'll call you with the details within the next few days."

"Well, then today we celebrate on me!"

Martinez' date walked up and Neco waved Hernandez back.

"Juni, Ada, this is Tarro," said Martinez. "Tarro, this is Juni and Ada."

The woman began to shake hands. "Juni, Ada . . . nice to meet you."

Neco started laughing. "Taro? That's a root vegetable! What, your parents didn't want to call you 'Turnip'?"

The woman did not look amused. "It's 'Tarro' with two 'r's in it."

"Why don't you just get it over with and buy a shirt with the words 'My name is Tarro, insert teasing remarks here'?"

As he said the last remark, Neco put his hands in a motion as if to 'frame' the imaginary wording in front of Tarro's shirt.

Tarro misunderstood the gesture for a groping action.

"Keep your hands off, pig!"

Tarro raised her hand and tried to slap her teaser in the face.

She never got past the backswing.

Neco let go with a right cross, snapping the woman's head sideways, followed by the rest of her body.

"Juni!" shouted Ada, as Tarro fell backwards into the arms of her shocked date trying to keep her from hitting the floor.

"Juni! What the *hell*?" exclaimed Martinez.

In the distance, even Alejandro found himself taken aback.

"*Nobody* smacks me!" said Neco, waving his index finger. "*Nobody*! She's lucky to be alive! I *pulled* that punch. When she comes to, you tell her what a lucky bitch she is." Then he turned around and stormed back through the loud, crowded casino.

Hernandez rushed after him.

Some people gathered around Martinez and the semi—conscious Tarro.

"What happened to her? Is she okay?" asked a man.

"She just fainted," answered Martinez. "Sometimes she gets a little too dehydrated in this weather."

A tall, dark Colombian man stepped in, offering some water. "She could probably use this."

"Thank you, sir," said Martinez. "She'll be fine."

She'll be fine."

"Juni! You hit a woman!" yelled Ada in the parking lot, as she walked rapidly next to her partner.

Neco never broke stride as he answered. "Nobody smacks me in the face! You can punch at me, you can kick me, but nobody *smacks* me!"

"She thought you were going to grope her."

He kept walking in the direction of their car, as if she wasn't even talking. His mind traveled elsewhere.

"Juni! You hit a girl!"

"She asked for it!"

"I don't care! There's no excuse for that!"

"But mama! It was my friend, Rosa, on the other end of Harlem. It was her seventh birthday party!"

"I know! I just got the call telling me, I've told you never to hit a girl!"

"But, mama! All the kids were spanking her as she crawled through our legs! It's called the spanking machine, mama."

"I never want to hear about you hitting a girl again!"

Mama Neco slapped her son across the face. Little Juni staggered back, keeping his footing, but wincing, trying not to cry. He then ran off to his room.

Zenaida, his sister, saw the whole incident.

"Why did you have to slap him? The girl knew she was going to be spanked. She wasn't even hurt!"

"Maybe next time he'll listen," said Mama Neco.

"I stayed in my room for the rest of the day and evening," said Neco to Hernandez, as they pulled out of the parking garage and followed signs for the Atlantic City Expressway. "Being surprised by my mother with a slap . . . it was the first and only time she ever hit me. I was real subdued for quite a while afterwards. Ever since then, nobody is ever going to hit me with an open hand.

You can't even be kidding around with me, even you. You can playfully punch at me, kick me, but do *not* smack me, or I will flatten you."

Hernandez had to gather her thoughts. "What about George? You punched out his girlfriend. How is he supposed to react to that?"

"Trust me. All George is going to do is open up another can of whores." They heard his car phone ring.

"This is Juni."

"Juni! This is Captain Blake."

"Well, long time no hear. How have you been, Captain? To what do I owe the honor of this call?"

"I've just learned of some news and was told to give you a call," said Blake.

"What's going on?"

"We've been keeping a tail on Arnie Schmidt since the arraignment . . . but we've lost him. It looks like he's jumped bail."

Hernandez observed her partner's face get serious again.

"*Who* lost him . . . the Prosecutor's Office? How does something like that *happen?*" asked Neco.

"I'm afraid so. We kept the phone tap on him and we tried to keep the tail on him from a distance, but we think he made our people," said Blake. Schmidt made a stop at an NJ Transit station in Haddonfield and our officers ran in after him, but the place was jammed. He disappeared into nowhere. His car never left the parking lot. I'm sorry to have to tell you this. I don't know what else to say."

"That's a big loss. He was still a source for other contacts, including who was getting him the military issue weapons at Ft. Dix."

"Actually we do know *who* was getting him those weapons."

"Who?"

"We received a report of two officers up there going AWOL after the arraignment. Sure enough, the inventory records did not match up with what was actually in supply. So at least we cut off that stream of guns into the hands of the criminals."

"What about Tortelli?" asked Neco "Dead."

"How?"

His car blew up this evening," said Blake. "He never had a chance."

"Why didn't you have a tail on *him?*"

"We *did* have a tail on him. But we didn't have his *car* under surveillance. Schmidt operates fast. And we have no idea where he is."

"Probably in some bomb shelter," said Neco. "He said he could disappear for years. I wouldn't be surprised if he had two or three of them."

"Well, that brings you up to date," said Blake. "I've got some other calls to make. Maybe I'll see you around some time."

"Maybe sooner than you think."

"What?"

Neco hung up the phone.

Ada asked about the phone call. "Do I understand that Schmidt is loose?"

"Unfortunately, yes."

"And what about Tortelli? Is he loose too?"

"Torelli's cold. He's cold . . . just like our trail for Schmidt's other connections."

The car phone rang again.

"This is probably Blake asking what I meant by seeing him soon," said Neco. "Hello, this is Juni."

"Juni, hi. This is Sandra."

"Miss Sandra!" replied Neco, who watched Hernandez grimace. "I'm glad you called. I wanted to apologize for my little outburst before. It was uncalled for. You did nothing wrong."

"That's okay," said Tomasson. "I just accepted the fact that you were still in 'Loco' mode. And that maybe sometimes it's tough to flip the switch off."

"You're right about that," said Neco.

"Anyway, did Blake call you?"

"I just got off the phone with him. He told me about Schmidt."

"There was something he didn't tell you."

"What?"

"When Schmidt was taken into custody, they looked through what was in his pockets and he had an appointment book," said Tomasson.

"And?"

"They saw he had an appointment for a corner on 56th and Walnut for that day at seven pm. Blake sent some people out there to see who might show up – to see if anyone would look like they were waiting to meet Schmidt."

"Did anyone show up?" asked Neco.

"Not that they could tell. But I think they blew it."

"How?"

"They only looked at the information as a meeting place. They didn't look at it as a piece of real estate."

Neco broke into a smile. "You've learned well, Miss Sandra. Now tell me the next thing I want to hear."

"I didn't tell anyone. I remembered how you took measures to limit who knew you were working on the case.

You said Schmidt had someone running drugs to a contact in government. So, you're the only one I'm telling about this. If you could find out who owns that corner, you might get your next lead."

"You're as smart as you are beautiful, Miss Sandra," said Neco, who noticed Hernandez clenching her hands and turning her head away to look out the window. He wished he could retract his last sentence. "And I know just the person I can trust to get me the information I need."

As soon as Neco hung up, the phone rang again.

"Who the hell's calling me now?"

"It's probably Tomasson calling to have you mail her lips back from your ass."

Neco shook his head and answered, "This is Juni."

"Loco, this is George. Are you all right? That was crazy, even for *you*."

"I'm fine, George. Hey, I'm sorry to have spoiled the evening. Is Carrot okay?"

"It's 'Tarro'. And despite my passing along your words of consolation, she feels like less than a 'lucky bitch'. Her face and lips are swollen and you chipped two of her teeth."

"She'll be fine," Neco said coldly.

"Only because we came to an agreement. She would keep quiet. In exchange, for which I pay for her dental bill, she keeps the mink stole she I gave her, and I let her stay alive."

"We can probably avoid future problems if you stop dating women from the produce aisle."

"That's a deal. Say, since we were interrupted, I wanted to take you up on your offer to come to your gym to show me a work-out routine. Then we can go over arrangements for your kilo. When can we set that up?"

"I'm working out tomorrow morning. Can you get your ass over to Bally's in Deptford."

"Just tell me the time."

Martinez hung up and turned to Alejandro. "Okay. We're on for eight tomorrow morning."

Alejandro nodded and pulled out his own phone. "I'm going to let the boss know another door has just opened up on Neco."

CHAPTER SIXTY-ONE

9 July, Glassboro, New Jersey

Petey watched his daddy help his grandmother clear off the breakfast table. "Daddy, can I go and play with my friends now?"

Neco began putting some plates and utensils in the dishwasher. "Sure, big man. Just go upstairs, brush your teeth and get your shoes on. Grandma will take you to Richie's and I'll pick you up later."

Petey ran upstairs as Carla spoke to her son-in-law and handed him some glasses. "Juni, is my daughter back with her doctor?"

"She's scheduled next week. Thanks again for watching Petey while I'm out of town."

Carla's eyes welled up. "Please don't let Sandy be committed. I wouldn't be able to take it."

Neco stepped over and hugged her. "I am doing everything I can to prevent that. Your help with Petey has been very important to keep things under control. We're going to get Sandy through this. Now don't let Petey see you crying."

Carla grabbed a paper napkin and dabbed at her eyes.

"I'll be okay."

Neco grabbed his gym bag, went outside. Before he could hop in his car, he recognized his wife's car pulling up. Sandy looked equally surprised at the sight of him.

She stopped in the middle of the street with the engine running and gave him an icy stare.

"Hon! I've been trying to reach you! So has your mother," said Neco. We need to get you back with the doctor."

"I *have* been back with the doctor. Maybe *you* should be the one getting with him. *You* seem to be the one with the problem!"

"What are you talking about?"

"I saw you meet with that blond tart in Puerto Rico!"

Her husband had to think for a second. "What? . . . I . . . that wasn't a *meeting*. She *surprised* me. I had no idea she had followed me there. And if you noticed, I walked away from her. Nothing happened. I told her nothing *could* happen."

"Something happened at the Phillies game last week."

Another pause. "Did you follow me to the Phillies game?"

"I didn't have to. You kissed her for all to see on the Jumbotron screen. My sister recognized you in the bar we were at."

"Did you tell her what I do?" asked Neco. "She thinks I walk a beat."

"No, she just thinks you're a womanizer. And so do I!"

"We were on a case!"

"When you told me you were accepting the job with the Attorney General, you said you wouldn't be working with her anymore."

"I believed that to be true! She was *assigned* to me.

She was the only one who *could* be assigned to me that night. Nothing happened. It was only a *case*."

"And, I suppose it was just a coincidence that you were assigned another one of the Camden women yesterday in Atlantic City?"

"What were you doing in Atlantic City? Are you following me?"

"No. I was at a bar there. I guess it was just another 'coincidence'." Then Sandy put the car in 'drive' and sped away.

Her husband looked around to see if Carla or Petey heard any of the exchange. He did not observe anyone.

Neco took a deep breath and realized he still had an appointment with Martinez. He hopped in his car started the drive to Bally's.

With Sunday morning traffic almost non-existent he arrived at Bally's within twenty minutes, well ahead of the appointment time with his sting target.

Neco went to the front desk where a young, perky blond receptionist greeted him. "Good morning, Juni."

"Good morning, Miss Cathy."

"So where have you been hiding yourself?" asked Cathy.

Neco handed her his membership card for swiping into the computer system. She looked at the computer screen which displayed of Neco' contact information and verified the membership as current. "I've had a lot of business to attend out of town lately. But, soon, I should be stably back in the area. Don't worry, you'll be seeing more of me than you want."

Like Ron Goldbach had discovered, Neco always kept his answers to personal questions cryptic around the gym.

"Well, then you better fork over some money soon. The computer says your membership expires in a month," said Cathy.

"I might have more inspiration to renew if you were to become a personal trainer here."

"Like you need that."

"I'm confident you would work my ass off."

"That would require you having an ass," grinned Cathy.

"I actually do have to fork over some money to you. How much is a guest pass?" asked Neco as he reached into his pocket.

"Your guest gets his first one for free."

"Cheap at twice the price. Please let me have one. Maybe I can rustle up some business for you."

"It's not like *I* get any more money," said Cathy.

"You would if you were a personal trainer."

"Leave me alone," blushed Cathy, as she signed and dated the pass. "Here."

Neco looked back out the glass front doors. "Ah, here comes my pigeon now."

George Martinez entered, gym bag in hand. "Good morning, Loco. Are you ready to put me through the paces?"

"Absolutely. Let's go to the locker room and change. Then I'll give you a little tour before we get down to business."

Bally's Holiday Spa had everything. The first floor featured state-of-the-art cardiovascular machines. Members had a choice of treadmills, stationary bikes, Stairmasters and low-impact stationary jogging machines. Off to one side of this area, Bally's provided a soft-surface running track. Rooms adjacent on the other side provided free weights, and next to those rooms members could do laps in a half Olympic-size heated swimming pool.

The second floor had large spaces for various aerobics classes and weight-lifting machines.

Neco showed Martinez some simple stretches to perform.

Martinez did as instructed and grimaced as he watched his host do more advanced actions. "Oh God! You do full leg splits? My legs are like tree trunks. Don't ever ask me to do that." Then he looked at his watch.

Next came the cardiovascular machines. Neco oriented Martinez to one of the stationary jogging machines that allowed the user to set resistance and degree of incline. He set his guest up for twenty minutes of low resistance jogging.

Martinez peeked over at Neco' machine. "An *hour*?

You go for an *hour* on this thing?"

"That's my minimum if I'm in a rush. Today I'm only doing an hour out of respect for you, so you don't have to wait long," said Neco. "Anyway, we have the area to ourselves. What news do you have?"

"Yes, arrangements are underway to get a kilo to you for the down payment. My boss is anxious to get things underway. As part of the preparations, you are being invited out to Colombia."

"What? Colombia?" said a surprised Neco. "I don't see myself going out to Colombia. I mean, I know The Badlands aren't Beverly Hills, but Colombia is just an *outlaw* nation. I probably have some enemies over there."

"You don't understand," said Martinez, as he talked through labored breathing. "You wouldn't be in the city.

You would be a guest on the finest estate on the planet!

The only time you would even be in proximity of a major city would be Medina, and that would only be to land and take off from the airport. And during that time, you would be given protection better than that afforded the president of our country."

"I don't know. I'll have to look at my calendar and think about that one. Right now I would be more interested in my down payment."

Martinez had to step off his machine. "Whoo! Maybe I'll tackle twenty minutes next time."

"Yeah, we'll find out your pace and build you up from there. Now you were going to tell me about the kilo."

"Slow down, Loco. You'll get your kilo on Saturday."

"Excellent! And once you pull that off, we can work out the logistics of the shipment. In fact, we will work out the logistics in style. I promise I will treat you right."

"I would share your excitement if my body didn't hurt so much," said Martinez. "Damn! I can't believe how sore I am. What do you do after this?"

"I do some free weights and then I stretch some more."

"How often do you put yourself through all this crap?"

"I try to do it six days a week," said Neco, picking up his pace.

Martinez shook his head as more members took positions on the surrounding machines. He looked at his watch again.

"You carry on, Loco. I'm just going to hit the men's room."

Back in the lobby, Martinez watched Cathy greet a new face coming through the door. "Welcome to Bally's Holiday Spa. Can I help you?"

"Yes, I'm looking to become a member here."

"Terrific. If you'll have a seat, I'll page someone to give you a tour and explain membership programs."

"Thank you, I've heard a lot of good things about Bally's."

"Oh, yes! The whole chain is growing and this is still one of the best facilities. The members love it here."

"You know, I believe I already have an acquaintance here. A member by the name of Juni Neco?"

"Oh gosh, I understand that there may be a member here who's a friend, but it's Bally's policy to not give out information about its members," she pursed her lips, "I'm sorry, Mr . . . um . . . what is your name?"

"Jimenez. Carlos Jimenez."

"Let me page someone for you, Mr. Jimenez."

"Actually, I just came in to see if I could get a brochure today. But, you can rest assured, I'm not just blowing you off. I promise I'll be a member before the week is over."

Martinez went back to the cardiovascular room.

"George!" said Neco. "I still have a half hour.

But the pool area has a whirlpool. If you want to go relax there for a while."

"No thanks. I didn't bring my swimming trunks. I think I going to leave it at this for my first work-out.

You finish your routine and I'll call you about where you're going to get your advance."

"All right, sir. We'll talk soon."

Martinez departed and Neco heard his cell phone ring.

"Hello, this is Juni."

"Juni, this is Gordo. I got your message. What's up?"

"Hey, Gordo! I need you to put out your feelers for the name of a dealer who operates on 54th and Walnut Street."

"No need to put out my feelers. He's one of my competitors . . . I mean . . . I *used* to compete with him. His name is Willie Greenwood. Do you need me to set something up?"

"Yes, in a way."

"What do you mean 'in a way'?"

"I don't want you to be there. I just want you to tell me where I can find him tomorrow night."

"Shit! I know *him*, but I don't know his actual address. I'm going to have to tell him I want to meet, and do what we would usually do – discuss a buyer who wants more than I can provide."

Neco thought for few moments.

"Juni? Are you still there?"

"Yeah. Tell Willie Greenwood that circumstances dictate you meet him at eleven o'clock tomorrow night. But you and I are going to put a different twist on this one."

CHAPTER SIXTY-TWO

10 July, Mt. Ephraim, New Jersey

Ray Diaz and Ada Hernandez manned a surveillance van outside of Rexy's Tavern on the Black Horse Pike. They listened in on Dexter Rasche conversing with the use of a wire to tape a drug dealer.

"I thought we'd seen the last of Opie when he was hired by the A/G," said Diaz. "And isn't he supposed to be at Indian Gap."

"It's the bittersweet result of the Special Task Force," said Hernandez. On the one hand, the new coordination between agencies lets us see more of Juni.

On the other hand, some cases will send Opie over here for help. Which is why he was excused to be here today. Let's just hope he gets what he needs to wrap it up."

"I don't know. I don't like all the background noise. It goes in and out."

Inside the tavern, Rasche kept the conversation in the direction of incriminating words.

His dupe—a young Puerto Rican with a tattooed bald head and goatee – began to cough up information for the bust. "My boss wants the shit on the 12th. Schedule your boys to bring it to a house on 5th and Elm Street at four o'clock that afternoon."

"Alright, Felix," said Rasche, scribbling down some notes. "Let's review the exact amounts one more time."

"Well, if the tape survives the noise, he's got what he wants," said Diaz.

Hernandez looked through some binoculars.

"Apparently, he thinks he's got what he wants. It looks like they're wrapping it up."

Rasche and Felix stepped outside and shook hands.

"I'm going back inside to hit the head, man. I'll see you in two days," said the man who looked like Ron Howard.

"Okay, Dexter."

Hernandez waited for Felix to leave. Then she stepped out of the van to stretch her legs.

Rasche emerged from the restaurant with a triumphant look on his face as he spoke. "Music to your ears, right, babe?"

"Hopefully not the wrong music. The bar music and those televisions with the golf tournament may have compromised the quality of the recording."

"Oh, hell! We have the technology to clean that up."

The two agents heard his cell phone rang. "This is Dexter.

Oh, good afternoon. Just a second." He cupped his hand over the receiver and looked at Hernandez. "I'm going to have to have some privacy for this one, babe." Then he walked over to the other end of the parking lot.

Hernandez bit her lip, marched back to the van and opened the door. "Ray, I'm hungry. I could really go for a personal pan pizza with mushrooms and onions."

"Then go. The tavern's right there."

"I'm asking if you would get it for me."

"I'm kinda in the middle of something," said Diaz, as he tried to listen to the recording. "Get it yourself."

"If you get it for me, I'll come in to work tomorrow with a tube top and a micro-mini."

Diaz whipped the headphones off and hopped out of the van. Hernandez shook her head. *Men are idiots.* She quickly took Diaz's seat and put on the headset. She whispered to herself, "Speak clearly into the wire, Opie."

"So you're coming back to Indian Gap for graduation, right? . . . Good . . . When? No, I'll have this case wrapped up on Wednesday . . . Where's Mt. Gretna? Yeah, what's the name of the restaurant? . . . If it's the only one in the development I'll find it . . . I've been introduced, but I really haven't spoken with him yet . . . What's the meeting all about? Hah! If you're not kidding, Neco will have an absolute bird . . . Sure, maybe I can get with him before our lunch . . . Yeah, talk me up. I'll see you at Thursday for graduation."

Hernandez rewound the tape as Rasche pulled out his pocket calendar, scribbled down a note and made his way back to the van's rear door.

"So how'd it come out?" he asked, popping his head inside.

"Better than I could have hoped," replied Hernandez.

Rasche came in and took a seat. "Well, let me hear it."

Hernandez hit the "play" button. "Sure." Then she casually rested her finger on the "stop" button.

Rasche nodded his approval and slapped his knees in drummer fashion as he took in the sting dialogue. "This going to be history. I'll be the first one to crack a case for the Special Task Force. And that is what you call 'going places', my dear!" He pumped his fist in the air.

Hernandez smiled at him and very matter-of-factly stopped the tape.

Rasche continued, "You know, you should apply for the Special Task Force, Ada. Then we could do more of this.

I've already put in a good word for you."

"Then all my letter writing has paid off."

"You make fun of it now, but soon you'll come around and see what you've been missing all this time." Rasche opened up his shirt and gently pulled the tape holding the wire to his chest. He left the shirt unbuttoned and got up as he addressed his female partner. "I'm going to go back and write up my report." Then he leered at her. "Ada, there's something in your eye."

Hernandez looked a little perplexed.

Rasche put his hand up to her temple and smiled. "Oh, look. It's *me*!"

After his departure, she pulled out her cell phone and dialed. The response came.

"This is Juni."

"Juni, this is Ada."

"Miss Ada! To what do I owe the pleasure of this call?"

"Why are you breathing like that? Are you working out?"

"Yeah, the Indian Gap training facility has a gym on the grounds. It's pretty good. What's up?"

Hernandez peeked out the window. "I don't have much time to talk."

"Where are you? Is everything okay?"

"I'm fine. I'm just short on time, so *I* have the floor."

"I'm listening."

"I've just listened to a wire on Opie," said Hernandez.

"You've just what? Why? How did you pull . . ."

Hernandez dragged out her pronunciation. "Flooooor!"

"Go on."

Hernandez rewound the tape as she spoke. "Opie was wearing a wire for a case here in Mt. Ephraim." She hit "stop" when the tape counter reached the right point.

"When he was done, he got a phone call and started acting a little suspicious. Well, he hadn't taken the wire off yet, so I held up something shiny and misdirected Diaz's attention so I could turn the system back on. I want you to hear it."

She peeked out the window again as she placed the phone against the receiver and hit the play button.

"Did you get that?" she asked.

Neco sounded disturbed. "Do you know what he was talking about? When is this meeting?"

"I don't know. That's all I got. I didn't have a tap on his phone. But sometime, somewhere in Mt. Gretna,

Pennsylvania, there's going to be a lunch meeting with Opie, and two other men. And one of the topics is going to be about something you would hate." She peeked out the window again and saw Diaz coming with the food. "I gotta go! Call me later." She hung up, hit "rewind" and clapped her hands together, "Screw you, Tomasson. Advantage:

Hernandez!"

Neco hung up the phone and placed a call of his own.

"Hey, Sensei. What's up?"

"Good afternoon, Ron. I've just had a strange call."

"From who?"

Neco reviewed his conversation with Hernandez and recounted the tape as best he could. "What do you make of that?"

"I don't know," said Goldbach. "Any idea who the mystery men are?"

"At first when I heard 'anti-Neco', my first thought was Blake and that Philly captain I roughed up.

But then I thought 'Mt. Gretna' and it didn't make any sense. Mt. Greta is outside of Harrisburg."

"Do you think it's Shurmur?"

"He's not anti-Neco. He hired me."

"Well, you did strong arm him a little to get hired," countered White Lightning. "And you were surprised to learn of his investigation."

"I still don't think he's one of the two men. But first I have to find out where and when this meeting is."

"Are we on for tonight?"

"No. Tonight a gentleman by the name of Willie Greenwood gets a little surprise."

That evening, one of Bally's latest members struck up a conversation with the woman on the adjacent treadmill.

"Say, I was looking for a gentleman by the name of Juni."

He held out his hand, palm downwards. "He's about this tall, Hispanic, great build, works out like a maniac . . . a friend of mine told me he could give me some good work-out tips. Do you know him?"

"No, I'm afraid I don't," replied the woman.

"Hey, don't worry about it. I'll ask around."

Alejandro stepped off the treadmill and proceeded to the free weights room, where he approached a man on the bench press. "Pardon me, are you doing several sets or just the one?"

"I'm on the first of three sets, but you can jump in between," said the man, as he got up. "Here, you take a turn."

"Thanks."

Alejandro posed the same question he had been asking other members throughout the day.

"Juni? Yeah I know *of* him, but I don't know *him*. He kind of keeps to himself," answered the man. "You're right though. When I've seen him, he's pretty intense. Good luck trying to get some tips out of him. If you get any, let me know."

"Yeah, you'll be the second one to learn of any tips."

Then he privately stewed. *This is getting nowhere! Time for the usual successful measures.*

An hour later, the last of the Bally's members emptied out of the building and into the parking lot. Cathy, the last of the skeletal evening crew, finished up the closing procedures. She finally stepped outside, inserted her key and clicked the deadbolt lock for the glass door into place.

Cathy walked to her lone car in the lot, got in and drove out of the parking lot and onto the highway.

From the parking lot of a discount outlet store adjacent to Bally's, the headlights of a black sedan clicked on. Cathy never noticed the other car pulling out from a distance onto the lane behind her.

The Bally's Holiday Spa receptionist lived over in Tacony, Pennsylvania. A light rain began to fall as Cathy crossed the Tacony-Palmyra Bridge and turned onto a dimly lit industrial section of State Street. With all the companies long closed, Cathy observed an empty road . . . except for one car behind her.

A mild concern prompted her to switch gears and press harder on the gas pedal.

Within moments, the trailing car accelerated too.

The mild concern turned generated into strong apprehension.
Who is that?

Again Cathy moved her four cylinder compact into a higher gear.

The trailing car more than matched the effort. The distance between her and the car rapidly closed. Cathy could see in her rear view mirror the type of car – a sedan. She knew she could not out-race the eight-cylinder closing in from the passing lane. Her body began trembling. "Oh, my god!" she said softly, her worst fear confirmed. *Somebody's after me!*

The skies unmercifully challenged her ability to cope and unleashed a rainfall creating a more treacherous road.

Cathy frantically groped inside her pocket book and fumbled around for her car phone as the other car pulled up beside her.

She found the phone, pulled it out and tried to make out the numbers for 911, but did not have enough light.

She hit a random button which lit up the phone. But before she could dial, she let out a scream as the sedan side—swiped her. Cathy used both hands on the steering wheel to keep her vehicle on the road, causing the phone to be dropped to the passenger side floor mat.

She flashed a quick look at the other driver and recognized his features. *Carlos Jimenez!*

Alejandro rolled down the electric window on the passenger side. "Pull over!" he screamed.

Through her window, he saw Cathy pronouncedly mouthing the words "Fuck you!"

The cold-blooded assassin pulled slightly ahead of her and veered into her left front end forcing the compact car off the road and into the chain-link fence of a closed warehouse.

He saw the left side of her forehead bang hard against the side window frame, opening a small gash above her temple.

As her pursuer screeched to a halt twenty yards from the disabled vehicle, Cathy jumped out and began running though the rain.

Alejandro did the same thing as he drew his handgun.

"Stop!" he yelled. "I don't want to hurt you!"

"Leave me alone!" she screamed back, never turning her head nor breaking stride.

Alejandro let out a curse. He did not want it this way. He wanted it to go the same way it did at Ott's – a successful extraction of information at knife point before the eventual slaying. Alejandro did not plan on chasing a young, athletically fit woman in her running shoes opening up ground on him.

Within seconds she would be in a dark stretch, making it virtually impossible to see her.

The hit man raised his revolver and began firing.

Three shots rang in the misty air.

A sharp cry filled the air as the silhouette's torso arched back.

Cathy fell forward to the ground.

Alejandro raced towards the prone body. *With luck, she'll still be alive!*

CHAPTER SIXTY-THREE

The rain in North Philadelphia, pouring down on Alejandro had not yet arrived to 58th and Walnut in the western part of the city. A heavy mist filled the air.

In the dark and the fog, the silhouette of Roberto Quintero stood alone, awaiting his fellow dealer. A peal of thunder warned him of what was to come. The man working both sides of the law pulled at the strings to the hood of his sweat shirt and alternated glances down the intersecting streets until he recognized a familiar outline of a man with his own hooded sweat shirt in the distance.

Willie Greenwood strutted the empty sidewalk with a bebop motion. He did not have on a headset – he just softly sang to himself.

Greenwood finally reached the corner. "Gordo! You're early! Don't you go tryin' to blame me for standin' out here too long."

"Yeah, you're as innocent as a newborn rattlesnake," sneered Gordo.

"So what's happenin'? Whatcha got for me?"

"I've got a client I've been selling dope to. His usual amount has been five to ten kilos a month. But he's found some high rollers that need more weight than I can accommodate. I want to work out a cut . . ."

Before Gordo could finish, the skies roared again and a figure darted out from behind a parked car to Greenwood's blindside. The West Philly dealer felt a forearm slam against his throat, half cutting off his breathing. Gordo saw a nine-millimeter Smith and Wesson trained on himself.

A whispering, steely-edged voice came from behind Greenwood's head and addressed Gordo. "Get your hands up and turn around! Right now! Turn around!"

Gordo complied.

"You are not the target here!" said the man with Greenwood in a chokehold. "I've been tailing this guy tonight and *you* are an unfortunate *complication.* Now you can choose to become an unfortunate *casualty*, or you can run like hell, not look back and forget this ever happened."

Greenwood watched his colleague sprinting away into the mist as he struggled to speak through the grip around his throat. "Why am *I* the target? Who are you? What did *I* do, man?"

"Shut the hell up!" said the assailant in a loud whisper.

The grip tightened, turning a potential scream into a gurgle.

A taxi cab drove down the street.

"I've just decided I'm not going to drag your ass back to my car!"

Greenwood felt his neck released from the chokehold.

With no time to appreciate the sensation of a full breath, a sharp blow came to his left knee, numbing the lower half of his leg. The drug dealer began to scream like a woman.

Before the scream finished, the attacker threw his body out into the middle of the street.

Lights came on in windows. Blinds cracked open.

Screeching from the tires of the taxi on the wet road matched the high-pitched wail of Greenwood.

The driver, an Indian in his fifties, managed to come to a halt about eight yards short of the writhing body that had come out of nowhere. The cabbie's shock quickly became more intense by the sound of his driver's side window being smashed open with a gun then being brandished at him.

"Get out of the cab!"

"What the hell's going on?" yelled the driver.

"Get out of the cab and pick that guy up!"

Shock paralyzed the cabbie.

The gun, now trained slightly to the right, fired – shattering the back passenger window into pieces outward from the other side of the car.

"I said, 'Get out of the cab and pick that guy up!'
You won't get hurt if you do what I say!"

"Just do what he *says*, man! He's *crazy!*" shouted Greenwood, still holding his leg.

The Indian held his hands over his ears as he felt himself being pulled through the now open car door. He ran out to Greenwood.

"Get him up and into the driver's seat!"

The cabbie tried to get out a question. "What's going to . . ."

"We're just going to borrow your taxi for a short ride. You'll get it back with all your fare money. Like I said, we're just taking it for a short ride. Now get him in there!"

While the cabbie obeyed, the attacker hopped in the back seat behind the new driver and gave him his next order. "Start it up and drive!"

"My leg is still numb, man!"

"Your right one is still good. If you want to keep it that way, shut the fuck up, start up the cab and drive.

Turn right at the corner."

Greenwood turned the key, straightened out the wheels, began driving and made the turn.

"Turn right at the next block."

Willie shot glances into the rear view mirror. He could see the man had Hispanic features but could not place him beyond that.

"Who are you? What have you got against me?"

Police sirens could be heard in the background and it started to rain.

"We're going to switch cars here, and then we'll drive off and have a nice chat."

The man in the back seat directed Greenwood to pull up to a silver Jaguar.

They abandoned the cab in the street and Greenwood drove off with the gun still trained on him.

"Are you gonna tell me who you are?"

"That's not important. What's important is that you tell me what I want."

"Anything, man! What do you want . . . how to get some crack? Speed? Just *tell* me."

"I want to know your connection to Arnie Schmidt. And don't bullshit me! I know he meets you at that corner back there," said his captor. "Turn left here, and then right at the next corner. We're going back to the Schuylkill Expressway. Now tell me about your relationship with Arnie Schmidt."

"Arnie Schmidt? No big deal. I run some stuff for him and he pays me. Sometimes I buy shit from him."

"Where is he now?"

"Why? Does he owe you money?" asked Greenwood.

The gun pressed up against his head.

"Just answer the question! And don't miss your turn."

"I don't know where he is."

"When did you last see him?"

"Arnie surprised me last Thursday. He had to collect some money I owed him – said he was disappearin'."

"Do you have any idea where he would try to disappear?"

Greenwood turned onto the Expressway. "Arnie could be anywhere. He once told me he had three different homes with bomb shelters. Wouldn't tell me where they were. He just said that if he ever had to disappear, he had enough supplies to lay low for a long time."

"Who else was he in contact with besides you?"

"Hell, I don't know! He wasn't loyal to anyone but himself. But it would only be those he could quickly contact in person. He knew phone lines would be tapped."

"I know that Schmidt was having you run dope for someone. One of our fine, upstanding civil servants. I want to know who that is."

"I don't know who it is."

More thunder roared and the rain came down harder.

"You are really flunking this exam, Willie."

"I don't know! But I just had one of my men go to a location to make a drop."

"Who makes the drop?"

"A guy I use—works for The Philadelphia Inquirer. I give him the drug packages and he delivers them durin' his route. We're not talkin' kilo's here. These are just little packets that can be tucked in the folds of the paper. Easy delivery."

"Where's the house of this friend in government?"

"There's no house."

"You said he made the drops for his paper route."

"He does. But this drop is put in the display copy of a vendin' machine for the Inquirer. After my man drives away, someone comes and gets that copy. My guy was ordered not to wait around."

"What if someone else gets to the vending machine first?"

"First off, this guy apparently makes sure he's somewhere in sight when the machine is loaded, so nobody can be ahead of him. Besides nobody gettin' a paper from a vendin' machine takes the display copy when there's a whole stack inside. Believe me, this has worked smoothly for a while."

"When's the next drop?"

"This mornin'. My man already has his packets. He's probably loadin'up papers within the next hour.

"Where is this vending machine?"

"Some suburb out in Harrisburg . . . Hershey! Yeah, Hershey!"

"Then you're going to take me there right now."

"Aww, shit . . . !"

Chapter Sixty-Four

11 July, Hershey, Pennsylvania

Hershey, home to the Hershey Chocolate Factory, displayed its own personality the moment you entered the town. Even a visitor, unfamiliar with the area, did not take long to figure out where he was.

If street names like "Chocolate Boulevard" and "Hershey Highway" did not tip people off, they could not help but notice the street lamps down the main street with the alternating silver-wrapped and brown-wrapped Hershey Kiss replicas covering the light bulbs.

Martin Shurmur stared at the alarm clock on the lamp table next to his bed. It read 5:47 am. He reached over and turned off the alarm setting to let his wife sleep some more. Mrs. Shurmur did not know about his plan concerning the investigation by the State Elections Bureau.

She only knew that her husband continued to reassure her.

We'll come out of this the other end, honey. And everything will be okay.

She also knew that Agent Michael Owens expressed great displeasure over the forty-plus boxes brought to him by Christopher Warner's office.

Shurmur mentally checked off another day on the calendar for his exit strategy. The State Attorney General began his morning routine for a work day. He stood in the bath tub with a mirror hanging from the shower head. As he shaved, he plotted some more stall tactics for Agent Owens. He had excused his star agent from combat training in Indian Gap. But Neco would be back for graduation on Thursday.

Neco will be a big key to keeping Owens at bay just a little longer.

Shurmur did not know his "key" sat in a car parked less than a mile away from his estate.

The sun rose higher on the horizon. Neco and Greenwood staked out the designated newspaper vending machine from a safe distance.

"You're sure that's the vending machine?" asked Neco.

"Of course, I'm sure, man," assured Greenwood. "I may not make the deliveries, but I sure as hell know where my shit is supposed to be put."

"Why hasn't your man made the drop yet?"

"Maybe there was a traffic problem . . . construction . . . a detour . . . I don't know. He should be here any minute. If not, he's supposed to call me. Then I call Schmidt and we reschedule it."

"You better hope Schmidt didn't cancel this drop."

"Not unless he personally drove out here," said Greenwood. "Like I said, he told me that I wasn't to call him because phones were being tapped." Greenwood looked in his rearview mirror. "Wait! Here he comes! That's him in the Inquirer truck."

Neco re-examined the street he had been looking at for the past four hours.

No one.

It would only make sense that the person picking up would have to do it immediately after the delivery before any potential witnesses arrived, Neco thought. He turned to Greenwood. "Give me the keys to the car."

"What's goin' on? You're not leavin' me here?"

"Only while I go in for a closer look. I don't want you driving away. And if you try to make a break for it, I *will* find you and I *will* kill you. Your role is almost done here. Keep being a good soldier. You were going to lose this client anyway."

Neco hopped out of the Jaguar they parked along a side street near the Hershey Golf Club – adjacent to the chocolate factory. Soon members would be arriving for their early tee-times. Several hours later, the aroma of fresh chocolate would be wafting through the entire course and town.

The factory featured expensive landscaping, including some huge bushes on a small hill sculpted to spell out "HERSHEY" for low flying planes to see.

This morning the bushes provided a good vantage point from which the vending machine could be seen.

Neco ensconced himself behind the "Y" in the bushes, as the truck driver finished filling the vending machine. The vehicle pulled away, but not before Neco made a notation of the license plate.

Once Gordo is safely in the Witness Protection Program, you and Willie will be dealt with, Mr. Delivery Man.

The quiet of the morning made it easy for Neco to hear footsteps clicking on the pavement. The sound came from around the corner. He could not see the person yet, but would by the time he or she arrived at the vending machine.

The footsteps became louder. A man came into view, but had his back to Neco. He faced the machine and placed some coins in the slot.

Even from behind, he looked familiar to Neco.

If he knows me, it'll make tailing him on an empty street impossible. And someone Hispanic in Hershey stands out like a sore thumb anyway.

The man removed the display paper.

A quick unfolding of the newspaper confirmed the contents for him.

Neco felt his heart racing faster. *Turn the hell around!*

The man casually looked around in all directions to see who might be around.

Finally, he turned in the direction of Neco.

The expression on Neco' face rivaled the intensity of when he was in Koblenzer's office and learned of his wife getting his gun in her hands in an effort to blow out her brains.

He stared in disbelief at the identity of the man who had just purchased the newspaper.

Anthony Sorvino.

CHAPTER SIXTY-FIVE

Clayton, New Jersey

Exhausted, Neco pulled up to his mother-in-law's house. Back in Harrisburg, he had stuffed some money in Willie Greenwood's hand and dumped him off at the Amtrak Station. The agent needed to be alone with his thoughts on the trip back.

Only he did not know what to think, who he could talk to, or who he could even trust with this explosive new incident.

Martin's already under investigation for illegal campaign finance funding. What the hell else is he into?

Is he running some type of side drug business with his Deputy Attorney General?

Is Sorvino acting on his own to get drugs?

Is he also in on the arms dealings with Schmidt?

Who's meeting with Opie in Mt. Joy?

He had nothing concrete that would get past a preliminary hearing in court.

Neco stayed in his car to make a call.

"Good morning, Sensei."

"Good morning, Ron."

"What's up?"

Goldbach found himself on the receiving end of an answer far longer and far more complicated than he imagined.

"Ron, get the gang together for a session tonight. I need to clear my head real bad. But first I'm going to get some sleep."

Neco hung up and as he opened the door to his car, he had to answer his phone.

"Yeah?"

"Whoa! Loco! It sounds like I woke you up."

"Who is this? George?"

"Of course it's me! Did you have a late night?"

"Yeah."

"Should I call you back later?"

"No, no," said Neco. "I should be up now. What's going on?"

"I do want to meet with you Saturday, around dinner time. And I *will* have something nice to bring to the table for you."

That kicked in some adrenaline for Neco. "Just name the place."

"There's a hotel off of Exit 13A of the New Jersey Turnpike. Are you familiar with the area?"

"Sure," answered Neco. "If I'm not mistaken, there's a Holiday Inn just off that exit."

"That's the one. The hotel also has a restaurant. Be there at five o'clock. Have your cell phone on and be ready."

"I'll be ready, sir."

Neco finally got out of the car and went inside his mother-in-law's house. He found Petey watching television in the living room where he gave him a big hug and kiss.

"Are you going to be home today, Daddy?" asked the son.

"I am. I just have to go back to our house and get a nap. Then I'm coming back here and we're going to have some fun today. So think about some things you want to do.

But Daddy really needs some sleep first."

"Is Mommy going to be home?"

"I don't know yet. Finish watching your program and I'll talk with Grandma about that."

Neco found Carla in the kitchen and thanked her again for watching his son.

"Do you know where Sandy is?" asked Carla.

"I was just about to ask you the same question," said Neco.

"Which means she's probably at her sister's place."

"Did she get back with her doctor yet?"

"She's seen Koblenzer once since we last spoke. I don't know if she's back on her prescription yet, but somehow I doubt it."

The mother-in-law sighed.

"Don't worry, Carla. I'm almost done with some vital out-of-town business and then I can concentrate on her more. But, even when I'm back in the area, I'll probably still need you for Petey a lot."

"I'm here for him. He's a joy to watch."

Neco went back home, grabbed a long nap and went back to take Petey to a nearby lake for swimming.

Evening came and he drove to meet Goldbach and the gang for a sparring session in Levittown.

He and White Lightning remained the last to get in the shower.

"So when's my next session for training with the 007?" asked Goldbach as they turned the shower heads on.

"Maybe next Sunday. "We'll make sure you can draw it from the pocket and snap it into the locked position in one motion."

"I think you'll be pleased," said Goldbach, sticking his head under the water. He grabbed some shampoo. "So, are you finally going to tell me where you learned that shit?"

"The Cut of a Thousand Deaths?"

"No, the Soap of a Thousand Lathers!" said Goldbach, his voice dripping with sarcasm. "Of course, I mean the Cut of a Thousand Deaths. Who taught you that?"

"You remember when I told you how I trained with Sensei Tony Echevarria?"

"Yeah, the Tenth Degree Black Belt – the guy who trained under the famous Tenth Degree Black Belt. I thought it might have been him. So at Tenth Degree training, you get into knives and shit?" He began lathering his hair.

"No, "chuckled Neco. "Knives are not part of Tenth Degree training. Sensei Tony was more than just a martial arts master."

"What else was he?" asked Goldbach, closing his eyes to rinse out the shampoo.

"A professional hit man.'

Goldbach went wide-eyed. "Get the hell out of here!

Aww, dammit!" His hands went up to his face.

"What happened?" asked Neco. "Are you okay?"

Goldbach held his hands to his face and rinsed the shampoo out of his eyes under the running water.

"A professional *hit* man?" Goldbach recovered and started to soap up his body.

Neco finished showering and stepped over to where his towel hung. "A professional hit man. Sensei Tony is the one who took a 007 knife and turned it into a whole new weapon."

"And you trained with him, knowing he was a hit man?"

"I didn't know at first. He didn't spring it on me until we were well into our training."

Goldbach finished rinsing off his body, looked down pensively and stepped over to his towel. "So, in between his training sessions with you, he's knocking people off?

And that was okay with you?"

"No. No. You misunderstand," corrected Neco.

"He had gotten really pissed off with his employers, so he stopped working for them."

"Oh, so, since he was on 'hiatus' from killing, you could rationalize training with him."

They kept talking as they went back to the empty locker room.

"Look," began Neco, "there were two masters involved here. One was Sensei Gorell – an ethical, good—hearted man. Gorell saw in me, someone that was part of a rare breed – a guy who could keep the upper level technology alive for future generations. Sensei Gorell himself didn't think he was able to do so." Neco took his clothes out from his locker and paused. "And the technology must *never* be allowed to die. The other master was, of course, Sensei Tony. Yes, he was a career hit man, but he never, *ever* tried to steer me in that direction.

This was not a matter of who had what background or future. This was all about to whom the torch could be passed. When you're at this level of martial arts, there's an understanding that transcends mortal law – the technology must not be allowed to die. And with that understanding, the bad will be balanced by the good. Tony had gone into organized crime. I went from his training into law enforcement."

"Phew!" exclaimed Goldbach, "So that was the overriding thrust.— you would train to someday use the technology for good?"

"Hell, no! I had no idea at the time I would become a cop. I just knew it was good shit and I wanted like hell to learn it."

"Are you still in contact with this guy?"

"No, I haven't seen him since my college days. For all I know, he could be either out of the country or dead."

They finished getting dressed and departed the building.

Goldbach had another question out in the parking lot.

"When you finish teaching me the 007, I can be available to race to your aid if you need me."

"If you even think about shit like that, the only "race" will be to see who kicks your ass first – me or that beautiful brunette you're married to."

Goldbach chuckled and then took on a serious look.

"So have you decided what you're going to do with Shurmur tomorrow?"

"No," said Neco. "I still haven't decided if can trust him. And I have nothing that I can take to court.

This wouldn't even get past the arraignment, let alone preliminary cause. I have to just keep working my case and looking for another lead."

"But it sounds like you're at a dead end now."

"I still think I can squeeze Greenwood for more information. But I terrorized him enough for one night. I have Gordo working on getting his home address. And somehow I have to find out what's happening with this meeting in Mt. Gretna."

"What's Greenwood's mindset on that whole episode?"

"In his universe, I'm just a nameless thug with a vendetta for one of Arnie Schmidt's contacts who screwed me," said Neco. "I told him that the guy at the vending machine was the wrong man and that I would keep looking on my own. Willie's just relieved to have me out of his life. And before this is all over, Martin may wish the same thing. Tomorrow I put a little demand on him."

Chapter Sixty-Six

12 July, Harrisburg, Pennsylvania

Martin Shurmur punched the speaker phone button and began his conversation with the agent from the State Elections Board. "Good afternoon, Mr. Owens. I was just calling to see how the audit was going on those files. I'd really like to get all this put behind me."

"Mr. Shurmur," began Owens, "I understand you're not wanting to have this drag out any longer than needed. But,

I'm short-staffed and it's going to take until the end of the month to go through dozens of boxes and correlate it with the information from all the tavern files. If I didn't know better, I'd say you and Mr. Warner were trying to hide something in the massive amounts of folders."

"Mr. Owens," said Shurmur. "If I wanted to hide something, I would do a much better job than handing it all over to you. Remember, I'm an attorney."

"Indeed," said Owens. "But I called you to schedule another appointment with you. Even though we've just broken the ice with your files, I do have some questions to ask to clear some things up."

"Absolutely," said Shurmur. "Today I have a drug bust in Mt. Ephraim. Then for the next few days, I have an agent setting up a huge drug bust. We're trying to put the hurt on a big fish. And I have The Special Task Force graduating tomorrow. What do things look like on your calendar for the 17th?"

"I'll make it happen. I'll be by first thing after lunch."

"I'm writing it on my calendar right now," said Shurmur.

Shurmur wrote on the page:

    9:00 am. Call and reschedule Owens appointment.

Moments after ending the call, his private line rang.

"This is Shurmur."

"Good afternoon, sir."

The Attorney General recognized the voice. "Good afternoon, Loco. Have you enjoyed your time off? Keeping out of trouble?"

"My parole officer is satisfied."

Shurmur laughed. "So what can I do for you?"

"George has scheduled a meeting for Saturday. He tells me he's bringing something for me up front."

"Perfect. Tomorrow, in Indian Gap, we'll have everyone we need to organize some surveillance for the drop. I'll have you brief everyone on the details for what you'll need."

"Very good, sir," said Neco. "And speaking of needs, I want to give you a heads up for something I'll need shortly after the drop."

"What's that?"

"I know Martinez has been anxious about this whole demand for something up front. But, he's coming through and now it's time to make an even bigger impression on him."

"What do you need?"

"A yacht," said Neco, who heard no response.

"Hello?"

"Yeah, I'm still here."

"Did you hear what I said?"

"A yacht. Yes. That's good! Organizing that will take a little time, but that's okay. When do you need it by?"

"I want it for the 18th. And I want this meeting on tape, so someone needs to wire up the cabin room."

"You've got my commitment, Juni. If we don't have a yacht impounded somewhere, we'll rent one."

Shurmur ended the conversation and placed his next call.

"Hello?"

"Dexter! This is Martin calling. Where are you?"

"I'm at the Camden County Prosecutor's Office. I have my bust scheduled in a few hours."

"Good man. So everything is all set?"

"Yeah, we'll nail this guy with four kilos of cocaine and about fifty pounds of marijuana."

"Not bad, Agent Rasche. You'll have the first official collar for The Special Task Force. Let me see you an hour before graduation tomorrow. I want to arrange for a commendation for you."

Rasche pulled out his pocket calendar and jotted down the time as he talked. "Thank you, sir. I'll make you proud."

"Good luck, Agent Rasche. Give me a call when it's over."

Rasche placed his phone and pocket calendar on his old, still-unclaimed desk and pumped both fists in the air.

The intercom buzzed.

"Yeah?"

"Opie, this is Blake. The officer running the surveillance wants to see you."

"I'm on my way."

Rasche left the room and less than a minute later Ada Hernandez stepped in the room and made her way to the desk.

She spotted Rasche's cell phone and pocket calendar.

Hernandez picked up the pocket calendar and quickly thumbed through it.

A voice from behind startled her.

"What are you up to?" asked Sandra Tomasson.

"For once in your life, just be quiet and leave me alone," said Hernandez, getting her breath.

"This smells. If you don't tell me what's going on,

I'm going to go rat on you."

"If you do, you'll sabotage Juni."

The word touched a nerve. "I would *never* sabotage Juni!

Who told you I want to sabotage Juni?"

"Settle down!" said Hernandez, who heard another set of footsteps approaching the door. "Oh damn!" She tossed the pocket calendar back on the desk.

Rasche entered the room. He looked cross. "What's going on in here? Why are you two in my office?"

"It's not your office anymore. But, I need to speak with you," replied Hernandez.

"About what?"

"I want to take you up on your offer."

"What offer?" asked Rasche.

"I want you to put in a good word for me with The Special Task Force."

"Me too!" said Tomasson. "I want you to put in a good word for me too."

Rasche got a gleam in his eye and grinned. "Well, you two are finally coming around." He nodded. "Yeah, my star continues to rise. I'll let you in on some breaking news.

Your man here is getting a commendation tomorrow from the Pennsylvania State Attorney General tomorrow for making the first bust in the history of the new unit." Then he picked up his cell phone and calendar. "These are what I came back for. I have to go now, but when I'm next in Harrisburg,

I'll be sure to put in a good mention for the two of you."

Rasche strutted out the door, to the delight of hearing two beautiful women expressing their thanks as he continued down the hallway.

"I have to make a phone call," said the Latino, stepping back into the office and pulling out her own phone. "I need some privacy now, Tomasson, so butt out!"

"No, I just helped you here," protested her partner,

"You owe it to me to let me know what's going on with Juni!"

Before Hernandez could reply, another voice from behind made them flinch.

"What are you two arguing about now?" said Jerry Cohen, walking in with a mug of hot coffee.

"Dammit, Jerry!" said Hernandez, lowering her phone and putting it by her side. "Ever hear of knocking?"

"The door was open. You're standing right there," said Cohen.

Tomasson crossed her arms. "Actually, it's good you dropped by. Maybe you could help us settle something. Ada thinks . . ."

"Sandra, we don't need to keep Jerry from his work.

I've just realized you have a point with what you said earlier. I think we can find some common ground."

"Excellent," grinned Tomasson. Then she moved towards Cohen, gently put one hand on the back of his waist and began directing him back to the hallway. "We just need some privacy now, but thank you for your offer to help."

"I didn't offer to help," said Cohen, digging in his heels, "I just smell something funny going on. What are you two up to?"

"It's none of your business. Now just give us some space," said Hernandez.

"This isn't your office," bristled Cohen. "You can't . . ."

"Get out, Woody!" said Tomasson, now shoving him into the hallway and shutting the door.

Cohen stood in the hallway. *Man, the women at the Prosecutor's Office are mean!*

Hernandez lifted her phone again and stared at Tomasson. "You just keep your mouth shut and let me do all the talking." She dialed up Neco.

"This is Juni."

"Juni, this is Ada."

"Miss Ada! I was just walking into Bally's for a workout."

"I have some more details for the meeting in Mt. Gretna."

"How did you . . . ? Never mind, I don't want to know."

"Please just listen. The meeting is for this Saturday at one o'clock. It's on the lounge deck at a Greek tavern called Acropolysis Now."

"Damn! We have the surveillance with Martinez later in the day. Now I have to figure out how to be in Mt. Gretna at one o'clock and then race back to Central Jersey by four."

"Maybe I could go there for you."

"No. You're not aware of it yet, but Shurmur is lining up you and Sandra to be the dates for me and Thomas on Saturday."

"Then maybe you could still do it. If anyone can pull it off, it's someone who can drive at ninety miles-per-hour with impunity along the PA turnpike."

"You're right. I can make that happen. Did you find out who else is going to be there? What they're going to discuss?"

"Nope. Don't know what it is you're going to hate. Oops . . . people coming. Let me go."

"Thank you, Miss Ada. I owe you again."

"I know."

Neco hung up and walked into the lobby area for Bally's where he greeted a young man at the front desk.

"Mr. Sal! How are you doing this afternoon? Where's my girl, Cathy?"

A serious look came over the man's face. "Cathy is missing."

"Missing? When was she last seen?" asked Neco.

"No one has seen her since she stayed to close up last night. When she didn't report for her shift today, the manager called her apartment, but there was no answer. Then he called her parent's house and finally found out the news."

Neco put his arms out with his palms upward.

"What did they say?"

"The police reported an abandoned car found on State Street near the Tacony-Palmyra Bridge. The plates came up on the computer with Cathy's name," said Sal.

"Was the vehicle disabled?"

"Worse. All signs from the police indicate her car had been forcibly run off the road and into the chain link fence of an industrial company. But, so far, there haven't been any witnesses." Sal paused. "Nor a body. So far they only have one thing."

"What's that?" asked Neco.

"Traces of her blood around the driver's seat, and more blood about one hundred yards from where they found the car."

Chapter Sixty-Seven

Des Moines, Iowa

That evening Senator Donald Carvey held a town hall meeting. He employed his usual successful tactics to sway public opinion. But, he had higher stakes now. With The Special Task Force underway, he now had to sell himself as someone who could be the leader of the free world. So he put in a new wrinkle.

As he addressed the crowd, he picked up a photograph that had been blown up to twenty-four by thirty-six inches and dry-mounted on foam board. He placed it on one of two easel stands positioned about four feet behind his podium.

"This is a picture of Elizabeth Schumacher," he began.

"Elizabeth is a fourteen year-old freshman cheerleader and a straight-A student. Her parents did everything good parents do for their child. They were always there to help her with her studies. They bought her countless hours of gymnastic lessons since she was five years old. Because, you see, this young cheerleader had aspirations of representing America for gymnastics in the Olympics."

Carvey made a dramatic pause. "She has her attention on other things now."

At that moment, the only other sound in the room was that being generated by the air-conditioning system.

The senator continued. "No, the Olympics are *not* going to happen. Mr. and Mrs. Schumacher *thought* they had their daughter in a safe environment. They were wrong.

Yes, Elizabeth has her attention on other things now – like charges of drug possession and intent to deal. Over a dozen other teen-agers in that neighborhood have their attention on 'other things' too.

"Within weeks of my Special Task Force Bill being enacted, our Pennsylvania law enforcement officials have already nailed their first low-life drug dealer in Mt.

Ephraim, New Jersey. And this dealer had his men processing cocaine for distribution to the state of Iowa!"

Carvey listened to the murmur prompted by that last remark.

"As your President, I will expand the Special Task Force nationwide, allowing maximum coordination between all your local agencies and the power of the federal ones. I will export the success of Pennsylvania to your state!"

Applause erupted. He raised his hands. *Now for some more preparation for my boy, Martin.*

CHAPTER SIXTY-EIGHT

14 July, Indian Gap, Pennsylvania

The supervisor running the program at the State Troopers Barracks stood at the podium in front of his audience and read through his notes for the graduation ceremony. He had the same percentage of chance for an uplifting and motivational speech as he had of his lottery ticket having the winning Power Ball number that night.

The graduates endured it.

He finally finished.

"Good luck, ladies and gentlemen!"

Martin Shurmur organized a meeting of some select recruits that he would use for the next assignment. He also wanted to introduce them to the author of The Special Task Force bill.

The group included Regional Director John Somerfield, SWAT supervisor Stan Logan, Surveillance Chief Hank Moller and Shurmur's prize hire – Juni Neco. Shurmur introduced everyone.

"Loco, these gentlemen have been assigned to your case. They're joining you on Saturday to perform surveillance on George Martinez during your meeting. Tell them what's happening and what you need."

"Thank you, Martin," said Neco, turning to the others. "The meeting is taking place in the restaurant of the . . ." He stopped mid-sentence as two more arrivals came into the room – Senator Donald Carvey and Anthony Sorvino.

"Don't let us interrupt, gentlemen!" said Carvey.

"We're just making the rounds to congratulate everyone.

Finish what you were doing and we'll just listen."

Neco maintained his social front and resumed talking. The revelation about the Deputy Attorney General had him more conflicted than ever about Shurmur. More thoughts raced through his mind as he outlined the plan for Saturday.

Why would Shurmur hire someone with my record of success for drug busts if he himself had connections to dealers?

But does he?

Is Sorvino operating independently?

Neco needed to find the next piece to the puzzle.

He finished briefing the group on what he needed. "I'm proposing to you we break out two surveillance vans for two video angles outside. For the first time since meeting Martinez, I'll wear a wire to start compiling our documentation for the bust. I also want a drug testing kit."

Carvey patiently waited for the group to finish its plan for Saturday. Then went about shaking hands and introducing himself. He asked everyone to sit down. "I want to tell everyone how impressed I am. This Task Force is only in the early stages and it sounds like you're already onto a huge case. Agent Neco, you must be *especially* busy. Now *you're* the one who looks like he can use some eye drops."

"I *have* had some long days, Senator."

Carvey rubbed his hands together. "Give me any dirt that you can, son."

Neco knew that he could not ask his boss for the privacy afforded him before. Fortunately, that was more for the Schmidt case than the one with Martinez.

"This case involves some Colombians . . ." Neco began.

"Hah!" exclaimed Shurmur. "Colombians. Senator, he's working his way into an arm of Escobar."

"Escobar? *The* Escobar? *Pablo* Escobar?" asked a wide—eyed senator.

"An *arm* of Escobar," emphasized Neco. "We don't know what kind of magnitude we're dealing with yet. But it should be big."

"Son, whether it's an arm or a leg, if you pull this one off, I may have to tab you as my running mate," said the senator, who received some polite laughter.

"On Saturday, we're going to get our first solid evidence and continue building from there," said Neco.

"Well, then what the hell am I doing holding everyone up?" said Carvey. "Please go home, get some rest and be fresh for Saturday."

Everyone started filing out when they heard a loud thud behind them.

They all turned to see Senator Carvey laying on the floor.

Shurmur darted back and got on one knee to help the senator up. "Are you all right? Oh, my god! Your nose is bleeding!"

"I'm fine, Martin. A little embarrassed, but other than that, I'm fine."

"What happened?" asked Shurmur.

Carvey grabbed a handkerchief out of his jacket pocket and placed it on his nose. "Aww, it's silly. I was looking out the window, and well, like I said, it's silly . . . I forgot where I was standing and turned right into the table. Then I stumbled and flopped right to the floor. I banged my nose."

"Is there anything we can get you, Senator?" asked Neco.

"Yeah, some self-esteem," chuckled Carvey through his handkerchief. "Seriously, I would be grateful if you can make sure there's no press people around. If anyone gets a shot of this, it'll be plastered all over the news."

"We'll run some cover for you, if necessary, sir," said Somerfield.

Everyone began leaving the room again.

Shurmur grabbed Somerfield by the elbow.

"John," said Shurmur softly, "I know you have no background on what I've been up against with Colombians lately. But I can tell you that someone has been out there slitting the throats of any of my people who've gotten too close to a big player. One thing you'll learn about Neco, is that he's fearless. But you make it clear to him that at the slightest hint of trouble, he's to pull out. Do you understand?"

Somerfield nodded. "Understood, sir. We'll have his back."

Down the hallway, Logan caught up to Neco. "Say, Juni. Did you hear where we're supposed to report tomorrow?"

"Some building near the Philly airport, right?"

"No. There's been a revision," said Logan. "The renovations are taking longer than expected. There's room for all the other agencies except ours. So, we're in a temporary headquarters on the other side of the city."

"That sounds a little unorthodox," said Neco.

"It's more 'orthodox' than you think."

The next day, Neco met Logan at the Gloria Dei Church grounds, located on the corner of Water Street and Washington Avenue, where church officials agreed to rent some temporary space to The Special Task Force.

The Church itself had been built during the early seventeen hundreds by Scandinavian settlers. Over the centuries, skilled craftsmen had taken marble tombstones of prominent religious leaders for the church and laid them down as part of the aisle from the front entrance to the pulpit. Other tombstones were imbedded into the walls. It had become something like a Reverend's Hall of Fame.

The front of the church faced Columbus Avenue which ran along the Delaware River. A graveyard took up space between the historical structure and a new red front annex, where The Special Task Force would conduct their business.

John Somerfield, in his late fifties, stood as tall as Stan Logan with more weight around his midsection. His temples had the grayest color on his otherwise brown hair.

He assigned Neco and the others a long banquet-style table butted up against the wall where the windows overlooked the courtyard before the cemetery. Among other inadequacies, the parquet-floored room had a shortage of phones for the initial ten recruits. They had to share.

Somerfield walked over to Neco and took a seat next to him and Logan. He spoke in a condescending tone.

"So I hear you need a yacht for next week. What's the status on that?"

"Martin said he would handle it."

"Well, I just spoke with Martin and he still has no resource for you. Couldn't you just make things easier and have us get a nice sail boat?"

"Martin said he would rent one if he has to."

"Hello, Neco! Look around you. Does this look like we have the budget to go around and rent yachts?"

"It's important for me to put the finishing touches on my reputation with these people as a high-roller. A yacht will do that," said Neco.

"Yes, a yacht," said Somerfield. "Of course! Now let me see . . . this is our first day as an operational unit and we have nothing in our immediate resources . . . so let me think . . . now what can we do? How can we stop wasting time and energy on this?" Then he stood up, turned around, started walking and threw his hands in the air. "Ah! I know! Let me just go outside, squat and shit one out of my ass for you!"

Logan leaned over and whispered to Neco. "I bet the pageantry follows you wherever you go."

Neco chuckled softly, "Yeah, this is what it was like in Camden. Maybe he wants me to feel at home."

"So what about the yacht?"

"I have an ace in the hole," said Neco. "The Camden County Prosecutor's Office has one impounded. I'm sure the captain over there can be persuaded to let us use it. I'll call Martin right now, and if he's still stuck, he can put that yacht to use." His phone rang. "But first, I'll take this call outside." Neco half-jogged to the courtyard and answered the phone.

"Loco. This is George."

"Good afternoon, sir. What's up?"

"Slight change of plans, Loco. Something's come up and I have to meet you earlier. Be at the Holiday Inn at four o'clock."

"Four?" Neco knew he could not even hint at a problem with that for fear of making Martinez suspicious.

"Four o'clock will be fine." *So much for Mt. Gretna.*

He ended the call and his phone rang again. "Hello, Ron."

"Hey, Sensei. How's your day going?" said Goldbach.

"Remember how I told you I was going to race back and forth between here and Mt. Gretna tomorrow?"

"Yeah?"

"Well, that's just been made impossible."

CHAPTER SIXTY-NINE

15 July, Mt. Gretna, Pennsylvania

At the tavern known as Acropolis Now, situated in the middle of a heavily wooded neighborhood, a hostess brought Dexter Rasche out to the lounge area on the deck.

Rasche took a moment to take in the unique décor.

Holes had been sawed in the wood, allowing trees to grow through the deck. Additionally, some of the round tables and benches had been built around the trees creating an effect commensurate with the artistic reputation of the community. The elevated deck, about eight feet above the ground, had lattice-style strips of wood composing the exposed sides. That allowed beautiful, thick layers of ivy to climb up them. The deck also gave a great view through the foliage of the township's open-air theatre just off in the distance.

The hostess directed Rasche to a table where he spotted the man who invited him – Senator Donald Carvey.

With him sat another familiar person – Deputy Attorney General Anthony Sorvino.

The two men rose from their seats to greet their connection to The Special Task Force.

"Hello, Dexter," said the senator. "Thanks for coming. You know Anthony."

"Of course," said Rasche as everyone took a seat.

"I've been curious to find out the connection."

"Order what you want, son," said Sorvino, handing him a menu from the table. "It's on the government. Then we'll get down to business. We've slipped the hostess a hundred dollars to not seat anyone around us, so we can speak freely."

Minutes later, the waitress came back and took their orders. Then Carvey waited for the server to move out of earshot. Then he addressed his guest. "Dexter, there are some things coming to a head politically very soon. This is going to necessitate some changes, and I want you to be an important part of it."

"Yeah, you put out a helluva carrot over the phone yesterday. You asked what I thought of the prospect of being Neco' boss. Is something going down with Somerfield?"

"Even better. Something is going down with Martin Shurmur," said the senator.

Rasche looked at Sorvino, then back to Carvey, who continued. "Shurmur is a lame duck with this campaign finance probe."

"Really?" asked Rasche. "For a lame duck, he's acting pretty cool."

"He has to," said Carvey. "Shurmur knows the State Election Board *will* find discover his campaign finance irregularities. And he *will* have to resign. His strategy right now is to stall the Board until July 16th."

"What happens then?" asked Rasche.

"That's when the statute of limitations runs out on his offense," said Sorvino. "He'll still have to resign, but he'll avoid jail time. Or at least that what he *thinks*."

The conversation took a break as the waitress brought out their drinks. Rasche resumed after she left.

"Are you gentlemen going to blow the whistle on him before the 16th?"

"No. That would actually spoil the timing of some things," said Carvey. "I want a couple of other things to take place before he's out of the picture. That's where you and Anthony come in. As you've seen, Martin is a Neco-man, not a Rasche-man."

"Everyone knows Neco wouldn't be half as successful as he is without strings being pulled for him."

"Exactly!" said Carvey. "That's the way it is for minorities. They get favorable treatment on small business loans, there's pressure to show a certain percentage of minority hiring. And if, on top of all that, Neco is the teacher's pet, how do *you* ever have a shot at working your way up the ladder?"

"I don't! It's not a level playing field!"

"That's where we come in," said Sorvino. "In the aftermath of this investigation, Martin-boy will be forced to resign. That's a foregone conclusion. What he doesn't know is that his last act will be to appoint me as the new Attorney General and you as the new Assistant Attorney General. Because we'll be damned if he has any ideas about keeping that crazy Puerto Rican around. With Shurmur gone,

Neco will soon be out too."

"And if Shurmur doesn't?" asked Rasche.

"Then he gets his head handed to him and goes to jail for a long time," answered Carvey.

"You make it sound as if it's all wired. What do you need me for?"

Sorvino took a long sip of his beer. "Let's just say there's been some drug dealing that definitely takes priority towards the senator's presidential campaign.

In fact, one could say now, they've had priority conducive to *your* campaign."

Rasche looked confused. "*My* campaign? *What* campaign?"

"Your campaign to be State Attorney General," replied Carvey.

Rasche dropped his jaw and held out an upward palm towards the Deputy Attorney General. "But . . . Anthony will already be the incumbent . . ."

"When I'm President, I'm going to appoint Anthony to be the U. S. Attorney General. He's going to need a qualified, experienced replacement. Over the next couple of weeks, our boy Martin will be taking measures to add to your resume. Then once you're on board as Deputy A/G, all you'll have to do is help Anthony here direct the Special Task Force in the right direction to bust cases per Anthony's priorities. Everybody wins."

Rasche got a gleeful look in his eyes. "Except for Neco."

"Except for Neco," agreed Carvey. "And when that day comes, I want you to join me and Anthony in a toast with that Remy Martin cognac waiting for us. So what do you say, Dexter?"

"Let's have a toast right now!"

They all raised their glasses.

"To a level playing field!"

"To a level playing field!" repeated Sorvino and Rasche.

Off in the distance, a man sat in a tan Mustang parked on an inclined street. He put down a pair of binoculars and put back on his thick-rimmed eye-glasses. Jerry Cohen took note of what he could from three tenths of a mile away.

So, the two missing pieces of the rendezvous puzzle everyone has been trying to figure out are Senator Carvey and Deputy A/G Anthony Sorvino. Not too shabby for 'Woody' . . .

CHAPTER SEVENTY

15 July, Elizabeth, New Jersey

That son-of-a-bitch is an hour late, thought Neco.

Sandra Tomasson and Ada Hernandez sat with him at a round table in the restaurant of the Holiday Inn. Thomas Bryant bored with his role as "bodyguard" over at the bar, stepped over and joined the other three.

Waiting for Martinez did not deter the group from ordering an expensive meal, complete with appetizers.

Outside, the surveillance vans had been in position ninety minutes before the two couples arrived. Hank Moller, the surveillance chief sat at the controls in one van with John Somerfield and Stan Logan next to him.

An impatient Somerfield squirmed in the cramped quarters and pulled out his cell phone.

Inside, Tomasson watched Hernandez grab Neco' chin and turn his face towards hers. Then she planted an opened-mouth kiss on her more-than-receptive partner.

Tomasson felt compelled to comment. "Hey, there are no bad guys to perform for, people."

Neco extricated himself from Hernandez mouth to rebut. "George Martinez could walk through that door at any moment. So it is *vital* for us to remain in character."

A ringing sound interrupted the banter. Everyone started feeling around for their cell phones.

"I think it's yours, Juni," said Tomasson reaching under the tablecloth.

Neco suddenly recoiled in his chair. "Sandra, that is *not* my cell phone. And, even if it was, *you're* not the one to decide to put it on 'hold'."

"George could walk through that door any moment."

"Uh oh," Neco muttered as he hit the 'talk' button. "This is Juni."

"Hey!" said Somerfield, "How much longer are you going to have us sit out here in these stinking vans while you're in there dining on lobster and filet mignon?"

"I'm sure Martinez will be here by the time we have our dessert, sir."

"We're not waiting out here all night for nothing.

You've got one more hour."

Somerfield turned to Logan. "He's insouciant. I don't like insouciance."

"Sounds like the natives are getting restless," said Tomasson.

"Yeah, we may have to run some leftovers out to them," said Neco.

His phone rang again.

Neco sneered. "It's been sixty seconds. What the fuck does he want now?"

"Loco! This is George!"

"George!" said Neco nodding at his fellow agents.

"We've been here at the restaurant for over an hour. Where the hell *is* your ass?"

"I'm pulling into the parking lot. Come out to the restaurant entrance, right away!"

"What the fuck is going on?" asked Neco.

"Please get out to the entrance, Loco – alone, right away."

Neco shook his head and stood up. "Lots of rude callers today."

"What's going on?" asked Bryant.

"I have to go out front. Just stay here while I see what's happening. Call Somerfield and tell them George is in the lot and to be ready."

Logan elbowed his director, who was falling asleep in the passenger seat. "Sir, Neco has just stepped out from the restaurant."

"Humph . . . what?"

"It's Neco. He's just come out," repeated Logan.

"And now he's looking expectantly at a car driving up to the entrance."

"Shit! Why didn't he phone us! Is everybody ready?

Shit! He better not get in that car! Is everybody ready?"

"We're all ready, sir," said Moller.

Somerfield's heard his phone and answered. "What?"

"Martinez is pulling up out front," said Bryant. "Get ready!"

"We're ready!" replied Somerfield, looking out the window. "Don't you get in that car, Neco. Don't you get in that car." He turned to Logan. "I've been ordered to keep him safe. Now he's going to get in that car, be driven off and get killed, and then you know what happens?

I get *fired! Fired!*"

Logan kept a straight face. "Yes. And *that* would be the tragedy."

Martinez' car came to an abrupt halt six eight feet to the side of Neco under the canopy. The passenger side faced Neco with the window completely rolled down.

"Catch, Loco!" He said, flinging a package wrapped and taped in brown paper through the open window at an open—mouthed Neco.

As Neco snatched the package in mid-air, Martinez gunned the engine and sped away.

With his mission accomplished, Martinez, who abhorred carrying drugs around, expelled a deep sigh.

Neco felt the package. It felt like a bag of flour. He glanced around to see if any public stood around.

The coast is clear, he thought.

"What just happened?" demanded Somerfield.

"Somebody – I can only assume it was Martinez – threw something out their car window to Juni," said Logan. "Now he's going back into the restaurant."

Somerfield looked at Moller. "Did you get that?"

"I'll check, but I doubt it. The driver was in motion and I didn't have the angle for the shot," said Moller.

"But Juni positioned the other van perfectly to cover our blind spot."

"I'm calling him!" said the director.

Neco settled back into his chair at the dining room table.

"Where's George? asked Hernandez. "What do you have?"

His cell phone rang.

"George was here and now he's gone." He passed the package underneath the table to Tomasson. "And *you're* going to tell us what this is." Then he answered his phone while she opened up a small section of the package revealing the white powdery contents.

"Yes, Mr. Somerfield?"

"What the hell just happened out there? Was that Martinez?"

"Yes, sir. That was George."

Out of sight, on her lap, Tomasson unzipped her sizeable handbag, while Hernandez sidled her chair over to her.

"What was that he tossed at you?" asked Somerfield.

"We are determining that right now, sir. We believe it's dope. It's being tested as we speak."

From the handbag, Tomasson pulled out a test tube and a tiny spoon. She and Hernandez used their bodies to shield their furtive actions from the other diners.

Tomasson handed her colleague the test tube.

"Don't test it in the restaurant!" said Somerfield.

"Let's take it to where we're all meeting afterwards."

"We're going to know in less than a minute," assured Neco.

"Oh, Jesus Christ!' said Somerfield to Logan.

"They're testing the powder right in public."

Balancing the package on her lap, Tomasson scooped a bit of the powder and put it in the test tube. Hernandez gently poured some water in the tube while Tomasson removed a vial from her handbag. The vial contained a clear liquid, which she added to the milky white concoction.

Bryant joined the table. "What's the verdict?"

Hernandez held up the test tube just over the edge of the table and displayed the now blue contents. "George is pregnant!"

Neco spoke into the phone, "We've got a kilo of dope, sir."

"Wow! Loco! You actually got a kilo up front. That's unheard of! But I knew if anyone could pull it off, it would be you."

Neco rolled his eyes.

Logan rolled his eyes too. Behind the director.

"We'll need more than what we got on tape, but with a payment up front, you have to know we're onto something huge," said Neco. "I smell something in the range of two to three hundred to five hundred kilos."

"Well, let's not get carried away here. I mean five hundred kilos, c'mon," said Somerfield.

"Sir, I just gotten a kilo without handing over a dime. And soon, there's going to be a huge shipment delivered with no money surrendered on our end. Trust me.

This is going to be huge."

The gang inside the restaurant wrapped things up. As they made their way to the door, Bryant approached Neco. "Okay. Tomorrow *you* help *me*, Loco."

"Relax. You can count on me to do my part. Just drive me back to Camden."

The two men got into their car.

As they pulled out of the parking lot, Bryant took it upon himself to quiz his partner on the schedule for the next day.

"So what time do we meet in Camden?"

Neco did not answer. He just stared in his side view mirror.

"I knew it! You don't even know the first thing . . ."

"Turn left onto the service road," said Neco, still staring in the mirror.

"But everyone else is getting on the turnpike. Why . . ."

"Someone might be following us. A car in the parking lot pulled out behind us. Just make the left."

Bryant turned and observed Neco' reaction to his mirror.

"Now he's turning left," said Neco. "Make the second left coming up. That'll take us into town."

The two men were quiet. Bryant studied the rear view mirror.

"He's turning. It could still be a coincident."

Neco pointed up ahead. "Go up to that traffic light up ahead and make a right."

"What are we going to do? You want me to call the others?"

"There's no time for that. We're going to turn the tables on this son-of-a-bitch by ourselves."

Bryant took a deep breath and made the right turn.

Moments later, Neco pulled out his Smith and Wesson. "Yeah. We're being tailed."

"Can you tell how many are in the car?"

"Looks like one. And whoever it is, is gonna pay for this – maybe with their life."

The last turn put them in a more congested retail area consisting of small eateries and shops.

"All right," said Neco. "Here he comes. Turn left into that alley and stop the car."

"Then what?" said Bryant as he turned and began to hit the brakes.

Neco never answered. Before the car came to a complete stop, he threw open his door, jumped out and sprinted along the sidewalk back to the corner. The instant the trailing car made the left turn, Neco ran up to the driver's side window. He began yelling an put the barrel of his gun up against the glass.

"*Stop the car, ass–hole! Stop the car and g*et both fucking hands on the wheel *right now* or I'll blow your *fucking brains* out!

The driver cried out, "Juni! Don't shoot! It's me!"

Neco' rage turned into shock.

Behind the wheel and next to a half-opened window sat a terrified, trembling Jerry Cohen.

Bryant, also out of the car with his gun drawn, stood frozen in bewilderment.

"Jerry! Why the hell are you following us? You dumb ass! Are you trying to get yourself killed?"

"No. I came to tell you some important information,

Juni. Please put down the gun. You made me piss in my pants, man."

Neco lowered the gun and tucked it behind his back. His demeanor transitioned from anger to amused.

"What? Are you shitting me? Roll down the window.

Let me see."

Cohen hit the button to lower the electric window.

"Look, I told you. I pissed in my pants. Please don't tell anyone, okay, Juni?"

"Of course, Jerry," said Neco with a mischievous grin. "I won't say a word to anyone."

Bryant tucked his gun behind his back and began walking towards them, but Neco waved him to remain by their car.

"What was so important to have you risk your life?"

"I know who Opie met with in Mt. Gretna."

Neco got serious again.

"It was Senator Carvey and Deputy A/G Sorvino. I was there. I saw them."

"How the hell did you know about that? Did Ada tell you?"

"In a way. She and Sandra were acting weird back at the office – acting sneaky, chasing me away from a room they were in. Well, expert in surveillance that I am, I went into the next room and listened to them through the air duct. It seemed kind of important, so I took it upon myself to go out there and observe. I couldn't hear what they were saying, but Carvey and Sorvino were getting Opie excited about something. He kept looking more and more pleased about whatever they were talking about. I didn't have your phone number, so I figured I better tell you privately in person, I drove it here to get with you after the meeting with Martinez. I wanted to see if I could get with you and Thomas after everyone else left, but you two drove off so fast, I tried to follow you. I never dreamed you would ambush me at gunpoint. God, Juni. Look at me.

I'm a mess. You said you wouldn't tell anyone right?"

Neco did not answer. He had stopped listening after the part about Opie looking more and more pleased.

Now his mind was spinning like a centrifuge, trying to figure out what possible scenarios would spark that reaction in Rasche.

CHAPTER SEVENTY-ONE

16 July, Olde City, Philadelphia

Physically, Juni Neco drove Thomas Bryant, Ada Hernandez and Sandra Tomasson in the direction of a ritzy townhouse near the eastern end of South Street. They used a fully equipped Ford Econoline van for their purposes.

Today Bryant played the lead agent with the girl friends and Neco played his body guard.

Mentally, Neco had his thoughts in Pennsylvania.

What the hell happened out in Mt. Gretna?

This section of South Street showcased the "hip" part of Philadelphia. Business owners coordinated to create a very eclectic image. Their shops lined the street with splashy, colorful signs for boutiques and antique shops.

Some spots featured large and loud neon signs reminiscent of the fifties. Hand-painted signs on gourmet coffee houses gave a "psychedelic sixties" feel. Still others displayed replicas of the disco era from the seventies.

And South Street had no shortage of establishments trying to display a cutting-edge eighties look.

Small playhouses for the performing arts punctuated the area; and huge murals took up the sides of at least a half-a-dozen buildings.

Neco pulled off Columbus Boulevard and navigated his way up Lombard Street into the heart of Olde City until they finally arrived in the designated neighborhood near South Street.

Someone at an outdoor art show got Tomasson's attention. "Wait a minute! That artist at the end . . . the one that looks like a hippie . . . is that . . . ?"

"Oh, shit!" said Neco. "That's Ray! What the hell is Diaz doing here? He wasn't at the meeting for this."

"Maybe someone couldn't make it and he got pulled in at the last minute," said Bryant.

"We're doomed!" joked Neco, who found a parking space near the townhouse.

The two couples got out of the car and noticed other agents staked out in their play clothes.

Neco observed other guests going into the townhouse. "They look as young as the kids I collared who we're doing business with Manuel."

"They are," said Bryant. "Only they have a lot more money. Just wait until those white-folk parents of theirs find out what their sons are doing with the townhouse while they were away this week-end."

"Holding a party and introducing their dealer to new recruits," said Hernandez. "They just don't know that the dealer is a cop."

"This type of crap is almost like a silver lining for people like us," said Bryant.

"How so?" asked Neco.

"Senator Carvey fought and fought for The Special Task Force bill, but it wasn't until drugs found their way to the upper-class white kids that the legislature received enough pressure from the public to sit up and take notice."

"Are you serious?" asked Tomasson.

"I'm dead serious," asserted Bryant. "In fact, the more I look at it, we probably owe our thanks to Juni."

"Why me?"

"When you made that triple-play with the two teens dealing with Manuel, they all flipped on the other teens out in the Main Line area. You set off a chain reaction that made big headlines, and more importantly brought enough public pressure to slam dunk that vote for the bill."

"It sucks that it took that to get the bill passed," said Tomasson.

"It *is* a shame," agreed Neco.

By two o'clock, all the guests had arrived and were contained in the townhouse. Tomasson signaled through the window that the hosts and their guests had all consumed various drugs into their systems and Stan Logan closed off the street. Bryant took the hosts and some new recruits out to his van to close their deals.

Logan awaited confirmation from Hank Moller that he had all he wanted from the wire in Bryant's van. Bryant gave the trigger phrase and all hell broke loose.

Officers closed in on the van and the townhouse and began arresting everyone. As Bryant, Tomasson, Hernandez and Neco had the cuffs put on them, they overheard all the denials in full gear.

"We didn't know they were dealing drugs outside!" cried one teenager. "We were just partying!"

"This was *more* than just partying, pal," said one male officer. "Everyone's eyes are so red, it looks like you all just came in on a midnight flight from L.A."

Another girl, in tears, wailed above the other protests. "I don't do drugs! I was just invited to a party! I don't do drugs!"

Ray Diaz, still in his hippie outfit countered

"Really? I wonder why your nose was bleeding when we came in. Do you know over what period of time you have to snort cocaine before it finally wears away the mucous membrane?

Nah! You wouldn't know that. You don't do drugs."

"What am I supposed to tell my parents?" she cried.

"That you were caught freebasing cocaine," said Diaz.

"What a waste of youth," said Neco in one of the squad vans.

Hernandez sat next to him. "And when you saw Ray, you said we were doomed."

"Sometimes even a rotten infielder catches a line—drive right at him in self-defense," shrugged Neco. He checked the time on the dashboard. He had plenty of time to wrap this up, go home for dinner and arrive at the dojo in time for their regular session.

Early in the evening, Neco came from the locker room of the Levittown dojo, dressed in his black gi. When he entered the training room, he was less than pleased with what he saw.

His four prize students were already sparring with each other—a huge no-no.

Goldbach spotted their sensei first.

White Lightning quickly withdrew from within arm's reach of White Sam and yelled for everyone to cease and desist on the fight. Mateo Meza and Black Sam lowered their arms. The four of them looked like guilty little children caught having a pillow fight by their father.

The father spoke.

"Who's going to explain to me what the hell was just going on here?"

Goldbach took a couple of steps forward. "Sensei, it's not what you think. This wasn't horseplay."

Neco crossed his arms. "I'm listening."

Goldbach continued. "We were trying out a new drill for if you have to fight in a riot. You know, you're fighting someone in a crowd. And all of a sudden, you get attacked from behind. You would have to switch off to another opponent without missing a beat, right? So, we paired off started to fight. The rule was that your fight had to stay within six feet of the other fight. And whenever you made contact with one of the other people fighting, you had to switch off and fight that guy. And the guy you were fighting had to attack the man you just stopped fighting with."

Meza chimed in. "It's like an advanced version of Shark Attack. We could demonstrate it for you."

White Sam and Black Sam winced at that last sentence.

They did not know the exact reaction it would evoke from their sensei. But they knew it was not going to be pleasant.

"So," began Neco. "You gentlemen want to know how to better fight in a crowd. That's good. We'll do two new things tonight. And clearly there's no need for running and stretching tonight, so," Then he clapped his hands.

"everyone line up!"

His pupils exchanged confused looks with each other.

"No running and stretching first?" asked White Sam.

"You heard me! Everyone line up!"

The four of them took their usual lateral positions, about five feet apart, and braced themselves.

Neco positioned himself in front of Goldbach, making a fist one inch from his student's abdomen.

"Tonight, I've just decided to teach you how to fight when your opponent is right in front of you and you don't have room to throw jabs, crosses and uppercuts."

From that starting point, he hammered the fist into Goldbach's stomach.

"Gunghh!" White Lightning stumbled backwards across the room and fell on his buttocks.

"*That's* for your new 'drill'. Now get back up on your feet, get back here and start breathing properly!"

Before Goldbach got back up on his feet, Neco swung his foot at White Sam and lodged the tip of his foot under White Sam's rib cage. The student let out a yelp of pain as the force of the blow lifted him up backwards ass over head. White Sam came down in a heap.

"That's for *encouraging* him."

Neco went down the line, back and forth.

Neco gave his next ruling from the Sensei High Court. "Okay! Positions for Shark Attack! Ron is the swimmer!"

Grim smiles came to the mouths of the other students.

White Lightning put his hands on his hips, looked to the heavens and walked to the center of the mat.

Neco assigned numbers to the trio surrounding Goldbach and began barking out a random sequence for the numbers.

But he found his mind wandering back to Cohen's revelations.

Willie Greenwood delivered drugs to Sorvino. Sorvino is in bed with Carvey. What's the picture being formed?

An Arnie Schmidt memory resurfaced.

Me, I served in Nam.

I have an old buddy, now in government, who asked if I could do a little drug running for him.

Then one with Carvey.

I received my Purple Heart for action when I was serving in Vietnam.

Then more memories with Carvey mixed with ones from Olde City yesterday.

You look like you had a late night on the campaign trail, Senator.

Oh, you mean my eyes . . . yes! It was a late night. You mean my eye drops didn't get all the red out?

"Everyone's eyes are so red it looks like you all just came in on a midnight flight from LA."

Senator! Are you all right? Holy Cow! Your nose is bleeding!

Do you know over what period of time you have to snort cocaine before it finally wears away the mucous membrane?

It all fit.

Senator Carvey is a user!

Then he stopped calling random numbers.

The four students turned around to see him gazing off into space.

"Sensei" asked Goldbach, "What's happening?"

Neco realized the cocaine potentially involved something worse than just the Senator's habit – something far worse. Another link existed right under his nose. *I'm going to need Gordo again!*

CHAPTER SEVENTY-TWO

Harrisburg, Pennsylvania

Martin Shurmur sat behind his desk with the speaker phone on. "Agent Owens. Thanks for taking my call."

"Yes, Mr. Shurmur. We're still on for this afternoon, right?"

"Yeah, that's what I'm calling about, Mr. Owens. I have to apologize, but something's just come on my plate.

I have to finish coordinating with the Camden County Prosecutor's Office on preparations on a yacht for that big case I told you about. It's going to tie me up for at least the next several days. I would like to call you back at the end of the week and reschedule."

"All right, Mr. Shurmur. *I'll* call *you* on Friday," said Owens.

Shurmur leaned back. *Phase I done. Phase II underway.*

His secretary's voice came over the intercom. "Mr. Shurmur, I have Senator Carvey on the line."

"Thank you, Mary." Shurmur hit the button. "Good morning, Senator. How can I help you?"

"Good morning, Martin. What do you have cooking today?"

"Some show prep for tomorrow. Neco is taking his next step on the big cocaine shipment. Why do you ask?"

"We need to have a talk today."

"Sounds serious," said Shurmur.

"It's important, Martin. I want to see you this morning before you get all submersed in your work."

"Senator, I'm really swamped today."

"Martin, you need to get with me this morning or you won't like what happens."

Shurmur got a sinking feeling in his gut. "Where?"

Shurmur spotted Senator Carvey sitting on a bench near a fountain several blocks away from Strawberry Square.

"Have a seat, Martin."

Shurmur came to a stop and folded his arms across his chest. "I'd rather stand."

"Suit yourself," said Carvey. "I'll stand too. Let me cut right to the chase. Your bid for the governorship is dead."

"Old news.'

"Your term as A/G is on life support."

"What makes you think you have a finger on the pulse of that?"

"I just do," replied Carvey. "Now it's just a matter of how you want to go out – with a resignation or a jail cell."

That remark unfolded Shurmur's arms.

"I know what you're up to with the stall tactics, Martin. You must have been like a little kid on Christmas Eve last night."

Shurmur's eyes widened.

"I can picture it. You were staying up late, waiting for Santa Claus to come down the chimney with your toys.

Only Santa Claus came in the form of midnight. And the toys were the statute of limitations running out on your illegal campaign financing."

Shurmur could barely get out his question. "How . . . how did you know?"

"Now you're just putting off Owens as long as you can to create a resignation on your terms."

"What do you want, Senator?"

"Before you're imminent departure, there are some things I need done to seal my presidential run. Before you resign, you will appoint Anthony to be your successor as someone who had nothing to do with your financial irregularities. Along with that, you will make sure that David Rasche is appointed to be his deputy."

"What have I missed here, Donald? Haven't we been helping each other all these years?"

"Don't confuse intensity with hostility, Martin.

We've been very good for each other. But you've fallen out of alignment with me lately . . ."

"What are you talking about? Is this about Neco being hired?"

". . . and the expiration date on your usefulness is fast approaching with this investigation. So this is going to get done next week. We'll be in contact again before that."

Shurmur looked off to the side, but perceived nothing except the realization dawning on him. "It was *you*! *You g*ave the anonymous tip to the State Election Bureau!"

"I always looked the other way for you on those video games, Martin. But, now you've crossed me. I told you not to hire Neco."

"Anything else?"

"Yes," said Carvey, "I can see your mental hamster running around in that wheel in your head. But, don't even think of crossing me on this. Remember, I used to be a criminal prosecutor too. Don't think you can play me like you're playing Owens. You still have crimes for which the statute of limitations is nowhere near running out."

"I don't know what you're talking about," said Shurmur.

"If you don't comply with my demands, you will be led away in hand-cuffs for mail fraud."

"Mail fraud? What the hell are you talking about?

I've never committed . . ." His voice trailed off with his second major realization of the morning.

"That's right," grinned Carvey. "Most of your illicit funds were sent through the mail. Dozens of them. That's enough counts to give a man in his fifties, the equivalent of a life sentence. So just do what you're told or else . . ."

The senator made a forlorn face and held up his wrists as if in cuffs.

CHAPTER SEVENTY-THREE

South Philadelphia

Neco sat at his "desk" – the long banquet table along the wall—in the Gloria Dei annex as he briefed Goldbach on the phone. "When I came home last night,
Sandy was there in bed."
"How is she doing?" asked Goldbach.
"She's on the 'up' part of her roller-coaster ride.
Of course, 'up' in her case doesn't mean happy. It only means not drinking. At least she's calmer."
"What changed?"
"Her sister has been out of town on vacation. Sandy definitely does better when she's not with her," said Neco. "I made her and Petey some breakfast. Then we all went out to the lake. It's not Puerto Rico, but it has a stabilizing effect on her. She has another appointment with Koblenzer today."
"I hope she can stay off the sauce."
"Since I'm done with Indian Gap, I'll be home more.
That should help. And I'm going to get word to Koblenzer about the sister."
"Is she okay about what happened with the women."
"I tried to apologize and explain everything, but let's just say it's dormant again for now."
"And what about the senator and his underlings?"

"Between the family and what I have to do for the Escobar case today, I can't invest any more time on what you told me . . ." Neco heard the call-waiting beep from his phone. "Hey, I got another call coming in. Let me go."

"Later."

"This is Juni."

He heard a Hispanic voice that he could not recognize.

"Good afternoon, Mr. Neco. Or may I call you, Loco?"

"Who is this?"

"This is Pablo Escobar! Are you in a position where we can talk?" Escobar heard no answer. "Hello? Are you there?"

"Yes. Yes, I'm here. I'm here and we can talk. I'm just surprised. I wasn't expecting a personal call from you."

"Mr. Neco . . ."

"Call me Loco."

"Loco, did you find the kilo to your satisfaction?"

"I certainly did. The kilo was very nice, notwithstanding the unceremonious delivery," said Neco, instinctively wondering if he could find a tape-recorder.

"What do you mean?"

"You've heard of a drive-by shooting?"

"Yes?"

"Well, this was a drive-by crack toss.'

Escobar let out a slight chuckle. "George hates to have weight in his possession, even his own. And I have seen George throw. He throws like a woman."

"*That* is an insult to women!" Cracked Neco.

The drug lord laughed harder. "I like you, Loco. You must fly out on my private jet to Colombia for an extended stay sometime. You will be treated like royalty."

"Yeah, George tells me it's like Bitchville out there."

"I am El Presidente of Bitchville!" Proclaimed Escobar.

"We can arrange for a celebration sometimes afterwards," said Neco.

"Which brings me to the purpose of my call. When I commit to something, I like to act fast, Loco. I have a sizeable shipment ready to go and I can have it to your people on the 24th of this month. When George gets with you for your next meeting I want him to have all the information you need to have your people be ready."

God, I have to get him to go through all this again with a phone tap. "Simply have George bring a copy of the bill of lading. Then have him tell me in what form they are arriving. For instance, if it's Bible's, I want to know how many layers deep the real ones go before we see the fake ones stuffed with your coke. I want to know so I can make the 'random' inspections look convincing."

"Done," acknowledged Escobar, "I am ordering my people to get the shipment to the docks today. As I have said, it will arrive on the 24th. You will be ready?"

"I'll make a couple of calls. Can you call me again in two hours?"

"Of course, my amigo."

Neco ended the call, turned and ran towards the annex.

Stan Logan stood in the door with his arms folded.

"What put a fire under your ass?"

"Where's Hank Moller?"

Two hours later, John Somerfield huddled in the annex with his surveillance specialist Hank Moller, Stan Logan and Juni Neco. Moller set up Neco' cell phone calls to be forwarded to a land line in the office.

They all stared at the phone like desperate salesmen waiting for their prospects to call back.

Finally it rang.

"This is Juni."

"Que pasa, Loco! What's happening, my man?"

Neco nodded to everyone, confirming the caller's identity. He pointed to a couple of other agents, working on the other side of the room, who got the message and stopped their activities.

"Is this Mr. Escobar? I'm sorry, you did say to call you Pablo."

Moller gave a thumbs up. He loved Neco' attention to detail – making sure to get the full name on tape.

"It is I! Did you reach your people?"

"Yes, sir. If you get that shipment of cocaine out today, my people will be ready on the 24th. They'll . . ."

"Please, no details. Give those to George. That's what I pay him for. Just consider the shipment on its way and make the necessary arrangements."

"Yes sir, Pablo."

Neco accepted high fives from his colleagues. "He wouldn't let me give him the details. We'll get those on the yacht. I *will* make George talk to me about that."

CHAPTER SEVENTY-FOUR

18 July, Penns Landing, Philadelphia

The Camden County Prosecutor's Office arranged for the yacht from their impound lot to get a fresh coat of paint and a new finish for all the wood.

Stan Logan privately ordered the painters to write "U.S.S. Loco" on the back – just to piss off Captain Blake.

Which it did.

They brought the vessel to an exclusive yacht club north of Philadelphia. It looked great with the rays of the sun bouncing off the glistening, inviting Delaware River. The lead cast for this performance included Thomas Bryant, reprising his role as bodyguard and the two hottest women in the local law-enforcement ranks—Ada Hernandez and Sandra Tomasson. They dressed in white halter tops and hot pants which only added to the tease of the skimpy swim suits underneath.

Supporting cast members took positions on board to operate the yacht and cater the affair.

Hank Moller had the cabin rigged with multiple hidden microphones and cameras.

Neco studied the "catering staff" composed of two men from the DEA, who began filling the heating trays with hors d'oervres, under which they lit the sternos. "What have got we here?" asked Neco. "It smells like seafood Neco. "And I definitely detect the aroma of garlic."

One of agents answered with a playful flair. "Today, sir, we have peppercorn encrusted ahi tuna with sun-dried tomato in a rich sauce of crushed garlic, egg yolks, lemon juice and olive oil. Plus another entrée, which I'm sure someone of your fine Hispanic descent will appreciate." He lifted a lid from a tray, "Pueblo corn-crusted Pacific halibut on a sweet potato pancake topped with a tomato confit.'

"And those?" asked Neco.

"Gougere Quattro Fromage – a crispy golden pastry filled with a creamy blend of four different cheeses."

Neco grabbed one and took a bite. The delicacy had just the right amount of gooeyness as it stretched from Neco' mouth back to the pastry. "Mmm. Like the ultimate deep-fried mozzarella stick."

Before he could finish telling the menu, a voice from the agent operating the helm interrupted him.

Looking through binoculars, he yelled out to everyone.

"I got our boy driving into the parking lot! He's got two babes and his bodyguard. Everyone get their game faces on!"

Neco had someone activate the sound system with some soft rock. Then he climbed down to the dock and walked into the club to have Martinez and his party admitted.

He spoke in a loud voice to the "receptionist" as he his arm and alternately pointed to Martinez and his body guard. "Let everyone in except those two big sons-of-a—bitches!"

The corpulent drug dealer laughed. "Oh no you don't,

Loco! I didn't drive over an hour-and-a-half to be stranded with another man!"

"Okay," Neco told the receptionist. "Let the big guys in too."

George introduced him to his two dates – two Hispanic beauties in tube tops and mini-skirts over their bikinis.

Neco already knew the body guard.

He then directed them to join his people on the U.S.S. Loco.

The two women stepped on first. Then the bodyguard surreptitiously "spotted" his employer from behind, placing his strong hands and muscular arms several inches below the butt of Martinez to ensure a safe boarding.

Neco, still on the dock, concealed a smile under his hand and watched with curious amusement as he wondered if the yacht would tilt to one side as Martinez climbed aboard. *That fat bastard will probably capsize my boat!*

The U.S.S. Loco did not give.

One by one, all the passengers followed the lead of the crew and donned their polarized sun-glasses.

With everyone on board, Neco gave a tour of the vessel as the anchor was pulled up and heavy, braided nylon ropes were untied from the dock.

The captain took a course going south.

Neco walked everyone into a spacious cabin area.

"George, after everyone's enjoyed the cruise for a while, you and I will have some privacy in here."

"Sounds good," said Martinez.

From there everyone went outside the cabin, found some seats and let an attendant take their orders for food and drinks.

All the guests settled in. While the men dug in, their dates stripped down to their bikinis.

Neco doffed their shirts in anticipation of a treat additional to the delicious fare.

As the host and his guests conversed and ate, the women took turns massaging their respective men with sun—tan lotion.

"How is everything, sir?" asked Neco.

"Loco, if your other people operate with half the quality of your cruise personnel, we're going to have a long and prosperous relationship."

"Thank you, sir," said Neco. "Eat to your heart's content and then we'll get down to business."

The two men finished eating and then massaged their ladies between sips of their beverages.

Eventually the two men climbed down into the privacy of the cabin. Attendants brought the females lounge chairs so that they could sunbathe.

Neco casually directed Martinez to take a seat on the couch. It was one of the seats that would provide the best position for the hidden cameras and microphones.

Martinez obliviously complied.

The host asked, "So, what did you tell your wife, Mrs.

Martinez you were doing today?"

"The wife thinks I'm visiting a client in Horsham."

"She sounds very understanding. But enough bullshit.

What have you got for me?"

Martinez reached into his back pocket and pulled out a slip of paper. Here's a copy of the bill of lading." He handed it to his colleague. "That also has the ship identification and arrival time written down."

Neco needed more incriminating statements. He read the slip aloud. Then added to the audio and video documentation. "Very good, George. It says 'ten crates of religious scriptures'."

"That refers to the Bibles I told you about back at the Moshulu."

"Ah yes, 'The Good Book', indeed," smiled Neco.

"How many kilos does ten crates hold?"

"That's tough to say. Whatever's left minus the twelve layers of real Bibles."

"Twelve layers?"

"Yeah, six layers on the top and six layers on the bottom. Sometimes in the process of shipping, crates get turned upside down."

"You have to hand it to Pablo Escobar when it comes to the details of arranging a shipment for his cocaine," said Neco. "And speaking of details . . . I get my ten percent of the shipment. So that means one of the crates goes right into my moving van."

"That's right," nodded Martinez.

"The shipment arrives around four o'clock. I don't want to hang around too much earlier than that. One of my men on the inside will call me with updates on the arrival and when it will be ready to be taken to the loading dock."

Neco reached for a pen and a pad of paper, which he handed to Martinez. "Write this down."

Martinez began taking notes.

"I want us in the same car for this,' said Neco,

"so you'll park your car somewhere near the intersection of Tulip Street and Allegheny Avenue. I'll pick you up there at two-thirty. Have your boys there in their own cargo van. My van will already be at the loading dock."

"Hold up a second. Let me catch up."

Neco waited for about thirty seconds. "When we get the word from my man on the inside of the arrival time, we'll wait another hour, until I get a second call indicating everything has passed through and is making its way to the loading dock. Then we'll go and wait outside Terminal D – the one with the old set of railroad tracks running through the gate. Your moving van will be parked about fifty feet in front of us."

"Hold up one more time . . ."

"Once my van is loaded up, my people will drive out of the gate and park right next to yours. Then your two men will switch vans with my men. Then we drive back to Allegheny and I take out my crate. You can take the van with the cocaine wherever you want and we can switch back vans the next day."

Then Martinez provided an unexpected bonus. He folded up the paper and placed it in his Hawaiian shirt pocket.

"I'll put this with my other val docs at home."

"What the hell are 'val docs'?" asked Neco.

"Val docs are valuable documents. You know, important papers. Miami and New York will still be sending stuff up here, as needed. So, Escobar gave me all the contacts for those locations and the needed bank account numbers. Plus there's names of competitors and outright enemies tortured out of people before they were killed. Like I said – val docs."

Neco kept tempering his enthusiasm. *The prize just keeps getting better and better.*

They wrapped up the business portion of the cruise and Neco had the captain reverse course back to the club.

Then he joined the others for dessert – another favorite for Neco: a rich, smooth flan. Finally, the guests were given their selection of some dessert cordials to sip for the rest of the cruise.

The captain brought the yacht back to its dock and everyone said their good-byes.

Afterwards, Moller played the recording in the cabin for all the agents to hear.

"The next best thing to a sexual orgasm is getting a truly incriminating recording. Juni got everything but his jock strap size. This is the type of tape that gives me what I call a 'recorgasm'."

Hernandez declared, "We have *got* to get you a girl friend."

Neco' phone rang.

"Let me get this one," said Neco, who stepped outside the cabin and answered his phone.

"Juni, Gordo here."

"Hello, Gordo."

"How's it going with George?"

"Funny you should ask. We just recorded all the details for a shipment next week. We're coming down the stretch. It's time to finalize your exit strategy for the Witness Protection program."

"Yeah, my family has already been relocated," said Gordo. "I want you to help me get five hundred thousand for this one. And some 'severance pay' for my guys."

"If it turns out to be as big as I think, we should be able to arrange that."

"And I want a house," said Gordo. "How much do you think is being shipped?"

"My gut tells me Escobar is sending at least five hundred kilos."

"Then I want a really *big* house."

"Yeah, yeah. Do you have that information I want on Willie Greenwood? He's suddenly become even more important than I thought."

"I'm gonna need another day or two."

CHAPTER SEVENTY-FIVE

20 July, Deptford, New Jersey

Sal unlocked the door to Bally's and went about performing the duties on the opening checklist. He finished the last step – turning on the music – and greeted the first member to walk through the door. Juni Neco.

"So has anybody found out anything about Cathy yet?" asked Neco, handing over his membership card.

"No, Juni," said Sal, taking the card and swiping it.

He saw all of Neco' contact information come up on the computer screen including verification of the membership as current. "We've tried to think positively and envision her back here, but now we've assumed the worst. We're looking for someone to take her place." He pointed to the "Now Hiring" sign on the front desk.

"That's a shame. My prayers go out to her family.

And I sure hope the police catch the son-of-a-bitch responsible for this. Because if *I* ever run into him, I will beat the living shit out of him!" He paused to take a deep breath and compose himself. "Is the TV remote back there?"

Neco picked out a Precor cardiovascular exercise machine and set the timer for two hours. As he had privately predicted, the TV monitors hung from the ceiling were all on morning talk shows, which did not interest Neco. With the remote, he hit the buttons that would put ESPN on the screen in front of his machine. Out of respect for any other members that might come in, he kept the volume on "mute" with the "closed caption" selection on. The work-out could now start.

As luck had it, the program was just beginning to show Phillies baseball highlights.

Moments later, another member climbed onto the adjacent machine. Neco did not recognize him. This was rare.

While he did keep to himself during stretching and weight training, he was more open to casual conversation while doing the cardiovascular portion of his work-out. As he result, he knew a lot of fellow members on a first-name basis. Even rarer was this man had Hispanic features.

Neco was sure he knew all the other Hispanics that came in during the morning time.

"Did they win last night?" asked the stranger.

"Yeah. They beat the Reds in Cinncinnati, 9-4", said Neco looking back up at the screen.

"That must make you happy."

"Nah. The Phillies suck! They won't even make the play-offs this year."

"Sorry to hear it. But good morning anyway, sir," said the Hispanic man.

"Good morning," replied Neco.

The man extended his hand. As Neco reached out to shake it, he noticed a lengthy scar on the forearm.

"Looks like you've had a nasty mishap with a knife."

"That's right. I had a little disagreement with a hoodlum who wanted my wallet. I didn't think he should have it. How did you know?"

"I know a little something about knives," said Neco.

"My name is Carlos Jimenez."

"I'm Juni. I haven't seen you around here."

"I've only been a member for a short while," said the man, as he started his machine. "How is it you know about knives?"

"I grew up in the setting for West Side Story. I was a Shark."

"Jimenez" chuckled. "I'm glad I wasn't a Jet back then."

"Damn," remarked Neco, "You've got another one on the other arm! How many times have people tried to rob you?"

"I've lived in some rough neighborhoods too."

Neco feigned a suspicious look on his face, "Let see those legs, Carlos. Let's see what *else* you've had going on."

"Don't worry. The ones on the arms are all I've got.
It was that same incident."

"Did the bastard get your wallet?" asked Neco.

"No," said his new acquaintance with a straight face.

The subject needed to be changed.

"So what does the ex-Shark do now?"

"I'm in the health care industry," said Neco.

"What's your specialty?"

"If people don't ask me too many questions, their health doesn't suffer." Neco noticed the other man's pace slow abruptly on his machine. He broke into a grin.

"I'm just joking. One thing you're going to learn quickly about me is that I mess with people."

"Awww, don't do that. I am such a sucker. Here I am just trying to make some conversation and you go messing with my head," joked the new member.

"I apologize," said Neco. "I'm just not in the mood for a lot of conversation this morning. I've got a lot on my mind and I want to focus on my workout, maybe catch a few sports highlights." He looked back at the TV screen.

"Fine, I can respect that," said the man. "I'll just go over to the walking track."

Neco glanced back. "There's no need for that. I certainly don't want to disrupt *your* routine either."

"That's okay. It sounds like you could use some space." The man turned off his machine and stepped off of it.

Alejandro walked away trying to think of another tactic. For the next two hours he went to all the various rooms for the machines and the free weights. But he simply went through the motions. All the while he covertly took opportunities to keep an eye on the man he knew as Neco, studying for anyone who might be a friend.

But, no one had any more success engaging in lengthy conversation than he did. Alejandro watched his target keep to himself as he performed intense stretching and weight-lifting until Neco finally went back to the locker room. Alejandro did not follow him. He paced around area, pretending to go to the drinking fountain or acting as if he was staring through one of the glass walls that lined the hallway to watch a game of racquet ball. All the while he kept thinking about what he might do when Neco emerged from the locker room to leave the club.

Alejandro quickly dismissed the idea of going out to his car to prepare to follow Neco from a distance. If he thought that would work, he would have had it done at any of those earlier meetings with Martinez. But Alejandro had the man called Neco pegged as too smart for that.

Trying to tail him would be an act of desperation. There was still time.

But what? Run into him again here tomorrow, and see if he could make Neco lower his guard and take a conversation further? Perhaps tomorrow he could observe where Neco's locker was, come back and break into it for his driver's license? That could risk a witness coming in at any time. Too many potential complications with that.

The hit man tried to stay focused through his growing frustration. *The shipment is arriving within days. I don't have time for another dead-end. There must be a chink in this man's protective armor!* Twenty minutes later, he watched his man go out the front door and wave good-bye to Sal, who was swiping a membership card to admit someone else to the club. Sal waved back and told Neco to have a nice day.

A sinister smile ran across Alejandro's face. *Of course!*

CHAPTER SEVENTY-SIX

West Philadelphia

That evening in a seedy row home on Sansom Street,
Willie Greenwood heard his doorbell ring. He did not expect anyone,
so he opened up a drawer and took out a pistol. He stood in front of the
solid wood front door.

"Who is it?"

"Pizza delivery!"

Greenwood sneaked over to the side of a window overlooking the
street. He saw a car with a magnetic sign on its roof. It read "Pine Street
Pizza". A man with a baseball hat on stood on the stoop held a pizza box
up to the side of his face in his left hand.

"I didn't order a pizza! You've got the wrong address!"

The voice on the other side became tentative. "The receipt says '5410
Sansom Street! That's here, right?"

"I said I didn't *order* a pizza. Now fuck off!"

The man persisted. "The name says 'Willie Greenwood'."

Greenwood lunged towards the door and whipped it open, raising his
gun. "I said fuck ughh . . . !"

Greenwood felt a forearm shoved into his throat. With a smooth
lightning fast motion, the 'delivery man' kicked the door shut and smashed
his prey against a foyer wall. A hand went over his mouth as he finally got
a clear look at the face of the man breaking in. The weasely drug dealer
tried to let out scream. But the hand over his mouth quickly transitioned to
the other hand, which had drawn a knife and jammed it between his teeth.

"Willie, I need you to be a gracious host," said Neco.

Greenwood's eyes bulged and he whimpered as his teeth chattered against the blade in his mouth.

"I'm not here to hurt you, Willie. I just need to talk to you like I did last time."

Greenwood slowly talked around the blade with slurred words. "Lath . . . time . . . yuh . . . thwoo . . . me . . . in . . . fwunt . . . of . . . a . . . cab!"

"Are we in the street? No," said Neco. "Now I'm going to remove my forearm and then my knife. And then we're going over to the living room for a nice chat.

You'll help me and I won't take you out to the street and get you a cab. Does that sound like a fair deal?"

The terrified hood looked like he wanted to cry. He managed to nod his head as his teeth chattered on the blade again.

Neco removed his forearm, withdrew the knife and grabbed Greenwood by the nape of the neck, pulling him to a tattered couch. He shoved him on one of the cushions and began the interrogation. "Where do you drop along the Main Line?"

"What?"

"C'mon, Willie. I know you've got some business out there in the towns with those rich white teenagers. Where do you drop?"

"All along Lancaster Avenue, man? Why?"

"Who handles the drop?"

"Now what? Why do you want to know that? Schmidt had no contacts out there."

"I'm actually here to help you, Willie. I want to talk to someone who knows your competition out there. Then I'm taking them out."

"Well, hell, I can tell you that."

"Then talk."

Within an hour, Neco drove along Lancaster Avenue in Ardmore. He parked his car on a side street and observed a corner with a closed convenience store. Then he spotted the dumpster Greenwood described along the unlit side of the building. Neco took a position behind the dumpster and waited.

Forty minutes later, a young Hispanic man, walked up with a small taped-up, brown paper package. He stood next to the dumpster when he felt a sharp blow to the back of his neck and suddenly everything went completely black.

When he came to, he found himself face down behind the dumpster. He twisted his head slightly and became aware of the heel of a shoe pressing down on his neck.

"You must be Juan," said Neco, who noticed his quarry attempting to turn his head. "Don't look up!"

"What happened? Who are you?" said the dazed young man. He felt the weight of the heel increase on his neck."

"Don't talk so loud, Juan."

Juan whispered. "What do you want? My weight? Take it!"

"The only weight you should be concerned with is the weight of my foot on your neck," said Neco. "I have other issues with you."

"What issues? What do you want?"

"I'm looking to work the kids in Nazereth. And the word is out that you've started poking your nose out there this summer. Now if that's true, you and I are going to have issues."

Juan tried to pick his head up to respond, only to have Neco increase the pressure. "Oww! I'm not working the area, man. The kids are finding me in Philly and I meet them out here!"

"Don't fuck with me, Juan," said Neco, pulling out his 007 and snapping it open.

Juan saw a silver blade being pressed against his ear and his whole body began shaking. "Damn it! I'm not fucking with you, man! I just started working the area last month when I heard demand starting up. Enough kids were finding me in the city to make it worth my while to come out here."

"I don't buy it, Juan," said Neco, pressing the flat of the blade harder. "Why did kids come from out of the woodwork to find you?"

"They didn't come to find *me*. They came to the 69th Street Station and started asking around to other to other kids. Eventually they found some of my customers. After four or five weeks, a handful of them have become suppliers up here. That's all I know. Now let me up! My face is soaking in a puddle of some shit here!"

"Just bear with me a little more and you'll be fine.

Where do I find one of these new suppliers?"

"One of them is coming to pick up that drop tonight."

Neco slightly eased the pressure. "When's she coming?'

"Any minute if you haven't scared her off."

"Juan, you're going to hang with me until she comes.

But you have earned taking your face out of the puddle."

Neco withdrew the blade and removed his foot. "Now stand up, face the dumpster and keep your mouth shut."

Four minutes later, a white Monterey drove into the lot and parked on the side of the building with the dumpster. A skinny young teenage girl in a black t-shirt and blue jeans came out of the car and walked to the dumpster looking for her contact.

"Okay, Juan. Take a hike and don't look back or I'll be the last thing you ever see."

Juan ran like a rat scurrying from the trash as the surprised teenager watched and tried to follow.

"Not you!" said Neco, putting a hand over her mouth from behind. "You're staying with me." He pulled her into the shadows and pushed her face first against the receptacle. "I'm going to remove my hand so that you can answer some questions. I'm going to wrap my arm around your neck while we're talking. If you scream, you better make it in the form of a prayer. Because if you scream, you'll be meeting God shortly afterwards. Do you understand?"

The teen closed her eyes and rapidly nodded her head up and down.

Neco removed his hand and wrapped her neck between his bicep and forearm.

"What's going on? I didn't do anything."

Neco spoke in a loud whisper. "Juan told me all about you. Now if you want to get home safely, you'll answer some questions right now."

"What questions?"

"Who introduced you to crack in Nazereth?"

She did not answer.

"Okay, suit yourself . . ." and he applied more pressure.

"No!" Her eyes welled up.

Neco felt her shoulders trembling. "Who introduced you to crack in Nazareth?"

"A man."

"Not good enough. What's his name?"

"I don't know. He didn't tell me. He was just some old dude in sunglasses who showed up at a playing field where me and a couple of other girls were watching our boyfriends. He said he wanted to report a suspicious—looking small plastic bag – said it looked like coke—and asked us where he could find the closest police station.

We pointed him in a direction and after he walked away, we grabbed the bag. He was right. It was coke. I grabbed it and took it to my house, where we divided it up between the three of us. One of our boyfriends knew someone who knew what to do with it, and we blew through it in about three weeks. But the man in the sun-glasses wasn't a dealer. He just found it on the bleachers and we never saw him again.

We heard that West Philly was part of The Badlands, so we took the train to the 69th Street Station and roamed around looking for other teen-agers and college students to talk to until we learned of Juan."

"Tell me more about what the 'old dude' looked like?" asked Neco.

"I don't know. I only saw him the one time. He was average height, average weight. He wore a baseball cap and sun-glasses but I could still see he had hair that was turning gray. He spoke in a nervous manner. That's all I know. Please don't kill me!"

Neco released her from the choke hold and grabbed her by the scruff of her neck. His instincts told him that was all he was going to get from her. "You dodged a bullet tonight. We're done." Then he shoved the girl to her knees.

The girl picked herself up and slowly turned to confront her assailant. But he was gone.

Neco made it back to his car and turned on the engine. *I have at least one more thing to check.*

CHAPTER SEVENTY-SEVEN

22 July, Harrisburg, Pennsylvania

Martin Shurmur sat in his office with Dexter Rasche.

"Mr. Shurmur, I wanted to thank you again for the commendation at Indian Gap the other day. I've just had it framed and matted."

"You earned, Dexter. And that brings me to why I called you up here this morning. I want you involved in something big. Your assignment involves disabling the moving van to be used by Martinez' men. I want them with no way out when the arrest is happening."

Rasche took a deep breath. "You want me in on the Escobar case?"

Shurmur kept a straight face. "I think you're going to be going places. So let's show people you have what it takes to play with the big boys. Come to the meeting on Sunday night when the final strategy is worked out."

"I won't let you down, sir."

"I know. Now, you'll have to excuse me for another call."

Rasche departed and the Attorney General dialed up Villages.

"Martin, what's the story with the home address for Martinez?" asked Neco, driving north on Route 55.

"We ran his plates right away. Piece of cake. We have an address for Exton, Pennsylvania. Someone has been out there already to nail down the best directions. But our wire taps haven't produced anything of note. You've been the only one to get anything incriminating on him. At least you'll know exactly how to get there. It's an old farm house."

"Great. Martinez is sending his family out for a big shopping spree the day of the bust. So the house will be empty. We'll act on securing his 'val docs' when the set up for the bust is under control."

"Okay. Are you ready for the meeting?"

"Yes, sir. I've spent the last two days with Somerfield studying the Tioga Marina area and coordinating with the marina personnel."

"Good. I'm tied up this afternoon, so Deputy Sorvino will be running the meeting with Somerfield and finalizing all the strategy for Tioga Marina." Shurmur heard no response. "Juni, are you still there?"

"Yeah, I'm still here."

"I said Deputy Sorvino will be running the meeting with Somerfield today."

Neco gnashed his teeth. "Yes, I heard you."

Later, the Special Task Force packed the room in the annex of Gloria Dei.

Juni Neco stood and pointed to a big street map thumb-tacked to a wall in the front of the room. "Here's where George and I will be parked. About forty yards behind that is a big elevated walkway that crosses the street. The sides are a green grating with openings large enough for rifle barrels. If you wear green and lie on the walking surface, he'll never see you while we're arriving."

"John," said Sorvino, "I want nine SWAT members stationed up there."

The Regional Director and Stan Logan nodded.

Neco continued. "Across the street is an oil refinery. There are two storage towers that directly overlook where we'll be parked."

"Three SWAT members on top of each tower," said Sorvino.

"Wear white. No one will see you Neco detailed other places from where more officers could hide at ground level.

The Deputy Attorney General then got the attention of Dexter Rasche and Thomas Bryant. "Dexter, you and Thomas will be driving the van to be used at the loading dock.

When all the crates are loaded, you'll drive over to the van with Martinez' people and trade vehicles with them.

Before you leave the van, Dexter, you'll hit the kill switch under the dash board."

Rasche nodded.

Sorvino continued. "Once you've rendered the ignition useless, get out of vehicle and let Martinez' people in.

That will be Logan' signal to have his officers move in and take everyone, including Juni and Martinez." He turned to Somerfield. "John, you have something for Juni."

Somerfield reached into his jacket pocket and handed a paper to Neco. "This is a warrant to search the Martinez premises."

"Thomas, since you've never met a safe you couldn't crack, you and Juni will go out there and grab the information on Escobar's banking accounts and his other smuggling contacts. Juni, have you confirmed when the house will be empty."

"George is sending his wife and kids and mother on a big shopping spree to 'occupy' them tomorrow. He knows that Escobar will have people watching them. He also knows that if he gets caught and coughs up any information,

Escobar's people will take the family out. But the house will be empty by ten o'clock."

Sorvino shook a celebratory fist. "Perfect. Because I want this done just before the arrest. Martinez can't have anytime to alert lawyers or anyone who can make trouble for getting those papers. So bring your toys,

Thomas."

Neco looked at the clock. It read three-thirty.

He had very little time for his next private assignment today.

Sorvino dismissed The Special Task Force and Neco sped off to the northwest part of the city until he arrived at 500 Wissahickon Avenue.

The Philadelphia Veterans Administration Building closed at four-thirty and Neco had no time to waste.

He ran up the steps, marched up to the registration desk and signed the guest book for an older man in a security uniform.

"Who can help me with military records? I want information from the war in Vietnam and I'm in a hurry."

The man directed Neco to the reference section. A woman brought him binders containing the military records of those officers who served during the war for the United State Marines.

Neco poured through the pages and finally found the unit for his man – Private First Class Arnold Scott Schmidt. *At least his parents gave him the right initials.* He read further. *Got your ass!*

CHAPTER SEVENTY-EIGHT

23 July, Deptford, New Jersey

Neco arrived at Bally's in the morning and found a new face behind the front desk.

"Mr. Carlos!" said Neco. "What are you doing back there?"

"I applied for the job of personal trainer. They needed someone after that tragedy with the missing young woman. Between my resume and the fact that I could promise them some new corporate accounts, they jumped at the chance to hire me."

Neco handed the man his membership card. "Then I wish you the best with your new job."

The new employee swiped the card, studied the computer screen and smiled. "Thank you, Mr. Neco. Enjoy your work-out."

Alejandro signaled his manager to come over to the front desk.

"What's up, Carlos?"

"Good news, Sal. I know I just started, but I've just received a call from one of my corporate contacts. If I could get someone else behind the front desk, I can go have a quick meeting and maybe bring back a big check for you."

Sal's face lit up. "Really? Should I go with you?"

"Nah, I've got a tight relationship with these people.

I don't feel comfortable suddenly bringing a stranger with me. Trust me. I can handle this. Just give me the rate sheets, get me replaced behind the front desk and you'll be a happy man."

"Oh hell! Just let me finish up some tours and registration cycles. Then *I'll* watch the front desk."

"Great!" The new employee watched his supervisor disappear into his office as a member came through the door and presented his card.

"Carlos" darted out from behind the front desk and strode right past the member and out the door.

CHAPTER SEVENTY-NINE

Clayton, New Jersey

The repetitive ring of the doorbell roused Sandy Neco from her sleep.

She went downstairs, under protest, and answered the door. "Sheila! What the hell are you doing here?" Why aren't you still on vacation?"

"Vacation was cut short," said the sister. "My boyfriend and I had a big fight. I grabbed a separate flight last night. I really *need* you right now."

"What time is it?"

"A little after eight. Come out and have some breakfast with me. I have to vent."

"I ate earlier and I was getting some more rest. Let me get with you for lunch," said Sandy.

"C'mon Sandy! I've been there for you lately.

Please! Please! Please!"

"Oh for God's sake. I'll go. Just shut up! We have to get Petey to my mother's first."

The two women drove down Delsea Drive with Petey in the back seat. They had no need to pay no attention as another car passed them in the opposite direction and pulled into a gas station. The driver rolled down his window and asked for directions.

"West Clinton Street?" asked the gas station attendant. "Just keep going down until you see the church.

The second street after the church, make a right. That's West Clinton Street. You're just minutes away."

"Thanks," said Alejandro.

Escobar's right-hand man parked about ten car lengths from the address gotten off the computer. He walked down the street and noticed a house with a "For Sale" sign one lot from his destination. A gray-haired woman with a dowager's hump carried a watering can and tended to her flowers on the lawn on the opposite side of the street.

There were no cars in the driveway for the Neco residence, but he had to wait until the woman went back inside her own home before breaking into number one hundred ten.

Alejandro decided to turn the situation into his advantage. He walked across the street. "Pardon me. I'm in the market for a home, and I'm considering moving to Clayton. I see that house for sale over there. Would you tell me a little about the neighborhood?"

"Oh sure. No bother at all," said the woman. "My husband and I have been here for over thirty years. The township hasn't grown a heck of a lot, but that's what we wanted – a place without a lot of commercial development."

"How are your neighbors?" Alejandro noticed the woman instantly frown. "What's the matter?"

"I want to be honest with you," she began. "Most of the neighbors are model citizens. But *those* people . . ." And she pointed to number one hundred ten. "Those people . . . we're just not too sure about. I don't mean to discourage you, but if you like Clayton, you may want to consider a different street."

"Why would that be? What's wrong with 'those people'?"

"It's a husband and wife with a small boy. They've only been here a short time, but no one has a handle on them. Beyond the fact that we know their name is Neco, no one knows anything. Except for the kid going out to play, they pretty much keep to themselves."

"That doesn't sound like such a crime," said the Colombian.

"Well, it's funny you should mention that because we all kind of have the feeling that the husband is a drug dealer."

"What makes everyone think that?"

"He doesn't seem to have any kind of work schedule . . . just comes and goes as he pleases. He definitely does not have a nine-to-five job, if you know what I mean."

"Perhaps he owns his own business. Maybe his employees keep a standard schedule for him."

"There's more," said the woman, "It seems like every month or so he's driving some fancy new car! And when I say 'fancy', I mean *real* expensive.

And each one has the name of some different car dealer around the license plate, so we all know the cars are *not* from some lot he owns."

Alejandro looked back, hiding his frustration as the woman continued.

I hope I didn't discourage you, son. Maybe it's nothing, but I'm telling you what we all think. If you have your heart set on that house, you'll still have me as a neighbor."

"Imagine my relief."

The woman looked at her watch. "It's time for me to get inside. I have to get ready for my soaps."

The woman's departure left the street empty.

Alejandro crept around to the back of the Neco home and worked on the lock.

Down the road in the Clayton diner, Sandy finished her coffee as her sister wolfed down the rest of her fried eggs and sausage.

"Looks like you were more hungry than upset," said Sandy.

"I was," said Sheila, sopping up the rest of the egg yolk with some toast. "Now I'm thirsty."

"Then get some juice."

"No, I mean *thirsty*, as in thirsty for some adult beverages."

"Sheila, it's only nine o'clock!"

"Great! That means that Jack's is open," said the sister. "And don't give me that holier-than-thou look!

We've been out drinking in the morning before."

"I know, it's just that I promised Juni I would be home when he got back. We have to get Petey back and I don't want him to smell alcohol on my breath."

"When does he get back?"

"Probably sometime this evening."

"Then what are you worried about? We'll go out for a couple of hours, get Petey, get you showered and gargled.

There's plenty of time to keep things under control."

"I don't think that would be a good idea. I should go get Petey now."

"No, not yet! You've got to at least come and keep me a little more company. I really, really need it.

Pleeease?"

Sandy waved her hands up and down. "No, Sheila.

Stop! Now you're getting on my nerves. Look at me – my hands are trembling. I'm going home." She opened up her handbag and pulled out a small container with her prescription.

"You know what I've found effective for a case of the trembles?" asked Sheila.

"No! I'm taking these. Then I going to my mother's for Petey."

Alejandro stood in the kitchen and shook his head in disdain at the bathroom off to the left. *Brilliant architects they have here in Hicksville. Why didn't they just put the toilet at the kitchen table? People could save even more time.*

He slipped on a pair of latex gloves and flipped the lid off the kitchen trash container. It proved to not be fruitful.

The Colombian prowled through the combination dining room-living room area. He checked under cushions and found nothing beyond some loose change.

Upstairs, he went through the drawers and closets, carefully replacing everything as found. Everything only backed up what the old woman across the street divulged.

Neco, who had led George to believe he was single, definitely had a wife and kid. But George Martinez also had a family in his double life.

Downstairs, he realized he had one more room to check – the tiny den to the left of the stairs. The room had a small wastebasket with some crumpled up slips of paper in it.

Alejandro unfolded some restaurant slips, supermarket receipts and a handwritten note. It read: "Secure five hundred thousand dollars for the arms in Camden deal twenty four hours in advance."

The Colombian hit man felt resigned. Juni Neco, if not without a false identity, dealt in drugs and weapons.

He crumpled up the papers in his fist and tossed them back into the basket.

As he walked back to his car, he made a call.

"Hello?"

"George. Where are you?"

"Oh, hello, sir. I'm just dropping off my family at The Gallery Mall here in Center City. I'll spend a little time with them and then I'm going to the meeting location."

"So, no surprises?"

"No, sir. Everything is on schedule. I'll be at my destination in plenty of time."

"Fine. Call me when it's over."

Alejandro hung up and his phone rang with the call he anticipated.

"Yes, sir."

"Alejandro! Que pasa?" said Pablo Escobar. "Is everything under control? Are George and Loco ready for their moment in the sun today?"

"George has told me that everything has been worked out to the last detail. I would have to say that I am satisfied all should go as planned."

"Excellente! Then I am officially taking my attention off that and am about to start my game. I'm leaving the locker room right now."

"What game is it today?" asked Alejandro.

"I'm playing a soccer game on my personal field. Our opponent is a team of nude women. I've hired professional announcers to give play-by-play over the public address system. The stands are packed with thousands of my employees, friends and adoring public."

"Your team will be kicking soccer balls at a nude female goalie?"

"You say that as if there's something wrong with that."

"Well, I hope you can slip one through the five-hole, sir. And I don't mean a soccer ball."

"What?"

"Just some American humor. Don't worry about it.

Good luck with your game." *As if you'll need it!*

"Call me with good news later, my friend."

"I will."

Escobar hung up and handed the cell phone to his personal assistant. "What is a 'five-hole'?"

The assistant shrugged his shoulders.

The boss turned and yelled out to the other men in the locker room. "I'll give five thousand dollars to the first man to tell me what a 'five-hole' is!"

CHAPTER EIGHTY

Deptford, New Jersey

Neco found Thomas Bryant waiting for him in the Bally's lobby area when he finished his workout.

"Hey, you son-of-a-bitch!" yelled Bryant.

"Hey, dumb ass!" retorted Neco.

Sal, still behind the front desk, wondering where Carlos Jimenez disappeared, did not know how to react to this banter. He pretended not to hear it.

"Are you ready for the big day?" asked Neco.

"I came out of my momma ready," said Bryant.

The two agents went out to Neco' car where Bryant pulled out a street map of Exton along with a slip of paper showing the Martinez address.

"From here," began Bryant, "at this time of day, no rush hour, we should be there in an hour . . . even if *I* was driving. Don't go ninety-miles an hour on Route 76. That would be too crazy, even for you."

"Hand me that phone," chuckled Neco. "I'm going to bust George's balls a little. He's probably been getting calls all day from his bosses."

Martinez forced himself to smile when he answered the phone. "Hello."

"George! This is Juni! Where are you?"

"Hello, again, sir," responded Martinez, disguising the call from his family members. "Yes, as I mentioned earlier, I'm just about ready to drop off my family here in Philly. What? Yes, of course I've brought the new software program. I can't wait to show it to you. I'll see you soon."

Martinez hung up and placed his phone in one of the beverage holders between the two seats.

Yolanda shook her head. "That meeting must be important. That's the fifth call you've got today to make sure you're on time."

"Yeah, this new client can get antsy at the drop of a hat. I'll be glad when this day is over."

Martinez drove his family to a corner near The Gallery.

His wife, Yolanda, along with his son, daughter and mother could not wait to be dropped off for their big shopping spree.

Martinez double-parked and put on his flashers.

"Okay! Everyone out! Go shop til you drop!"

The words left his mouth when, all of a sudden, the family felt a jarring impact from behind. Yolanda's purse flew off her lap and hit against the dashboard, spilling some contents – lipstick, eye liner, a cell phone and a ring of keys—to the left of her feet. Her husband's cell phone came loose from the beverage holder and also landed on the floor at her feet.

Her husband slammed his fist on the steering wheel.

"What the *hell?*" He looked in his rear view mirror and saw a van with a teenager slamming his own fist into his steering wheel.

Yolanda turned to the backseat. "Is everyone all right?"

The grandmother had an arm around each of the children. "We're a little shook up, but we're okay. But George's boss will be mad if he's late for his meeting."

Martinez jumped out of his vehicle to confront the other driver as Yolanda composed herself and groped on the floor to retrieve the contents of her handbag. The grandmother rocked her body back and forth to keep the kids calm.

"What the hell are you *doing?*" bellowed Martinez. "Do you *always* run into parked cars, you dumb bastard? That's a new Lexus!"

The teenager stayed in his van and talked through the car window. "You stopped to park in an illegal space! You surprised me!"

"Are you high! I had my flashers on! They're *still* on!" Martinez then saw some other flashing lights. A police car pulled up. "Oh shit!"

The police officer came out with a clipboard holding some forms. Martinez went back to his car for the documents he knew the officer would want.

"Yolanda, reach into the glove compartment and hand me the manila envelope."

The wife looked up as she groped for the items from her purse. She paused from retrieving her things, opened the glove compartment and gave him the envelope. Then she handed him a cell phone from the floor. "Maybe you should call your boss and let him know what happened."

Martinez already felt overwrought with all the unnecessary supervision. He did not want to tolerate anymore. So he decided how to *not* invite any more such quality control nonsense.

"No. I'm only twenty minutes away from where I have to be," he said, taking the phone. "I've got plenty of time," said Martinez. "If my bosses hear about this,

I'll get ten more calls between now and the appointment.

Screw that! This is a little ding and I'm just going to get this over with."

CHAPTER EIGHTY-ONE

Clayton, New Jersey

Alejandro had some time to kill. He needed food and a good stiff drink. The hit man remembered a place up the road he had passed on the way to Neco' house.

He pulled into Jack's Tavern.

Inside the two sisters sat at the bar.

"I can't believe you talked me into coming here," giggled Sandy, sipping some Johnny Walker and waving an index finger at her companion in fake protest. "You are a b*ad* girl!"

"We're *both* bad girls!" said Sheila. "And by the way,

I don't notice you trembling anymore." Then she pointed towards the entrance of the tavern and whispered at her sister. "Look what's walking through the door, Jen – some big, brooding, sexy Hispanic. Just the way you like your men."

Alejandro walked in, a Cuban cigar already lit, and chose a bar stool one away from Sandy. He had plenty of time to drive back to Philadelphia.

Sandy whispered back to her sister, "Are you saying I should try to pick him up?"

"If you don't, *I* will."

"I don't know . . ." said Sandy, flitting a glance at the man one stool away."

Sheila nudged her sister with an elbow. "Puerto Rico.

Driftwood. Sun-tan lotion. Jumbotron."

Sandy's heart began racing.

"Your husband can't be the only one allowed to play roles. With him acting like that, you're not really married." added Sheila.

Her sister got a playful look on her face and turned to her right, as she dangled an empty glass. "Hey, tall, dark and menacing . . . buy a woman a drink?"

The killer stared back at the flirtatious woman and raised his hand to signal the man behind the bar.

"Bartender! I'll have a scotch – the good stuff, Johnny Walker Double Black! I want none of your house swill. I also want that special on the blackboard. And give these two women another of whatever they're having on me." Then he peeled off a hundred dollar bill and placed it on the bar. "I'm going to be here a while, so keep them coming."

The two sisters lit up.

"Looks like he's doing all right for himself," whispered Sheila.

The bartender brought them their beverages.

Sandy addressed the man treating them. "So, I'm Sandy. And this is my sister, Sheila. Who are we thanking for the drinks?"

"My name is Carlos," said Alejandro, feeling his prospects increasing.

"We've never seen you around before, Carlos. Are you new in town?"

"I'm just handling some business in the area."

"I'm an importer."

"What do you import?" asked Sheila.

"I distribute mostly neck-ties," Alejandro said with a straight face.

"Oooh," cooed Sandy. "Sounds like you travel a lot."

"I get around."

"Do you *fool* around?" asked Sandy.

"Ah! A woman with a gift for turning a phrase," the man said, looking down at her ring finger. "And apparently a woman with a husband. I like a woman who lives dangerously."

CHAPTER EIGHTY-TWO

Pennsylvania Turnpike

Thomas Bryant took over the wheel at a service area while Neco called his favorite Jew.

"You sound a little down," said Neco. "Are you okay?"

"I've been better."

"What happened now?" asked Neco.

"I was just made the laughing stock of the office."

"What did they do?"

"It wasn't the staff! It was the dumb-asses at the trophy shop. I ordered customized t-shirts with the words 'White Lightning' printed above a picture of me wearing my gi."

"And?"

"I put the shirt on to debut it at work. When I walked through the door, everyone looked at me and started howling."

"Why?"

"Because the shirt read 'White *Lighting*'!"

"White Lighting!" Neco repeated through his laughter. "I order you to wear it at the next training session."

"Thanks. Did you call for any other reason than to laugh at my misfortune?"

"Yeah. In your travels today, I want you to stay clear of the Port Richmond section of the city. It's going down today."

"The big job?"

"Yes," said Neco. "And I do not want you within miles of that neighborhood. Clear?"

"Oh yeah," said Goldbach. "I really don't need you and the others to beat my ass again."

"I'm serious, Ron. Just stay away until I call you."

Chapter Eighty-Three

Clayton, New Jersey

Alejandro had the sisters on their third glass of hard liquor. He decided to make his move.

"So, Sandy, if Sheila doesn't mind, maybe you and I could get out of this place."

Sandy drew a deep breath as Sheila nodded.

"We could go back to my place. It's just over on Clinton Street."

"And your husband?"

"Out! First he has business in Exton, then in Philadelphia at the Tioga Marina. That'll keep him busy all day," said Sandy.

Alejandro stopped mid-sip and slammed his glass down.

The significance of Clinton Street just sunk in. "He's *where?*"

"In Exton trying to put some bad boys away for the government. Are *you* a bad boy? You said you like a woman who lives dangerously."

"And this one *does,* honey," interjected Sheila, "She's inviting you over, and her husband's a little on the loco side, if you know what I mean."

"The *'loco side'*?" roared Alejandro.

"Don't get all bent out of shape, sweetie. That's his nickname," said Sandy giggling and making 'quotation marks' in the air. 'Loco'." Then she put a consoling hand on the arm of the man with the suddenly anxious expression on his face. "But, don't you fret now. I told you, he's away all . . . Hey! Where are you going? What did I say?"

Alejandro dialed the number of his boss as he bolted towards the door.

Pablo Escobar charged the opponent's net, prompting the roar from the standing-room-only crowd. The women made sure to offer only token resistance. He kicked a shot from a side angle that went past the "overwhelmed" goalie.

Escobar's personal assistant stood on the sidelines.

He could not hear his phone ring over the crowd and the announcer on the public address system.

"GOAL, GOAL, GOAL, GOAL, GOAL, GOAL, GOOOOOAL . . . PABLOOO ESCOBARRRRR!"

Escobar bowed and milked the applause.

Alejandro furiously cursed as he got into his car and waited for the voice mail to activate. "Pablo! This is Alejandro! I've just learned Neco is an agent! This whole arrangement is a sting operation. And it sounds as if he knows about the documents you gave George! I'm calling George and then I'm rounding up some people to secure the documents and eliminate Neco!"

Then he dialed the number for Martinez.

The cell phone for George Martinez rang from inside a woman's purse lying on the bench of a fitting room of a clothing store inside The Gallery. About a dozen feet away, Yolanda Martinez modeled a dress for her mother-in—law. "So what do you think about this one?" she asked.

"So far, I like the second one the best," said the mother-in-law. "But, did you see that emerald one over there?"

"Oooh, no. Let me get that one to try on," said Yolanda.

"Is that your phone ringing back in the dressing room?"

"Whatever it is, it can wait. Hand me that emerald one. I think I saw some shoes nearby that would match up great with it."

Alejandro sped down Delsea Drive with his phone pressed up to his ear. *Pick up, you dumb bastard!* He cursed as a voice mail came on for Martinez. "George!

This is Alejandro! Neco *is an agent!* Do *not* go to Port Richmond! Call me *immediately!*"

The Colombian hit man pulled into a gas station.

An attendant came over. "Fill 'er up?"

"No! Tell me the fastest way to get to West Chester County from here!"

"Go up the road a little further until you see Route 322 West. Make a left and stay on that until you cross the Commodore Barry Bridge. Get back on 322 and that will take you all the way to West Chester. Where in . . . ?"

Alejandro peeled out of the lot and raced north. He knew if those papers fell into the wrong hands, there would be no place to hide from Escobar's brand of justice.

He punched in another number.

"Yes?"

"It's me! We have an emergency. Round up every man you can within the next fifteen minutes. Have them grab their weapons and drive out to Exton and meet me at this address!"

In Exton, Neco and Bryant followed a long dirt driveway back to the farmhouse.

"My god!" said Bryant. "These homes are really spread out around here. You can't even see your neighbors."

"It's not like Clayton," said Neco.

They walked up the front steps and Bryant, carrying a valise for his tools tried to turn the knob on the front door. "Let me just jimmy this lock."

"Please," said Neco. "Allow me."

Neco planted his feet and then kicked the door open with one blow.

"Yeah," said Bryant. "That's a valid way too."

The two agents divided the house by floors – Bryant took the upstairs and Neco did the ground level first floor. They looked behind pictures for wall safes and tapped the floors for hidden removable panels.

Nothing turned up. That left only the half—underground, half-above ground lower floor.

They saw it. A large steel combination safe sat next to a half-dozen propane gas tanks.

Bryant reached into his valise and pulled out a high—powered drill with a long diamond-tipped bit. "Let me just find an electrical outlet and I'll crack this baby open.

How about if you stand look-out upstairs?"

"Let me know when you're done," said Neco going up the stairs.

Bryant plugged in his drill and placed some goggles over his eyes.

He softly voiced his progress. "That's one hole . . . That's two holes . . . and three . . ." Then Bryant heard his partner call.

"Thomas! We've got company!"

Bryant took off the goggles, sprinted upstairs and took a position opposite from Neco at a window overlooking the front of the property. "Who the hell knew we were out here?"

"At least ten guys with guns," said Neco.

"They're spreading out around the house."

"Man, we have to hold them off until help arrives.

Where's a phone?"

"Over there."

Bryant crouched down and crawled over to small table at the end of a couch. "There's no dial tone."

"Then use your cell phone, quick. They're closing to within firing range."

The screen on the cell phone flashed "no signal".

"There's no service out here!"

"No! George has called me from here."

"Well then he must have used his land line! And now it's been cut!" said Bryant. "What are we going to do? We can't guard every window and door from ten guys."

"Let's see if we can quickly reduce the advantage. I don't think they're aware that *we* know they're here," said Neco.

"Then let's announce we do."

The two agents busted some panes of glass and opened fire. They heard cries in the distance. The Task Force members had taken out two each.

The return fire came immediately. It became clear the enemy had Uzi's. The thick stone walls could easily withstand the barrage, unlike the windows.

"They're trying to get to the left and right sides of the house," said Neco. "Get to a window over there and shoot anything that moves." He then let off a couple more rounds.

Alejandro laid on the grass with a Kalashnikov rifle and fired off a shot at Bryant. The bullet missed and ricocheted off the stone section of a fireplace. Bryant snapped back his torso in reaction and tripped headfirst into the corner of a coffee table.

"Thomas! Thomas!" yelled Neco, who shielded himself from shards of glass as the Uzi's sprayed from three sides of the house.

Covering three sides of the house with two people provided an extremely difficult task. Having Bryant out of commission made it impossible.

Neco had seconds to think. He had a situation worse than the one in Camden with Julio and his gang. At least there the cavalry evened things out. But no outside help could be counted on here. Even neighbors would never hear the shots from such a distance.

Even if he could somehow overcome one of them and hold him hostage, it would do no good. Neco knew one thing about these animals – they held no life sacred except their own.

Except their own!

Neco knew the only chance he had left – one crazy, insane chance!

The six killers gave each other a shower of bullets as cover to move closer and closer.

Neco had just precious minutes to set up his plan.

Stan Logan had all his SWAT team units in position at the Tioga Marina. Following the plan laid out yesterday,

Logan had a squad of snipers standing inside the overhead walkway. Once word came that Neco was on his way with Martinez, they would all lie down until the delivery was underway. Another unit dressed in white clothes and pull—over white hats blended in on top of the water towers across the street. It would be very difficult to spot either unit unless you were looking for them.

No one wore any "play clothes" to be hot dog vendors or homeless people and such. Such characters in this neighborhood would be suspicious. Everyone at ground level stayed concealed, wearing jackets with the clearly identifiable bold lettering for their agencies. Agents, dressed in plain clothes, pretended to be ordinary public driving back and forth in unmarked cars to create the illusion of an ordinary day when the street became blocked off.

Inside the marina, some agents did have play clothes to look like customs officials and dock workers who would transport the crates.

Logan stood next to John Somerfield in the overhead walkway with the snipers.

His Regional Director glanced over. "Why haven't we heard from Neco and Bryant?"

Logan looked at his watch. "I wish I knew. Neither will answer their phones."

"I know they're still not due for a couple of hours, but they should have been done in Exton by now," said Somerfield. "I want to know that Neco is on his way to Allegheny Avenue to meet Martinez. And we need Bryant to get ready with Opie in the van being used for the switch with Martinez' men. The last thing I want to hear about is Neco going off-script and gumming things up."

Logan shared Somerfield's concern about Neco. Like his Regional Director, he had very little confidence in Neco sticking to any script. The difference was that Logan knew that whenever Neco went off script, it was being done for the right reason.

Still, he did not like being kept in a vacuum either.

"I know, sir," said Logan. "But, if Neco hasn't called yet, I'm sure there's a good reason. We'll probably hear from him shortly. I'm not worried."

What the hell are Neco and Bryant doing?

Silence filled the air at the Exton farmhouse.

Alejandro and his men cautiously approached the front door and side windows. They entered the premises from the different sides and met no resistance. The Colombians hoped to find two dead bodies in pools of their own blood.

They only found an unconscious one.

Alejandro signaled for two of his men to check upstairs.

They came back down shaking their heads.

Their boss knew this house. The basement remained the only place left to check. Alejandro cracked open the door at the top of the stairs and heard a voice greet him.

"Are you afraid to die, gentlemen?"

"Loco!" said Alejandro. "Or should I say, 'Mr.

Neco'?"

The agent recognized the voice. "Carlos? Carlos Jimenez? Is that *your* sorry ass?"

"You can call me 'Alejandro' now. And speaking of sorry asses, we have your friend up here. Unless you do exactly as I say, I'm going to bring him to, and personally fit him for a Colombian neck-tie."

"That's been *you* killing off the Attorney General's agents?"

"Guilty as charged," came the reply. "But if it makes you feel any better, I am not without mercy." He paused.

"I only *shot* your friend Cathy. You'll be happy to know she died a *quick* death."

Neco clenched his jaw. "You chicken-ass coward!

Shooting a defenseless young woman? Did that make you feel like a big man?"

"I'm big enough to bring your friend's life to an end.

Unless you do exactly as I say, your fellow agent is going to suffer a gruesome death."

"You're going to do *that* anyway! So think again, bright boy!"

Alejandro bristled. He quickly glared at his men to study their reaction to his being insulted. "Shut up! If you think you're in any position to bargain, then *you're* the stupid one!"

Neco now knew how he could unnerve the enemy.

One of Alejandro's men spoke up. "I say we surround the basement and *blast* our way in!"

"Go ahead!" came the voice from the dark basement.

"But before you do, I'm going to pull the switch on all your electric chairs."

"You're even a bigger nut job than George thinks," said Alejandro.

"Funny you should mention George. I have something of his . . . what did he call them . . . ? Oh yeah, his 'val docs'. His valuable documents on your dealers in other cities and bank accounts. What would happen to you and the gang if these papers fell into the wrong hands, bright boy?"

Alejandro gnashed his teeth. "You and your friend will not be leaving here alive, you fool!" Then he turned to his men, "Surround the basement and shower the room with bullets!"

Another man spoke up. "Do you smell something?"

Alejandro took a deep breath.

"That's propane gas," said Neco. "George loves to barbeque. Did you know he has six tanks of propane gas stored down here?"

"So what?" said Alejandro.

"So, if you try to shoot off a gun, or create a spark in this room, there's going to one blazing inferno underway."

Alejandro looked perplexed. "Why should I give a rat's ass whether you get shot or burned to a crisp?"

"Never mind me," said Neco. "I'm not afraid to die. You and your men better think of themselves. If this room goes up, the whole house is going up."

"You and your friend will be the only ones in it."

"A fire like that is going to attract attention.

Maybe the neighbors can't hear bullets going off, but they'll sure notice the massive black smoke coming from here. *Someone* will alert the police and firemen."

Alejandro snorted. "We'll be long gone before they arrive."

"Without the safe?"

Alejandro went quiet, finally comprehending the significance of Neco' message.

The gang listened to the seemingly disembodied voice coming from below. "And if there's a full blown blaze underway, how will you get to the safe? Who's going to charge through the raging fire? And it's pretty heavy . . . probably going to take two or three of you. Do you have that many goons not afraid to dare getting that safe out of here? The safe will endure the blaze and you'll never get to it before the first responders get here. How will you explain *that* to your boss?"

The Colombian did not know what to say as his men looked at him for the next command.

Neco continued to bait him. "How about if we just settle this? You and the rest of your girls come on down and we'll have it out without the guns. You aren't afraid of one little cop are you?"

Alejandro's face turned red.

"It's your move," said Neco. "But if you don't secure this safe, I can't see Escobar just settling for giving you all Colombian *neck*-ties. I wonder what a Colombian jock-strap looks like. So what do you say, bright boy?"

The assassin erupted. *"We're going to cut you up!"*

One of the men flipped on the light switch and they all rumbled down the stairs single-file and spotted Neco standing in the center of the room. They reached into their pockets and pulled out their switchblades.

"Let *me* take him," said one of the men. "I'll show him who the girl is."

He began brandishing his blade and made some jabbing motions in an unsuccessful effort to make his opponent flinch. Neco gave no ground.

The hood closed within five feet and Neco reached down to his side pocket with the speed of a gun-slinger.

His middle finger threaded through the leather loop of his 007. In the same continuous motion, he yanked out the Cut of a Thousand Deaths, snapped open the blade to the locked position and whipped it across the neck of his assailant.

The man's previous bravado changed into a loud cry as blood spurted out of this neck. That one instant of despair created an opening for a swift kick to the chest, turning the choking man into a writhing heap on the cement floor."

Alejandro dropped his jaw with the rest of his wide—eyed minions.

"El Diablo!" shouted another man. "I'm getting out of here!"

The man whirled around to the stairs, only to have his chest intercepted by the cold blade of Alejandro. He watched the man collapse dead to the floor and bellowed to the others. "No one leaves until that cop is *dead!*"

The other three men nervously took a wide path to form a half-circle around the agent. Neco whirled the Cut of a Thousand Deaths in a figure eight motion. He alternated that move above his head and to his right side.

"You idiot! Don't just *stand* there watching him. Get him! He can't stop all three of you at once!"

The man on the right saw Neco swinging his blade on the opposite side to ward off his partner. He lunged at the agent, who dodged the blade and used the leather strap to flip the 007 handle back to his palm. Before he saw it coming, the thug received a counter stab – right to the lung. He crumbled to the side of a work bench.

The goon on the opposite side tried to close in as Neco withdrew his knife. Alejandro watched his man receive a kick to the face that snapped his head up and back. His arching torso became the next bulls-eye.

Neco released the handle and again used the leather strap to whip his blade. This time into the man's heart.

In desperation, the last man of the trio bull-rushed the agent. Neco evaded the knife, but not the crash of the man's torso against his own. The thug managed to grab Neco' knife hand. He knew he could now thrust his own weapon before Neco could free up his other hand to defend himself.

It would be the final plan to go through his mind.

From one inch away, Neco formed a fist and hammered the man in his diaphragm. Before he even realized he could not breathe, the thug slammed against the stone wall and fell to the floor – his own blade plunging into his chest as he screamed.

Neco tried to pivot back towards his last opponent. Before he could fully turn, he barely managed to ward off a heavy metal tool box thrown at him. The tool box crashed into his head and forearm. The 007 fell to the floor and Neco staggered backwards with a gash on the wrist. Alejandro pounced at him, lashing out with his own knife.

The agent dodged the blade but could not avoid a backhand to the side of his head, sending him to the floor.

The Colombian hit man closed in and found himself on the receiving end of a leg sweep that dropped him to the ground. Alejandro rolled, grabbed his knife and sprang to his feet as Neco got up off the floor.

They squared off in a circling motion.

"You're not dealing with those other incompetents now," said Alejandro. "I can't wait to see the look on George's face when he finds out you were just another bumbling agent who received a Colombian neck-tie."

Neco answered the best way possible – with a swift kick to the wrist. Alejandro's knife flew off to the side.

A second kick to the mouth sent the assassin backwards into a set of shelves.

Alejandro felt blood running from a loose tooth. He grabbed at cans and small boxes on the shelves and furiously threw them at Neco, who either dodged them or batted them away with this hands.

The Colombian retreated to another set of shelves and found a container of nails. He threw handfuls at Neco, but Neco protected the only body part that mattered against the nails – his eyes.

But Alejandro bought himself the precious seconds he needed to lunge to the space underneath the stairs. He grabbed a spray gun filled with pesticide, and a crowbar.

Neco looked for his 007.

It laid off to the right of his killer, who taunted him. "Even if you could get to your little toy, it wouldn't help you if you can't see." Alejandro quickly moved in and pulled the trigger of the spray gun.

Neco shielded his eyes even as Alejandro took a swing at him with the crowbar. He dodged the crowbar and used his hand to block another release of pesticide. But even though he covered up from the direct burst, some of the pesticide dripped from his forehead into his right eye.

The sting of harsh chemicals made the eye involuntarily close as he wiped at it with his wrist.

"That's *one* down!" shouted Alejandro. "You know,

Loco, I've reconsidered. Don't worry about the Colombian neck-tie. I'm going to use your own knife to send Escobar your head in a box. Now your wife and child? *They'll* get Colombian neck-ties!" Neco almost charged him right there. But instead he ran to the far side of the room and picked up a rubber ball next to some infielder gloves.

Alejandro chortled. "A rubber ball? Hah! So, the great undercover agent is now a playground pitcher. What are you going to do, Mr. Pitcher? Throw me a fastball?

Give me a little chin music?"

Neco planted his feet. "Maybe more like the high heat!" Then he hurled the rubber ball at the light bulb.

The bulb smashed apart, creating sparks. The sparks instantly turned into a wave of flame rapidly bleeding from the ceiling and throughout the room.

Alejandro screamed louder than any victim he had ever tortured.

Neco leaped onto the work bench and spring-boarded fists and arms first through a glass window with exploding flames licking at his feet. He hit the grass and jumped to his feet to run for safety.

Thomas!

Neco sprinted to the front of the house and ran through the doorway.

Bryant still laid on the floor, but the smoke began to began to make him cough, bringing him to consciousness. As his vision cleared he recognized his partner standing over him.

"Juni . . . what the hell is going on?"

Before Neco could answer, the basement door blew open. Alejandro emerged from the opening, his body engulfed in flames and howling like a wild boar. Between the flames from him and the open door, other parts of room – furniture, carpeting and walls began to catch on fire.

The Colombian reared up and ran towards his target –

Bryant.

Neco grabbed a poker rod from the fireplace and impaled the Alejandro from the side. He swung the assassin around by the rod and let him drop to the floor. The sound of his screaming overrode the roar of the flames from his blazing body and other parts of the house.

"C'mon, Thomas!" said Neco, as he helped his friend to his feet. "I need you to run now."

"I'm not arguing!"

The two agents ran through the front doorway as the whole living room became ablaze.

They gathered their wits from about one hundred yards away. Sirens sounded in the distance.

"Where are the papers?" asked Bryant.

Neco pointed at the house. "I saw you had put two holes in the safe. Somehow I doubt the papers are going to make it through that heat."

"Do you think he tipped off George?"

"No, he made some remark indicating George doesn't know yet," said Neco. "We'll proceed according to plan. If George acts the least bit suspicious, I'll do what I have to do. But first we need to find the closest hotel. Then I'm going to wash the smell of smoke off while you find a department store and buy me some clean clothes."

CHAPTER EIGHTY-FOUR

Port Richmond, Philadelphia

George Martinez sat in his car at Tulip Street and Allegheny Avenue. He looked at his Rolex and felt himself getting a little antsy. He knew Juni Neco as a man who prided himself on punctuality. And now he found him to be eighteen minutes late. He decided to call him. Before he picked up what he thought was his cell phone, a tapping on the car window startled him. Neco smiled and waved to him.

Martinez rolled down the window and greeted his fellow dealer. "Loco! You had me a little worried there."

"I must apologize, sir. Some unexpected developments that had nothing to do with our transaction slightly detained me. But, rest assured. I've just gotten a call from my people and the shipment has arrived. All our planning is about to pay off."

"Pay off," repeated Martinez. "I like the sound of that."

"Yep. You're one step closer to getting what you deserve."

Juni Neco and George Martinez pulled in to the target area. Dexter Rasche and Thomas Bryant followed them in a cargo van. The other two men helping Martinez trailed everyone else in another cargo van and watched Neco park near the designated gate with the old railroad tracks going through it. They passed his cargo van and assumed a position a little further up the street.

Martinez and his people remained oblivious to the small army watching them.

The police sealed off the street from the public.

Other officers told the employees of the marina to not leave their respective work sites until given permission.

The crates carrying religious scriptures came out where Bryant and Rasche helped load them into their cargo van. Then they drove out through the gate and pulled up next to the cargo van with Martinez' men.

Bryant watched Rasche hit the kill switch and they stepped out of the vehicle. The two men, already out in the street, waited to swap transportation.

Stan Logan looked through binoculars from the overhead walkway and patiently waited for the drivers to trade car keys and get inside the vans. "All units move in now! I repeat, all units move in now!"

Agents jumped out from behind parked cars and ran in from all directions.

"Police! Police! Everybody freeze! Freeze!" yelled one officer.

"Hands on your heads! Now! Right now!" shouted another.

Bryant and Rasche put their hands where directed.

The hood in the passenger seat shouted, "Let's get out of here!"

The driver frantically turned the ignition key to no avail. "Shit!"

Resigned to their fate, they put their hands on their heads.

Neco and Martinez sat motionless and watched a group of officers rushing their car.

Neco put his arms out with palms upward. "What the fuck, George. Did you set me up?"

"No, man," said George. "Just don't say a word! I have excellent lawyers. We'll get out of this!"

Everyone had handcuffs put on them and put in squad cars and drove off for a local police station.

About a half-hour later an officer took Neco from the holding tank in the North Philadelphia precinct. Once out of view, he took him to a private room where Somerfield and Logan waited to shake his hand.

"Congratulations, Juni!" said the Regional Director.

"Tremendous job, Loco!" added Logan.

"Thank you, gentlemen," said Neco. "Did we get a count on how many kilos were hidden in the Bibles?"

"Eight hundred," answered Logan. "We're talking over a billion dollars of street value! Over a billion dollars!

That blows away the record for a hand-to-hand job!"

"And not only did no money exchange hands," said Somerfield, "you actually made *them* pay something up fRont to do the deal. Amazing!"

"Generations from now people will be singing songs next to their camp fires, telling of the Legend of Loco," said Logan.

Neco laughed and they opened some drinks while they talked.

"Say, Juni," said Somerfield, "You want to go for broke on this one?"

"What do you mean?"

"How about if you go back to George's cell and tell him we got him dead to rights and see if he'll cough up some more information?"

Logan became incredulous. "You want him to reveal he's an undercover cop? What are you thinking? This is not a case with the Asians or the Mac Boys. We're dealing with Colombians here! Escobar! Remember?"

"Exactly!" said Somerfield. It's Escobar – the biggest menace on the planet. I saw Martinez sitting in the holding tank. He's absolutely freaked over the prospect of never seeing his kids again. I don't know if he'll ever be more vulnerable than now. He'll know it was Juni when he hears the tapes from the yacht anyway. If we can exploit this before he lawyers up, we may be able to get a lot of the information we lost in the fire."

"The Director has a point, Stan," said Neco.

"Plus, somebody, somehow found out about me anyway. So what the hell, let me give it a shot. Have George put in a room by himself."

Neco walked down the hallway and received an unexpected greeting by a couple of familiar faces.

"Juni!" shouted Ada Hernandez.

Sandra Tomasson raised her arms in the air and joined in. "You did it!"

"Ladies!" said Neco embracing with them. "What a delightful surprise! What brings you two across the river tonight?"

"Are you kidding?" said Tomasson. "The news has already spread to the Prosecutor's Office. That was a record hand-to-hand!"

"So, they told me," smiled Neco. "Hey, listen I would love to stay and talk, but I've got to work on someone before they call for an attorney."

"Okay, we'll catch you later," said Hernandez. "Maybe you can tell us over lunch tomorrow."

The women started to walk away when Tomasson stopped and quickly walked back to Neco. "I thought you should know that my husband and I have agreed the right thing for us to do is to get a divorce."

"Oh," said Neco, "I hope things go smoothly."

"Hopefully. We're off to an amiable start. Call us tomorrow."

"I will, Miss Sandra. Have a good night."

Hernandez waited for Tomasson to walk back to her.

"You just had to slip that in, didn't you?"

"What? Look me in the eye and tell me you haven't laid some groundwork too."

Hernandez did not respond.

"Yeah," muttered Tomasson. "I thought so."

A guard let Neco into the interrogation room containing Martinez. He sat with his head in his hands.

He lifted his head. "Loco? What are you doing here?"

"George, we have to talk."

"Don't worry. I promised you I had good lawyers for us. They'll be here shortly."

"You're lawyers can't help you, George. You'll be going away for life."

Martinez stood up and suspiciously squinted his eyes.

"Why? What did you do? Did you flip on me?"

"No. I didn't flip on you," replied Neco. "I'm a cop. I orchestrated your whole arrest. We've got tapes from the yacht. I even have a tape of you being in the car with me back there. I'm telling you, there isn't a legal team in the world who's going to get you off the hook."

"I can't believe you're a cop! How could you do this to me?" He started pacing. "We had a relationship. I treated you like my friend. How could you do this? Do you realize what you've done to me and my family?"

Do you realize the lives you were going to destroy with 800 kilos of cocaine? Thought Neco, as he bit his tongue. "Sorry, George. I was just doing my job."

"You've ruined my life! Do you realize that? You've ruined my life!"

Neco continued ignoring the hypocrisy and kept his diplomatic, good-cop approach. "Maybe I can help you with that, George. Give me some information I can use. I promise I can make things better for you than your lawyers can."

"Information? On who? Escobar?" asked Martinez.

"You don't know it, but I work with his lead assassin. He was checking out your past behind the scenes. Do you know what he does to informers?"

"You don't have to worry about him," said Neco.

"Neither of us don't"

"You caught *him* too?"

"Let's just say he's way too burnt out to bother you anymore."

"Huh?"

"C'mon, George. You have valuable information to make a sweet deal for yourself. We can have you and your family protected."

Martinez sat back down in his chair. "You know how it works, Juni. Escobar has people on all my family members right now. My mother, wife and two kids are probably at Le Bec Fin restaurant having a five-star meal. And they don't even realize they're being watched by killers. If there's one whiff of trouble out of me, they'll all die horrific deaths. I can't count on the police protecting me or anyone."

"I get it. But I had to try," said Neco. "If you change your mind, let me know if there's anything I can do to help."

"How about waving a magic wand, so that I can be released on bail and go back to my house."

"Oh . . . umm . . . George . . . I've got some more bad news for you, man."

George Martinez knew bad news would be reaching someone else too.

Pablo Escobar waved and blew kisses as he basked in the cheers of his adoring fans. Some beautiful women brought out a trophy and the professional announcers proclaimed Escobar to be the Most Valuable Player.

Escobar finished his acceptance speech and his personal assistant handed him a towel and his cell phone.

They walked off the field to the locker room and the drug lord noticed he had a message. He punched the buttons to hear his voice mail.

The time it took for his victorious facial expression to transition to maniacal rage took mere seconds.

"Why didn't I get this *message!*" he bellowed.

The personal assistant cowered before him. He stammered a reply. Sir . . . I wasn't aware the ph . . . ph . . . phone had even rung! There was the crowd . . . the announcers . . . I never heard it!"

Escobar attempted to call Alejandro and Martinez to no avail. He threw down the phone. "Bring me my car! People will pay with their lives for this!"

CHAPTER EIGHTY-FIVE

23 July, Philadelphia

The rage of Pablo Escobar permeated The Badlands like a rapidly spreading virus, with dozens of gangs of hired guns assailing people for information in exchange for money or their lives.

Two cars, packed with armed Colombians, came tearing into the parking lot of Roberto Quintero's auto garage.

They did not see a single car parked on the premises and they found the door locked. One man took his rifle butt and shattered the glass door. One car load climbed through the opening and ransacked the place for any clues to the whereabouts of the man called "Gordo".

The other car load dispersed into the surrounding businesses.

The leader assailed, an old Caucasian man, the owner of an adjacent store. "Where's Gordo!" He trained an Uzi on the man.

"I don't know," trembled the gray-haired man behind his counter.

"Where does he live?" shouted the leader.

"I don't know! We're not friends! We're just business neighbors! Please don't shoot me!"

The leader's rage grew. He kept pressing. "Who *does* know?"

The old man began crying.

Down in Center City, Juni Neco parked his car in the private lot for the Federal Building on Seventh Street, just off of Arch Street. He still felt tired after a celebration with the gang from the dojo. But the view in front of the building got his attention.

He noticed a highly unusual amount of activity, including armed security guards stationed near the entrance. They supervised long lines of people slowly being admitted into the building.

Neco flashed his badge and ID, and went to the front of one of the long lines where a young Asian Federal agent greeted him.

"Juni Neco!" said the agent. "What the hell are *you* doing here?"

"I'm here to see if anything else is required of me concerning the arrest yesterday," said Neco. "What the hell is going on *here?* What's with the lines?"

The FBI man pointed through the glass front door.

"Look right there. You see that?"

Neco looked and got a bewildered expression on his face when he saw metal detectors, like those used at the airport, had been set up in the lobby. Additionally, he observed all bags and briefcases being opened and inspected.

"What's up with all the detectors? asked Neco.

"They've never had those before."

"By the end of yesterday, we were receiving phone calls from Colombian drug cartel reps threatening the building was going to be bombed. This is the first time in *history* we've *ever* taken measures like this. You've created a big effect, my friend. People are hunting for you."

"I'm flattered," said Neco.

"Be more than flattered. There's a ten million dollar price tag on the head of Juni Neco."

Neco' eyes widened. "Ten million dollars? Damn,
I must have really pissed someone off."

"*That* amount of crack confiscated? That had to cost over *ten times* the price of the bounty. Plus word is out you may have damaging information on Escobar. I'm surprised to see you even out in public today."

"I don't have damaging information. But those low—life scum bags don't scare me."

"You're a better man than I am, Loco. Come on, let me get you around this checkpoint."

"I appreciate that. I have another important meeting after this."

CHAPTER EIGHTY-SIX

Harrisburg, Pennsylvania

Shurmur stood before the door to the press room of the state capital building. A large packed crowd of media members awaited his announcement concerning the record cocaine arrest yesterday. This press conference stood to be his second-to-last one. He would shortly, in the near future, hold another and announce his resignation on a high note.

He had still heard nothing from Michael Owens and the State Board of Elections. Secure in the knowledge he could not be prosecuted, the Attorney General knew that would not last much longer. So, he continued to plan his end game—including being a good soldier for two people he used to consider friends. Two people he now had to go out and make look good.

Shurmur stepped into the press room. To one side stood Deputy Attorney General Anthony Sorvino. And on the other side, fresh from a swing through West Virginia stood presidential candidate, Senator Donald Carvey.

Shurmur led off the briefing. "Members of the press, thank you for being here this morning for the announcement of this momentous day in the early history of The Special Task Force. With me here today, are two gentlemen, without whom, we may have never seen such an unprecedented arrest in the war on drugs."

Between the announcement and the subsequent questions and answers to the three men, the press conference lasted just less than an hour.

Afterwards Carvey gave Sorvino a subtle nod. It was time for them to get together for one more action today.

CHAPTER EIGHTY-SEVEN

Merion, Pennsylvania

A couple of hours later, Donald Carvey emerged from the passenger side of a white Lincoln Town Car. In place of his usual tailored suit were a pair of blue jeans, a Philadelphia Phillies tee shirt and matching baseball cap.

Replacing his imported Italian shoes was a pair of old sneakers. The final touch, aviator-style sun-glasses, gave Carvey the complete opposite image of an impeccably attired congressman.

Anthony Sorvino, dressed in similar garb, remained in the driver's seat and watched Carvey stride off to a local high school field where some teen-age boys were playing a pick-up game of soft-ball.

The senator took an isolated seat on the third row of some aluminum bleachers behind the back-stop and inconspicuously placed a latex glove on his right hand. Up and over to the side of him, about ten yards away, three young girls in tee-shirts and hot pants approached their boyfriends who waited their turns to go up and hit.

One of boyfriends, a teen-ager wearing a muscle shirt to display his tattooed arms, started ribbing his girl.

"Hey, babe. You're looking righteously slutty today."

"Shut up, Sean!" protested a blonde, who punched him on the arm.

The others all laughed.

They look like suitable air-heads, thought Carvey, who patiently waited for the right diversion to evolve on the field. Minutes later, two batters reached base on singles, putting runners at first and second. The senator stared at the next batter. *Okay, let's get one more hit with a play at home plate.*

The batter hit a line-drive into the gap between the center fielder and the right fielder.

Perfect!

Carvey had the distraction he needed. With everyone's attention on the field, he reached into his pants pocket and removed a small plastic zip-lock bag with about four teaspoons worth of cocaine in it. The senator placed it on the surface next to him during all the yelling. He removed the latex glove, calmly rose from his seat and walked towards the "airheads" until he was within hearing range.

"Pardon me. Pardon me. Uhh . . . excuse me." Carvey said, getting their attention. The six of them looked at him with expressions of annoyance and boredom as he kept talking. Carvey continued, speaking in a manner that sounded unsure of himself. He also mixed in some nervous laughter. "I was just sitting in the bleachers over there . . . you know, to watch the game and I noticed a funny—looking little plastic sandwich bag . . . There's some type of white powder in it." He kept talking while the teens all looked in the direction to which he pointed and noticed the plastic bag. "I'm . . . I'm no drug expert . . . but that looks like it might be cocaine. I was wondering . . . wondering if any of you knew where the nearest pay phone was. I was just thinking I should . . . uhh . . . call the police and have someone who knows what they're doing to come out, you know, and have it examined. If it's what I think it is, the police will probably want to, you know, confiscate it. Is there a payphone around somewhere?"

The youngsters all looked at each other for several moments before the one called Sean answered him. "I don't know, man. I think the closest payphone is back out on Lancaster Avenue near one of the bus stops."

"Okay. Okay. Uhh, you don't think there's one in the school over there," asked Carvey, already knowing the answer.

"The school's locked up, sir," said the blonde. "You probably have to go to Lancaster Avenue like Sean said."

"Okay. Okay . . . thanks. Thank you," nodded Carvey.

"I'll go find it. I'll find something. Thanks. I think I should just leave it there until, you know, someone who can check it out comes, right?"

"Right. Yeah," replied Sean, trying to look serious.

"Leave it there until the authorities come. You're doing the right thing, sir."

The others nodded in agreement.

"Okay," said Carvey, "Well, umm, thanks again. I'm gonna go find a phone now."

And he departed as the six teen-agers stayed quiet and watched him leave.

That pouch will be gone as soon as I'm out of sight,

Carvey thought as he kept putting more distance between himself and the field. When he reached one of the large street signs for the high school, he went behind it and peered back at the field.

The six teen-agers were gone. Carvey smiled, confident that the plastic bag had disappeared with them.

Feeling satisfied, it was time to go back to the car.

From what I sow, so shall I reap. But when he did an about face, he was startled to find a cross-looking young Black man with dread locks standing in front of him. He spoke to Carvey with a Jamaican accent.

"You think no one knows your game, man?"

Carvey's previously smug look instantly became a mix of surprise and concern. He tried to brush the man off and walk around him. "I'm just coming from a baseball game.

Nothing to concern you, my friend."

But the Jamaican stepped right in front of him again.

"I've seen you in the suburbs out here. And I know what you do. You plant some drugs for the kids, let them get hooked and you create a demand for yourself. Then you must hook them up with someone who can come back and charge them. It's the oldest gateway to addiction in the world."

"I don't know what you're talking about friend, but I assure you this is a misunderstanding," said Carvey, stealing glances to see if anyone was observing this. He saw Sorvino getting out of the car. Carvey did not want the Deputy Attorney General joining in and possibly drawing attention to the confrontation.

"You listen to me, man. This is *my* territory! I don't want to see your ass here, in Ardmore, in Bryn Mawr or any of these neighborhoods along the Main Line."

There was no time to argue. Every second risked unwanted exposure.

Carvey riveted his eyes on the Jamaican, "I'm leaving now. You do whatever the hell you want with this territory, but I'm leaving." And he brushed the man aside and stepped past him.

"Don't you go diss'ing me, man," said the young man as he grabbed Carvey by the shoulder and roughly spun him around towards him. The sudden move jarred Carvey's sun—glasses from his face.

An angry Carvey did not hesitate. Before the man could get a good look at this face, Carvey brought a quick knee up into his assailant's groin, doubling him over.

The senator followed up and crashed an elbow down on the back of the man's neck, who crumpled to the ground unconscious.

Snapping up his sun-glasses from the grass, Carvey quickly strode back to the car, motioning for Sorvino to get back in the driver's seat.

Sorvino sounded rattled as Carvey jumped in the passenger side seat. "What the hell was that all about?"

"Dumb jack-ass! Thinks I'm trying to take over his territory," said Carvey.

"I *told* you this was no longer necessary when you got the bill passed!"

"And I told *you* that *now* when I'm planting coke, I'm getting some names. Then I can anonymously call in leads to the Special Task Force and make the unit look brilliant in the eyes of the voters. Now just drive! Before someone sees us."

Sorvino pulled out, forcing himself to not let the tires squeal.

CHAPTER EIGHTY-EIGHT

Hershey, Pennsylvania

Senator Carvey arrived at his gated home and used a remote control to open the door to his three-car garage.

His wife left a message that she would be at her mother's until after dinner. So he had the place to himself, which suited him fine.

He grabbed a copy of the Wall Street Journal off the kitchen table and made his way into the living room where he was greeted by a surprise visitor.

"Senator Carvey!"

The startled congressman dropped his paper on the floor. "Agent Neco! Lord, son, you scared the piss out of me! What are you doing here? How did you get in past the alarms?"

"You should ditch all your fancy surveillance equipment and place cages of birds around the premises."

"Why are you here, Agent Neco? Have you come with a search warrant?"

"No. No search warrant is required," said Neco.

"This is just an informal visit from someone in your sphere of influence."

Carvey's initial fear started growing into impatience.

"Listen, son. You may be the 'golden boy' with Martin Shurmur, but I wouldn't count on that much longer."

"I've learned not to count on anyone. Martin is not the subject today. The subject today is *you*."

"What the hell are you talking about?"

"You've been very busy behind the scenes, Senator."

"Tell me what you think, Juni."

"I'll do better than that. I'll tell you what I *know*.

You're a crack user, Senator. At first, when I saw Sorvino picking up some cocaine at the vending machine by the chocolate plant, I wondered if it was for Shurmur."

Carvey's face took on a more serious look.

Neco continued. 'But then I was reminded of some of the physical symptoms of cocaine users during a bust – red eyes, sudden nose bleeds – and I remembered your repetitive need for eye drops and, coincidently, your 'stumble' out at Indian Gap with the bloody nose."

"That doesn't prove anything," said Carvey. "And I don't think your word against Anthony's will prevail anywhere, let alone a court of law."

"Not by itself, but there's more," said Neco.

"When I was working the arms dealer case, Arnie Schmidt told me about an old war buddy, now in government, whom he was running cocaine for. I had no idea until some more pieces fell together."

The senator remained silent, looking more and more grim.

"The meeting at the tavern in Mt. Gretna established your link with Sorvino. Then I remembered your Purple Heart from the Vietnam War. The VA Building in Philadelphia has files showing the military records for you and Arnie Schmidt. You were his commanding officer. You're the 'old war buddy'!"

Carvey finally spoke. "All you've laid out is hearsay evidence, and some circumstantial information.

Have you got anything better than that?"

"I also tracked down a dealer in the Main Line area,

Senator. I learned about some anonymous white guy playing candy man for the upper class white teens in the region.

Your Special Task Force bill was never going to get the votes you needed until there was pressure from the wealthy families – the high-rolling donors for the politicians in the congress. *That's* how you got your bill passed. You actually *introduced* drugs to a useful demographic for yourself. That's what you were using most of Schmidt's drugs for."

"I can see why they call you 'Loco'. You're nuts!"

"You've been out on the campaign trail inflaming communities with tragedies of your own making. The coincidences are adding up, Senator. You secure your victory in the primary and ride the success of The Special Task Force to the White House next November. Putting Sorvino and Opie into positions of power. Now they can be selective about who the

Attorney General's Office goes after. So no one steps on your toes. When I heard all the dealers crowing about how much better things were going to get for them, I never dreamed that they were including your actions with Escobar's!"

"They didn't know who they were referring to either."

Carvey went over to his bar, grabbed a snifter and poured himself a brandy. He took a sip. "You've certainly been an industrious fellow, Agent Neco. I admire your resourcefulness. I admire your stick-to-it-ness. You've assembled a lot of information. But being a former prosecuting attorney, I know you would have to do a lot better than that. You have nothing that could stand up in court, my loco friend."

"Maybe not," said Neco. "But there may be enough to cast a big cloud over a presidential campaign. Maybe even enough to have you join Martin in the ranks of the unemployed. What do you think, counselor?"

Carvey took another sip of brandy. "You're not looking at this the right way, son. Take for example what you do as an undercover agent. You hook up with some small-time corner drug dealer. You give him some money for some drugs. You make higher demands to move up the ladder until you finally nail some high card. It took you forking over some money to a criminal, who could use that money to purchase more drugs to sell. But you're looking at the big picture, right?"

This time Neco stayed silent.

"Well," said Carvey, "it's the same with the 'hypothetical' situation you present to me. Smaller wrongs get dwarfed by the bigger rights. Without The Special Task Force, maybe you don't nail an arm of the Escobar cartel.

But with it, you do! So now other states are *clamoring* for this program. Under both scenarios, the street drug industry gets hurt far more than it gets helped.

And maybe that knucklehead Arnie Schmidt *has* helped his 'buddy' in government to dupe some drug dealers. What they don't realize is that initially there *would* be more small—time traffic. But with more small-traffic comes more Special Task Forces throughout the country to nail the big fish."

"And greatly enhances your re-election as President," said Neco.

"Just like your record gets enhanced when you give money to drug dealers. You and the man you describe are a lot alike."

"I am *nothing* like you! I don't deliberately take measures to get teens hooked on crack!"

"Don't be naïve. The money you give to the dealers is used to buy more drugs that find their way into the hands of all kinds of users – *even teenagers!*"

"The authorities *know* what I do. They have no *clue* about what you're doing. But if they were to find out . . ."

"Then such a man would be dragged into depositions, probably have to testify in open court, and in the process bring up the *name* of any agent involved in the whole scheme of undercover work. And all of a sudden that *agent* is brought into court to testify. And this is open court, you understand, where Colombians, who are looking to collect ten million dollars, could learn the identity of that agent. Even worse, they would be out to get his wife and son."

Neco fumed. "If your actions *ever* resulted in the harming of my family, I guarantee you would *truly* regret the consequences."

Carvey's expression stayed the same – smug. "Here's a proposal, Agent Neco. You are now entitled to a huge bonus for your latest efforts."

"I will *not* be bought off," said Neco.

"Juni, I'm *not* suggesting that. What I *am* saying is that you *should* get some substantial reward on sheer merit.

I know with Anthony in power, I could get that enhanced.

Not for the purpose of buying you off. Hear me out.

You take a year-long paid vacation. We send you down to Puerto Rico. And right now, you *need* to be far away until this whole bounty business dies down. All expenses are on the government. I'll bet you and the whole family would like that. Expenses include a tutor for Petey, so he wouldn't fall behind in school. And I would bet Sandy would benefit a great deal in that environment."

Neco clenched his jaw over the senator's knowledge of his family issues.

"During those three months," said Carvey. "You sit back and take a good hard look at what you want to do.

Maybe you come back and take your chances with me in court.

Maybe you just resign with a golden parachute in Puerto Rico. Or you come back after the heat dies down and you do what you do best – work undercover."

"I'll get the whole Puerto Rico package without your influence. No thanks!"

"Well, of course, you'll get something. I'll just make it sweeter. The important thing is you don't make a rash emotional decision. You need to step back and look at what's best for your *family*. In any event, you really need to disappear from the area immediately until the heat dies down.

There are *bad* people looking for you." The senator walked over and picked up a bottle from a small wine rack.

"Look, I have a three hundred dollar bottle of Remy Martin, I've been saving to celebrate a special occasion.

Which I must admit was supposed to be for you demise in the agency. Maybe *this* is the special occasion. You and I forging an alliance—creating a win-win situation."

Neco stared back. "Answer this question for me.

How does a high-profile, public figure like yourself make all the rounds in the suburbs and not get recognized? How can you not be afraid of getting caught?"

Carvey laughed under his breath. "High profile? Hah!

The only demographic being dealt with is teen-agers. These kids couldn't tell you the name of the *Vice-President* of the country let alone the name of a state senator. And a smart man wouldn't go out there in a three-piece suit. All he would have to do is throw on a plaid shirt with a pair of jeans and add a pair of sun-glasses with a baseball cap.

He would blend in very nicely. And he wouldn't make any *exchanges* with anybody – no trunk load of kilos, no bag of cash. All he would have to do is just point them in the right direction until somebody took the bait."

"What do you mean, 'point them in the right direction'?"

"This man could go to some upscale high school area, walk around and look for a place to deposit a small sample of cocaine . . . maybe a spot on a deserted stand of bleachers near a field where some local neighborhood kids are playing. Then he could tell the young dolts that he spotted a suspicious-looking bag and needed to know where the closest police station was. Trust me, I bet that sample would be gone before this man had left the field in his pretense to find a cop. The sample is enough to get some of them get hooked and then a few of them make their way into the inner city where we've given them some leads on locations for a regular supplier. Now *they* become the 'supplier' for *their* neighborhood. That is until the real suppliers get their middlemen operating out of the area."

"So, you've got your ass covered from all angles."

"Hypothetically, I would," said Carvey snickering.

Neco did not share in the laugh.

"Play ball with me and we'll get the Special Task operating nationwide. And Juni Neco will have his seat at the power table, getting the recognition he deserves.

What do you say, Loco? Can I open up this bottle?"

Epilogue

25 July, Cabo Rojo, Puerto Rico

Upon their arrival, the Neco family checked in with Zenaida to begin their year-long paid vacation.

Once again, Sandy became a new person just by stepping into the environment and being away from the sister. The whole experience with "Carlos" unnerved her enough to drop the alcohol and get back on her medication.

She never learned the real identity of the stranger in the bar. And for now, she kept the whole encounter a secret from her husband.

Neco put on a swim suit and left Sandy with Petey at his sister's home.

He needed some time alone. And he could still catch the sunset from his sanctuary.

Neco walked along the beach and eventually waded out to his 'island', where he sat on the driftwood facing the western horizon. Purple and yellow colors dominated the sky.

In his left hand, Neco held a 'souvenir' taken from his visit with the senator – a bottle of Remy Martin cognac. In exchange, the senator had received a bloody nose – no cocaine required.

Neco did not drink alcohol, but he *did* want to see what a three hundred dollar bottle of French brandy tasted like.

He opened the bottle and took a sip.

That gave him the experience. *Three hundred dollars, my ass.*

Clutching the bottle, he stared out over the ocean sunset and heaved the bottle as far as he could. Then Neco reached into his pocket and grabbed his badge issued by the Attorney General's Office. He clutched it tightly as he again stared out at the sunset.

Before he could take his next action, his cell phone rang. Neco removed the phone from the plastic zip—lock bag and answered it. He heard Goldbach's voice.

"Sensei, have you heard the news yet?"

"What news?"

"God! You actually haven't heard, have you?"

Neco sounded as if he had no interest.

"What happened?"

"Senator Don Carvey and Deputy Attorney General Anthony Sorvino are dead!"

That got his interest "What?"

"The two of them were part of a crowd just gunned down by a Jamaican Shower Posse on a street corner in Merion!

And no one knows why! No one knows what those two were doing there. And no one knows why a Jamaican Shower Posse was even *in* Merion. They're *unheard* of outside of The Badlands. The local and state government officials have said they have no comment until their investigation is completed."

As he kept listening to Goldbach, the agent Martin Shurmur had labeled "Kha Kahn" continued to stare out at the sunset and placed his badge back in his pocket.

9 781543 445954